The Ones We
Remember

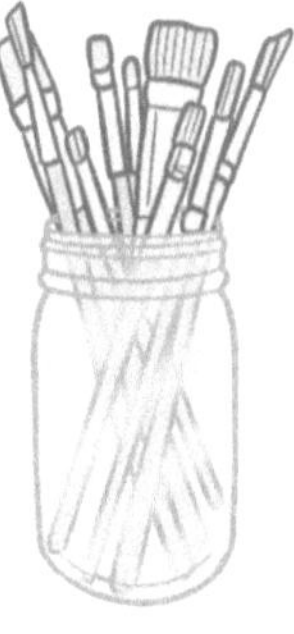

Katie Golightly

ISBN: 979-8-218-53883-5

ASIN: B0DJ1J5V8B

Cover Design by: Sam Palencia at Ink&Laurel

Editor: Maryarita Kobotis

Formatting: Kristen Hamilton at Kristen's Red Pen

Sensitivity Reader: Danielle Hoegy

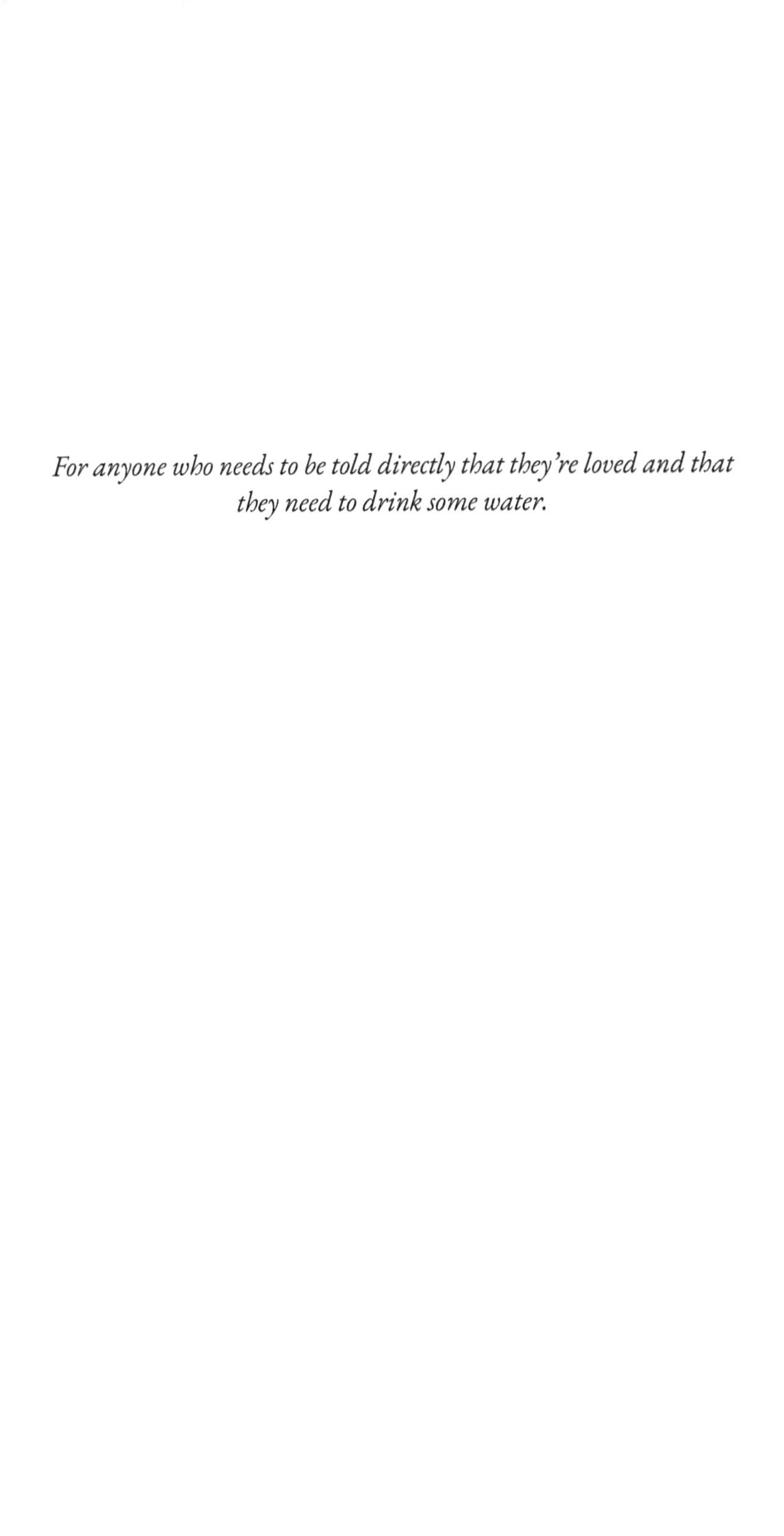

For anyone who needs to be told directly that they're loved and that they need to drink some water.

PLAYLIST

right person, wrong time by Henry Moodie
Home by Good Neighbours
Here You Come Again by Dolly Parton
Weird Science by Oingo Boingo
Unknown (To You) - Timbaland Remix by Jacob Banks,
Timbaland
What A Time (feat. Niall Horan) by Julia Michaels, Niall Horan
I Want You Back by *NSYNC
Crazier Things (with Noah Kahan) by Chelsea Cutler, Noah
Kahan
Young Blood by The Naked And Famous
Somebody's Heartbreak by Hunter Hayes
Mamma Mia by ABBA
Check Yes, Juliet by We The Kings
The Very First Night (Taylor's Version) (From The Vault) by
Taylor Swift
Heaven by Niall Horan
Till Forever Falls Apart by Ashe, FINNEAS
You Are The Reason by Calum Scott
Teenage Dream by Katy Perry
Glue Song by beabadoobee

Someone To You by BANNERS
Red (Taylor's Version) by Taylor Swift
18 by One Direction
Make You Mine by PUBLIC
Back To You by Selena Gomez
I Was Made For Lovin' You by KISS
Power Over Me by Dermot Kennedy
Addicted by Simple Plan
Ho Hey by The Lumineers
Only Love Can Hurt Like This by Paloma Faith
I miss you, I'm sorry by Gracie Abrams
Too Little Too Late by JoJo
There It Goes by Maisie Peters
bad idea right? by Olivia Rodrigo
Diet Pepsi by Addison Rae
Tie Me Down (with Elley Duhé) by Gryffin, Elley Duhé
If You Love Her by Forest Blakk
Everywhere, Everything by Noah Kahan
This Love (Taylor's Version) by Taylor Swift
Coming Home by Leon Bridges
Belong Together by Mark Ambor
Yellow by Coldplay

Author's Note

We've made it to book three, and like every book I've set out to write, it was exactly what I planned and not what I intended. I thought that this book would be the least personal to me. I figured I wouldn't have much in common with an artist who loves cats and can keep a lot of plants alive when I am decidedly a dog person who has exactly four plants that are always on the brink of death. I thought I wouldn't connect with an autistic man who is way smarter than I'll ever be, so much so that the research required for this book had me reevaluating why I didn't try harder in my chemistry classes in high school. Needless to say, I found so much in common with these characters that I was flat-out wrong to assume otherwise.

There's something that happens with every novel I write at around the 75% mark in draft one. I get to a scene, and I suddenly know exactly who these characters are despite having written them for months. I had that "aha!" moment with Colin, and I realized that it was there all along, just waiting for me to decide to finally go there, to dig in. I even had a moment where I desperately didn't want to go there, and I looked up statistics like Colin would, trying to prove that I didn't have to take it that far. The statistics were a slap in the face to the idea that I could ignore it.

I sat at my desk and cried for probably thirty minutes after reading the staggering information on autism and suicide or suicidal thoughts. One study suggested that people with autism are seven times more likely to die by suicide than the neurotypical populace, while another cited that it was nine times more likely. Yet another study done in the UK said that 35% of people they interviewed with autism had considered it.

As upsetting as it was when I knew I had to include this, I couldn't ignore it any longer. While the majority of this plotline is a recollection or a discussion of things that happened during the five-year time jump between the past and present, it may still be difficult to read. I want to assure you that I always write with intention, and all my books have a heavy thematic focus on healing because I continually have to examine things that are uncomfortable to put down on a page. I encourage you to guard your heart regardless of what my intentions are.

In addition to Colin's plot, we have a woman who fell in love too young and had to figure out who she was on her own. I was basically a fetus when I met my husband (I was sixteen), and when you are that young, you simply don't know shit. You don't even know who you are. The logical next step for us was, of course, to get married way too young and then struggle for years to find footing as people outside of the relationship. In the past timeline of this novel, you'll meet a girl so in love that she's willing to give up everything for it. She latches onto this identity of being with someone and decides that is who she wants to be. I don't encourage this as a healthy relationship dynamic, and I hope that is clear from how juvenile I wrote some of the scenes. Slapstick, happy love, while fun, is not always grounded in rational thinking, and neither is trauma bonding.

Lastly, there is a moment that may be considered dubious consent, where a line is crossed for **both** characters during an experimental scene. Throughout the entire book, Colin and Scarlett are adamant about obtaining consent for everything they do during intimacy, but there is a miscommunication in how that is handled and what each person needs to get that consent. The scene does not go very far, but I again want to assure you that it is handled with care, and I think a lot of people will find it relatable. This incident is resolved through direct communication, character growth, and future scenes that make it obvious they learned their lesson.

As always, if you know me in real life, reading this book will probably scar you and make you reconsider looking at me from across the Thanksgiving table. At this point, we're on book three, and I've made the astute observation that if you want to read it, you're going to do it with or without my blessing, so enjoy the explicit on-page sex scenes, I guess.

To the rest of you, hydrate yourselves, because this will make you thirsty... because you're crying, of course. Get your mind out of the gutter.

Prologue

Four Years Ago

Colin
18 Years Old

"Carter." The choking sound that left Colin's mouth was followed by a heavy intake of air that failed to help him breathe.

"Colin? Where are you?" Carter's voice sounded panicked through the phone speaker. It had been a great enough feat for Colin to find and hit his brother's name on his favorite list to call him, so holding a conversation was going to be a problem, especially because he now realized he couldn't ask Carter the questions burning in his head. If he could see or think clearly, Colin would have pulled up a map or ordered a rideshare, but logic was not his strong suit at the moment when he could barely breathe.

Sniffing and wiping a hand down his tear-streaked face did not further compose him. New tears sprang up in place of the ones he had smeared across his cheeks. "I'm on a bench," Colin croaked.

"On a bench *where?*" Carter's voice felt even more distant

now as Colin's heart rate spiked again. It had been doing that for ages. He would start to come down from his soul-crushing dysphoria only for his brain to replay the last twenty-four hours and send him spiraling into another fit of uncontrollable emotion.

"I don't know," Colin got out. It felt like an admittance of guilt or stupidity. He was never one prone to stupidity, but it was as if the last day were an alternate dimension he had been propelled into. A dimension where *he* had been the stupid one for years. Since birth. Since the moment he'd had a cognizant thought in his head and didn't realize that everything was fundamentally incorrect or altered in some way.

"Are you okay?" Carter was usually one for a quick joke or a sarcastic comment that would have to be explained to Colin after the fact, but, for once, the tone in his voice was unmistakably one of fear. All of Colin's siblings were quick to assume the worst because that was the hallmark of their experiences. A statistical bell curve would show that they had deviated from a normal amount of tragedy the day they lost both their parents. In the case study that was Colin, he had now lost four people: two to a freak accident, one to distance and words, and one more—himself—to no longer caring.

The sweaty shirt sticking to Colin's skin felt like a vise suctioning against his worn body. He had been walking for what felt like both an eternity and no time at all. The concept of time was a mere nuisance to him when he would spend the rest of his days without meaningful companionship. He knew Archwood like the back of his hand, but he had been out walking for so long that he might be in a different city now.

"We broke up." The words soured in his mouth and cracked appropriately on the word 'broke.' Someone had fed him poison. No, more likely, he had fed himself poison. Even lying flat on his back with his legs dangling over the side of the bench hadn't helped. He thought that he should maybe just lie down for a bit, and the swooping feelings in his head and chest would cease so he could think straight enough to do what he wanted to.

"What happened? You're scaring me." Carter sounded frantic on the other line, and Colin almost wanted to laugh at the irony of Scarlett saying those exact same words earlier.

"I did it. I did the right thing, I think." His chest heaved. "But it doesn't feel very good."

"I—fuck, I can't help you if I don't know where you're at." Carter sounded almost shrill now. "Why did you break up with her? You didn't tell me anything was wrong. What the hell happened?"

"Everything and nothing," Colin said, blinking up at the spinning sky that was starting to splash with deep pinks and oranges. It wasn't as beautiful as one of Scarlett's watercolor paintings, though, nor the sunset over the lookout. Not now, with his perpetual tunnel vision hued with dull grays. The last few months had been in vivid color, hints of blue sadness masterfully painted over with joyous yellows, deep, lustful reds, and warm, comforting pinks. He had been looking at that painting upside down and backward the whole time, and when he finally flipped it over, he'd taken a torch to the center of it, turning everything to dust.

"Colin is on the phone!" Carter yelled before a murmured conversation was whispered through the speaker, incoherent to Colin's ears. The deep tenor of the other voice had to be his uncle Walker, but Colin was still breathing too hard to hear much of anything other than the thrumming heartbeat in his skull. It was as though he had ripped his beating heart straight from his chest and held it up to his head to listen to the life dwindle away.

"Where are you?" Walker came on the phone. "Can you see anything?"

Most everything was blurry. "Trees," Colin replied simply.

"No shit, we live in Oregon," Walker huffed. "We've been calling you nonstop for three hours. They just found your car at Scarlett's. We thought you were fucking dead somewhere, Colin!"

Walker was angry, and Colin knew he should say something to ease his uncle's worry and anxiety, but he didn't care about anything or anyone at that moment. And maybe that was his fatal flaw—he lacked empathy. His therapist had suggested that his emotional empathy was well intact, but he could feel the lack of emotion he had now like an object he could grasp, a numbness that took over as his tears dried against his tacky skin. *Three hours.* That was how long it had been since he had wrecked everything.

I might as well be dead, Colin thought for what felt like the hundredth time that day. He knew for a fact that his death would hurt people, though, and the reason he had blown up his life was to avoid more harm, so caring *too* much seemed to be his problem. If he cared less, he could continue hurting people without thinking twice about it. So he grasped onto the numbness, his vision still hazy and his breathing erratic at best. "Sorry."

"I called Roscoe a while ago," Walker explained. "He's out looking for you, and now that I know you aren't coming home anytime soon, I'm leaving everyone with Talia and coming to find you." The sound of keys jingled on the other end of the line, and Colin thought that maybe the warped auditory issues he had been having since he left Scarlett's house might be fading, but he was still barely processing a word Walker said. It was all meaningless to him.

"Roscoe," Colin repeated, finally placing the name. It should matter to him that Walker's best friend was out looking for him, no doubt in his police cruiser, but it didn't. The flashing lights would be all the more disorienting when he was eventually found.

"You're scaring me," Walker breathed into the phone. There it was again. The same phrase everyone had been using with him today. Colin hadn't thought of himself as very frightening, but maybe he should after Scarlett, Carter, and Walker had all said it. He half-expected the trees to start whispering the same thing. "You're breathing really hard. Are you injured?" Walker asked.

"No," Colin replied. His heart was permanently damaged, but he had enough common sense left to know that his family would want to know about broken bones or car accidents like the one his late parents had been in. "I broke up with her."

"I heard." Walker's tone dropped and leveled. "That's why you're not okay." It was said more as a statement instead of a question, and Colin bobbed his head without responding. Walker would know better than anyone how Colin felt about Scarlett because he and his uncle had both fallen in love at the same time. The major difference, however, was that Walker got to keep Talia. In the end, Colin wouldn't have a happy ending, and he didn't care to talk it out with someone who'd had to deal with him out of obligation and familial duties to begin with.

The only person he wanted to talk to was Scarlett, and he had made sure he could never go back to her. He made sure she hated him. Nothing between them could be water under the bridge because there was no bridge. He had set it on fire and watched her sob and beg for him not to do it. It had never been harder to turn around and leave her standing rigid amongst the half-packed boxes strewn about her bedroom. A life he could have had if he weren't himself. If he were normal.

The room Colin had spent countless hours in, losing himself in vibrant copper hair, smooth, freckled skin, and soft, full lips was forever tainted by today. Would it be like that for her, too? Would she remember him broken with a cold demeanor in the same room they had shared 'I love you's in and pressed hands of intention into each other's skin? Would she dream of him? Or would she replay how he had left her in tears and made her cry more than the one time?

"It'll be okay," Walker soothed, bringing Colin out of his thoughts enough to realize he was crying again. Not just crying, but audibly sobbing. "We'll find you, I promise."

But Walker was wrong. Colin would never be found again. And there was a large part of him that didn't want to be found. A part that wished he would fade away into the night like a mist to be forgotten because Scarlett had found him once, body and soul, and he had purposely destroyed that simply because he knew she wouldn't do it herself. She was too kind to ever call this what it was: an experiment that had failed epically, because while she would forever be the right person for him, he would never be the one for *her*.

And so, she would remember him that way: *wrong person, right time*.

One

Present Day

Colin
22 Years Old

The box Colin gripped under one arm was practically disintegrating under the torrential downpour. He picked up his feet and sprinted faster, hoping the cardboard wouldn't completely fall apart by the time he got to the door. Rain pelted his face and glasses, making it nearly impossible to see. Luckily, he could get to the front door of his childhood home blindfolded. Everything about coming back to Archwood was muscle memory.

The second Colin got to the porch where the cement below his feet was decorated with the handprints of his parents and siblings, the front door swung open.

"Colin!" his younger sister Pearl squealed and stepped to the side to let him in.

"Hi," Colin replied as he quickly entered the house and skirted past her. He realized a second too late that the lack of enthusiasm in his response was probably rude given that he hadn't seen the majority of his family in eight months and, before that, only sporadically during the last four and half years. He quickly shot back an "I missed you!" to make up for it as he sprinted up the stairs. And he did miss her, truly, but the wet box in his hands was about to burst out the bottom, and the feeling of his wet clothes chafing against his skin was about to make him lose his mind.

Running had been a part of Colin's morning routine since his freshman year of college, and it came in handy as he just made it into his bedroom before the contents spilled out the bottom and the box was no longer a box, but a wet, sopping hunk of cardboard in his hands. The cardboard was pliable enough to bend, so he folded it into a tight rectangle and looked around the room for the wastebasket that was exactly where he had left it, beside the wooden desk in the corner of the room. One of the better parts about moving back into his childhood home was that the routine he had left behind—the routine he was comfortable with—was still here, ready for him to pick it back up again. While he wouldn't be living here for long, and finding his own place was high on his list of things to do, he liked the idea of knowing all the streets in Archwood. Knowing all the restaurants and which dishes had the right textures. Knowing the people who lived in town. Knowing that the one person he loved most was still here, even if she despised him. The proximity to her alone made him feel high on both possibilities and grief.

Once the cardboard was disposed of, Colin quickly moved back over to the random assortment of his belongings piled on the bed and sifted through them until he found what he was looking for. He turned over the sealed bag in his hands, looking down at the several sheets of paper scrawled with his and another, more bubbly handwriting. The papers were crumpled, and no matter how many times he had tried to flatten them, they never got as smooth as they were the day Scarlett Wallace balled up each one and threw them at his head. He always felt a bit guilty for thinking that that day was tied for the worst of his life, along with the day Walker showed up at the house with a police officer to tell him and his siblings their parents were never going to come home from their date night. Colin had no idea why he kept the damn notes, but it was something of a reminder now. A reminder to do better. His parents had been his safety net, and so had Scarlett. Relying on other people to save him had never worked out well for him. Something bad always happened, and even when it was his fault, it felt out of his control.

A knock on the open bedroom door pulled Colin's attention back out of the chaos of the past. "Hey, I brought your suitcase in, and whatever the hell this is." Walker was drenched in rainfall and dragging Colin's gray-blue suitcase across the floor. The duffel bag he held up was equally wet, and Colin's vision lasered in on a drop of water rolling down from the black handle to the hardwood. His fist balled up in discomfort only once before he released it, reminding himself that the floor was already wet due to his own dripping clothes.

"Thanks." Colin retrieved both bags and set them in the middle of the floor.

"Figured you'd want to change," Walker said. He was right, too. The longer the wet clothes stuck to Colin's skin, the more he started to feel overwhelmed. "Is this really all you brought? You don't have any other stuff?"

"Nope." Colin shrugged and unzipped the duffel first, running his hand along one of the corded ropes inside and regaining a little bit of his control. "I have a few textbooks and my steamer in the backseat. I packed all my clothes pretty tightly, so I'll have to de-wrinkle everything." There would have been more books to bring, but for efficiency's sake, Colin sold the ones he had already read and wasn't planning on rereading back in Maryland. A lot of his personal collection still took up the floor-to-ceiling wall shelves his mom had designed specifically to fit his room and his tastes.

"Right, so, your clothes, a steamer, and an entire bag of bondage rope. Normal, everyday stuff." Walker chuckled.

"Yep," Colin agreed.

"I didn't realize you were into that."

The way people beat around the bush was always frustrating to Colin, because "that" meant absolutely nothing to him. Deductive reasoning said Walker must mean the shibari rope, but he wasn't one hundred percent certain. Walker wasn't the type to steam his clothes, so maybe that was what he meant. Colin pulled a cloth from a side pouch to clean his glasses.

Walker seemed to realize his lack of clarity because he cleared his throat awkwardly. "I mean, I didn't realize you were into bondage."

"Oh." Colin bobbed his head. "I use it as a self-soothing sensory thing. My therapist back in Baltimore recommended it. If I'm at home reading or something, I usually just tie some double columns across my thighs and connect them to another double column across my ankles and lie on the floor or something."

"And that helps?" Walker peered down at the bag.

"It does. It would probably help with your anxiety, too. Plus, I have an entire book on different knot options, and I like learning new ones."

"I just figured you got into some kinky shit while you were gone." Walker grinned.

Colin let a small smirk pull up the corner of his mouth. "I would definitely not have been opposed to that." He was the exact opposite of opposed. Some of the new knots he had been practicing required a partner, and he'd had to practice those on a pillow instead. The lack of a partner was a problem if he ever did want to try out even more complicated things, but he could never get past a first date with anyone. He hadn't even tried to. No one would ever come close to *her*, and Colin had finally accepted the likelihood that he would be on his own forever was high. He swallowed and pulled at his wet clothes again. "But that would require me to date people, and that's not going to happen."

"Why not?" Walker asked. Colin hit him with an irritated expression. Not only was this the last thing he wanted to talk about when coming home to the very town where he had destroyed his love life, but the cloth against his skin was starting to feel like a serpent coiling around his torso and suffocating him. Not the kind of pressure he enjoyed. His short fuse was getting shorter by the second.

"Scarlett." Colin figured blunt was the best way to go about ending this conversation. At the mention of her name, Walker's playful demeanor shifted to concern.

"You're going to beat yourself up over this forever, aren't you?"

Colin rolled his eyes. "Don't act like you wouldn't do the same thing."

Walker grimaced. He knew just enough about how Colin had blown up his life back then to know that the way Colin had done it was a mistake, one that had hurt both himself and Scarlett so badly that it was hard to come back from. "Yeah, you're right. The Hartrick family seal should just be someone punching themselves in the face."

"Do we even have a family seal?"

"We do not. Know any artists?" Walker quirked a brow.

"None that will ever speak to me again." Colin sighed.

"Shit. I walked right into that one."

His hand pulling at the collar of his shirt, Colin nodded his head toward the doorway. He was going to lose his damn mind if he didn't change out of his clothes immediately. "Your name is Walker, so clearly you were born to walk into things. Now kindly *walk* out of my room."

"Technically, I think your sister is the one who does the most walking into things," Walker said, finally moving toward the door. He wasn't wrong. Colin's oldest sister, Piper, had been slamming her head on corner cabinets and letting doors actually hit her in the ass since Colin could remember. When they were younger, he had stopped a toddler Piper from falling face-first into a lit fire pit despite being a toddler himself at the time. He couldn't remember that moment, but his parents used to bring it up as proof of how smart he was. When Walker made it halfway through the doorway, he tapped on the door frame twice with his knuckles. "I missed your constant puns, Colin. Welcome back."

The door shut behind Walker, and Colin yanked his wet shirt over his head immediately. Once he had stripped completely naked, he felt a bit better—a little cold, sure, but he no longer wanted to peel his skin off, and that was a plus. As he slowly pulled on his new boxer briefs, he hoped the rest of his insides would settle with the warmth of clean, dry clothes. It was wishful thinking, though, because his equilibrium wouldn't return. He knew exactly why his body was having trouble with it, yet he had no control over the outcome. Normally he would practice some knots to calm his inner turmoil, but for now, a change of clothes would have to do. He couldn't hide away from his family or this town any more than he could escape the feelings that had followed him thousands of miles away from home.

The quick fix to what felt like an overwhelming flood of senses lived only four blocks away. Sometimes, just imagining Scarlett's embrace would calm an influx of anxiety. Right now, all the memory did was remind him just how royally he had fucked up four years ago. No—not fucked up, but learned a lesson, he quickly corrected his thoughts with his therapist's catch-all. But really, there was no way around it.

Any hope of a future for anything other than his career died the day he left Scarlett. Any hope of a relationship with anyone else had died the day he met her.

Two

Four Years Ago

Scarlett
18 Years Old

While Scarlett could face objectively harder things head-on, science classes always made her want to crawl into a hole and hide. Her career aspirations were far from set in stone, but the *last* thing she would ever be was a scientist. Anything that involved complicated math went in one ear and out the other. She tried to pay attention, but she just couldn't imagine a single time in her life when she would ever need to use the equation for radioactive decay. Her father used to say there were two kinds of people: those who were good at algebra, and those who were good at geometry. She fell into the latter. Shapes, symmetry, distance—all were things she could easily portray on a canvas. Her father fell into the former category, and it was why she had nothing in common with him other than their shared trauma. They were on opposite sides of the coin when it came to that, too. Her father's logical brain said that no amount of love was worth suffering that much, and he left. Scarlett had come to believe that if you could leave so easily, then you didn't love in the first place. It was probably why she could so easily leave the AP Chemistry class her best friend Kashvi had convinced her to take to hide out in the art room. She didn't love chemistry at all.

Today was different, though, because Scarlett's mother had finally caught wind of her declining grade and read her the riot act for it before making her promise to try harder. Out of all the days to attend this class, this was probably the worst one. As Scarlett stepped into the classroom, Ms. Matthews locked eyes with her and waved her over. Scarlett was appropriately hesitant as she walked toward the desk in the corner of the room, her chunky wooden earrings swaying with each step and her hands smoothing over her center part to catch the flyaways. No news was ever good news when it came to this class, and Scarlett had a feeling that whatever Ms. Matthews had to say, it wasn't going to be that she had somehow pulled a one-eighty with her grade and test scores.

"Scarlett, what a treat to see you live and in person again today," Ms. Matthews greeted her. Scarlett did not miss the subtle dig at her formerly shoddy attendance record, but she had been religiously attending this class for the last month, so the comment seemed a little out of left field. Until, of course, she saw the piece of paper Ms. Matthews handed over with red ink at the top. The percentage scrawled out made Scarlett's stomach bottom out. Twenty-three percent was quite possibly the worst she had ever done on a test before.

"I-I..." Scarlett blinked, stammering as she raked her eyes over her detailed answers. "I studied. I tried. I—" All of the hours she had spent poring over the textbook, desperate to understand, were to no avail.

"I know you tried." Ms. Matthews gave her a sympathetic look and folded her hands on the desk. "I spoke to your counselor and confirmed that you still need a science credit to graduate. It's too late in the year to drop this class and switch to a different one, but I think I have a possible solution."

Still reeling from the possibility of not graduating, Scarlett eagerly bobbed her head. "Anything. I'll do whatever. If there's extra credit, I could—"

"I'm swapping your lab partner."

"And that will help my grade?" Scarlett glanced across the classroom at her usual lab table, where Kashvi was giggling with a guy from the baseball team. She had already gotten her new partner, apparently, and didn't seem to be minding the arrangement. And that was when Scarlett realized what the switch meant. Her eyes darted to the back corner of the room and traveled up the tall length of...

"Colin Hartrick has the highest grade in this class." Ms. Matthews tilted her head in Colin's direction.

A dry swallow did nothing to alleviate the nervous energy that took over Scarlett's body. Despite being in the same grade as Colin since she moved into town at eight years old, she knew virtually nothing about him other than that he was shockingly intelligent and elusive as hell. Girls in her class whispered about him and passed scandalous rumors because the mysterious energy he gave off coupled with his over-six-foot height, ocean blue eyes, and sandy blond hair gave Colin the want-what-you-can't-have edge. That nerdy guy in every high school TV show that was inexplicably attractive? Colin Hartrick to a T. While Kashvi and other girls—and, okay, Scarlett herself—had whispered about his appeal, the boys in her grade used his antisocial tendencies as fodder and fuel to poke fun at him. Colin's two younger siblings, also attending Archwood High, were the only people he spoke to apart from the precise answers he offered up in class. He didn't seem to care about or even notice people's feelings about him, and that made him even more of an enigma. Then, when news of the car accident that killed the Hartrick siblings' parents hit the school, even the sexual commentary came to a grinding halt, because while high school kids were canonically assholes, there had been an invisible line drawn in the sand, and no one wanted to cross it.

No words sprung from Scarlett's lips. She was rendered

speechless, which was saying a lot considering whenever she was nervous she tended to ramble, and she was suddenly so nervous she might throw up.

"I think this could be a mutually beneficial agreement, if you make it one. He helps you understand this class a little better, and you... talk to him." Ms. Matthews' words fell flat, but the concerned look she tossed in Colin's direction said it all.

While the car accident was common knowledge, so was Scarlett's connection with grief. Her elementary school had held annual fundraisers for her brother's cancer treatment, and her middle and high schools had fundraised every year after his passing for the memorial foundation that her family founded in his honor. It was why she knew that platitudes and attempts to talk to Colin Hartrick about his grief would be fruitless. She didn't know him well enough to be digging into his suffering. They hadn't had a single conversation before, and yet Ms. Matthews seemed to think that Scarlett was the perfect person to talk to him. While the dead relative club connected lots of people, grief support wasn't as uncomplicated as simply asking someone how they were holding up.

"Okay," Scarlett said. There was no use in arguing with her teacher or going into the complexities of grief and why it would be inappropriate to ambush Colin with a conversation while they completed their assigned lab work.

The somber expression left Ms. Matthews' face, and she smiled. "Perfect. You can go join your new partner. I'll allow you to retake the test after you spend a little more time understanding the material."

"Thank you, I-I'll figure it out. I promise." The nerves bouncing off the walls of Scarlett's body were making her childhood stutter come back. She had mostly overcome the speech impediment, but if she got nervous enough, it came back in full force. It was probably why she never got super far into the dating scene. She always clammed up. Not that she had ever liked anyone enough to get very far, but when her words started to dissolve on her tongue, it ruined any intimate moments she was a part of.

As Scarlett turned toward her destination, she braced herself for another awkward encounter she would no doubt have when she got to Colin's lab station. Sure enough, when she got there, Colin barely looked up from his textbook, just shifted off to the side a bit to give her more space. She wasn't exactly expecting a warm welcome, but a cold-shouldered brick wall was a bit much.

"So... I guess we're lab partners?" she managed to squeak out. Colin didn't respond, but reached for something to the right of his backpack on the connected cabinet countertop. Before she had time to wonder what was important enough to interrupt their introduction, he slid a waxed brown paper bag over to her. Scarlett furrowed her brow in confusion, but curiosity got the better of her, and she picked it up to peer inside. "A maple bar?"

Colin still didn't meet her eyes, but he shifted his torso to somewhat face her. And then he finally spoke. "Happy eighteenth birthday."

THREE

Now

Scarlett
22 Years Old

"Fucking amazing, Letti." Harper stood back and looked at the new artwork hanging on the wall above the espresso maker.

Scarlett smiled beside her but kept a cautious eye on her watercolor painting. She felt as though it could suddenly burst into flames and prove it wasn't worth a spot on the wall. Her sister was always complimentary, even with paintings Scarlett had made when she was a novice. "I feel like I could have made the steam coming out of the mug a little better. See how it's a bit off on the left side?" She pointed to where the gray paint faded, twisting and billowing up from the coffee mug in the picture.

"Nope, I see nothing but perfection." Harper smiled, and when Scarlett frowned, her sister set a hand on her shoulder. "Really. It's beautiful. I truly don't see a single flaw."

Scarlett let out a breath. The thing about art was that it was never going to be perfect, no matter how hard she tried. "All right," she gave in with a real smile. It was time to let it go.

"So, how was last night?" The suggestive eyebrow pump was quickly followed by Harper's face falling flat when Scarlett attempted a good-natured smile. She was absolute shit at hiding things from her sister. "Nothing happened? You didn't do the dirty with Braiden? He seemed like he was all over you at dinner."

"Yeah, we slept together," Scarlett confirmed with a shrug and nervous adjustment of her bangs. In the end, her lack of excitement must have been a dead giveaway.

"Dammit. I was hoping he didn't suck this time."

"He's very nice!" Scarlett argued. And Braiden *was* nice. He was thoughtful, and sweet, and kind to her cat, even though her cat barely gave him the time of day. Most importantly, though, in the six months they had been together, he hadn't left once. That was more than she could say for some of the people she had dated. So what if he didn't seem to know where any of her parts were... even with direction?

Harper ignored her. "Why are all the men you date bad in bed?"

Not all of them, Scarlett thought.

Again her sister was too astute at reading her facial expressions because she glared at Scarlett. "Okay, fine. They aren't *all* terrible, but if they're good, then they're also an asshole."

"Can we stop talking about this, please?" Scarlett groaned. "This is completely normal. I mean, when's the last time you had good sex?"

Harper smirked. "Last night."

"Really?"

"Really." Harper flushed slightly and bit her lip, the picture of newlywed afterglow. As much as Scarlett loved her sister and brother-in-law, seeing two people so sickeningly in love when she was bound to never have that again made jealousy swarm her heart. "I keep telling you that Marcos has two available younger brothers."

"And I've told *you* a billion times that Varo is flighty as hell. He's fun to hang out with, but I'm not about to live in his converted van. He's bound to leave, and I don't need another Dad or another..." She trailed off, avoiding *his* name entirely.

Harper jumped in to save her. "Leo is pretty stable, though."

"He's both not in town and also fucking terrifying," Scarlett argued. The youngest Diaz brother had a domineering presence that suggested he probably had whips stashed in his bedside table. She had discovered a long time ago that she was not into that kind of pain during sex. "You and Saanvi took the two stable and non-threatening male Diaz siblings, and as much as I love Mariana, I don't love her like that. And she's also a bit young for me."

"Maybe Varo will chill out as he ages," Harper considered.

"Look, I'm fine." Scarlett waved her off. "Braiden is sweet. He made me breakfast in bed this morning."

"As an apology?"

Scarlett cringed and pressed her fingers into the bridge of her nose. "He said it was to celebrate."

"Oh my God. You faked it, didn't you?"

Scarlett quickly diverted the conversation to something else. "Want to see the other art pieces my class made?"

"Okay, we are not done talking about this, but—" Harper peered over her shoulder, excitement sparking behind her eyes. "Did you bring more from that one kid?"

"Theodore," Scarlett clarified and broke into a grin. "And of course I did." It was wrong to have a favorite student in her after-school art program, and she would deny it if any of the kids asked, but Theodore would always be her favorite. The squeal Harper let out at the mere prospect of seeing more of Theo's artwork was exactly why. Pure talent couldn't be taught, and while Scarlett had some, she could admit that Theo's talent far outweighed her own, even at eight years old.

"What'd he paint this time?"

"DNA. It's his best work, I think." Scarlett walked into the back room, picked up the largest of the frames leaning against the wall, and flipped it around to display the vibrant colors and hundreds of thousands of tiny dots that made up the picture.

Harper gawked appropriately. "Holy shit."

"Right?" Scarlett looked down at the painting and grinned wider, recalling how focused Theo had been for the last two months during the creation of this particular project. Unlike all of her other students, for whom she conducted an art lesson each time, Theodore always came in, went to his corner, pulled his headphones over his ears, and started to work. The pointillism pieces he created had only gotten more and more dynamic. For this particular painting, he had used the paintbrush Scarlett had gotten him for his birthday. All of the kids got gifts for their birthdays, but this specific brush was made for Theodore. It was easy to grip, and the material wasn't as hard or irritating to hold on to, which was important because Theo had once stripped down to his underwear right there in her studio because he couldn't escape the scratchy feeling of the tag on his shirt. Scarlett had quickly removed the tag and had him change back into his shirt in her office, away from the prying eyes of the other students, while she continued the art lesson. She could tell he was a little embarrassed afterward, but sometimes he couldn't help the way his body reacted to things.

Scarlett had learned the hard way that Theo not only disliked fire but would completely shut down if he was anywhere in the vicinity of it. She had once tried a burnt-edge art piece with some of the older kids, and Theodore's panic was enough to strike fire art from any future lesson plans. On second thought, she probably shouldn't have been doing fire art in a studio with flammable chemicals and barely up-to-code wiring. "This one will sell quickly, I'm sure," Harper said offhandedly as she continued admiring the painting.

"I'm sure it will. Does it kinda... in an off-handed way—"

"Make me think about Tucker?" Harper's sister telepathy was on point today. When Scarlett nodded and gave her a sad smile, Harper returned one of her own. "It does. Our bodies are so complex, and if something's off—one dot out of place—the whole thing is thrown off."

"He got the short end of the stick," Scarlett said. She had only been nine when their brother passed away at eleven, but it wasn't something she forgot or healed from easily. Grief was a fickle thing, especially when you knew someone's life was cut way too short. Scarlett took another glance at the painting and all the colors that bloomed and intertwined to create something whole. "But he made that short stick a sparkler."

"He made his mark," Harper agreed. "Did you finish his piece?"

"If by finish, you mean that I'm agonizing over every detail and I'm still in the sketching period, then yes." Scarlett looked down at her feet. She hadn't even started sketching. The fundraiser gala was months out, but she normally didn't put things off like this. She was a creative type, sure, but she usually hyperfixated on projects with deadlines, sometimes well into the night until they were done. This time was different. She would never capture her brother in the exact way she wanted to. While she was good at portraits and landscapes, and those kinds of commissioned pieces were where most of her income came from, she enjoyed freehanding with only her inspiration to go on even more. She knew when she finished the piece of Tucker she would be disappointed that she could never perfectly portray her brother's laughter or the way his nose crinkled at the bridge. He had freckles and green eyes that matched her own, darker auburn hair like Harper's, and he would forever be stuck at the age where fart and poop jokes were the funniest things ever. Something told her that donors would not want a freshly painted poop emoji as an auction item, even as a representation of her brother's humor.

"It's going be wonderful, Letti." Harper patted Scarlett's shoulder and looked toward the glass doorway, where the first customers of the day were starting to file in. Scarlett quickly took the painting from her sister's hands so she could get to work. "Oh, look, my favorite people!"

"Girl, you can't flatter me this early in the morning." Amala Winston, the co-owner of the local grocery store, sauntered up to the counter with a yawn. "I need coffee to get over the fact that I have a teenage girl at home. She's driving me up a wall. *Save me*."

"Jayla can't be that bad, can she?" Harper giggled.

"She said this blouse I'm wearing makes me look twenty years older, then requested twenty dollars to go out to lunch with her two best friends, who, mind you, are both teenage boys," Amala grumbled.

"Okay, that shirt is far from aging. You look hot. And teenage boys are the absolute worst." The look Harper tossed over her shoulder made Scarlett roll her eyes. Harper was very good at holding grudges on her sister's behalf, and the slight at teenage boys was a subtle dig at Colin Hartrick. Considering Scarlett tried her very best every day to not think about Colin, it didn't exactly help that she lived in a town where his name popped up like a phantom memory, taunting her at every turn. One of the teenage boys Amala was referencing was his younger brother, for God's sake. The old wounds had barely even scarred over before Scarlett was stitching them back up again. "*Hartrick* teenage boys especially," Harper tacked on, just to drive home the point that Colin was on her shit list.

"Nah." Amala tossed her hand in the air, mistaking the dig as a lighthearted one at the youngest boy. "Cooper's mostly harmless."

"Mostly," a voice called out from behind them. Scarlett looked up to see Talia Hartrick wandering up to the counter. The Hartricks were fucking everywhere, not that Scarlett could be mad about it. Talia and her husband Walker had donated to her after-school art program numerous times. She could never quite figure out if they were doing it out of some sort of pity because they knew how brutally their nephew had destroyed her heart, but she did appreciate the donations nonetheless. "Wait until Jayla's sixteen. Pearl is so obsessed with boys that I want to rip my hair out."

That was the other thing about the Hartrick siblings—there were five of them. *Five*. Back when she was fooling around with

Colin, it was nearly impossible to sneak around because he had a constant entourage. That, and Colin's uncle, Walker, who was the stand-in parent after his mom and dad passed away, watched everyone like a hawk back then. And for good reason. But Scarlett and Colin were both technically legal adults at the time and horny enough to find a way to do whatever the hell they wanted to do, which, admittedly, was a lot. Scarlett was lucky enough that the next two oldest siblings, Piper and Carter, were both away at college, or she would probably have to stitch her heart up even more when she saw them around town. She had heard rumors that Piper would be back soon, but at least Colin had fucked off to Maryland and seemed to be sticking to his plan of never contacting Scarlett or seeing her again. She would never ask, but she assumed that Colin had probably gotten a job somewhere far away. She could easily picture him traveling to remote places to take soil samples from long-dormant volcanoes. It was easier that way. If he didn't want her, then at least he didn't want her from a distance.

"I'm going to go make the display cards in the back for these," Scarlett said, tucking Theodore's art piece out of the way of the espresso makers. She only looked up briefly to catch an unreadable expression on Talia's face before hightailing it to the back to bury herself in work. She would spend the rest of the afternoon hanging up her students' artwork around the coffee shop and forcefully shoving any thoughts of Colin Hartrick into the back corner of her mind behind a brick wall. The problem with her brick wall, however, was that the bricks seemed to be made of sand. It never took more than the sight of a maple bar before the bricks were crumbs at her feet.

Four

Colin
18 Years Old

"Happy eighteenth birthday."

Scarlett reeled back like Colin had slapped her across the face, and he again reconsidered getting her a donut. Maybe that wasn't a normal thing to do for a new lab partner. Maybe she didn't like maple bars. That seemed to be the likeliest option, so he asked out loud.

"Ms. Matthews told me you'd be my new lab partner a few days ago, and it's your birthday, so I got you a donut. If you don't like maple bars, I can give it to someone else." Colin reached for the donut Scarlett had dropped on the lab counter as if it had caught fire and burned her. He had barely even stretched his long fingers toward the brown paper bag before Scarlett snatched it off the counter and held it away from him.

"No! I will stab you with my pencil if you try to take this away from me." Scarlett clutched the donut to her chest, and Colin did his best not to drop his eyes to where her shirt scooped to reveal the tops of her breasts. Quite frankly, it was hard because Scarlett was objectively the kind of girl who turned heads. It might have been her wavy red hair, but more than that, Colin thought it was her lips. They were full and pouty, and redder than usual, like she had applied lipstick that morning, but he had only ever seen her use a swipe of Chapstick. The scattered freckles that danced across her face were oddly symmetrical in their placement. Or maybe it was just that there were so many of them that there was no telling what wasn't symmetrical. He would have to sit down and map out her face, which he had suggested doing once for Emma Stone when he and his brother Carter were arguing about her general appeal. But apparently mapping someone's face with math was serial killer behavior. Sometimes Colin's ideas came across as over the top, which was probably why Scarlett wanted to stab him so soon after becoming his lab partner.

"Okay." Colin lifted both hands in a sign of surrender. Today would be a very bad day to get stabbed. Not that any day would be great, but today in particular wouldn't be the best. "If you're going to stab me, can you wait till tomorrow?"

"Are you..." Scarlett blinked and stood up straighter. "You know I'm joking, right? I'd never legitimately stab you with a pencil."

Colin released a breath and bobbed his head. "Oh. I mean, I don't know you or your murderous tendencies very well, so how was I supposed to know you weren't going to stab me?" He hadn't meant it as a joke, but the giggle Scarlett let out made the corner of his mouth quirk up.

"I'm just very serious about my food. I love donuts." She smiled, and he almost wanted to mimic it. "And you don't know me, but you know when my birthday is?"

"It's pretty easy to remember." Colin reached beside his backpack again and grabbed his own waxed paper bag, dangling it between two fingers for show. "It's also my birthday. Both our moms used to bring in cupcakes for the class in elementary school on the same day." He swallowed back the lump in his throat he had acquired just from the mention of his mom.

Scarlett's mouth dropped open. "I-it's your birthday? I didn't know that. I would have... I, um..." She floundered around in her backpack for a moment, and Colin stood awkwardly, unsure of what to do with his hands while he waited for her to get to the point. By the time he had shoved them into his pockets, pulled them out, and shoved them in again, Scarlett had retrieved a sketchbook and ripped off a page, passing it over to him. "Here." He took the piece of paper hesitantly, his fingers skimming over hers. Her hands were warm, and he fought the urge to press into the touch. The gentle grazing of skin made him almost itchy with discomfort.

What finally pulled him out of his hyperfocus was the drawing. It was almost like she had been reading his thoughts earlier about mapping out her own face. The sketch was of a face, but only half of it resembled one, while the other half spiraled and bloomed from the center line above the nose in chaotic wildflower bouquets.

"It's not my best work, but it did take a while. The concept was cool in theory, but my execution was not the best." Scarlett tucked a strand of her copper hair behind her ear, getting a piece tangled in her oval-shaped wooden earring and wrangling it free before she pointed to a small spot on the picture that she must have decided was a mistake. Colin stared down at the drawing, cataloging everything about it, and concluded that he had no clue what she was talking about.

"It's perfect." The smile that was threatening to come out earlier spread. "I can't keep this. You should give it to someone important."

"Who's to say you aren't important?" Her eyebrows rose, and she leaned closer to him, dropping her voice into a low murmur. "I mean, I don't know if you know this, but we share the same birthday."

"Is that... a joke?" He floundered for some sort of sign that she was teasing, but now she just looked confused. "Because I do know. That's why I gave you the donut?"

"Not a fan of sarcasm?" *Sarcasm.* He sighed heavily and

shook his head. He had the absolute worst time figuring out whether someone was dead serious or just being sarcastic. Sometimes the bitter way people delivered a line felt true, even after they said they were joking.

"No, sorry. I can't tell when it's sarcasm unless I know you well. I can usually tell when my brother and uncle are being facetious, but I'm more of a pun or punchline kind of guy."

"Got any good ones?"

"I make them up on the spot. And... most of them are dirty." He grimaced, knowing this was probably the worst introduction ever. He had read a few books on job interviews and meeting someone new, and no matter how much he had studied Scarlett from afar, this was probably supposed to be similar to that. It was decidedly uncouth to bring up anything sexual at a job interview.

"Oh?" She seemed genuinely shocked by this, and he was weirdly pleased he could surprise her.

"You can blame my brother for encouraging it."

"I can take a dirty joke. Half of the male population at this school come up with the most vile things to say every day, so what's new?" Colin had to agree with her on that considering that the very large breasts on her chest (which he was attempting to not home in on) were the frequent subject of his previous lab partner's commentary. He supposed Scarlett's womanly figure was shocking to people whose prefrontal cortexes weren't developed enough to determine appropriate topics of conversation. "Plus, we're legally adults today. Bring it on."

"I, uh, well..." Colin looked around for something to pull inspiration from other than Scarlett before his eyes landed on her drawing and a half-thought-out idea popped into his head. He slid the paper across the lab table and pointed at it. "It looks like someone planted their seed on her face." The pregnant pause with no viable response from Scarlett made his skin crawl. Then it made him explode into a frantic explanation so she would get it. "It's a play on words because wildflowers come from seeds, but also, people call ejaculation 'seed' sometimes. I guess that's more old-timey, but—"

Scarlett burst into laughter. It was so loud and bubbly that Colin flinched before his ears regulated the sound a bit better. It wasn't quite loud enough to set off the claustrophobic feeling he always got from loud situations, so he shouldn't have been feeling any sort of pang in his chest, but the sound had a strange effect on his body anyway. It wasn't altogether a bad feeling, so he watched her, enraptured in the way the red on her collarbone spread up her neck. A second later, Scarlett had slapped her hand over her mouth, muffling her laughter. She wheezed behind the press of her palm. The whole class was looking at them now, and Colin was no longer sure of what to do with his body. Not that he was ever really sure how to carry himself, but with everyone's eyes on them, he felt like he was the animal at the zoo everyone was pointing at.

Their teacher, who had been dutifully writing on the whiteboard as everyone got settled, raised her eyebrows as she looked over at them. "Scarlett, do you have something to share with the class?"

Hands fidgeting in front of himself, Colin grasped for an explanation to give Ms. Matthews to save them both. "Sorry," he announced, voice wavering. "It's my fault. I told her a joke about—"

The back of Scarlett's hand smacked against his sternum, and he let out a surprised whoosh of air. When he jerked his head to look at her, she started coughing violently all while shaking her head. "Don't..." she wheezed under her breath. "Please don't tell her."

"Can you breathe?" Colin whispered somewhat frantically. Her reaction was starting to make him panic. It was quite possible that she wasn't laughing at the joke, but at *him*.

"I'm okay," Scarlett squeaked out and managed to find control, giving the class a timid wave. "Sorry."

Scarlett's breathing slowly leveled as her chest heaved in and out. For all of Colin's self-beratement about sustaining eye contact with people, he seemed to have zero problem dropping his gaze again to watch her heaving breasts. She still didn't look like she was getting enough air, and he had just enough mental forethought to not take a pair of scissors or his bare hands to the front of her shirt to help her breathe better. While he had recently read one of his uncle's ghostwritten novels—a historical bodice-ripper—he was fairly certain that this was not the time to destroy the front of her shirt.

Eventually, Ms. Matthews ignored Scarlett's outburst and began her lesson. Colin would normally pay attention to the lesson, but he had already read ahead to prepare for this class, and he knew the material. His focus today was Scarlett: to help her understand the basics, and, apparently, to gawk at her chest, which was finally taking steady breaths again.

"Well, that was embarrassing," Scarlett whispered.

"Me?" Colin asked.

"What?" She looked up at him, and he met her eyes briefly, counting to two Mississippi in his head to make sure the gaze held for an appropriate amount of time before he could break eye contact. "No, I meant me. I was expecting a knock-knock joke with a pervy punchline or something even more ridiculous, and you just came out swinging with a," she dropped her voice even lower, "cum play joke. And one that was so highbrow that it took me a second to recognize the genius of it all. And who says ejaculation with a straight face like that?"

He shrugged. "I can say most things with a straight face." He kept his voice at a low hum so as not to disturb the class. Most students were chatting amongst themselves anyway because it sounded like Ms. Matthews was gearing up for a lab.

"Should we test that theory?" The corner of her mouth twitched.

Colin tilted his head to the side. "Shouldn't you be listening to the lesson? Ms. Matthews said you needed help understanding the material."

"I hate to break it to you, but listening to the lesson isn't going to help me. I've tried that. I don't get it, and I hate science."

This argument was his favorite argument to ever exist. Colin frequently had the same conversation with his brother Carter, who claimed the same thing as Scarlett. No one *really* hated science, though. They maybe weren't good at learning all the different facets of it, or they were confused by it, but hate it? Impossible. "You can't just say you hate science. Everything is science. All of our surroundings are science. *You* are science." *And very attractive science at that*, he thought.

Scarlett sighed. "I'll look up some YouTube videos on this information later. My brain doesn't work well with lectures. I try to listen, but it all goes in one ear and out the other. I need visuals to make sense of anything."

Considering the artwork she had gifted to him, he agreed that she seemed to do very well with visuals. "YouTube videos aren't the same as hands-on experience in the classroom, though. I can watch a thousand videos and read a thousand books on sex, but I can't say I know it completely because I've never experienced it."

Scarlett blinked up at him, her green eyes flicking across his features. "You were not kidding about saying everything out loud with a straight face."

"I don't like to beat around the bush."

"And have you?"

"Beat a bush?" He pulled his eyebrows together.

"Read a thousand books on sex."

A mental calculation of the number of books he had read on the subject jump-started in his head as he pictured the covers of each one on the shelf in his room. "I've read seven in total."

Scarlett gaped at him and squeaked out, "Seven?"

He nodded. "You want my Goodreads username?"

"I'm not much of a reader. I get distracted and end up reading the same page fifty times over, so the book has to be really good for me to finish it."

"Right, because you need visuals." He flipped through the

covers of the books in his head again. "Two of them had very detailed diagrams, if you want to borrow them. You'd have to be careful with them, though, because I hate cracked spines and page smudging."

"Oh, um." Scarlett tapped her fingers on the counter, and it reminded him a bit of the way his fingers twitched when he didn't know what to do with them. "That's nice of you. Maybe I will. I mean, I've seen diagrams before, but maybe your diagrams—er—the book ones will be different."

Ms. Matthews interrupted their conversation with a direction to the class to start the lab from the packets she was passing out. They stood in silence for a moment until the chatter in the room picked up again, and Colin felt the odd sensation that he wanted to keep their conversation going. Scarlett was easy to talk to. She seemed to genuinely think he was funny, too, which was a first for anyone outside his immediate family and the occasional teacher.

"I have books on all of this, too." Colin gestured to the classroom. "Most of them don't have pictures, but if you come over I'm pretty good at the Play-Doh thing in all those timed trivia games. Maybe I could show you with that? I'm not as good at drawing as you are, or I'd sketch it for you."

A smile returned to her face. He liked the way she brightened after he said things. "Really? You'd do that for me? We could study at my house. I have like thirty different-colored containers of Play-Doh because my uncle bought them preemptively for his baby, as if she could even play with it yet. At least, I don't think babies can play with Play-Doh. But maybe Play-Doh is non-toxic?" Colin opened his mouth to tell her that he would probably be more worried about the Play-Doh being a choking hazard for a baby when she continued to rattle off more thoughts. "She's not even on a full solids diet yet, but she'd probably like it if I waved the colors in front of her face. That's a good sensory thing, right?" Colin opened his mouth again, and she cut him off. "Babies and me, we both need visuals." She seemed to realize a second later that she had veered off track and redirected. "I'll pay you for your tutoring services. I'm desperate for the help if you still want to after that tangent. If you're any good at math, too, I would love to ace my stats final. I can't promise there won't be more Play-Doh monologues in your future, though. I ramble and stutter when I'm nervous."

"And I make you nervous?" Colin asked, curiosity sparking.

She bit her lip. "A little."

"Interesting," he contemplated. He was usually the most overwhelmed person in a room, so this concept was foreign to him. "You make me nervous, too."

"But not nervous enough to back out of being my tutor, right?"

Colin chuckled. "Right."

Scarlett bounced on the balls of her feet with a squeal. "Thankyouthankyouthankyou!" And then before he even knew what was happening, her arms were tossed around his midsection, her breasts pressed into him in a hug. He was so shocked by it that he could feel his muscles stiffen under her touch before they released the tension and sank into the embrace. Usually, he hated when people touched him, but Scarlett's hug was so enthusiastic that the pressure lessened some of the tightness in him before she jerked away from him, her arms curling into her chest like a T-Rex. "S-sorry, I don't normally hug strangers. That was... I-I don't know what that was. I'm sorry."

"It's okay," Colin assured her. It was better than okay. He wished it would have lasted a little longer so the relief from it was a bit more permanent. "We're not strangers now, remember? I'm your tutor."

FIVE

Colin
22 Years Old

Colin stepped onto the asphalt of the Roaster's Republic parking lot and adjusted his jacket, running his fingers over the corduroy textured elbow patches once before shutting his car door and meeting Walker around the front of the minivan. This place was familiar, and it would soon eclipse the out-of-place feeling he got just from riding in the new car Walker and Talia had gotten. He missed the old one. It had been outdated, and repairs were starting to outweigh the cost of just buying a new vehicle, but Colin was the type to drive one car and *only* one car until it died a slow and painful death. He still had the same Audi he had gotten in high school, and he meticulously cared for the thing so it would last longer and he wouldn't have to get used to a new car. There were too many memories in the backseat to junk it.

"You still drink it black?" Walker asked as they walked inside the coffeehouse.

"Yep. Cognitive function and all that." Colin nodded. He had always wondered why caffeine made him feel less hyperactive when it seemed to have the opposite effect on other people. Now he knew exactly why.

"Remember that time we tried to go on a health kick and we cut out coffee for a month?" Walker asked as they approached the counter.

"Worst month of my life," Colin said. And he meant it, too. Not because of the lack of coffee, but because it had been right after his high school graduation and right after his and Scarlett's relationship went up in flames.

"I agree," Colin's aunt, Talia, called out from behind them. She was seated at her normal couch beside her best friend Amala and sipping out of a mug, high ponytail bobbing behind her head. When he arrived at the house that morning, Talia was already gone, so Colin was happy to see her now. More routine and more familiarity for him to latch onto for comfort. "You two were the grumpiest assholes ever that month, and I hope you never go on a health kick again."

"It was Colin's idea." Walker pointed a finger at Colin.

"I said I wanted to start running. You're the one who added all the diet stuff to it," Colin countered.

"True." Walker grimaced. "I can't cook, either, so I don't know why I thought that was a good idea."

"If I recall, it was because you said you were losing your abs and you wanted to look good naked again," Colin informed. His statement was immediately followed by snickering from Talia and Amala.

"Jesus," Walker huffed. "Maybe don't announce that to the whole coffee shop?"

Colin winced. "Sorry." Sticking his foot in his mouth was his forte. If there was a fact or explanation he could provide, he had a hard time keeping it to himself, and occasionally people didn't want to remember things or to know about every single chemical that had been known to cause cancer when they were just trying to heat their leftovers in a styrofoam container. A fact Colin had learned from living in the dorms at Johns Hopkins University and watching his roommate use the microwave like it was his job.

Luckily, Walker knew him well and just slapped his back with a grin and called back to his wife, "I don't know what you're laughing about, Ponytail. You directly benefit from all of this." He gestured up and down his body.

"That she does," Amala piped up.

"You two need to stop telling each other everything," Walker grumbled.

"Why?" Colin asked. "I would think communicating about sex would help increase the use of contraception and decrease sexually transmitted diseases."

"Well, at least he knows about protection," a voice said from the doorway to the back room. Colin should have thought twice about coming to Roaster's Republic, but he had zero idea that Scarlett's sister, Harper, was still employed there. The new name tag on her black apron said "manager," so he was already calculating how long he had to be in her presence before he could make a quick exit. He wasn't good at reading social cues, but he could tell that Harper was staring daggers at him despite him not making eye contact. That, and about two months after he left for college, she had called him up to tell him he was "a good-for-nothing asshole who thinks he's better than everyone." It didn't bother him that she had said that because she was so far off base that the words held no meaning. What bothered him at the time was that she had refused to answer his questions about how Scarlett was doing, so he had to have Carter keep tabs on her for him. That ended when Carter left for college, and Colin felt a little sheepish about asking Walker or Talia to do the same. His youngest sister, Pearl, wasn't discreet enough for the job, and his youngest brother, Cooper, would end up making an investigation out of it and stalking Scarlett a little too well. So, instead, Colin heard virtually nothing about Scarlett for several years other than through her social media, which he only allowed himself to look at once a week. Mostly, there were pictures of paintings she had finished—all painstakingly beautiful—or pictures of her with her sister, who was currently glaring at him like he had kicked a puppy.

"Harper." Walker's tone was drawn out and cautionary. The way Colin's father used to sound when Colin did something wrong.

"It's fine," Colin assured him, but kept his eyes on the floor. Eye contact was always uncomfortable. If he had to use it, he usually counted out the seconds for a designated amount of time. When he interviewed for his current job, he had practiced on FaceTime with Carter to make sure he wasn't looking away too quickly or staring for too long, which often happened when he overcompensated. He didn't know why eye contact was so important when the job he was applying for entailed working in a lab forty hours a week with little to no contact with anyone other than the research team, but he had gotten the job, so whatever he'd done during the interview process must have worked.

"So, I guess you're visiting?" Harper made it to the counter, and Colin was grateful for the physical divider between them.

"I'm back permanently," Colin said. "I got a job in Merrick." The neighboring town was widely known for its oncology center and research facilities. It was in part why he had chosen to pursue cancer research because even when he wasn't planning to come back, his subconscious had wanted to. The main reason he had chosen his occupation, though, had nothing to do with routine and everything to do with his favorite person on Earth. Not a single thing had changed in the last four years on his end. He was still in love with and would always be in love with Scarlett Wallace, no matter how much she and her sister despised him.

"Lovely," Harper huffed out.

"For the love of God, can you just take our order?" Walker cut in.

"Sure. A black coffee and... the tears of a thousand women for him?" Harper gestured in Colin's peripherals to him.

Colin's hands started to fidget at his side. "Just another black coffee." His eyes zigzagged across the floor, searching for anything to make a focal point to calm his anxiety. That was when his gaze landed on the perfect object to focus on, leaning against the floor cabinets. The painting, with all its tiny blue and red dots, spiraled into a DNA double helix. It was similar to the one hanging up in his childhood home, which he had stared at enough to get lost in. An open book that Walker had bought Talia for their wedding anniversary. This piece had a similar style and had to be by the same artist. And suddenly, he *needed* the painting. Once he had his mind set on something, it was hard to redirect. The need was so visceral that he couldn't think of anything else until he had it. DNA made up everything and anything alive or dead. DNA was the reason he was the way he was. DNA was so complicated and intricate that humanity would never solve every puzzle related to it. It was his job. His life. Everything in between.

"How much for the painting?" Colin pointed.

"That's not for sale," Harper bit off. That statement alone made him panic a bit, but he was sure he could convince her.

"Why? Because it's not up yet? I'll pay you double whatever you were going to ask for it." He could tell his voice was getting somewhat frantic by the way his hands were starting to quake, but the small amount of control he had in the painting was now on shaky ground, and his body wanted to revolt against the idea.

"Colin," Walker's voice soothed with a hand on his arm. "I'm sure we could work something out. Why isn't it for sale?"

"I don't make the prices, so I couldn't tell you what it costs," Harper said. "And even if I could, I wouldn't sell it to Colin on principle."

"Oh, come on—" Walker started.

"Who prices them? Can I speak with them? *Please*," Colin begged. "I need—"

A flash of copper hair and the swing of the door to the back room caught Colin's attention mid-sentence. Then Scarlett's sweet voice made all his thoughts about the painting halt in their tracks.

"H, can you make me tea or something? I'm starting to see double, and—" Soft green eyes shifted over to Colin, and she froze, her feet jerking to a stop.

The mug Scarlett was cradling in her hands dropped to the floor.

Six

Scarlett
18 Years Old

The sound of Scarlett's keys hitting her concrete front step mimicked glass shattering. She reached down to pick up the ring, loaded down with various key chains, and looked sideways at Colin, nervous that he was judging her for the excessive trinkets and for fumbling with them to begin with. "I lose my keys a lot," she explained. "And my aunt had this event thing that I went to with her where they had a bunch of free key chains, and I thought if my keys made a bunch of noise and were clunky, I'd be able to find them better. Last week I thought I might lose them forever because I—" She cut herself off, realizing she was about to go on another long tangent while her poor tutor suffered through it because he was too nice to tell her to shut up. On second thought, he might not be nice at all. He was probably annoyed to be here and annoyed to be her lab partner. His looming presence and her inability to get a read on him were what had made her drop the keys in the first place.

"Because you..." Colin raised his eyebrows like he was genuinely waiting for the rest of the story. "I assume you found them because of the added key chains? Or did this story take place before you added the key chains and that was your catalyst to acquire all of them later on? I don't know when the event you went to with your aunt was."

Scarlett slid her key into the lock and smiled to herself. "I was actually trying to find my keys in order to go to the event with all the key chains."

"Ah." He nodded. "I hadn't considered that option. Where did you eventually find them?"

"In the fridge," she said, unlocking the deadbolt.

"That's hilarious." It was said in such a deadpan way that she thought he was poking fun at her, but he didn't have that haughty twinkle in his eyes that people got when they delivered sarcasm, and he had already told her once that he didn't do sarcasm.

"Welcome to my humble abode." With a push of the front door, Scarlett brandished her hand outward to the open living room. There wasn't much time to second-guess her exaggerated introduction to her house as she stepped inside, but she grimaced at her word choice. From the second she had introduced herself to Colin at their lab station the other day, she could not stop talking to save her life. Words flew out of her mouth at the speed of light, so there was no way to retract them once they popped into her head. All of Colin's words, on the other hand, seemed to be carefully chosen, and yet some of the things he shared were so jaw-droppingly truthful that she couldn't imagine they had been planned.

"Nice." Colin followed behind her, his backpack slung properly over both shoulders.

"So we can do it in the kitchen at the table."

"It?"

"Studying," Scarlett clarified. Everything felt sexual in under-tone with Colin, but he also seemed to be none the wiser to it. He was either relentlessly flirting with her, or it was all in her head and she would embarrass herself if she called attention to all the double meanings. Colin didn't hang out with many people at school, and she couldn't imagine being the exception to the rule. She wasn't special in any sense of the word. Everything she did in life felt exceptionally average. There was no way someone who read nonfiction as a hobby and collected facts like Pokémon cards would ever be interested in her. "How much am I supposed to pay you, by the way?"

"I don't know, ten bucks?" Colin said as they moved out from the entryway into the hallway.

Scarlett stopped to guffaw at him. "What? No. That's ridiculous."

"Too much?"

"Too little," she said.

"Scarlett, I *really* like science. This is fun for me." Colin's eyes lit up like a Christmas tree, so if she'd had any qualms about him telling the truth, they were no more. "Plus, I'm rich. I don't need your money."

"He likes science, and he's rich." Scarlett grinned. "What a catch."

Colin pinched his brows together. "I can't tell if you're joking or not."

"I'm joking, but I'm also serious," she explained, moving down the hallway again.

"That makes no sense."

"Science is awful, but the people that are into it are a catch. I was more or less just teasing you about being a ladies' man with your fat stacks of cash and the telescope or... microscope you most likely have in your room?"

"Microscope," he confirmed. "I used to have a telescope, but space freaks me out too much because it's mostly uncharted. I gave it to my brother Carter, and I think he uses it to drape dirty clothes over."

They had made it to the end of the hallway when Colin stopped his progression abruptly, pausing to look at a framed picture hanging on the wall. Scarlett dry-swallowed when she realized which picture it was: an old one of her and her two siblings.

Her sister Harper was beaming at the camera alongside a five-year-old version of herself. Tucker still had all of his hair, and his smile sliced through her heart like a shard of ice.

"Is this why you hate science?" Colin asked. She could tell his eyes were fixed on Tucker in the picture, but not in a pitying way like so many other people. He just looked sad.

"It's definitely part of it. If everything around us is science, then so was that, and no one fixed it." She looked away from the picture, afraid she would start crying if she stared at it for too long. "Science is out of reach to me. I'll never be extraordinary enough to solve that kind of problem. But you, you *are* the kind of person that will change the world."

"I think you'll change the world, too." He said it as a whisper, so quiet she could barely hear him, his eyes still locked on the picture. She couldn't tell if he was looking at the younger version of her or at Tucker anymore.

"Why do you think that?" she couldn't help but to ask.

"Because you're kind." It was so simple, and yet her heart cinched and pulled taut. "And you remind me a little of my parents."

Her heart skipped a beat. "I do?"

"Yeah." Colin looked up at the ceiling. "You don't seem to mind when I say something socially unacceptable or if I'm blunt."

"It's refreshing," Scarlett said, meaning it. "Your parents sounded wonderful."

"I don't have very many friends that aren't family members. It's pathetic that they were my best friends, right?" His eyes weren't glassy with tears, but the sadness behind them was so poignant that her face fell, and she reached out to touch his arm.

"I don't think that's pathetic at all. My brother was my idol. I was probably the uncool little sister to him, but I was desperate to be his best friend. And my sister *is* one of my best friends. If she thinks I'm uncool, then that's too bad, because she's stuck with me." Colin leaned into her touch, and Scarlett let her fingers wrap around his bicep.

"I think you're cool," he said. "I've been trying to figure out how to get you to think *I'm* cool."

"I was sold from the second you made a cum joke." Scarlett grinned, and Colin looked briefly down at her hand on his arm, slowly cracking into a smile.

"I can make more of them."

"Don't tempt me with a good time." She smirked.

"Maybe I want to tempt you," he said. Her face felt instantly hot, but when she looked at Colin's expression to gauge whether he was flirting, it gave nothing away. "What are you thinking about?" he asked.

"I don't want to tell you that," Scarlett admitted.

"Why not?"

She let out a long sigh and dropped her hand away from him. "Because it has the potential to be embarrassing for me. Would you tell me what you were thinking if I asked?"

Colin nodded toward the dining area with his head and started to move out of the hallway, calling back over his shoulder. "If you ask, I'll tell you."

Scurrying after him, Scarlett got to the table and started unpacking her backpack, trying to calm down enough to ask him when he slid two books across the table to her. Her eyes practically bugged out of her head. "Oh, these are... *the* books?" She picked one up and almost dropped it when she read the title *Kama Sutra*.

"That's one of the books with pictures," Colin explained. Hesitantly, she opened to somewhere in the middle where there was, in fact, a contorted sex position stretched across the page. She didn't even realize Colin had come to stand behind her to look over her shoulder until he spoke. She flinched and fought the urge to shut the book immediately, berating herself with a chant of *you're an adult, act like one*. "That position looks painful to me. I don't think I'd be into that. Can't say for sure, obviously, because—"

"Right, right, because of the lack of experience," Scarlett

interrupted. She couldn't for the life of her figure out *why* he wasn't experienced. Besides his towering height, daunting eyes, and hot nerd appeal, he was also genuinely nice and truthful. And maybe that was his problem. Too many green flags when the girls her age seemed to always be into bad boys who were bound to break their hearts. Scarlett had zero interest in red flags. She already had enough of those because her mom had fallen in love with one. No one would think it from her father's accounting degree and stable appearance, but he was the charismatic jock in high school that had women flocking to him. Which is why it took him exactly zero seconds to find himself a new wife and family after Tucker died. It wasn't lost on her or Harper that their father acted as though he was no longer a dad after his only son died despite having two daughters that were still very much alive.

Colin moved around her to casually pull out his science textbook like they had just been talking about the weather and sat down at the table, all business. Carefully closing the litany of intimidating sex positions in her hand, Scarlett set the book back down, her eyes landing on the second one Colin had brought. It had a bright pink cover with a picture of a tan zipper peeled back to reveal a red fabric and the white lettering on it read *Come As You Are*.

"That one doesn't have pictures." Colin pointed at it. "But it's my favorite one I've read. It's mostly about women, actually, so I thought you might like it. It's all information everyone should know. It does have science in it, but I promise it's titillating."

"*Titillating*," Scarlett parroted back.

"Weird word, right?" Colin popped his head up from the textbook he was looking at.

For a split second, she thought his eyes dropped to her chest. It wouldn't be the first time a guy had looked at her breasts. All the women in her family were going to have some serious back problems when they were older. Usually, she tried to avoid that kind of attention, but this time she had the urge to bend over more so he could see. She just wanted to know if he was interested. She wouldn't act on it, she just wanted to know for certain, because he kept delivering lines in a statuesque manner that had her second-guessing herself every three seconds.

The curiosity won out, and she finally bit the bullet. "What are you thinking about right now?"

Colin drummed his fingers on the table. "Tits."

"Right, because of the word titillating and your love of a good pun?" Scarlett reasoned, her face flushing.

"And because I'm having a really hard time not looking at yours." His eyes dropped—for sure this time—to her chest before he shook his head and looked away. "I'm your tutor, so the power dynamic is not really appropriate."

Scarlett's nerves were practically vibrating as she edged a little closer to him, almost brushing against his arm. "Well, you're more than just my tutor, right? We're friends?"

Colin leaned into her a little bit, the lengths of their arms connecting. "No, we aren't. I don't want to be your friend, Scarlett."

She swallowed and pulled away from his side. "Oh." Curling her lips over her teeth, she shook her head. "Okay. Yeah, that's fine. I don't know why I thought—I assumed that you liked me or at least tolerated me. I know I ramble a lot, but you didn't seem to mind. Maybe you *do* mind, and I just thought you didn't. Did I do something to—"

"Wait." Colin held a hand up, and she instantly snapped her mouth shut. "What did you think I meant by that? I mean, I can only handle you in this setting because I have to tutor you. I have a specific goal to achieve."

It really felt like slapping her in the face would have hurt less. "Wow, okay. I get it. I'm intolerable."

"Exactly," he agreed. "This tutoring agreement works because I have something to focus on. I don't think you're supposed to want to fuck your friends, so anything outside of this won't work. Granted, I don't have a lot of friends, so maybe that's normal behavior, but it seems like it'd be violating to you if you're expecting friendship and I'm constantly thinking about you naked."

Her stomach somersaulted, then her brain replayed everything out of order, trying to make sense of it before looping the same sentence over and over again. *I don't think you're supposed to want to fuck your friends.* "You don't hate me or think I'm annoying? You want to hook up with me?"

"I thought that was obvious, assuming that 'hook up' means sex to you." She sat down at the table beside him, and he stiffened, his spine going ramrod straight. And she might have been tempting fate or doing it on purpose at this point, but now that she knew she had some sort of an effect on him, she couldn't stop herself from reaching her hand out to touch his arm. Colin let out a shaky breath and forcefully flipped a page in his textbook. "Can we please focus?"

"Honestly, I don't think I can now," Scarlett snorted.

"Well, you have to. You're paying me to tutor you, so." He gestured to his textbook.

She wiggled in her seat. "No one has ever blatantly told me they wanted to hook up with me before."

"Surely the people you've had sex with have." Colin rolled his eyes, and she bit back a smile at how sassy he was being.

"Do you think I'm some sort of a maneater or something?"

"I think sex is a normal thing people our age are engaging in. I have no opinion on your sexual tendencies, nor does it matter for our tutoring sessions."

"So," Scarlett pushed ahead. "You don't think it's normal to be a virgin at our age? Even though you are one?"

"I am one due to lack of opportunity, not lack of wanting to, but even so, no, I don't think it's unusual to be a virgin, either."

She nodded slowly. "And do you think—"

"I *think*," Colin said pointedly. "That we should study, and you should go get the Play-Doh."

"And then you can make me Play-Doh figurines of all the sex positions you want me in?"

He sighed loudly. "Scarlett." He wasn't super great at telling when she was joking, but he seemed to get that she was messing with him this time.

"You're kinda grumpy," she teased.

"We are *studying*. You're purposely making me grumpy."

"Getting laid would probably help that." She was sure she had never been so overt about sex in her life, but she couldn't help herself.

"Does it actually help?" Colin fidgeted with his hands.

The question made her retract, folding in on herself and looking away. "I wouldn't know," she said.

"Because you're always happy?"

She mumbled the next part, the last word unintelligible. "Because I'm a hmm-mmm."

Colin's face screwed up. "A what?"

"I'm a virgin, too, okay? No sex-goddessery happening here!" She gestured to herself from head to foot then immediately wanted to set fire to the word "sex-goddessery." The tendency to invent words and phrases frequently popped up when she was nervous, along with rambling stories that were so long they could be developed into novels if the plot wasn't a clusterfuck of epic proportions. They always included too many extra details and tangents that didn't matter. No one needed to know that it happened on a Tuesday at ten p.m. and her mother's birthday was the following day, which they had lemon poppyseed cake for. Also, if she took a drug test after eating said poppyseed cake, would she fail it? Was that still a thing? What were they talking about again? Right, sex, or the lack of it, at least.

"Oh. Okay." The unbothered way Colin was still looking at his textbook made her want to pull her hair out. *Okay.* Like she hadn't just divulged a semi-embarrassing fact about herself.

"How are you this cavalier about everything?" she huffed. She had about three hundred follow-up questions, but she held her tongue in the greatest show of self control since that time she didn't eat an entire bag of potato chips the day prior.

"I'm not. I just think we should study, and you can't seem to focus on anything other than me thinking about you naked, so, clearly, I shouldn't have told you that. Your sexual history or lack thereof doesn't have to do with chemistry or statistics." In the most dramatic display of his height, he sighed heavily and leaned back in his chair, stretching out his long legs. Her eyes immediately went to his crotch, because he was right and she was just a vessel for thoughts about sex now. If cocks were proportionate to the size of the person, then Colin was packing a fucking horse in his pants, she just knew it. "I'll level with you. If you let me tutor you for at least an hour, then we can talk about my less-than-professional tendencies."

"I can ask you any question I want?" She raised her eyebrows. "Even if my question is just asking exactly what you've thought of me? No matter how inappropriate?"

"Yes, but first," Colin pointed down at the book, "let's review the basics, so I can gauge how much you already know about chemistry."

"I know nothing. I learn it, then I immediately forget about it." Scarlett got up from her seat, wanting to postpone how dumb she was about to feel. "Shouldn't I make you coffee or tea or something? My sister works at the coffeehouse, but I despise coffee, so I don't actually know how to make it."

"Scarlett." Colin's voice darkened, and her body immediately jolted to attention. "Sit down, or I'm never going to tell you any of the dirty things I think about you."

Properly threatened, it was truly shocking how fast her ass dropped down into the seat. "Fine. Just don't be annoyed when you have to reteach me everything, okay?"

"Like I said, this is fun for me. You not knowing anything means that I get to tell you. I won't be annoyed, I promise."

Colin sat up straighter, genuinely looking excited as he slid their chemistry textbook toward her.

SEVEN

Scarlett
22 Years Old

Scarlett must have done something to piss off the powers at be because Colin had only gotten hotter since he left. At eighteen, he had looked like a nerdy wet dream, but now? Now his jawline had sharpened, and while he was clean-shaven, she could tell that there was stubble right under the surface. There was no way he would ever let it grow out, considering he had once told her that the small amount of hair he had to shave off back in high school had felt like a foreign object on his face, but just the shadowy illusion of hair was annoyingly attractive.

On top of the new manly features Colin now possessed, he had clearly figured out what to do with the cowlick just right of center at his hairline. Every hair fell perfectly on his head and swooped in all the right places. Wire-rimmed, round glasses had always looked good on him, but he had traded black for brown, and the softer color brought out his daunting blue eyes. From the brown knit sweater to the tan jacket with corduroy elbow patches, Colin looked like he had fallen straight out of a dark academia magazine. Either that, or he was about to star as the sexy scientist villain in a highbrow indie film. The latter was especially fitting because Colin Hartrick was absolutely the villain in her story. And there he was, standing there and staring at her like he knew exactly what was under her clothes because, unfortunately for her, he did.

"Hi, Red." *Fuck.* Colin's voice was deeper now, too, which made the high-pitched squeak that came out of Scarlett's mouth even more mortifying.

"P-please, leave me alone." Out of all the fire and brimstone things she had thought to say to him when they met again, this stuttering and begging version of herself made her feel weak and pitiful. The way her eyes were already pricked with tears left a bitter and resentful taste in her mouth. *We do not cry over men,* she reminded herself. *It's been five fucking years.* Then, she straightened her spine and quickly added, "I think it's best if we don't cross paths again, Colin." Scarlett went to cut and run, but a large hand grabbed at her wrist, holding her in place. She looked up to find that Colin was behind the counter now and blocking her from leaving. *He* was the one who had left before, so she didn't see how her leaving the vicinity now was of great trouble to him. Her eyes dropped to where his hand warmed her skin, and he must have noticed his error because he let go.

"Just don't move, okay? There's glass all over the floor," Colin murmured. She looked down at the shards in a daze, disconnected, with all her focus still on the spot where he had touched her. All the nerve endings in her body were dancing under her skin like eager little traitors.

"You aren't allowed to fucking hop the counter, Colin!" Harper yelled, moving over toward them.

"He's preventing your sister from getting hurt. Calm the hell down," Walker shouted from behind the counter.

"Your nephew is an asshole, and I can help my sister without him."

"Okay, you don't get to talk about Colin that way. You don't know what you're talking about, Harper." Talia jumped into action beside her husband, and Amala was quickly at the counter with her. The walls felt as though they were closing in on her. Everything was overwhelming, the voices bouncing off the coffee makers and slamming into her one by one like tiny daggers to her heart. As if her brain had already reverted to her eighteen-year-old self, she suddenly realized who the shouting would affect the most, and it wasn't her.

Sure enough, when Scarlett jerked her head to look up, Colin's eyes were squeezed shut, his hands pressed over his ears in his classic defense, and she could tell he was shutting down. She reached up quickly and pressed his hands harder against his ears before turning her head to shout to their family members.

"*Stop it!*" The room went silent other than a muffled "*shit*" from Walker. When Scarlett met her sister's eyes, they were wide and surprised. "Please go get a broom and stop yelling. It's too much noise." Her voice was calm and even. The one she used in all of her art classes to tame children and wine-drunk adults. Colin's breathing was still erratic as she pulled him down a little, his forehead resting against her shoulder and her fingers pressing into the back of his head to massage. "Breathe. It's okay. I'm here." She wasn't exactly sure if that would be a comfort to him at all given how badly they had ended things, but he seemed to be coming out of his trance when something touched her arm. A pair of headphones she assumed were like the ones Theodore wore to art class were dangling over the high counter from Talia's hand. It was a new tactic that Colin must have figured out since he had been gone, but Scarlett was surprised no one had thought of headphones before. He had worn earplugs plenty in high school, but these looked much more comfortable. She carefully maneuvered them over his ears, and Colin relaxed a bit in her grasp, his eyes fluttering open as she pulled him up to his full height, cupping either side of his head and pressing against the headphones to block out any sound, including Harper below them, sweeping up the ceramic particles scattered all over the floor. Scarlett looked into Colin's face for a brief second and mouthed *okay?* Colin took two deep breaths before responding with a small nod of his head. She let her hands fall away from his face, but his arms, she realized, were wrapped around her waist like the start of a slow dance. She stiffened, revolting against the feeling of her body wanting to relax into his touch.

After a few more deep breaths, Colin finally spoke in a hoarse voice, like he had just run a marathon. "I'm sorry."

Scarlett looked away and slowly unfurled herself from his embrace, gripping his wrists and pulling them off her. "It's fine." She swallowed. "I think we're good with the mug now. You should go sit down." But Colin didn't move at all, just stood there breathing with his eyes flicking from her head to her feet. As much as she wanted him to be okay, she also needed him to not be in her presence. She was done being examined, so she took a giant step away from him and folded her arms over her chest to make it clear he no longer got to look at her or his favorite parts of her body.

"Colin," Walker said calmly from the sideline. Colin's head slowly swiveled toward his uncle, his brows pinching together. "Come sit down. We'll get you some coffee."

"On it." Harper stood up from the floor with her dustpan, and Scarlett took another giant step away from Colin, who had turned to face her again, clouds forming behind his sky blue eyes.

"Do you hate me, Red?" Colin asked, a look of hurt so potent behind his eyes that she almost stepped forward.

Steeling herself against the emotions welling up inside her, Scarlett slowly shook her head and murmured, "you don't get to call me Red anymore," before turning on her heel and barging through the swinging door to the back room.

EIGHT

Colin
18 Years Old

"Okay, and a nonpolar covalent bond?" Colin raised his eyebrows expectantly, passing over the atoms he had configured out of Play-Doh.

"When... two atoms love each other very much and share a bed?" Scarlett grinned at him, and he tapped the table with his finger for her to get to the point. "Okay, okay. When two atoms equally share a pair of electrons."

"And when the atoms are glued together?" Colin reached out to press the arms of the atoms—ridiculous, considering atoms didn't have arms—together to make one double atom with two rounded balls as makeshift electrons.

"They become one, like during intercourse." She flashed a toothy grin at him. She had been doing it the entire study session, slyly slipping in sexual references to remind him of their agreement. It wasn't likely he would forget with the way she kept leaning over to rearrange the Play-Doh, giving him a straight shot down her shirt.

"You really want to make it to the question portion of the

evening?" He took the bait, and she nodded. "Tell me what they're called when they're glued together."

"A molecule?"

Colin broke into a beaming smile. "Correct. And nonpolar covalent bonds are an extremely important part of proteins because of..."

"Peptide bonds," Scarlett finished for him. "I remember that one because of Pepto Bismol." He had purposely used light pink Play-Doh after she mentioned that word association earlier. A quick rearrangement of some molecules and all their parts created the display for his next question.

"And how does the Pepto Bismol bond form?"

"It's a chemical bond between the carbolic—"

"Carboxyl," he corrected. It wasn't a huge mistake, so he let it slide with a wave of his hand for her to continue.

"—carboxyl group of one amino acid molecule reacting with the amino group of another amino acid molecule." Scarlett looked deep in thought, but she was pretty much nailing what they were covering, so he kept going.

"And the reaction between the two causes what to happen?"

"A water molecule is released? Or... wait, is that right?" Scarlett massaged her temples.

"That's right," Colin assured her. "Last review question, and then we can talk about—"

A sudden wailing from just beyond the front door interrupted him, and he blinked in confusion.

"Shit, I think my baby cousin is home. She was supposed to be in daycare until my aunt and uncle were off work, but..." Scarlett looked toward the door where, sure enough, the handle was jiggling, and a beefy trucker of a man wearing a flannel barged through the front door gripping an infant car seat. The wailing got louder, and the nerves in Colin's head started to bounce off the walls of their enclosure. *Not now*, he scolded himself. But the chaos continued as the man who he assumed was Scarlett's uncle made his way toward them, a now-unbuckled baby screaming and writhing in his grasp.

Colin's head was going to explode. Or implode. He couldn't think anymore.

"Hi, Letti. Sorry to intrude. The daycare said Lindy was sick, and—"

There weren't any words past the screaming that he could comprehend anymore. Nothing intelligible broke through the surface of the panic that stiffened every muscle in Colin's body as he froze up and started to shake, pressing his hands into his ears harder. *Too loud, too loud, too loud.* Every receptor in his brain was shouting at him to escape, to enter fight or flight. But all his body could do was rock back and forth in his chair, his hands against his ears his only safety against the onslaught of overwhelming noise that was a battering ram to his head. A warmth seeped into his arm a moment later, and he focused on it, the piercing sound fading into the distance like an emergency vehicle siren passing by.

Colin's eyes fluttered open to find Scarlett standing beside him on her front porch with her hands rubbing up and down his arms. "Are you okay?"

"I'm sorry." Colin slowly unclasped his ears and grimaced. "I have really bad noise anxiety. If I don't know a loud noise is going to happen or if it happens for an extended amount of time, I kinda shut down. I should have warned you, I just didn't really think it would come up."

"But are you okay?" She raised her eyebrows. "You didn't actually answer the question."

He backtracked in his head, realizing that she was right. Usually, people just accepted his apology as his statement of health. "I'm okay. I don't think I can go back in there, though."

"That's okay. I'll go get our stuff, and then we can sit out here. Or not, because now my uncle Marty is here, and talking about... what we were going to talk about is not a great plan if you don't want to be murdered. He's a big teddy bear, and normally pretty happy-go-lucky, but he can be scary if you're on his bad side."

"My family is all at my uncle's birthday party at a different house. No one's home. We could go there?" The idea of not making it to the conversation he had been building up in his head since the start of their tutoring session rubbed him wrong. He was never one to break a promise or leave something incomplete, and he was legitimately excited for a conversation for once.

"Perfect. I'll go tell Uncle Marty."

"Tell him I'm sorry for freaking out. I'm sure his baby is very nice." Colin looked sheepishly down at his feet. He wasn't entirely opposed to children, and if they weren't so loud, their squishy arms and cheeks would be appealing. At some point, he would be that uncle who came over while the babies were asleep and rocked them for hours in a rocking chair. When Pearl and Cooper were babies, that was exactly what he had done. He couldn't be trusted to get a baby to calm down, but he could keep them calm easily enough.

"You don't need to apologize. Lindy is too loud for *me* sometimes, let alone someone with noise anxiety." Scarlett moved toward the door, her little multicolored dangly cassette tape earrings swaying as she walked. "I'll be right back with all our crap!"

"Awww. Look at your little hand. And, oh my God, baby handprints!" Scarlett pointed to where Cooper and Pearl's concrete handprints from ages six months and three years old, respectively, were imprinted down the line from his own at age ten. He could still remember the shock of his parents telling him about Cooper's imminent arrival. They had already decided that four was their cap on children after adopting Pearl, and Cooper was frequently called the "happy little accident."

Cooper, and even Pearl, would grow up not knowing their parents to the extent that Colin did. They wouldn't quite remember the tiny details, and a lot of their memories would be lost to the recesses of their minds. But Colin could remember the exact day they had pressed their handprints into the step. He could remember that Cooper put up a fight, and his dad took one look at Colin and knew it was too much noise, taking him to the backyard to decompress.

"Cooper was a really chubby baby. And Pearl was really screechy." He smiled. "She still is, actually."

"Harper used to pull my hair when I was," Scarlett raised her fingers in air quotes, "being annoying."

"I think it's ingrained in older siblings to torture their younger siblings. Piper hates bugs and reptiles and whatnot, and I put a snake in her sleeping bag once because she took my last hot dog." Colin opened the front door and heard Scarlett gasp behind him.

"You didn't!"

"It was a garter snake. It wasn't going to hurt her or anything. We were having fish that night that we had spent all day catching, but I fucking hate fish. The texture of it is just…" He shivered. "And then I get all freaked out by all the possible tiny little bones in the weirdly squishy yet flaky meat. Anyway, my parents knew this would be a problem because we were already away from home and I tend to like routine, so they brought me hot dogs. The snake idea wasn't an even trade for Piper's thievery, because she ended up screaming bloody murder, which as you can imagine was not fun for me," he recalled. Like his body was on autopilot, he started up the flight of stairs to his bedroom, Scarlett taking his lead and following. "There's a pretty big desk in my room we could work at."

"I thought I only had one question left," Scarlett whined.

"Right, but I have a billion more books on sex on my shelf in here that could explain my mental state so you're not weirded out," he explained.

The twinkling of laughter behind him made him look over his shoulder at her. "Colin, I'm not going to be weirded out. Just curious."

"Curiosity killed the cat," Colin said.

"But *satisfaction* brought it back," Scarlett replied.

"You know the full proverb." He couldn't help the slow smirk pulling at the corners of his lips.

"I'm a cat person." She shrugged. "I don't like the idea of dead cats. But I can tell you're thinking more about the word *satisfaction*, Colin."

"I wasn't trying to hide my thoughts or facial expressions. I don't even know if I'm making the right one half the time to hide them. But you're the one who overenunciated the word."

"I can't help it. We haven't even done anything yet, and you've already ruined me," Scarlett said. Colin stopped dead in his tracks, only one stair from the top. "I—er, I mean, not that we would do anything. I didn't mean to suggest that. I just meant... I don't know what I meant. I guess I mean you're ruining me with knowledge or something because of all the sex books? I know nothing, and—"

"Scarlett," he said calmly. It was a toss-up with him on whether he should interrupt her during one of her rants because she always got flustered, and it was terribly endearing. The less self-indulgent side of him could tell her anxiety seemed to ramp up when she started to over-explain, and she had done him a favor earlier to ease his anxiety, so he figured it was his turn to offer the same courtesy. "I know what you mean. It's okay." He marched down to his room and swung open the door. Stepping into one of his safe spaces always made his shoulders slacken in relief, even if he hadn't been particularly stressed. He occupied the room farthest from any of his siblings' or his parents'—now Walker's —rooms.

"Okay, this is exactly what I thought your room would look like." Scarlett wandered immediately over to his desk and pointed at the object sitting on the end. "Microscope." She pointed to the far wall. "Extensive bookshelf." She pointed to his bed next to her, face flushed. "Where you read all your sex books."

"And my non-sex books," he confirmed, pulling out his desk

chair for her to sit. There was only one chair in the room, so he took his position sitting on the ledge of his desk, facing her in what he hoped was a casual stance. If Scarlett was nervous, he was more so. He had zero clue what questions she would ask, and the unknowns of that made him a bit itchy and eager to lay it out in some organized form.

"Are you going to ask me the last question?" Scarlett asked.

"How are bioactive peptides beneficial?" Colin rattled off.

"They've been used to do a whole slew of things like lowering blood pressure and helping with infections." She was quick to recite the answer, and he barely had a second to respond before she was jumping into her questions. "Okay, so, how many times exactly have you thought about hooking up with me?"

"Uh..." Colin screwed up his face in thought. "All time, or just in the last few days?"

"You've thought about it before we were lab partners?" Scarlett gasped.

"Yes." He nodded. "Sorry."

"No, it's fine, I just—okay, um, we'll say in the last few days, then."

"Hard to tell, maybe around thirty times? I don't really know." Colin briefly looked at Scarlett as she shifted in her chair. He hadn't realized that his leaning position had him staring down at her and, therefore, at the tops of her breasts. "Thirty-one."

Scarlett's face turned a deep shade of red before she coughed and bit into her lower lip. "Okay, and you already said you're a virgin, but have you ever had the opportunity to hook up with someone?"

That was an easy one. "No. I've never kissed anyone, Scarlett. I doubt it'll happen anytime soon. I technically had a girlfriend last year—someone from my Mathletes team—but we didn't do anything physical. I didn't even know we were dating until she started telling people we were. It was more of a studying relationship, and we mutually parted when she left for college. I got the impression she just wanted help on her college applications. I haven't spoken to her once since she left."

"Oh. That's... strange." Her head started to bob slowly. "I've kissed people, but I've never made it past second base. I always start overthinking, and then I can't handle the idea of actually doing it when I'd probably embarrass myself." She blew out a breath. "And I have no idea why I just told you that."

"I think first times are routinely awful," Colin said "Especially for women because of the lack of knowledge about female anatomy and false ideas about female pleasure in general. It's all in that book I gave you." He was trying not to seem too eager for her to read it, but he was desperate to talk to someone about the science behind it all.

"Wouldn't it be nice if we could have a chart of data to tell us exactly how to be good at it? Like they just hand you a form when you turn a certain age that says 'congratulations, you have a foot fetish!'"

He cringed at the thought. Feet were of no interest to him. Socks were weird and often irritating because they stuck to his toes uncomfortably, and then he would become all too aware of his toes like he did when his hands became foreign objects. Being highly aware of his toes was decidedly unsexy. But he didn't want to kink shame all the same. "*Do* you have a foot fetish?"

"I can confidently say no. But wouldn't it be nice if they just handed you a map of all your parts with red circles over all the important bits telling you exactly where you like to be touched and how?" She got up and started to pace the length of his room, and he watched with amusement. This girl was wildly entertaining. Everything that came out of her mouth had him hooked from minute one. The way she told stories felt as though she was pulling spooled yarn from the center instead of an open end, and the chaotic metronome of her cadence sped up and slowed down at random intervals, making him constantly wonder what she would say next and if it would match her enthusiasm. "I want someone to just stick me with a needle and my bloodwork to come back with, 'You have a large rack that will give you back issues starting in your mid-twenties, and you're also only into missionary sex.' Or, 'Gee whiz, did you realize you enjoy being whipped in bed?'"

"I assume people do the experimenting for most of their twenties till they figure it out. It would be nice to just be able to look at a chart, though, or at least have one to reference while you're trying to figure it out," Colin agreed. He tipped his head to the side in thought, and the more he thought about it, the more he liked the idea. "I think I'm going to make one."

"What?" Scarlett stopped dead in her tracks and whipped around to face him.

"I think it's a good idea. I can keep track of my performance and the things I like when I get to college since I can already predict that I won't have the opportunity to have sex with anyone until then, and hopefully someone will take interest in me enough to get that far." He smiled good-naturedly.

Scarlett scoffed. "I'm shocked you don't have women lining up to volunteer as tribute."

"Things outside of extremely thought-out and planned events freak me out. And I told you that my parents were my best friends, so technically I don't have friends anymore other than my uncle and siblings. What on Earth would make you think that I could manage to get a girl naked long enough to want me in that way?" Now *he* was the one scoffing.

"You're... you know." Her hand gestured lazily at him.

"No," he said. "I don't."

"Don't make me say it," she groaned.

He looked over at her and scanned himself, then the room, for some sign of what the hell she was talking about, but came up empty-handed. "You're going to have to say whatever you mean because I have no idea what you're talking about."

"You're hot, Colin!" Scarlett practically shouted. "You're, like, what, six-seven? And you look like you just got back from filming a porno where you play a scientist in a lab coat named Lead comma Rod, but lead is spelled like Pb on the periodic table. And, yes, in case you were wondering, Rod definitely uses his microscope to just really," she jabbed the air with a curled hand like she was stabbing it, "get in there and see it all."

"I'm six-two, and that was," he paused, "weirdly specific."

"It's similar phrasing to what I've heard from at least five girls at our school."

"Good to know that all I have to do to attract a mate is generally avoid them and be uncomfortable," Colin said.

"Sounds about right. We also love massive red flags if you're interested in obtaining an especially awful personality." Scarlett was fiddling with the hem of her color-blocked sweater, and he flashed on the distinct image of her pulling it over her head.

"Thirty-two," he whispered. "That's probably my red flag. I'm sorry, I should just stop looking at you." Colin patently looked away and focused on the books on his wall, scanning for anything to take his mind out of the gutter.

"Four." Her voice was so quiet he wasn't sure he had heard her right.

"Four what?" Colin asked.

"That's how many times I've thought of you naked." She bit her lip back, dropped her eyes to a notebook on his desk, and started fidgeting with the corner of it. "It's not fair that you're going to use my idea without me, you know. I want to know how to be good at it, too."

"We could always..." His brain jumped the gun a little bit, and he blinked hard, suddenly so nervous that he could throw up.

"Figure it out together?" Scarlett continued his thought, not looking at him but meticulously straightening the pens on his desk into a line.

Colin swallowed. "Yes. We could practice and figure out what we like before college. We'd make it a science experiment, and at the end of the summer, we'd collect all our data and summarize it so that each person knows exactly what they like and how to perform for at least the other person."

"So, what, we just... do it?" Her voice cracked, and she cleared it before restarting. "We could start slow? Work our way up to bigger stuff, then when we get there, we try different things?"

Hesitantly Colin asked, "You're serious? Because I really can't tell if you are or not, and I don't want to misconstrue anything."

"I'm serious," she breathed. "I promise. I-I think I want this. I want to know what I like, and I don't want to be nervous about this forever. You were patient with all the chemistry stuff, and I think I understand some of it now because of you. If I'm going to lose my virginity at some point, you seem like the safest person I can figure it all out with."

Colin nodded, drumming his fingers on the desk. "I feel the same way," he said, and it wasn't because he found her attractive, it was because she was considerate and seemed more nervous than he was.

In a world where he didn't feel safe most of the time, Scarlett felt like a warm blanket and a hot cup of tea. Coffee, actually, because unlike Scarlett, he fucking loved coffee. That was why he liked her. Scarlett was like a direct shot of caffeine to his head, and the way she kept conversations going made him feel like he didn't have to try so hard to exist. And maybe that was how sex would be with her, too. She would fill in the social gaps where he couldn't, and he would fill in the knowledge gaps. This could work. This could be good.

"Okay." Scarlett nervously sat down on the end of the bed. "So, should we just start, then?"

"Right now?" he asked.

She shifted and patted the spot beside her with a shaky nod. "Right now."

NINE

Scarlett
18 Years Old

Colin was wringing his hands together as he made his way toward the bed. When he slotted himself directly beside her, goosebumps broke out on Scarlett's skin, and her thoughts started to war with one another. She had only kissed a few people, but the idea of kissing Colin made her even more anxious than usual. He was so proper and precise that she had to wonder if she had done everything the wrong way before him. Colin seemed like the type to get it right the first time, whereas she could now see all of her possible failings like they were laid out on a table to choose from. Unlike their new arrangement, she didn't have a chance to ask any of the two guys she had kissed if she was terrible at it.

"I'm worried I'm going to do it wrong," Scarlett blurted.

"Just follow me," Colin said.

"You haven't kissed anyone. I know I haven't gone all the way, but I have kissed before, so aren't I supposed to be the one teaching *you* this?"

He shrugged. "I've practiced it. I'm a quick study."

Her brow furrowed in confusion. "You've practiced? How?"

Colin raised one hand into the air. "The back of my hand." Scarlett couldn't help but break into a smile. The thought was so innocent and wholesome that a giggle escaped her lips. "Are you laughing because that's not going to help?"

"No, I—" She pressed her palm over her mouth to stop herself from laughing more. "I do think it might help. That's just not something people normally admit to."

"Oh." Colin looked down at the floor and rocked back on the bed a little, his face falling. "Is it bad that I did?"

Scarlett leaned toward him and touched his arm. "No. I swear, I'm not laughing at you. I was just surprised by how honest you are. I've done that, too. I think most people have. And I like that you say whatever you're thinking. It's nice to not have to guess."

"Okay." He sighed and briefly made eye contact before he looked away again. "Then maybe I should tell you that I get a little confused when you don't say the actual word for things. I assume 'going all the way' means sex, but maybe it doesn't. And I think if our goal is to have sex, shouldn't we be able to say the word? I don't want any confusion about what we're doing, and I think I need you to explicitly tell me when you don't want to."

Scarlett swallowed and straightened her spine. He was right. It might be uncomfortable to start using the actual words instead of dancing around the subject, but she was an adult now. Sex was a part of life, and she needed to be able to talk openly about it. "That makes a lot of sense, and I agree. I'll say 'sex' in the future." Her mouth tightened around the word, but when she finally said it, it wasn't as bad as she originally thought it would be.

"Great." Colin let out a sigh of relief. "Can you tell me what exactly we're doing right this second?"

"I'm a little too nervous to have sex."

He gave a concise nod of his head. "So, we just kiss, then."

"Yes," she agreed.

"Okay..." Colin trailed off and looked around the room. "Right this second?"

Scarlett blushed and turned toward him. The round, wire-rimmed glasses that made him look like he had fallen out of the fifties or an academic brochure slid down his nose, and he quickly pushed them back up the bridge. He was classically handsome, but his glasses were her favorite part about him. They made his eyes look even bigger, and they softened all his features until he looked boyish and curious.

"Before we start..." Scarlett wiped her clammy palms on her thighs. "You know that you could probably have your pick of anyone at our school, right?"

"Pick?" he questioned.

"Like, the experiment doesn't have to be with me. If you're interested in someone else or something, I could set you up."

He looked genuinely dumbfounded. "Why would I want someone else?"

"I-I don't know." Her insides were roiling. This was why she didn't do shit like this. Everyone assumed she had dated frivolously, but she had never made it far enough to be worth talking about. No one really made her feel so out of control with lust that she wanted to have sex with them.

"Maybe I'll want to kiss other people at some point," Colin said slowly. "But right now it's just you." The breath whooshed out of her lungs, and she scanned his body quickly to take stock of him. Was this really happening? She was really about to kiss Colin Hartrick? And even more than that, she was sitting on his bed, and he *wanted* to kiss her. The direct way he spoke always caught her off guard in the best way. There was no question about what Colin wanted because he would just say it outright. He wanted to. "And," Colin looked away and started to rock in his seat, "at some point, I'd like to see you naked."

If Scarlett had any oxygen left, it was gone now. Her body felt hot, and after he had been so open, she figured she should do the same. "I think I'd like that, too. I-I mean, I'd like to see *you*, too. But, kiss me first?" She twisted her torso to fully face him, trying to find some semblance of bravery.

"Okay." Colin bobbed his head, still rocking back and forth in his seat, almost as though he were on a boat. She thought he must have been nervous, but before she even knew what was happening, on a rock forward, his face was an inch from hers, then a centimeter, then... warmth. His lips were pillowy, the bottom one plump and soft. It was just one careful press of his lips before he pulled away, his eyes darting from her face. "Thank you."

Thank you?

She could feel her cheeks go red with embarrassment. Was she really that bad that he had to go so soon? "Um, you're welcome. You can keep kissing me if you want to."

As if that were all the permission he had needed, Colin turned toward her again, reaching out to cup the back of her arm to pull her in. When his lips descended, they weren't soft this time. They were firm. Demanding. Like he had gotten just one taste and could barely stop before he needed more. Her mouth slanted over his, and she found herself leaning into each touch with an almost desperate longing she couldn't quite place. His hand slid up to her shoulder blade, pressing into her. Her limbs were stiff originally, but she finally relaxed, taking his suggestion to follow his lead and copying his movements with her own hands. The heat was spreading through her body, and she couldn't pinpoint one location she needed him most. She wanted him touching her everywhere. All at once.

And then Colin did the hottest thing Scarlett had ever seen anyone do. He pulled back with a gasp for just a second and ripped the glasses off his face, folded them, then threw them on his night stand before his lips crashed against hers again, cupping the back of her head and lacing his fingers into her hair. She scooted even closer and dragged her tongue along his bottom lip, practically begging for more. It was all too much and not enough.

"You," he gasped against her mouth before cutting himself off with another indulgent kiss. "You have to tell me when you want to stop."

"*Colin*," she pulled back, already hating the lack of contact.

"Please don't stop." She edged as close to him as she could without sitting on his lap.

"Good. Can you hug me?"

"Hug?" Scarlett choked out, suddenly nervous that it was all in her head and that he didn't like kissing her. If he already wanted to backtrack to something more tame, then that couldn't be a good sign. While she had felt about ten seconds away from asking him to move his hands all over her body, he must not have felt the same. Despite how much she enjoyed the press of his fingers at the base of her neck, everything had felt wound tight, her breasts heavy and aching for attention.

"Yeah. Is that okay? I like pressure. Maybe we could lie down?" Colin moved to the head of his bed and looked over at her hopefully, not quite meeting her eyes. Her mind whirred with insecurity and confusion until she remembered how direct he normally was. The facts were that he wanted to lie down and that he liked pressure. If this was an experiment like they said it was, then she needed to take what he wanted in stride and use it to be good at sex. So, she boldly moved over to him and lifted her leg to straddle his hips before adjusting her body to be practically lying on top of him. He didn't say anything for a moment, and she thought she might have severely miscalculated how much pressure he really wanted until his arms wrapped around her, pinning her harder against him. "Perfect. I like this."

Scarlett liked it, too. Especially now that she could physically feel that he was turned on. The hard ridge of his erection climbed up his stomach in between them, and her body had the urge to rub against it. Even more so when Colin tentatively closed his eyes and craned his neck to kiss her again. She was hanging on by a thread. Colin was right about the pressure. It felt good, but she still needed more. And maybe that was why she didn't notice she was grinding on him until Colin groaned against her mouth. Normally, she would panic. She would get caught up in the *idea* of doing it, instead of doing it, but this was a need. It was carnal the way she was desperate for this. The awkward tension they had earlier was no longer, and it was replaced with an aching want between her legs and the need to be touched. What was first a gentle rock of her hips was now a harsh dragging of that spot between her legs over his hard length. She felt so reckless and grounded at the same time. Everything was so naturally good that she couldn't help herself. Even her nipples were hard, like they were pointed to search for him.

Colin's head flew back, and his chin tipped up with his eyes firmly shut as he breathed hard, his chest rising and falling in rapid heaves of air. "Scarlett," he moaned. "This feels so good."

"We can go further, " she breathed. "I want more. Do you want to? I—God." A soft whimper left her lips when the seam of her jeans and Colin's cock knocked against her clit.

"Yes. Can I touch you here?" He moved his hand near one of her breasts, and she enthusiastically kissed him as her answer before remembering that he had asked for her to be direct.

"Yes. Please touch me. I need you to." She rolled her hips again, and they both panted as his hand cupped her and squeezed. It still wasn't enough. There was no relief with any of it. She could almost tell how good it would feel to do this without clothes. To have more pressure.

"Stop me if you don't want what I'm doing," Colin murmured. His hand left her breast, instead slipping under her shirt, then over her bra before he burrowed his fingers under the fabric of her cup, grasping her flesh. She didn't stop him. Didn't want him to slow down at all. "It's so warm." Colin started to massage with his fingertips, and it felt so good that she didn't care anymore about boundaries. She wanted them shattered. She wanted to feel his silky skin against hers.

"I know we said we were just going to practice kissing, but..." She swiveled her hips, pressing down hard onto his cock to give him a taste of what she hoped it would be like. "We can keep going if you want to."

To her utter shock, Colin jolted upright, practically catapulting her off him. She had only a moment to contemplate being mortified by his rejection before he was rocking back and forth again in his sitting position. "Sorry, I didn't mean to toss you around. I just don't have any condoms in the room, and I need to go grab some. My dad gave me one forever ago, but I'm ninety-nine percent sure that it's expired at this point."

"Oh." Scarlett blinked, coming back into her body a bit. She could see how people had gotten carried away enough to have unprotected sex, because she wasn't thinking sanely when the persistent ache between her legs was in charge. "Right. Of course."

"Can you just tell me what you mean exactly? How far is 'keep going'? Did you mean sex? You did, right?" She leaned toward him and pressed her lips to his in a reassuring kiss. He still looked slightly panicked when she pulled back, so she scooted closer to him, applying pressure to his chest with her palm over his heart so that she could feel it racing.

"Colin," Scarlett started and then opted to take a page out of his playbook. Absolute honesty. If he thought she was uncool or lame, then they could end this now. "I meant sex. I just keep getting in my head about whether you want that, too."

He let out a slow breath and nodded. "I want whatever you want. Everything feels so—I don't know how to explain it. Heightened, maybe? I should have been doing this forever ago. I thought it would feel the same as masturbation, but it's not even kind of the same."

Scarlett let out a small giggle. She was obsessed with the way he spoke. His lack of a filter made her less nervous. With Colin, what she saw was what she got, and it was comforting to know that she could trust him. "Okay... then, you have a condom somewhere?"

It only took Colin point two seconds flat to swipe his glasses off the end table and get to his bedroom door, practically sprinting into the hallway. His eagerness made her smile. He clearly wanted this. But while he wasn't gone long, it was just long enough for some of the heat to die down and her nerves to ramp up to a thousand. How could she not worry about this? First times were supposed to be mind-altering, right? But how did one make it mind-altering when they had never done it before?

What if she was so bad in bed that she ruined Colin's first time, too?

Ten

Colin
18 Years Old

Scarlett was fiddling her hands when Colin returned, much in the same way he did when his palms started to get clammy in social situations. All his fingers would feel like they had suddenly developed a low-level arthritic ache and felt too real, too present. Now, he could barely feel his fingers at all as the excitement took over his body. His feet tipped forward and rocked back to allow his torso to sway like a branch in the breeze. That usually helped ground him when his emotions were out of his control.

"Hi," Colin said, letting the condoms unfurl from his hand in a flashy accordion down to the floor, still rocking from ball to heel. He had just enough sense to realize that "hi" was probably the dumbest thing he could have possibly said pre-coitus. "I got the condoms." Again, she could clearly see that, so he didn't know why he was spouting useless information. He quickly folded the condoms back into his palm in a rapid retraction of his contraception reveal.

"One hundred of them?" Scarlett's eyebrows shot up.

"There's twenty," Colin clarified. "Does it bother you that

I'm overly prepared for this? Technically, I wasn't prepared at all, I just figured if I was going to steal from my brother's stash, I'd take the whole thing."

Scarlett's mouth quirked up. "Isn't your brother like fourteen? And he's already more experienced than both of us combined?"

"He's not as experienced as he makes himself out to be. But girls do tend to like Carter. They typically stay away from me because I'm awkward... like right now."

She tipped her head to the side, her full lips parting into a half smile. "I kinda like that you're awkward. It makes me feel less weird that I'm also being awkward. And you tend to say whatever's in your head, so I know exactly what you're thinking. It's nice."

"I'd like to know what *you're* thinking, actually." He tapped his fingers against the foil wrappers in a repetitive tic. It was decidedly uncool that he couldn't keep his shit together for two seconds, but at least she didn't find his lack of bodily autonomy off-putting

"I'm thinking..." Scarlett trailed off before restarting with a spew of words. "I'm thinking that I'm really fucking nervous, and it was a little easier to get lost in it when we were in the middle of it and now that we had to stop in order for you to get the condoms, I don't know how to pick up where we left off." She heaved in a breath of air, and his eyes automatically dropped to her chest to watch the air expand her shirt. "What are you thinking?"

Colin let his eyes roam over the rest of her body. "I'm thinking that I really want to see you naked."

"Oh." Scarlett's voice came out breathlessly, and he briefly looked up to her face to see a splash of red coloring her cheeks and nose. She stood up slowly from the bed, biting her bottom lip. "Maybe we could do, like, one article of clothing at a time so the scales are even and one of us isn't more uncomfortable than the other?"

"Whatever you want." The eagerness of his body was overshadowing any of his nerves about the actual act. Since he couldn't stop rocking, Scarlett probably thought he was just as nervous, when really all he wanted to do was drag her back to the bed to continue exactly where they had left off. Preferably without clothes.

"Okay." She sighed. "You first?"

Colin nodded and walked over to his nightstand to deposit the condoms before carefully pulling his shirt over his head and glasses, folding it meticulously and setting it on the end of his dresser. There was a small wrinkle in the fabric when he set it down, so he swiped his hand over the raised ridge to flatten it. "Now you?" he asked, going back to standing in the middle of the room across from her.

The distance felt more uncomfortable than anything. Scarlett already knew Colin liked pressure, so he started inwardly wondering how strange it would be if he held on to her while she was taking her clothes off. *Probably very strange*, he decided. Then again, he could see her body better this way as she slowly took off her sweater. It was all he could do not let out a small groan when he saw the plain red bra she was wearing. He liked how no-frills everything was. In all the porn and in most of the ads with hot underwear models he had seen, the women all seemed to be wearing lace. All he could ever think was that it must feel scratchy and irritating.

"I like your bra," he said aloud.

Scarlett slowly let her arms fall away from her chest. "I didn't do it on purpose, but my underwear are the same color, and it's very rare that I match, so you caught me on a good day."

"Can I see?"

A slow grin spread across her face. "It's your turn to take off an article of clothing. What kind of underwear are *you* wearing?"

Colin's hands reached for his belt, and he ripped at the buckle, eager to get to her turn again. "They're blue. And Fruit of the Loom, if it's important for you to know the brand."

Scarlett let out a small laugh that fell off when Colin dropped his pants and stepped out of the legs, ripping his socks off in the process. Again he carefully folded his clothes and set them out of the way. He looked down at the floor and saw Scarlett's sweater laying haphazardly on the ground. His thoughts homed in on all the reasons why leaving it there would cause Scarlett grief later. It would get wrinkled, and then she would have to deal with it the rest of the day, and then she would forever associate him with wrinkled shirts, and...

Scarlett picked the sweater up off the floor and handed it to him. "I can fold it myself, but you look like you maybe want to so it's done right?"

Colin's shoulders sagged in relief. His hand reached out to close around the fabric. "Thank you. I like routine and order. I didn't mean to—"

"You don't have to explain it to me. It's your room. I have stuff in my room that I want done a certain way, too."

"Okay." He was so used to having to explain every facet of his idiosyncrasies that it felt almost unnatural to not have to. "Hand me your pants?" he asked, looking down to where Scarlett's high-waisted jeans hugged her hips and thighs before he remembered that she wasn't wearing the shirt he had just folded and set next to his clothes, and his eyes traveled up to her breasts again. The freckles didn't stop at her face and arms. Scarlett bit her lip again and started unbuttoning her jeans, doing a cute little shimmy to drag them down and over her round ass to reveal even more freckles on her thighs. It was excruciating how much he wanted to help her. To take her clothes off himself. Not only that, but there was so much skin to touch now, so much space between the two of them, and so many different things to look at that all the thoughts bouncing around his head were competing for his attention.

Scarlett's underwear was red just like she said it would be, but Colin found himself woefully unprepared for how the creases where her hips folded into her legs were like little arrows deliciously pointing to the apex of her thighs, her freckles dots on a map to the places he desperately wanted to investigate. Matter of fact, every single thing about her body felt like a manual on how to turn him on. He fucking loved instruction manuals. It was almost painful how much he ached behind his underwear, his cock straining to break free. His boxer briefs felt like a restraint now, and the distance between himself and Scarlett, the force of two magnets desperate to snap together.

"Scarlett, I—" Colin took a deep, grounding breath and continued to rock. "I really want to help you take the rest off."

"If you want to, you can." Scarlett brushed her hands over her arms and took a shaky step forward. "Do you want me to take yours off? I think I'm a little too nervous to help you."

"I don't mind doing all the work." Not only did he not mind, but he preferred it. The control of it all would help with the out-of-body experience he was having. He stepped forward and lifted his hand to her breast, cupping it like he had before. The sigh that she let out sounded almost relieved, and he thought that maybe they were both having the same issue until she reached out and grazed her fingers over his chest. He sucked in a sharp breath through his teeth and practically jumped away from the touch. He wasn't astute at tracking emotions just from facial expressions, but he knew enough to see that Scarlett looked hurt by his reaction. Her face pinched as she looked down at the floor, her eyes glossing over with moisture. "I'm sorry. It was too gentle. If you touch me, can you be sure about it? Harder?"

Scarlett's throat dipped on a swallow. "Right. You already told me that. I forgot already. I-I don't know what I'm doing. I'm kind of panicking."

"Can I help?" Colin stepped toward her again and warily reached for her hand, lacing her fingers in his. It felt better that way, to be somewhat entwined. He couldn't quite meet her eyes, so he looked at her lips instead. "I wish I could be gentle with you, but I don't think I can. Do you need that? For someone to be gentle?"

Warm lips met his a second later, and he breathed in through his nose, sinking into it and chasing the warmth until Scarlett backed away. "No. I don't need you to be gentle, just slow."

"I can do that." Unlacing their fingers, Colin slid a firmly pressed hand into her back and dragged it up to the clasp of her bra. His other hand reached up to help, but his fingers were blind and unpracticed as they fumbled around, yanking at different pieces, trying to release it.

Great, you said you wanted to do all the work, and now you don't know how to take a bra off, he chastised himself. In all the books he had read, none had mentioned anything about the mechanics of a bra clasp. Soon, he'd start to get overwhelmed by his lack of control, and everything would go to shit.

"Colin?" Scarlett's voice cracked. "I can turn around if that makes it easier?"

Oh. Turning around. Yeah, that would make it easier. He had been so focused on her front and her breasts that he hadn't even thought of that. "Please? I guess I need to research how to take a bra off."

"Or I could just tell you." Scarlett chuckled and flipped around. "You can probably see it now. There are three little metal clasps that each have a hook. You have to push in so the clasps —*oh.*" It was easy once he saw what he was working with. Her bra fell away, and he gripped it tightly in his hand, not wanting to set it with the rest of their clothes just yet. That would mean he'd have to leave her backside. His fingers reached up of their own accord to touch the red marks on her skin that her bra had left.

"Are bras comfortable?" he asked. It seemed almost cruel to mark her freckled skin like that until he imagined himself making some sort of a long-lasting proof of his touch. *That* was possibly wrong, but it didn't change the fact that he wanted it.

"Some are more comfortable than others, but it's always more comfortable without them." She still had her back turned to him, so he stepped into her, his groin hitting her ass. Scarlett sucked in a sharp breath, and he thought it might have been too much until she leaned into the touch and stretched on her tiptoes, as if she were trying to rub against the right spot, the way she had been grinding against him on the bed.

His hands wrapped around her and dipped under the hem of her underwear. "Is this okay? Is this what you want?"

Her back arched against him. "Please, take them off."

"It's my turn. You've gone twice now." Colin reminded her, still teasing the seam of her underwear. He had to go with the rules they set out because his comfort always fell within the guidelines, but his body kept revolting against him and chanting at him like it would be perfectly okay to take her underwear off now instead of in the proper order.

"Take yours off and then mine?" Scarlett suggested.

"Deal." He was dying to see her completely naked, so he made quick work of yanking his boxer briefs down his legs and stepping out of them. He was a little more deliberate about Scarlett's, following her request to go slow. She bent in half slightly when she leaned over to remove her underwear from around her ankles, and her ass knocked into his bare cock. The sound that came out of his mouth was inhuman. "Scarlett," he pleaded. "Give me your underwear." She did as told, and he set a hand on her shoulder. "I'm going to put this with our clothes, then you can turn around on three?"

"Okay." Her voice was high and squeaky, her hand moving to cover herself again. As much as he loved order, he was a little more haphazard with their clothes this time. Snatching a single condom, ripping it open, and sliding it on before ditching the wrappings in the waste bin near his desk and practically jogging over to her, his cock lazily bobbing as he went, hard and at full length.

"I'm back," Colin murmured. "Ready? One... two—"

"Wait! Just... I, uh, didn't shave or anything, and maybe if you want that, I should go do that?"

"What?" He furrowed his brow, confused by the sudden interruption.

"My, um, m-my hair? Like, between my legs? It's trimmed, but it's not, like, gone or anything," Scarlett stuttered.

Still confused, he answered slowly. "But I don't get it. Does the hair prevent penetration or something? I haven't read anything where—"

Scarlett groaned, and not a breathy one like she had been doing when they were clothed and on his bed, but more of a protest. "Never mind. Forget I said anything. I'll just turn around now." And she did, flipping quickly to the front so fast that her hair whipped around and smacked him in the face, the auburn strands falling into his slightly ajar mouth. He gagged and wiped frantically at his mouth to pull the hairs away. "Shit, sorry!"

"It's oka—" He cut himself off in the split second it took to take in Scarlett fully nude and standing in front of him. Her large breasts were perky but hanging heavy on her chest. His tongue swept over his bottom lip as his gaze traveled down over her pale nipples to the flat expanse of her stomach that looked smooth to the touch, all the way down to the matching patch of auburn hair between her legs.

"Holy..." Scarlett heaved out a breath, and Colin looked up to track where she was looking, down at the hard length between his legs. The stricken look on her face made him blanch, and then double-check that his cock hadn't grown a second head or something. It hadn't, and he had seen plenty of them via porn and in men's locker rooms to know that his was a normal, circumcised penis.

"You okay?" Colin asked.

"Remember that time Jeff Bezos went on his vanity space trip and the rocket was shaped like a giant dick?" Scarlett huffed out a small laugh.

"Yeah, it was shaped like that to save cabin space."

She pointed downward. "Well, that thing looks like it's going to blast off, and there *isn't* extra cabin space. I don't see how it's going to fit. I-it's too big." She was rambling now, continuing her perusal of his apparently too-large cock. He kind of liked when she started spewing everything in her head. He had figured out that when she stuttered, she was nervous, and it was oddly endearing to watch her flounder. Even better without clothes. Her face, neck, and chest were flushed as she gestured wildly with her hands, making her breasts sway with the motion. "I didn't know that it could be that big. Are you half whale? Whales are the ones with the giant dicks, right? You probably know because you're into all the science stuff. M-maybe you don't know because you're not specifically into marine biology? I mean, that's *a lot* of biology right there." She gaped at his cock again. "I assume whales are the same size as you because you're part whale?"

Colin's eyebrows pulled together. "It's not possible for me to be part whale. They do have large penises, though. Around eight feet long."

"Fucking hell." Scarlett gasped.

"Mine isn't that long, obviously," he stated. It was odd that he felt like trying to downgrade the size so she would feel better. "It's on the high end of average. I promise."

"You measured?" She shifted on her feet like she was preparing to take him bluntly between the legs.

"Of course I measured. It should fit fine. The human vagina can stretch up to eight inches."

Scarlett scrunched her eyes shut. "C-Colin, I like that you know things, but can we not talk about how much vaginas can stretch?"

He winced. Carter had kept telling him that there was a time and a place for certain facts, and apparently when he and Scarlett weren't wearing clothes was not the opportune time for anatomy facts. To him, it seemed like the *exact* time he should be sharing things like that, but he nodded anyway. "Facts aren't sexy. Got it."

"It's not that. I mean, I think sometimes facts *are* sexy, it's just that some of your facts feel clinical. I realized that I started up the measurement conversation, but I don't want you to be my doctor. I want you to touch me like you want me, not like you want to chart my growth spurts."

That made more sense to him. Unless they were in some sort of role play where he was playing a doctor, some things could be left unsaid. "Okay," he agreed. "But you still like facts about the here and now? What I'm feeling? What we're doing?"

Her voice was lower and throaty when she responded, "yes," stepping into him. Colin's hands wrapped around her back. "I still want to be walked through it. Just no more measurements."

"No more measuring," he promised and dipped his head down a bit. "And if you want me to touch you like I want you, that's an easy request. I think you should shoot higher, because how could I not want you, Scarlett?" Her breasts pressed into him harder with a short inhale. "And I think I should kiss you now."

A small smile hitched up the side of her mouth. "I think you should, too."

With her body pressed up against him, warm in all the right places, he bent his mouth all the way down to hers, full force but also remembering she wanted it slow. His tongue dragged in a rough swipe along her bottom lip, and Scarlett's tongue came out almost hesitantly, brushing over the corner of his mouth. His hand wandered around her body, overwhelmed by everything he wanted to touch. Every inch of her soft skin pressed against him was making him lose it. One of her hands was planted around his back, pressing into his spine, and the other was cupping his face, angling him where she wanted to go. He was aching to be even closer despite already touching her everywhere they could be. The next step was to be inside her.

"Bed?" Colin rasped out before his desperation to keep kissing her cut off whatever answer she was planning on saying. Scarlett didn't respond, but her fingers moved down from his face and pressed into his arm, pushing him toward his bed.

When they stumbled over to it, she broke free and sat down on the edge before backing her way to the headboard, her eyes trained on him. He met her gaze for a brief second, counting to two Mississippi before breaking eye contact. The problem with that, however, was that he had been so focused on trying to keep her eye contact that he hadn't moved at all with her onto the bed, and she was staring at him and waiting at the headboard, no doubt wondering what the hell he was doing. He gave a little shake of his head to refocus and climbed onto the mattress and over her, balancing on one arm.

"Now we... do this?" Scarlett asked.

"This?" Colin hesitated.

"Sorry. Now we, um, have sex?" Her voice kicked up at the end, going pitchy.

"Right. And I put the condom on, so we're good to proceed."

"Okay, then, maybe you should proceed."

Colin gripped his cock and angled it toward her center. "Is that a question?"

"No, no." Scarlett shook her head. "Sorry. Just go slow."

His breathing was erratic as he leaned forward a bit, hitting what he assumed to be the right spot. The head of his cock was swallowed up, and his eyes fluttered shut. They both took deep, sucking breaths. It felt like every nerve ending in his body was now in his cock, pulsing with need. He could barely think or hold himself back, but Scarlett hadn't said a word, so he opened his eyes to clock her enjoyment. Her eyes were screwed shut, her face pinched in a wince. "Are you okay?"

"Um," her shaky voice called out. "You tell me. Is it supposed to stop hurting at some point?"

"Supposedly," Colin bobbed his head. "It might hurt a bit before you relax a little. But I don't know for certain, and if it hurts the whole time, then that's irregular."

Scarlett hadn't opened her eyes, but she bobbed her head. "Okay. Go ahead."

He edged forward. It was surprisingly hard to do so. From what he'd read, Scarlett's body could naturally lubricate itself to help him slide in, but everything was so tight and felt more like when something was in the process of drying and almost sticky to the touch when you ran your hand over it. "Should I keep going?"

"I-I don't..." Scarlett's back arched like she was trying to give him a better angle. "Does it feel good for you, at least?"

"Yes," he answered honestly. It still felt good, but he was fastly losing his enjoyment. She still looked like he was stabbing her, not fucking her.

"Maybe once you're in all the way it'll feel better."

"Maybe," Colin agreed. "So, keep going?"

"Sure." Scarlett winced again as he pushed forward, and he hated it. Other than the pleasure of it, nothing felt right. She was too dry, and his brain was starting to work overtime on why nothing seemed to fit the way he had told her it would. But he had somehow forgotten everything he'd ever read in that moment that could make it better. He could feel his cock starting to lose pressure and slacken. He took one last look at Scarlett, who still had her eyes squeezed shut.

"No. I don't like hurting you. I'm done." Colin shook his head fervently and slowly pulled out, watching her still-pained face finally release when he was fully out.

He wasn't sure what he was expecting, but it wasn't for Scarlett to shoot upright in his bed, covering her face. "Sorry."

Everything was so disorienting that he tried to grasp onto anything to keep his emotions in check. Logic and facts were the best option. "You need to be wetter than that. I think that's why it didn't work and why it hurt you so much. There needs to be more lubrication."

Scarlett's voice was choked, but he couldn't see her face. "I ruined it."

"What?" Colin's mouth opened and closed several times, trying to make heads or tails of anything until he saw a tear roll down her forearm where she was covering her face. Panic lanced up his body. "Fuck. Did I hurt you? Are you okay? Do you need to go to the doctor?"

A broken sob came from behind Scarlett's hand, and her red hair started shaking with the movement of her head. "No, I'm not injured."

"But you're crying," he pointed out, scooting toward her. Maybe she wasn't crying. Maybe there was another explanation for the liquid coming out of her eyes. One of his hands gingerly wrapped around her wrist and pulled it away from her face to find that, no, she was definitely crying. His heart freefell in his chest as she yanked a pillow from behind her to cover her naked body. He swallowed. "I don't know what I did wrong, but clearly I did something."

"Y-you didn't," she whispered. "It's my fault it was bad. I was supposed to be wetter, right? There's something wrong with me?"

Colin's eyes widened in alarm. "What? No! There's nothing wrong with you. I just meant that it's either arousal non-concordance where you're not wet despite being turned on, or it's probably more likely that you just weren't feeling into it. It was probably all my stupid, unsexy measurements earlier. We also had to stop in the middle to get condoms, and that killed the momentum. We were both nervous. I really didn't mean it was your fault."

"I'm sorry."

"Scarlett, please stop apologizing," he pleaded with her. He didn't like making people feel bad, but it occasionally happened when he was too blunt or tactless in the way he delivered things. "I just need to learn how to make you aroused, and I need to be better prepared with lube or something. That's all. I don't want to hurt you. I want it to feel good for you, too."

Instead of responding, Scarlett covered her face again, and Colin had the sinking feeling that he would never get the chance to find out how to turn her on because he had royally screwed up. Everything in the books suggested taking things a hell of a lot slower and practicing foreplay before intercourse. He had ignored everything to jump to the main attraction, and now she would probably never want to see him again. That thought made him somewhat desperate for the connection again. His body needed safety, what they had before he ruined it all with sex. He reached out a shaky hand and pulled back his bed covers. For some reason, they had done everything on top of the comforter, and maybe that was yet another place he had gone wrong. It had to feel better cocooned in blankets than open and exposed with all the lights on. He crawled up to the headboard and slipped under his bedding as Scarlett peeked out from her hands. He reached out and tugged on the pillow she was holding with a loose grip, and she let him drag it up beside his. The pillow made a soft thudding sound when he patted it in invitation. Scarlett took the hint and crawled under the covers with him. When they were both fully covered, but not touching, he scooted closer and put his hand on the back of her head, pulling her in and tucking her under his chin.

The crying stopped a few seconds later, and Colin's own heart rate and anxiety leveled as time dragged on, their bodies pressed together again. Scarlett's breath ghosted against his collarbone, a warm rhythm he timed his own breathing to. Her palms moved to rest on his bare chest, and his arm curled around her.

"This feels good," Colin whispered. Scarlett's head tipped back to look at him.

"It does." Her eyes flicked to his mouth once, twice, and three times before she finally met his lips, unhurried this time. Each press was languid and comforting, and she moved back to her spot under his chin, pressing herself closer to him.

"We won't do that again until we're ready, okay?" he said. "I think we should stick to our original plan to slowly work through the steps."

Scarlett sighed. "I can be a bit impulsive sometimes without thinking, and I jumped a little ahead."

"*We* did," he corrected. "This was the point, though, right? We'll learn from this and get better at it. We'll start with smaller things, and I'll learn what you like."

"Okay." Her head nodded against him. "If you still want to try with me? You don't have to if you don't want to."

Colin let out a deep breath of relief. "I thought *you* might not want to after this. I was supposed to be an expert, but none of the books really translated that well to the actual act, which is confusing. It's also really hard to think about books when you're naked underneath me." A small chortle burrowed into Colin's chest, and he clutched on to Scarlett tighter, taking the opportunity to be even closer, her warm skin pressing into his. He wanted to be bruised from her touch and marked everywhere she was pinned against him. A brand on his skin. "Are you laughing at my statement, or at my apparent lack of sexual prowess?"

Another giggle. "I don't even know why I'm laughing. You're just so *you*. I mean, you just used 'sexual prowess' in a sentence, and you keep openly telling me that you like my body, and I'm so used to having to pry that kind of information out of guys. It's nice to not have to guess."

"I don't know why no one would tell you to your face," he murmured against her hair. "If you like it when I tell you that, I can tell it to you more."

He could feel the way her mouth stretched into a smile against his chest. "I'd like that."

"Okay. I also think you need a nickname."

Scarlett pulled her head off his chest and looked up at him. "Oh? Like we're secret agents? But *sexy* secret agents."

Colin grinned in amusement. "My uncle keeps calling his best friend 'Ponytail,' and Talia wears a ponytail ninety percent of the time."

"Oh, so, you want to be my friend now?" she asked, curling into his side again.

"Well, Piper and Carter keep insisting that Walker's actually in love with Talia, but yeah, I think we can be friends. So I'll start calling you 'Orange.'"

"What?" Scarlett jerked back from him. "Like Agent Orange? Like the fruit?"

"No, I'm not naming you after a pesticide or a fruit. It's because of your hair."

"I'm a redhead." She pulled on a loose strand of hair for show, and he took it from her, twirling it between two fingers.

"Sure, that's the term everyone uses, but your hair isn't red, it's orange. Do you not like the nickname?" Colin asked.

"Not really. Orange is, like, my least favorite color. Can't you just call me Red?"

He considered for a moment. "I can call you Red, but it won't be about your hair."

"Then what would it be about? My name?" Scarlett had barely gotten the question out before she seemed to notice where his eyes had landed: on their folded stack of clothes and the not-so-neat folding job he had done on the objects of his immediate attention. "You're going to call me Red because of my underwear?"

"And then every time I call you that, you can add another tally to the number of times I've thought of you naked."

Eleven

Colin
22 Years Old

The car door slammed shut, and Colin immediately pulled out his phone as Walker got in beside him. Talia and Amala piled in the backseat after them, and Walker turned around with a furrowed brow.

"Are we being hijacked right now?" Walker asked. "You both drove here in your own vehicles."

"We want the tea." Amala shrugged.

"*You* want the tea," Talia said. "I want to help my nephew."

Colin leaned over the center console to peer back at them. "You can all help me by staying quiet for a second." He tapped into his contacts and hit the one at the very top of his favorites list.

"Put it on speaker," Walker directed after he caught sight of who Colin was calling. Colin obliged, tapping the right button and turning up the volume to full blast as the first dial tone rang out. Carter picked up after the second ring.

"What's up? I'm walking to class."

Colin leaned toward the phone and spoke clearly. "How do

you woo a woman?" Talia and Amala both gasped behind him, and Walker shifted in his seat, a smile pulling on his lips.

"Wow," Carter said. "Coming in hot with the questions on a Monday. Is it safe to assume you mean Scarlett? Also, no one says 'woo' anymore."

"Yes, I mean Scarlett." Colin closed his eyes and pressed into his temples with his free hand. "I still..." He trailed off in misery. "I blew everything up the last time, and I don't want to do that again. I don't even know if it's possible to win her back, but I have to try. You're clearly good at getting women for some reason. You've always had a girlfriend since you were five. Tell me how you do it."

Carter hummed on the other line. "Can I get some context? Have you seen her yet?"

"Yeah, I saw her. She dropped her mug, told me to leave her alone, and almost started crying. Then Harper and Walker started shouting a lot, and I had a meltdown, and she helped me." Colin glanced at Walker beside him, who coughed guiltily. "So, I guess you could say it went really well."

"Is that sarcasm?" Carter's voice held a smile.

"Was trying it out. How did I do?" Colin asked.

"Not bad. Wish it was under different circumstances, though. Okay, so, there's not a whole lot you can do if she specifically told you to stay away from her. You don't want to come off as obsessive and stalker-ish. There's a fine line between wooing and being a creep." Carter paused for a moment, and Colin waited. When there was only dead silence on the other line for at least ten seconds, Colin gave up the waiting game.

"That's your tip? Stay away from her? Can't I at least be her friend? I mean, she told me to hit her with a whip once, and I didn't listen to that, either. It turned out that that was a good decision on my part."

"I do not need to hear this," Walker muttered beside him.

"Oh, am I on speaker phone?" Carter asked. "Walker, you're a dick for giving Colin a meltdown."

"I know." Walker sighed. "I already apologized. Harper really hates Colin for obvious reasons, but it hasn't really come up that much before now, so it threw me off guard."

"She was being unreasonable," Talia said.

"It's not that unreasonable. She's just protective of Scarlett," Colin argued. Harper's hatred almost felt like a proper punishment and what he deserved for what happened back then. It probably wasn't healthy to think that way, but he couldn't help it.

"I still think it was overkill," Amala said. "You didn't murder Scarlett, you broke up with her."

It was so much more than that. None of them really knew just how in deep they both had been when he did it. None of them truly understood *why* he did it.

"How many fucking people are with you right now?" Carter wheezed into the phone. Fletcher University, the college both Carter and Piper were attending, was built into the side of a massive hill, and it sounded like Carter had been scaling stairs for the entirety of the conversation.

"Walker, Talia, and Amala," Colin answered.

"While we're all here and inserting ourselves into your love life," Amala said, "I also think it's stupid that you're calling Carter, a manchild, to—"

"Hey!" Carter protested, but Amala barged ahead.

"—help you woo a woman. Clearly, this question deserves a woman's touch."

"You think I should ask a woman?" Colin considered. He always ran immediately to Carter with social issues because Carter was well-versed in them and had no qualms about Colin asking questions, regardless of how direct those questions might be. But maybe Amala was right. "Should I call Piper?" Colin asked. When Walker, Talia, Amala, and Carter all shouted some variation of 'no' and 'don't do that,' Colin flinched.

"I think what we're all trying to tell you," Talia lowered her volume, "is that Piper dates assholes and wouldn't know how to be wooed if it hit her in the face."

"And that's putting it lightly," Amala agreed. "If she wastes her time on any more losers, I might drive down to Fletcher to smack some sense into her."

"Think about it, Colin," Walker said. "Have you liked a single one of your sister's boyfriends?"

Colin didn't have to think about it before he was shaking his head no. The only one he had ever met was Piper's high school boyfriend, and Harden was quite possibly the biggest tool on the entire West Coast. That, and Colin had personal reasons to hate the guy beyond him being a dick to his sister. He rubbed at his right hand, a phantom pain aching in his knuckles. "Okay, I won't call Piper, then. Scarlett's still friends with Kashvi per her Instagram. I could try that?"

Amala turned to Talia. "I'm insulted."

"Colin, there are literally two women sitting right here." Talia gestured to herself and Amala.

"Oh." Colin blanched. "I was looking for a more modern take on this."

"Did he just call us old?" Amala gasped.

"He did." Talia folded her arms over her chest. "We are both still incredibly young and lively, Colin. What the fuck?"

"While we're at it, don't ask Walker, either," Carter said.

"Rude!" Walker protested beside him. "I am not old."

"You *are* old, but I meant more because you are absolute garbage at wooing women," Carter retorted. "You have game, but you don't know what to do with it."

"I did just fine. I'm married. I know exactly what to do with it." Walker looked back at Talia, who was whispering something into Amala's ear.

"You barely did anything," Colin noted. "Not even after we forced you to go on a date with her."

"He's not wrong," Carter agreed.

"I would like to point out that if you're asking how to woo a woman, I highly suggest *not* doing what you did to us when you were in high school, Colin," Talia grumbled.

Colin shrugged, unfazed. "It was a very specific circumstance, and for a good cause," he said. The circumstance being that Walker and Talia weren't speaking at the time, and Colin, Piper, and Carter had collectively decided to use the school live auction as a way to throw them together under the guise of fundraising for their respective sports teams and clubs. Yes, they had technically offered up a date with Talia as an auction item without her consent, but everyone knew Walker would save her.

"Right, the Mathletes team?" Talia scoffed.

Colin fidgeted with his fingers and looked out the window guiltily. That was a lie he had never been caught in, and now that he was a full-ass adult, he figured it was as good a time as any to clear his conscience. "I was never in Mathletes my senior year."

Walker twisted toward him. "What?"

"I wasn't in Mathletes," Colin repeated louder. "The auction money I raised was just split between Carter's basketball and Piper's soccer teams."

"I heard you, I'm just trying to reconcile what the fuck you were doing one day a week for months." Walker had his parenting tone on, the stern one he had only ever really used a few times with Colin. Most notably, the time Colin had overreacted to the knowledge of Piper getting drunk at a party, and, of course, the live auction. Things that were out of his control back then had made his emotions feel like chemical explosions rather than something he could manage. Now, he knew exactly why emotional regulation was hard for him, especially during that period after his parents died. Recently, his self-soothing tactics had worked so well for him that things like shibari and lying sprawled out on the floor kept him better tethered to his emotions.

"At first I was using it to visit my parents—er, their grave, I guess," Colin said.

"Oh." Walker hung his head. "Why would you need to hide that from me?"

"No offense, but I didn't want anyone to come with me. I just wanted time to myself." That filled Colin with a pang of guilt, too. It was normal for him to want time to himself, away from socialization of any kind, but it almost felt like a betrayal to his siblings and uncle for using that time to visit the family they had all lost. Walker was probably the one that understood the most what Colin specifically went through. Cole and Paisley were his best friends, too, the way Carter was Colin's best friend now.

"You could have just said that," Carter called out from the phone Colin was still clutching in his hand. Colin blinked and came back to the present, shoving down the guilt and reminding himself, once again, that his behavior wasn't something to feel guilty about.

"I know that now," he said. "I didn't at the time."

"You said 'at first,'" Amala noted. "You stopped going to their grave?"

"I still went sometimes," Colin explained. "But a lot less after Scarlett and I got together."

"You were having copious amounts of sex, weren't you?" Walker sighed and ran a hand through his hair. Carter was snickering on the phone, knowing exactly what his brother had been up to. Half the time when Colin needed a scapegoat after everyone found out about Scarlett, Carter freely volunteered. And when Carter wasn't available, Piper was. While growing up with a lot of younger siblings had always been a constant invasion of privacy, it was also very convenient at times because they all had things they wanted to hide from Walker and Talia.

"Kids are getting sneakier and sneakier nowadays. What the hell are we supposed to do about Cooper and Jayla when they get older?" Amala asked. "Do you think they're already lying to us about shit?"

"Oh, they definitely are." Carter chuckled. For once, Colin knew exactly what Carter was talking about. Their sibling group chat was sworn to secrecy, and Colin now owed Carter twenty bucks for Cooper's first kiss being none other than Amala's daughter Jayla.

Walker jerked his head around his seat to look at Talia. "What about Pearl? She's not... doing that, is she?"

"I wouldn't tell you if she was," Talia said. Again, per the sibling text chain, Pearl was as innocent as ever.

"Really? Because you have zero problem telling me all the shit Piper is up to," Walker huffed.

"She's still currently dating Tim, in case anyone was wondering," Carter said.

"Todd," Talia corrected.

"Douchebag name starting with a T, we get it," Walker groaned. "Fuck, I was... *am* a terrible guardian."

"No, you weren't." Colin shook his head earnestly. "I was eighteen, so there wasn't much you could do about it. And it's not like I wasn't protected every time. We were careful. Plus, you and Dr. Thomlinson are the reason I know anything about myself, so I should be thanking you."

"Have you set something up with someone now that you're back?" Walker asked, clearly sidestepping the thanks. Praise was never something Walker took easily, and it would also require him to acknowledge Cole and Paisley's one massive failing if he did, which Walker would never do. Colin was the only one who didn't see his parents as the epitome of perfection. While he loved them, their failure had made the formative parts of his life a hell of a lot harder to figure out. Mistakes were a part of their memory just as much as the good things were. The good outweighed the bad by a long shot, but he was still allowed to be occasionally pissed off that that his parents, medical professionals, and the education system had royally fucked him over on getting the resources and knowledge he should have had from a young age.

"I'm back with Dr. Thomlinson on Monday," Colin said. It would be strange to go back to his old therapist, the one who had diagnosed him with autism at eighteen, but if anyone knew how in love with Scarlett he was, it was Dr. Thomlinson.

"Good, good." Walker nodded. Despite how reluctant Walker had been in the beginning to join therapy himself, he was the one who had pushed Colin and all his siblings into therapy after their parents passed. Now, Walker was a staunch supporter of mental health, including his own.

"Maybe he knows how to woo a woman," Colin considered.

"Can we stop saying woo?" Carter chuckled. "You're not about to ask Scarlett's dad for a dowry for her."

"Uncle," Colin corrected, a pinch of irritation in his voice. "Scarlett's dad is a bit busy fucking his interns and leaving his family high and dry for him to be worried about a dowry."

"Damn," Amala muttered.

"Was that not an appropriate thing to say?" Colin asked, then shrugged. "Because I don't really care."

"As the president of the shitty dad club," Talia raised her hand like she was in a lecture hall, "I think it's perfectly appropriate." Jeff Cohen, Talia's father, was none other than the man who had drunk driven himself into the collision that killed Colin's parents, so he figured she was definitely a good judge on whether his hatred for Scarlett's dad was unfounded. "I also think that you should just talk to Scarlett. See where you stand exactly. Figure out whether she just needs time to get used to you being back or whether she wants you to stay away forever. And then, whatever that is, respect it."

"Talk to her," Colin said slowly, mulling it over in his head for a moment. "Okay. Bye, Carter." He hit the end button while Carter was in the middle of asking what was going on, and he reached for the handle.

"What are you doing?" Walker set his hand on Colin's arm.

"I'm going back in there, and I'm going to talk to her."

Twelve

Scarlett
18 Years Old

"I need to talk to you," Scarlett whisper-yelled, jogging across the hallway to Kashvi, who was standing at her locker. Her best friend looked up, eyebrows raised as she slammed the locker shut.

"You good? You look more jittery than usual," Kashvi said.

She wasn't wrong. Scarlett was practically brimming with information, and she needed to tell someone. After she and Colin had parted ways the night before, she had drafted a long string of texts to Kashvi, ranging from a borderline novella with thirty paragraphs and an epilogue to a simple one-sentence text that was so underwhelming for what had happened that she decided in person was the way to go.

"I need to tell you something, and I need you to not tell your sister," Scarlett said, looking over both her shoulders for listening ears.

"I don't tell her anything anyway." Kashvi shrugged.

"Yes, but for real this time. If you tell Saanvi, she'll tell Harper, and I don't want her to know yet. Promise me," Scarlett begged. There were perks to their sisters also being best friends, but the free flow of information wasn't one of them. Since their sisters had introduced them on that fateful day many years ago at a bowling alley of all places, there was no room for secrets between Scarlett and Kashvi. They had commiserated over how lame it was that their sisters were trying to force friendship on them, only to become attached at the hip from that point on. Over the years, both of them had learned to keep their sisters on a need-to-know basis, and Colin was certainly not something they needed to know about. Just as Scarlett had kept every single one of Kashvi's sexual exploits a secret, she knew Kashvi would do the same for her.

"I promise. Now spill. It must be good if you're keeping it from Harper." Kashvi leaned toward her, dark eyes focused and alight with interest.

Clearing her throat and carefully watching as a group of people passed by, Scarlett pulled Kashvi a little farther from the masses before putting a stiff hand up to her mouth to block the sound from leaving the immediate area. "I hooked up with someone last night."

Kashvi's eyes widened like a cartoon character as she gasped. "What?" she whispered, darting her eyes around to make sure no one was eavesdropping. "You mean, like, all the way? With who? And, more importantly, how was it?"

"Hi, Red," a voice said behind them, making Scarlett jump. She whirled around to find Colin standing a few feet away, straight-backed and holding an envelope in his hand.

"Shit." Scarlett clutched at her chest, coming down from the jump scare.

"Sorry. I didn't mean to scare you." Colin's eyes softened on her, and a small smile tugged on the corner of his lips. There was only a short amount of time to register that he had used her new nickname before he spoke again. "I like these." He reached up and brushed his fingers over her teal macramé earrings, and her body responded immediately, cheeks flushing.

"Th-thank you. Is that for me?" Scarlett finally found some words and pointed to the envelope in his hand.

"Yes." He nodded and started to pass it to her, but pulled it just out of reach before she could grasp it. "It's a performance chart. I was up until like two AM making it. I filled one out for you, but I'm not going to give it to you until you're done with this so I know that nothing I say will impact what you say."

"Chart?" Kashvi finally piped up from beside her. "Fuck. Do we have a chemistry project I forgot about?"

Scarlett ignored her and took the envelope from Colin's now outstretched hand. "How thorough do you want me to be?"

"*Very* thorough."

"And you won't be offended?" Her eyebrows rose probingly.

"No," Colin said. "You can always be honest with me. But at some point, these charts are going to read like the reviews of a five-star restaurant. I can promise you that." There it was again: the heat. It spread over her body as Scarlett imagined what exactly he would be feasting on at the Michelin-starred restaurant.

"Right, because you're a quick study?" Scarlett asked, trying to hide her face from her best friend.

"Aren't I?" Colin reached a hand up and thumbed her bottom lip. "I at least feel like I mastered one thing." Suddenly she felt like liquid, and she wanted to fall into a pool of herself on the ground at Colin's feet.

"Oh my God," Kashvi gasped beside them. Scarlett blinked, coming into her body again, and whipped her head to her best friend as Colin's hand dropped away. Kashvi jabbed a finger in the air, waving it between Scarlett and Colin. "You two hooked up?"

"*Shh!*" Scarlett hushed.

"Depends on what you mean by 'hooked up.'" Colin stated. "It seems people use that phrase for a wide array of physical acts."

"I thought you were tutoring her," Kashvi hissed at Colin.

"I am," Colin defended. "We went over the basics, and we'll move on to harder things next time."

"What do chemistry basics have to do with seduction?" Kashvi asked wryly.

Colin shifted uncomfortably and jerked his head to look at

Scarlett before his gaze darted away again. "Seduction? I wouldn't know how to lure a woman into talking to me, let alone have sex."

"Is he for real?" Kashvi cackled.

"He is." Scarlett glared at her. "Colin, when are we... um, when is our next tutoring session?" She tried to give her voice the appropriate undertone so he would realize what she was really asking, but Colin didn't catch on.

"Any time you're free. I think I can get you ready for the test in two weeks if we study enough."

"No, um..." Scarlett looked around again. "I mean for *this*." She lifted the envelope, and Colin's eyes flashed with understanding. "Other than yesterday, because Lindy was sick, my family isn't usually home till five thirty."

"Is she still sick? My uncle thinks I'm in Mathletes every Wednesday, so if that works for you, we can practice on Wednesdays."

"She's okay. So... today?" Scarlett shifted with nervous excitement. The first time didn't exactly go as well as she would have hoped, but everything up until that point and after they had curled under the covers together made up for it. When she had calmed down enough, Colin had gone into an extremely logical monologue about why it didn't work. They had skipped over foreplay. They had enough of a break in between to make Scarlett's brain believe that sex was no longer happening. Then, she was too nervous and catastrophizing everything that could happen, at which point doing anything without proper lubrication wouldn't work. All of that information probably would have mortified her coming from anyone else, but curled naked into Colin's chest while he spoke, slowly stroking her hair, it was almost enough to lull her to sleep.

"Humping on hump day. Nice," Kashvi noted with a smirk.

"What do you normally do on Wednesdays?" Scarlett once again ignored Kashvi's comment.

"I go to the cemetery," Colin said. The amused smile on Kashvi's face fell.

"We can do this on a different day, then," Scarlett said. "Go visit your parents, Colin, that's—"

"It's a stone and a grave. It's not my parents," Colin stated bluntly. Scarlett looked up at him, trying to catch his eyes, but he wouldn't look at her, so she timidly reached out her hand before committing and setting it firmly on his arm.

"Why do you go if not for your parents?" Kashvi asked. Her voice was soft now, forgetting all semblance of the teasing tone she had before.

"The psychology of visiting graves says I should feel a connection being in the same space as where they were buried. I thought if I—" His Adam's apple dipped on a swallow, and he looked down the hallway, his eyes growing distant. "My parents used to be part of my old routine. I made a new routine that I thought would include them." His voice had grown cold and detached. "It doesn't work, other than occasionally getting me peace and quiet from my family. I have therapy in an hour, and I think that will be enough time spent talking about my parents, so I'd rather have sex."

Kashvi started coughing loudly, and Scarlett reached up to slap her hand over Colin's mouth, startled by his abrupt conversation change. Colin encircled her wrist and tugged, removing her palm from his mouth, eyebrows raised. "I, uh, sorry," she whispered.

"You really need to get used to saying things out loud," he said.

"It's not that—well, I mean, it's partially that, but it's also that you'd probably get praised for what we're doing, while I'll get called mean names." Scarlett grimaced and looked up to find Colin scowling, his body stiff. "So, if it's all the same to you, I don't really want people to know."

"Except for me. I get to know everything," Kashvi chirped.

"Except for Kashvi," Scarlett confirmed.

"I won't tell anyone. I don't want to hurt you, and I won't be the reason someone hurts you," Colin said. The fluttering feeling in her stomach intensified. "Text me or pass me a note or something if you have questions about the chart?"

Scarlett clutched the envelope close to her chest and squeaked out, "okay."

With a flick of his eyes to her lips, Colin hesitated before he stooped forward, his mouth going to her ear instead. "I want to kiss you right now, but I can wait." While she was left gawking and trying to convince herself that she shouldn't tell him not to wait, he was gone, leaving her to watch with flushed cheeks as he met his brother at the end of the hall. The incredibly suspicious look on Carter's face was enough to make her pull her attention away from Colin's backside.

"What the fuck is happening right now?" Kashvi whispered beside her.

"I'm in trouble," Scarlett groaned and turned to press her forehead into the cool metal of her best friend's locker.

"I'll say. That was erotic in, like... a really weird way." Kashvi had no qualms about looking down the hallway at Colin's retreating backside, and with his height, Colin stuck out like a sore thumb in the sea of students.

"I'm so into it." Scarlett flushed and covered her face with both her hands.

"So," Kashvi leaned forward, her voice hushed, "the sex was good, then?"

"No, actually." Scarlett shook her head, cheeks still hot, and opened the envelope, pulling out a slip of paper. "Both of us were virgins. It was really terrible."

"So why are you all heart eyes for him, then?" Kashvi pulled her eyebrows together in confusion.

"Because he's so sweet. I was sad it wasn't good, and I kinda started crying."

Kashvi's mouth dropped open. "Oh, honey."

"I know. It was mortifying. But then he wrapped us up like a burrito while he explained everything scientifically so I wouldn't be embarrassed about it, and we talked about a plan to make it better next time. I mean, he made a grading system for it, look at this." Scarlett flashed the sheet, and they stood in prolonged silence while they read over each of the categories that were followed by a "circle your answer" grading system of one through five and a freeform section for notes.

Knowledge: Describe anything learned during the session, questions that arose, or things you would like to learn prior to the next session.

Pacing: Record the time elapsed during different activities, whether it was too fast or too slow, and any notes on tempo.

Skill: List all areas where improvement is needed or what was most enjoyable for angle, positioning, pressure, hand placement, etc.

Productivity: Any improvement from the last session? Where is the trajectory of the sessions headed?

Orgasm Achieved? It was the only category that was followed by a "yes or no" and a grading of one through five for the *strength of the orgasm* instead of a performance meter. The first set of categories was repeated a second time, she noticed, before she found he had split up the chart into two brackets: "foreplay" and "intercourse." And, finally, at the bottom of the chart, after an additional uncategorized freeform section, was a "total time elapsed" box and a spot for the hypothesis and conclusion of the session.

"This is incredible," Kasvi whispered.

"Right? It was my idea, and he just ran with it. It'll be nice to know exactly what I like and how I like it." Scarlett reached for her backpack and pulled out a pen. She had never been more excited for a science project in her life.

Thirteen

Scarlett
22 Years Old

"Are you okay?" Harper's voice was calm as she set a mug of tea in front of Scarlett, who grimaced and shrugged, trying to look indifferent.

"He was bound to come back at some point. I saw him once in Lydia's Grocery two years ago, so it's not like I didn't know he'd be back every Thanksgiving and Christmas at the least," Scarlett reasoned.

"That's a hell of a lot different than moving back permanently," Harper noted.

"I'm over it." It sounded false coming out of her mouth, so when Scarlett clocked her sister's reaction, she wasn't shocked to find that Harper didn't believe her at all. "I need to be over it," she corrected herself.

"Just start thinking of him the way I do, and you'll get there." Harper stood up and smiled down at her.

The problem with Harper's train of thought was that she was wrong. Colin wasn't some evil man, luring women to his bed so he could purposely hurt them later. *That* was why it hurt so much. It would be so much easier if Scarlett could say that he had cheated on her or something equally awful so she could call him a womanizing asshole and move on to someone kind like Braiden. Instead, she had had the time of her life right up until the end, when Colin's demeanor changed so drastically that it didn't even feel like him. The Colin she saw today felt like the old one, before the day he broke up with her.

"Yeah," Scarlett said, her voice fading with her complacent response.

"Oh, come on. What the fuck do you want?" Harper called out. The outburst caught Scarlett off guard, and she peered toward where Colin was standing—alone this time—near the entryway. "I already told you the painting isn't for sale." Scarlett had no idea what her sister was talking about, but it didn't matter, because the only person she could focus on now was Colin as he slowly approached her table, nervously playing with his hands. She already wanted to cry again, and it pissed her off that she couldn't hold it together for two seconds around him.

"What do you need?" Scarlett asked bitterly as she rose from her chair.

"I just want to talk to you," Colin said. His voice was almost shy, the movements of his body timid as he finally made it to the table she was seated at. "I know you told me that we should stay away from each other, and if you still want me to do that at the end of this conversation, then I will."

"I can kick him out, Letti," Harper said.

Scarlett shook her head. "It's fine. I can deal with this."

"Are you sure?" The concern on Harper's face made Scarlett feel like a child.

"I'm sure." Scarlett made her response strong this time. She could do this. She could have one conversation with him and not be a wreck after. Colin slowly sat down at her table as she reseated herself.

"Let me know if you need me." Harper called back as she moved toward the counter.

At first, Colin said nothing. They sat in silence as the people in the coffee shop around them sipped their drinks. It unnerved Scarlett that he wasn't talking, but she refused to be the one to break the silence when he was the one who had demanded to speak with her. She took a sip of her tea instead.

"I want to be your friend," Colin finally said. The tea sliding down her throat made her choke. She coughed violently and took another sip to calm the burning sensation.

"We can't be friends, Colin," she finally said.

Face falling, Colin looked at the floor. "Why not?"

"How can you not know why?" The scoff Scarlett let out sounded so hurt that even she was surprised by it.

"Explain it to me like I don't know why," Colin said.

"Well, for starters, you have no idea who I am anymore. We don't know each other. You've been gone for five years."

"Four," he corrected. "Four years, six months, and twelve days."

"Semantics." She set her mouth in a flat line.

"You've changed that much since I've been gone? Because I haven't." Colin apparently failed to notice how his own body had changed, but she could see that his personality was still the exact same.

"I've changed enough to know that you don't know where I work or what I spend time doing anymore." Not many of her aspirations had changed since high school, but it didn't change the fact that he hadn't been around for the last four years to catch on to any of the little differences.

"You work for your brother's foundation. And I assume you still spend a lot of time painting because you also run an after-school program for at-risk youth. You're on a rec league soccer team in the fall. You have bangs now, and tattoos that I assume you designed yourself because they look like the watercolor flowers you used to paint all the time," Colin rattled off.

Scarlett frowned. "So, what? You're stalking me on social media now?" If Colin had any social media, she probably would have done the same, to an unhealthy degree, but she wasn't the one that had ended things.

"Not just now," he admitted. "Once a week for the last four years."

Her heart almost stopped beating completely. "Why?"

"Because I think it probably would have been unhealthy if I did it more than that, so I scheduled it for Wednesdays."

"No, why did you stalk me at all, Colin?" Scarlett's mind was whirring and spinning with the information. "You're the one who blew us up. You decided it was over, so why are you looking at my Instagram every week on the day we used to..." She trailed off, shaking her head from the memories.

"You still can't say the word?" Colin asked.

"I can say 'sex,' Colin." Scarlett folded her arms over her chest, self-consciously covering her breasts. "It's not the word that's throwing me off, it's you. Why are you stalking my Instagram?"

"I like seeing you happy," he said. "You're happy, aren't you?"

"I am." It came out rough from her mouth. Right this very second, she wasn't sure that she was. "Are you?"

Colin folded his hands on his lap and shrugged. "Sometimes." He looked toward the counter, and something crossed over his face that she couldn't read. "Did you paint the art above the espresso maker?" He pointed to the canvas she had just hung up earlier that morning.

"Yes." She swallowed. "It's new. It's not my best work."

"It's beautiful. I can see the improvement, even though I never understood how you were doing it to begin with."

"Is that the one you were trying to buy? Harper commissioned it for the coffee shop, so it really isn't for sale." She watched as Harper took someone's order behind the counter and casually looked over at them, keeping a watchful eye.

"No." Colin shook his head. "There was one leaning against the cabinets behind the counter. A double helix?"

For some reason, the knowledge that Colin was going to buy Theodore's art was what hit her the hardest. Years later, Colin still was able to pick out the things that were important to her. She didn't care about the mug piece above the espresso maker at all. The DNA painting was much more special. So, she surprised herself when new words came out of her mouth. "That piece *is* for sale."

"It is?" Colin sat up straighter.

"Yes. I hadn't decided on a price yet, but a quarter of the profits go to the art program I'm running for supplies, and then the rest I stash away for each of them until they graduate high school." For some reason, out of anyone, it felt like Colin was the one who should own the piece. Maybe it was because she had that same feeling about Theo as she did with Colin forever ago. They were both going to be somebody. They were both irrefutably special. The type of minds to change the world. The type to see everything differently. Theo's autism allowed him to see the world at a different frequency, enough to make masterpieces that she could only imagine in her wildest dreams. Colin's straightforward way of thinking and desire to find the knowable in everything was going to get him places. "That piece was made by my favorite student, so if you plan on buying that one, you have to promise me you'll take care of it." Colin's mouth flatlined, and he cocked his head to the side. "Right. You keep everything pristine. Who am I kidding, I'm sure you'll keep it safe. You take care of the things you love. I guess I'm just the exception to that rule."

"Scarlett." His voice cracked as if he were shocked by the statement, but she just lifted her eyebrows in a challenge. "I never wanted to hurt you. I know I did, but I'd like to explain, and—"

"No," she cut him off. "I'm not interested in dredging up the past. I'm sorry I brought it up. We didn't even date, right? It was all just one big experiment."

Colin looked stricken. "It wasn't just an experiment to me."

The shrug she gave him was as nonchalant as she could make it. "Well, I won't hold you to anything you said back then."

"I meant everything I said back then," Colin said with a bitter edge to his voice. "You watched me cross off the no strings attached rule on our chart, Scarlett."

"We agreed originally to an experiment, and that's what it turned out to be in the end. No matter how convoluted it got." It was a blatant lie, and she waited for only a split second for him to call her on it, watching his mouth open in protest before she spoke again. "I have some bubble wrap in the back, and I can wrap the piece up for you if you still want it. But I was serious about not wanting to cross paths, Colin. As much as we can avoid each other, that's what I want. I can't be your friend. I'm *trying* to be happy, and you make me..."

"Sad?" he asked, his expression somber as he looked down at his hands.

"And mad." Scarlett let out a long sigh. "I never want to be blindsided again the way I was blindsided by you. I don't even want to be having this conversation right now. I want to be done wondering what I did wrong. If I was too much. I want to be done ever thinking about it. I want to move on, and you moving back here is going to really suck if you keep coming around."

"Okay," Colin whispered. He looked up at the ceiling and closed his eyes for a brief moment. The look of misery on his face made her heart ache in her chest, demanding that she say something to ease his pain. But all it took was the memory of him watching her break down in tears and choosing to walk out the door anyway, and she was cured. "I won't bother you again, and I'll try to keep my distance." He lowered his head a second later and started to get up. "Sell me the painting?"

"Sure." The silence between them felt like a ticking time bomb as she walked over to the counter. Harper looked between the two of them warily as Scarlett cleared her throat. "I'm going to go get bubble wrap for that." She pointed to Theodore's painting, still leaning against the cabinets, before turning to Colin. "I normally sell Theo's work for three hundred."

"Okay." He pulled out his wallet as she moved to pick up the painting, walking it past her sister to the back room.

The second Scarlett pushed through the door, the emotions lodged in her chest finally released. There wasn't a way to hold back anymore, and she finally decided, just once, that she could allow herself to cry over a man, because *fuck it*, being fully known and then subsequently unwanted was never not going to sting. A broken sob escaped her lips. That all-consuming sorrow she had been better about fighting off lately was still there. It was lurking in the shadows and waiting for Colin to come back and remind her that love was a fleeting thing she couldn't hold on to. It left like her brother. It left like her father. And it left like Colin. No matter the magic of the feeling, it wasn't there to stick around, because the men in her life either had no choice but to leave or had left of their own accord. She could forgive her brother for dying. She could decide that her father wasn't worth her time. But Colin? She really hoped he wouldn't forever be the gaping wound that constantly reopened, letting all her worst fears in.

Tears fell silently down Scarlett's cheeks for only a minute before she collected herself enough to wipe them away and wrap Theo's painting in the bubble wrap she had packaged it in earlier that day. She regretted selling it to Colin now because it almost felt like he was getting yet another piece of her, but it was too late. She always ended up paying for her impulsive tendencies. Even having sex with Colin the first time had been a snap decision. And now the painting. Colin made her brain foggy and her heart plummet when it was no longer his to hold on to.

A final sniff, and Scarlett had her tears dried and a carefully wrapped painting ready to hand off. Colin was holding a check when she pushed out of the back room, careful to not hit the painting on any edges. He slipped the check onto the counter, sliding it toward her as she moved to pass the painting to him. Their hands barely grazed, and Colin sucked in a breath, no doubt due to his hatred for soft touch. She almost pressed against his fingers to soothe his problem, but fought against it, letting go and releasing the painting into his hand.

"Is there anything I can do to help you at all?" Colin finally asked, gripping the painting hard. "I won't come around, but if there's something you need… I'm here. I'll be your biggest supporter." He tipped his head to the side and added, as an afterthought, "from afar. Miles away from you. So far away that you'll wonder if I even exist anymore."

A small laugh pushed up Scarlett's throat, and she was surprised that it wasn't bitter or hurt. Colin had always been funny to her, even inadvertently, though it seemed like he was intentionally trying to make a joke this time. And maybe that was why she felt she could ask, at least not for her own sake, but for someone else. She already felt guilty enough that with her schedule, she couldn't volunteer herself. "My aunt runs a mentorship program through the children's advocacy center. They're hard-up for volunteers. The kids are older, anywhere from seven to seventeen, so it shouldn't be a noise issue for you. And I know it doesn't help me directly, but—"

"Done." Colin gave a firm jerk of his head. "I'll sign up."

"Great." Scarlett drummed her fingers on the counter and saw her sister pretending to make a drink in earshot. There was no good way to end this conversation, and she seemed to be locked in place, waiting for the ground to swallow her up or for Colin to become a mirage and fade into oblivion like one of her dreams. In the end, she could always count on Colin to get right to the point.

"I'll leave now." He held up the painting. "Thank you for this."

"You're welcome. I'll tell Theo it's in good hands." The awkward nod she gave him did nothing to alleviate the discomfort of watching him turn to walk away. It was as if the sight of him leaving were ingrained in her on a cellular level, her chest tightening around her heart just like it had the last time. What she wasn't expecting was for him to freeze halfway to the door, turning slightly back over his shoulder.

"For what it's worth, you were never too much, Scarlett. You're everything good and right in the world." Without another word, he opened the door and left, leaving her to stare after him with her mouth slightly parted.

"Letti," Harper soothed, coming up behind her and rubbing a hand up and down her arm.

"I'm fine." Scarlett took a shaky breath and finally reached for the check sitting on the counter, noticing first that Colin seemed to know exactly who to make it out to, and second the incorrect amount he had written on the check. Her eyes widened.

"Holy shit," Harper whispered. "Didn't you say it was three hundred?"

"Yep." Staring at Colin's neat script that she had seen a hundred times didn't change the numbers he had written. One thousand dollars was a far cry from what she had told him to pay, but the note on the memo line seemed to explain it all.

For your favorite student.

Fourteen

Colin
22 years Old

Eden Wallace's office was not an office at all. Instead, she was crammed into a cubicle at the back corner of a room beside several other social workers, with a mess of paperwork on her desk. As she guided Colin back to her space, he could feel her eyes on him like a sniper's laser, tracking his every move and clearly none too thrilled by his presence. Every member of Scarlett's family was privy to the worst mistake of his life because of course they were. They had been there to pick up the pieces when he wasn't.

There wasn't much conversation when Colin first arrived at the advocacy center, but he had never been there before, so he figured that might be why. Either that, or the office was still in a food coma after Thanksgiving. He hadn't expected when signing up for the mentorship program that he would actually have to speak with Scarlett's aunt. Since the second she had assigned herself to him, Colin had been paying for his past.

"Break any windows lately?" Eden asked, taking a seat behind her tiny desk scattered with loose papers and manila folders.

Colin had almost forgotten about a different mistake he had

made back in high school that probably would have been a fun story to tell at his and Scarlett's wedding if they'd never broken up. Now, however, Eden brought the memory up with clear malicious intent.

"Only ever the one," he said.

"Good to hear," Eden replied coolly. "Scarlett warned me that you'd be signing up for the program. If that's why you're here, then we need to fill out the application and background test forms. And you need to get CPR and First Aid certified."

Colin nodded and reached for his leather satchel bag, riffling through it to find his wallet and subsequently his CPR and First Aid certification card. "I had to get this for work." He slid the card across the desk, and Eden gave him a curt nod.

"Then just the applications and background check information. I'll need to scan your ID as well." He obliged, sliding over his driver's license. "Do you have a certain age bracket you're looking at?"

"No preference, except I can't do small children or really screechy kids."

"Right." Eden's voice softened a bit. "I remember from when Lindy was little."

"Lindy." Colin smiled hesitantly, remembering Scarlett's baby cousin. "She's what, six now?"

"Mm hmm," Eden said, pointing to the frame on the corner of her desk, where Scarlett's Uncle Marty was beaming up at a small girl sitting on his shoulders.

"She's beautiful." He meant it, too. Lindy had the classic Wallace green eyes, just like Scarlett's.

"Thank you." Eden reached down and pulled a few forms out from her desk drawer, passing them over. "Any other concerns?"

"I, um..." He paused, fiddling with his hands. "I don't know if this matters or if it disqualifies me, but I'm formally diagnosed with autism."

Eden blinked in surprise for a second then quickly recovered, shaking her head. "No. I wouldn't think that would be a problem."

"Okay. Then I'll just fill this out and get it back to you?"

"Yes, I actually—we have a child who has ASD. Do you think that would be a good fit? We've had trouble with him connecting to anyone. It might help him to get to know someone with his same diagnosis who is... thriving." Eden looked somewhat uncomfortable, and he assumed it was probably the same odd response he always got from people when he simply stated his brain didn't work the same until she spoke again. "I wouldn't suggest it if I didn't think it would be good for him. He spends most of his time painting in Scarlett's art program, and as much as I don't think she'd want to see you around there, I think she'd agree with me that Theodore deserves a role model, and her art studio is where he's the most comfortable."

Colin's heart hammered in his chest, eyes wide as the painting Scarlett sold to him flashed in his mind along with the neat signature at the bottom. "Theodore Whitlock?"

"Yes. You've met?" Eden's eyebrows rose.

"No, but I own one of his paintings," he explained. His mind was whirring with the new information and all the possible outcomes. If Theodore was in the program and Colin became his mentor, then he'd get to see Scarlett frequently. It was a loophole of sorts because although Scarlett had told him she didn't want to see him, this was a valid reason to see her anyway without crossing a boundary. Rocking in his seat from the small amount of hope that gave him, he bobbed his head. "I'd love to be partnered with him."

"Perfect. I'll set it up, but I need to be certain that you will be committed. He has enough trouble with the lack of routine from being a foster kid that bounces around from house to house. To be frank, Colin, I don't want to partner him up with you if you're planning on leaving any time soon."

It wasn't a subtle dig at his character, but Colin appreciated her being forthright. "I'm permanently in Archwood. As long as I have it on my calendar and in my own routine, I'll be at every meeting provided that I'm not sick or injured."

"It'll probably end up being sometime after the New Year because background checks are always backed up from Thanksgiving and by the time they're caught up again, Christmas rolls around," Eden explained.

It was further out than he would have liked, but beggars couldn't be choosers, so Colin just bobbed his head in acknowledgment. Luck was a fickle thing he wasn't even sure he believed in, but he thought, for once in life, he might have hit the pot of gold at the end of the rainbow. There was just one small problem. "Can you not mention this to Scarlett?"

"I wouldn't normally disclose work matters to my niece in general," Eden said. "But I don't enjoy blindsiding her, either."

"Not that." He shook off the idea. "Don't tell her that I'm autistic."

"You don't want her to know?" Eden drew out the words slowly, like she was trying and failing to understand the significance.

"I'm not embarrassed by it, but I don't want to use my diagnosis as an excuse. Everything she thinks of me now, she should think of me with or without that knowledge," Colin explained. "I'll tell her myself."

Something seemed to pass through Eden's eyes, her mouth opening and closing several times before she finally said, "Can I ask when you were diagnosed, Colin?"

"The summer before I left for college," he replied. Eden sat back in her chair, a spark of understanding washing over her facial features.

"Then it's your story to tell." Eden nodded. "I won't mention it."

FIFTEEN

Colin
18 Years Old

"You seem less downcast today." Dr. Thomlinson clipped a sheet of paper onto his clipboard and paused. The pause was so long that Colin shifted in his cracked leather chair and started to feel his fingers too much again. His psychiatrist wasn't usually one to cause discomfort. From the time Walker had made therapy mandatory for Colin and all his siblings after the death of their parents, Dr. Thomlinson had usually been a mellow person to be around, with his Bible Belt accent and soft demeanor. Nothing in his office was loud or invasive. The plants lining the bay window were a comforting range of greens, with ethereal rays of sunshine hitting them like tiny rainbows through Colin's glasses when he tilted his head just right. Some of the rays were hitting the desk near the window, and he followed them for a bit, tilting his head from side to side to watch them dance across leaves and cherry oak.

"Am I supposed to respond to that?" Colin finally asked when the silence outweighed the visuals in the room. "It wasn't a question, just a general statement."

Thomlinson hummed and nodded. "You are correct. It wasn't a question, but usually I find I can make a statement like that and my patients will immediately confirm or deny my observation. I frame the statement like a question by making the end higher in pitch."

"So if I go 'you're wearing blue today,'" Colin upturned the end of his statement like a question. "Do you then immediately tell me why you're wearing blue?"

"I might be inclined to." Thomlinson smiled. "Let me frame it as a question. Are you in high spirits? If so, why?"

"I am." Colin sat up straighter. "I made a friend. I'm tutoring her in AP Chemistry, and I also lost my virginity to her yesterday. We're meeting again after school." There was a choked sort of coughing sound from his therapist, and Colin's eyes widened in alarm. "Do you need water?"

With a shake of his head and a clearing of his throat, Dr. Thomlinson clicked his pen. "I apologize. The way you delivered that news felt abrupt, and I wasn't prepared. You hadn't previously mentioned any romantic interests despite that being high on the list of priorities for someone your age."

That was true, Colin hadn't mentioned it before, but there wasn't yet anything of note until recently. "Isn't it normal to have some sort of dramatic change right now? Carter keeps skipping class and forging Walker's signature on absence slips, and Piper dated the worst guy imaginable from our high school, got drunk at a party, and had to throw his keys into a bush when he was going to drive her home drunk. All of that seems way worse than me liking someone and wanting to have sex with her."

"Grief doesn't present the same way with everyone," Dr. Thomlinson said simply. "So, this girl is a romantic interest, then? Not just a friend, as you said earlier?"

"Currently she's a friend with benefits sort of person," Colin explained. "We were talking about science and the conversation fell into her saying she wished she could take the guesswork out of sex like we do with science. For example, someone would turn a certain age, then medical professionals would run some blood work and come back with a profile of your sexuality, what you like, dislike, et cetera."

"Intriguing."

"I thought it was a great idea, so I said that I would create a chart of sorts so when I did end up having sex, I could track my progress and performance. And then Scarlett—" Colin bit his tongue. "Shit, I wasn't going to tell you her name because we agreed to keep this quiet so that people at school wouldn't make mean comments."

"Unless you are a danger to yourself or others, I'm legally bound to confidentiality and will not share anything from our sessions with anyone." Dr. Thomlinson crossed one leg over the other and folded his hands atop his clipboard. "You are also a legal adult now, so I don't even have to inform your uncle about medications or diagnoses."

"Are you planning on prescribing me anything?" Colin asked.

"Let us continue on with your explanation, and then we will discuss further action with your care."

The answer seemed like a blatant skirting around the question Colin had asked, and he could feel the anxiety in his bones from the not knowing. "Scarlett and I then decided to conduct the experiment ourselves because she was also a virgin. The experiment is going well barring a few mishaps, and I'm enjoying myself. I have received all the pros from a release of endorphins, oxytocin, dopamine, serotonin, and other hormones I've read about in research books on sex and relationships. Oxytocin the most out of anything, I think, because I'm experiencing strong affection toward her." The words flew out of his mouth in the quickest explanation possible before he jumped back to his question. "Now, what further action are you implying?"

Thomlinson blinked and then slowly nodded his head. Colin met his eyes for a count of two Mississippi before looking away. "Am I correct in assuming that you sped through that explanation of your newfound relationship because you are too focused on the question I didn't answer?"

"You still haven't answered it," Colin said bluntly. "I don't enjoy not knowing where things are headed."

"Right, you stated previously that you love the idea of routine." Tomlinson scribbled something on his clipboard. "I don't mean to keep you in suspense, it just seemed like the explanation of your sexual relationship with another person could potentially discredit my thoughts. I now feel fairly confident that they did not. In our future appointments, I would like your permission to evaluate you for Autism Spectrum Disorder."

Colin snorted with amusement. "They evaluated me for that when I was five. I'm not autistic."

"It is very hard to assess children, and frequently people are misdiagnosed or underdiagnosed."

"I didn't have speech delays," Colin argued.

"Autism is a spectrum. Not having speech delays used to be associated with something called Asperger's Syndrome and was a separate diagnosis from Autism Spectrum Disorder, but it was very hard to distinguish between Asperger's and ASD. Eventually, researchers decided that the two were so similar that they were all under the same umbrella."

"What are you getting at?" Colin demanded, waving his hand for Dr. Thomlinson to get to the point.

"They removed the diagnosis in 2013, meaning when you were evaluated at five years old with your lack of speech delays, I believe that they most likely would have been looking for Asperger's or another condition instead of ASD, causing you to be undiagnosed. Often children with ASD who have challenges with social skills seem mature for their age, and I can't say for certain, but I imagine you would have been written off as someone who was simply intelligent for their age."

The urge to roll his eyes was strong as Colin remained unperturbed. His mother would have noticed something was wrong with him. Growing up, he never missed a single important appointment. Paisley Hartrick had everything down to a science with her color-coded whiteboard calendar. Once, she had decided that one of Colin's moles needed to be looked at, and he came down from his room to find a new dermatology appointment on the books. And his father was Colin's best friend. Out of anyone, Cole Hartrick would have noticed something was off given the amount of time they spent together. The idea that either of his parents would miss something this big was preposterous. Even more preposterous would be getting a diagnosis simply because he went in for grief counseling *for* his dead parents.

"You realize I'm here to wax poetic about depressing things, right?" Colin asked bitterly. "I didn't realize a diagnosis was on the table when I came in here to talk about my late parents."

Thomlinson sighed and then reaffirmed what Colin already knew. "You are definitely here to talk about grief."

"Okay."

"But," Thomlinson drew out the word hesitantly. "If your brain does not work in a neurotypical way, the approach to healing could be quite different."

"And you think you need this evaluation so you can check ASD off your list and proceed with grief counseling?" Colin raised his eyebrows in a teasing manner, but he was surprised when Thomlinson's response was short.

"Yes."

Confident that Dr. Thomlinson wouldn't find anything, Colin shrugged and said, "Go for it."

"Great." Dr. Thomlinson smiled good-naturedly and clicked his pen again. "Now, let's go back to the sexuality experiment. I don't want to breeze past this. I at least need to make sure that you're both being safe."

"If you mean contraception, we're doubling up. If you mean consent, I had it and I will obtain it every time," Colin said in slight irritation. The idea that he would be anything other than thorough when it came to Scarlett's safety or even his own angered him. He wasn't a reckless person. "We have a list of rules we stick to and an understanding that we can amend anything on that list whenever we want to to account for changes we didn't anticipate."

"Safe sex and consent are important, but that's not what I was referring to." Thomlinson set his clipboard back on his desk and folded his hands contemplatively. "You are in a very fragile time in your life, and I want you to be very careful with your heart. A list of rules won't save you from real emotions when you feel them."

Sixteen

Scarlett
18 Years Old

"Okay, somehow, I don't think staring at the bed in prolonged silence is going to further our agenda to be naked and thriving," Scarlett said, and then immediately cringed when an amused smile emerged on Colin's lips.

"Naked and thriving? Is that our new catchphrase?"

"Please, God, no," she huffed. "But I can't deal with long, drawn-out silences. I get nervous, and then I have to fill the empty space, and I don't know if you know this, but I ramble when I'm nervous, and then I start think about how I wasn't prepared for more sex things to happen this immediately, and I'm not wearing a matching bra and underwear today like I magically was yesterday when we first…"

"Say the word, Red," Colin said sternly. The tone he took with her was surprisingly hot.

"When we first banged."

"*That* is not the word. We didn't have a shootout like an old Western movie," Colin huffed.

"Well, I think maybe if I got you there, you would have shot out *something*," Scarlett mused and peeked over at him. Colin's face cracked a bit, a smile begging to get out as he shook his head.

"We really need to stop with the cum jokes and focus. Say the damn word, Scarlett," he scolded, and again she felt the heat from him telling her what to do burn through her core.

"Sex," she finally gave in.

"Great, so, I went over your critiques. We seem to agree on the majority of what went wrong last time. I don't think you can tell me that I need to," he cleared his throat and read right off her scoring chart, "get a smaller dick."

"There has to be a reverse Viagra pill somewhere. Their ads would probably be something like, 'do you suffer from whale syndrome and frequently injure your partners with your giant schlong? Then have we got the pill for you!'" Scarlett expected Colin to laugh at her joke, but instead his face just paled.

"Did I actually injure you?" Colin's concern was so palatable it sobered her teasing manner immediately. "I asked you if you needed to see a doctor, and you said you didn't. Maybe I should have taken you anyway."

She shook her head vigorously to dispel his worries. "I promise I'm fine. I was just making a joke. Nothing hurts, see?" She lunged forward and turned to rock from side to side in the most egregious display of her undamaged vagina. There was only a split second to panic about the stupid yoga moves she was performing before Colin took her idiocy in stride and steered the conversation back to their common goal.

"Okay, good. Did you agree with all the rules?"

"Yes." Scarlett unfolded her chart, looking over the hand-written list at the bottom.

Rules:

1. All parties must consent to every activity planned before and during.

2. A condom and the birth control pill will

be used simultaneously when engaging in intercourse to prevent reproduction.

3. The experiment will come with no attachments or expectations for a further romantic relationship after the experiment has concluded or been terminated.

4. All sexual activity is monogamous between the two parties unless otherwise discussed during the course of the experiment.

5. If at any time the participants no longer want to continue the experiment, the experiment is terminated.

6. The experiment's scheduled end is August 18th, pending Colin's move to Johns Hopkins University.

7. Each party will fill out the above chart for the respective party to the best of their abilities, and the participants will converse to write down ways to fix any issues or variables that arise.

And finally, the last one, written in earlier after they spoke by the lockers:

8. The experiment will be kept a secret between both parties, with the exception of Kashvi Mehta.

"Perfect. For this trial, I think we should do a sort of control group," Colin stated.

"Control group. So, like, we do the experiment without any variables?" Scarlett scrunched her eyebrows together, trying to work it out in her head.

"Right, so, I would be the variable in this scenario, and instead of touching you, I'd watch you bring yourself to orgasm." The words came out of Colin's mouth so directly that if she had been drinking water at the time, she would have done a spit take.

"Y-you want me to get myself off?" she squeaked.

"Yes. In front of me, so I can observe what you're doing. And then we'd do the reverse, where you watch what I do."

"Okay, but I-I—" Scarlett's cheeks flamed with embarrassment.

"Tell me what you're thinking, Red." Colin's voice was a balm to her anxiety, and the soothing way he leaned into her, bringing his hands up to press against her arms, quieted the fog of chaos in her head.

"I haven't masturbated very much," she admitted. "I've orgasmed, but it's usually by accident. I've masturbated one time to orgasm with my hand, and it took forever. Maybe I just don't know what I'm doing."

"Okay, well, that's why we're doing this, isn't it?" he asked. "We have around two hours to kill, and if we use up all that time to figure out what you like, I'm okay with that."

"I'm nervous about how it looks down there and how it smells and how to conduct myself with you watching me. I don't know how to start."

Colin let his hands fall away from her. "Do you need a good reason to start?" She nodded. "Will kissing you help? Because I've been dying to kiss you all day." She nodded again, and like a moth to a flame, Colin's lips crashed against hers, his hand moving to take the chart from her hand as he backed her toward her bed. He groaned against her mouth, pressing into her spine to force her closer a moment longer before he pulled away, leaving her head fuzzy. "Sit down, Scarlett." She immediately did, and he came back for seconds, nipping at her bottom lip and then dragging his tongue over it as he stood between her legs. "Now I want you to take your pants off for me first. Go as slow as you want to go. I'll keep your brain distracted." His mouth trailed hungrily down her throat, and she gasped as she frantically tried to unbutton her pants and wiggle them down her ass while maintaining contact with Colin, who was pressing his lips into her collarbone.

"Fuck," she breathed, hurriedly stepping out of her pantlegs.

"Good job, Red," Colin murmured. "Get on the bed and take your underwear off."

"Okay." Scarlett obediently bobbed her head and backed herself onto her blue comforter, then lifted her hips off the bed to slide her underwear to the floor. Colin, still standing between her legs, took a long, shuddering breath before he spoke again.

"Now use your hand." From the looks of it, the hard erection Colin was sporting in his pants said that he needed to be taken care of, too. Maybe he liked to watch. The original idea was just to figure out what she liked, but he seemed to be enjoying this as much as she was, and she hadn't even done anything yet. That knowledge made her feel invincible. "I can't be a variable for you anymore. I need you to spread your legs and touch yourself. Show me what to do. I want to know exactly where your clit is and how many fingers you use to fuck yourself."

A small amount of courage—or maybe just pure lust—coursed through Scarlett as she pointed to a small chair in the corner. "Sit down and watch, Colin." She had never seen him move so fast before, parking the chair right where he would have a front-row seat.

"Tell me what you're doing while you're doing it." His voice was all gravel as he dropped into his spectator seat.

Her hand moved almost of its own accord down her stomach, blocking his direct view when she slowly parted her legs, pressing the pads of her feet into her mattress. "I'm starting to move the tips of my fingers around to find what I need."

"How are you moving them?" Colin asked.

"I'm swirling them and—" She gasped, arching a little into her hand and spreading her wetness up her slit to where the pulsing ache was. "I found my clit, and I'm pressing into it."

"Do you want even more pressure? Or does it have to be just the right amount?"

"I-I..." Her eyes fluttered shut as she tested his theory, pressing harder. "Shit, it feels good when I press harder. Not faster, but harder."

"Got it. Slow, but firm." Colin adjusted in his seat, and she watched with heavy-lidded eyes as he pulled at the fabric near his crotch where his cock was tenting his pants. She found a rhythm between her legs but kept her eyes on Colin, stroking herself from side to side. He wasn't talking anymore, just watching her and raking his eyes over her body as she squirmed under her fingers. The excitement was still there, but she liked it better when he was asking questions and suggesting things.

"Keep talking to me," she urged.

"Doesn't that make me more of a variable?" Colin asked, his voice dark and heady, like he was on his last thread of patience and close to snapping and giving in to anything she wanted.

"Fuck the control group, Colin." Scarlett bucked her hips off the edge of the bed and whimpered as the thrumming ache heightened, her eyes falling shut.

"Fine." It was almost aggressive in tone, so unlike the calm version of Colin she knew that her eyes fluttered open just in time to watch him shove her legs apart. "But you need to listen to me this time. I said spread your legs. You're not letting me see, Red. I need to see, or I won't know what to do to make you come later."

"O-okay." She jerked her head up and down and let her legs fall open even more, brazenly baring herself to him, her body even going so far as to tip her hips in his direction.

"That's good." The sound of him unbuckling his belt had her mouth watering. "Now, try using your thumb instead, and then push two fingers inside you. I brought lube if you need it."

The slick feeling of Scarlett's fingers suggested that she didn't need lubrication, but she tested her hypothesis carefully, letting her thumb take over on her clit as she gently pushed two fingers inside her heat. There was only a little pushback before she slid completely in and coated her fingers with her wetness, allowing her to pump more freely. "I don't need it."

"Good." His voice cracked as he unbuttoned his pants. "I do, though. I need to do something about this before I ruin my underwear." She eagerly watched him snatch a small bottle of lube from the backpack he had set carefully on the floor earlier, and he pulled his cock from his pants and coated himself in a small dollop, working it over his shaft. His breathing was so erratic, and she was enraptured by the way his chest was rising and falling, sometimes in sync and then out of time with the stroking of his hand. "Don't stop, Scarlett. Tell me what you're doing."

She picked up her pace again, realizing she had stilled to watch him. "It feels better when I curl my fingers. Tell me what *you're* doing."

Colin groaned, sliding his hand over himself faster. "I'm mostly using three fingers, and I'm pulling a little when I go up, pushing when I go down and—Jesus, this is happening way faster than I—" His head whipped backward, his mouth falling open as pearlescent white pooled at the slit of his cock. Distracted by him enough to stop the motion of her own hand, she paused to sit up on her forearms to watch his hand jerk up again, slower this time as his whole body went taut as another stream of cum rolled over his hand. When he released his cock, his chest still heaving with exertion, he looked down with a grimace at his covered hand. "Dammit."

"What?" Scarlett sat up all the way in alarm. "That didn't feel good?"

Colin shook his head. "It felt amazing, but you stopped, Scarlett. Now I have to wash my hands because I can't deal with being all sticky. I have to leave the room, and when I did that last time, it killed the momentum. I ruined the experiment because I got too turned on too quickly." He scrunched his eyes shut. "I'm so fucking bad at this."

"Colin, It's fine," she assured him. "Really."

"Piper said when a woman says she's fine, she's not actually fine." He recited this knowledge like it was a fact, and she couldn't help but smile.

"This time I actually am, though. I promise. I just got distracted watching you." Her legs were firmly closed now, and she was sure if she felt around down there, she would be wet from the memory of her arousal rather than anything new.

"Can you try again now?" Colin asked hopefully. His hand was held at a stiff, awkward angle away from his body, like he was desperately trying not to be bothered by the fact that it was still soaked in his own release. Scarlett kept her legs mostly closed as her fingers traveled back down to the apex of her thighs. It didn't feel good anymore. Before, her clit was swollen and aching to be touched. Now, it felt like it was hibernating somewhere and was pissed off that she was even trying to wake it up.

"Um, I don't think so." She tried forcefully swiping her clit, and it felt more sensitively painful than erotic. A long-suffering sigh left her lips as she watched Colin's discomfort grow tenfold, his shoulders hiking up around his shoulders. "Just go clean yourself off. It's okay."

"Are you sure? I'll be quick, I promise." He didn't wait for her response before he was bolting from the room, using his clean hand to twist the knob and escape into the hallway. When the door shut behind him, her mind started replaying everything on a loop, analyzing it the way she figured Colin would as soon as he was back. A pros and cons list started in her head as she slipped her underwear back on. It was a bit easier to think without an anxiety-ridden guy standing at the foot of her bed with a fistful of cum, expecting her to continue on as if she couldn't tell he was wildly uncomfortable.

Pro: she liked the feeling of her fingers against her clit.

Con: she couldn't figure out the timing of both her fingers and her thumb simultaneously. Her rhythm was easily thrown off by one or the other.

Pro: Colin's directions and the blunt and bossy way he delivered those directions was a massive turn-on.

Con: her fingers inside of her didn't feel like much. Bent fingers helped, but not enough to get off from.

Pro: she was definitely wet this time, so the passage Colin had made her read in his scientific sex book about the brain's ability to register that something sexual was happening definitely proved true this time. She wasn't distracted for the first part, and therefore, she was wet.

Con: she couldn't really do two things at once, so watching Colin get off, despite her loving it, killed her own momentum.

Pro: she really liked watching Colin get off.

Con: Colin really did not like the messy aftermath. Despite all their cum jokes, she had to agree with him that the actual substance was not as appealing.

A myriad of possible fixes for all the cons ran through Scarlett's head. She couldn't quite come up with a fix for her tendency to get distracted, because, after all, if she could fix that, she probably wouldn't have needed Colin as a lab partner to begin with. Colin's problem, however, seemed like more of a simple fix, with several possible solutions.

"I think I should swallow," she declared when Colin reentered the room.

Colin blinked several times, adjusted his glasses, met her eyes for maybe a millisecond before shifting his gaze down to the floor. "What?"

"You don't like the sticky aftermath when you get yourself off."

"Yes, the ac-cum-ulation of issues we're running into seems to be growing." The joke was again delivered with a nonchalance that made her think the word play was an accident, but Colin never pronounced words incorrectly.

A slow grin unfurled across her lips. "A cum joke about your distaste for cum? And using the word 'growing' in the same sentence? So many layers. Well done."

Colin smirked. "I thought of it in the bathroom while I was literally washing the cum off my hand. It was too good to pass up."

"Well, I think I can fix one of our cum-plications." Her eyes sparkled as she watched his reaction, which was understated but amused nonetheless.

"This is getting out of hand." He cracked a smile.

"I think it was actually *on* your hand. That was the problem."

"Red." His tone held a warning to finally get down to business, and she obeyed.

"Blow jobs," she said, pleased that she sounded so sure of herself. "If I swallow, then you don't have to deal with it."

Colin's throat bobbed. "I love your ideas."

"I figured you would like this particular fix." Scarlett gave him a cheeky smile.

"We'll have to try that later. For now, I need to touch you." A hand gripped hers, and she was yanked into the firm wall of Colin's chest, his arms wrapping around her on a sigh. "This is better." She closed her eyes, burying her face into his shirt and breathing deeply. Colin smelled like something calming. He wasn't overly fragrant, which she loved because she had smelled enough Axe body spray for a lifetime. "Can we talk like this?"

"Mm-hmm." Her dreamy response was muffled, but Colin heard it and tightened his hold on her. She didn't complain, sinking even deeper into the touch. Out of everything they had done, this was what quieted her mind the most. The safety of it took away all her insecurities.

"I liked my idea originally, and clearly I was turned on by it, but it was almost painful not to touch you. I didn't like that part," he said. "Why'd you stop?"

She pulled her head off his chest a bit so he could hear. "I couldn't focus on all the different moving parts. I couldn't time my thumb and my fingers, and then I wanted to watch you and couldn't multitask."

"Okay…" Colin drew out the word like he was thinking. "So then I'd conclude that we need to do foreplay one at a time, and we can probably cross sixty-nineing off the list."

"Agreed. That sounds like my own personal hell."

"I also like seeing you, and if you were to be flipped like that, I'd only be able to see your legs. You have nice legs, but you have nice everything else, too." Colin's hands dragged up and down Scarlett's sides, and she smiled to herself. She wasn't sure she would ever get used to how forward he was about her body, but she didn't mind being blindsided by the compliments. Who would?

"You also have a nice body," Scarlett said. "I also don't know if you noticed, but I really like it when you tell me what to do. You got a little grumpy with me, and—"

"Sorry. I didn't mean to get short with you. I was just irritated that I couldn't touch you."

"No, I'm saying I liked it," she explained. Her head was laying against his chest so he couldn't see what she was sure was the bright red coloring of her cheeks.

"You like it when I'm mean to you?" Colin's voice held a hard edge of confusion. "Why?"

That was a good question, and it took her a second to ponder a response. "I don't think 'mean' is the right word. I like when you're demanding, if that makes sense. When you take charge, it means I don't have to, and that clears up some of my brain fog. I'm constantly wondering if I'm doing things wrong, and when you tell me to do things a bit aggressively, I know I can just do that thing and be doing something right."

"That makes sense. I like control, so I'd rather you just do exactly what I say anyway. We're well-matched." *Well-matched.* The word ran through her head several times on a loop, giving it too much emphasis, then barely any emphasis at all. He couldn't mean anything as drastic as breaking rule number three. *No attachments.* That was what they had agreed on. They could be well-matched but then go their separate ways. He was leaving in a few months, anyway, so that would make it easy to cut ties.

"We are." Scarlett finally decided on a response.

"I think with whatever we're doing, if we could just... keep some form of hard contact, that would help a bit. When there's space between us, I almost feel... itchy." The last word he'd landed on didn't seem to do his thoughts justice, so he continued. "I don't know how to explain what I mean. It's kinda like this thing my brother used to do when he was little and annoying where my parents would tell him to stop touching or bothering me, and just to be defiant he'd hold his pointer finger out from my arm or something just enough to say that he wasn't actually touching me. It always made me want to lose my shit."

"Ah, siblings. Can't live with them, can't live..." She trailed off, a wave of grief slamming into her chest at the thought of Tucker.

"Without them," Colin whispered. "I'm sorry I'm complaining about my brother."

"No, no. I, um, I get it." Scarlett choked back her emotion. "I'm pretty sure I used to do that stupid not-poking thing to Tucker and Harper. It's a classic sibling move. Occasionally something just hits me, and I get super emotional. I'm sorry."

"When my parents died, I threw a massive tantrum like a toddler." His voice was almost so quiet it was nonexistent.

"You did?"

"Yeah," Colin murmured. "I told the police officer, who is now my uncle's best friend, that he was a liar, and then I told Walker that he wasn't allowed to take my parents' room because I was so certain they were coming back. I just kept rambling on about how they weren't dead until I guess I... I don't remember much after that, but Carter says I ended up in a ball on the floor, shaking and screaming nonsense, and Piper had to kind of hug me until I came out of it, so whatever you think is super emotional, I doubt it's as bad as the things I've done. I was supposed to be a role model for Pearl and Cooper. That's what I should have done. I mean, Cooper's only eight years old, and his reaction was more sane than mine. I don't know, I just couldn't control myself. It was like all the cells in my body were ripping down the center, and my entire routine and life were suddenly on fire and burning me from the inside out."

"I refused food for several days when Tucker died. My mom and sister were obviously depressed, too, so eventually we ended up eating ice cream and Hot Pockets for every meal for like a month. I'll never fucking touch a Hot Pocket again. Just the sight of those makes me want to throw up now."

"What about your dad?" Colin asked.

"My dad went to work. He pretty much never came home, and then he slowly left. His presence just became less and less until he was packing up his stuff and moving out of the house." Scarlett shrugged, trying to act indifferent.

"He left you?" The bafflement in Colin's voice made her heart clench. It was like he genuinely couldn't fathom a world where someone would leave her.

"He couldn't handle it. He couldn't handle *us*. I don't know. I guess he decided he got dealt a bad hand, and now he's remarried to his receptionist with a second kid on the way. I'll have two half-siblings I barely see because he barely talks to me." That was the worst part to her. She was so easily replaceable. Even her own father decided he didn't get it right with her and set out to make a better family that didn't include her.

"Well, now I feel better about my reaction, because at least I'm not an idiot." The sentiment delivered was so straightforward that she burst into laughter.

"I don't think you could ever be an idiot. You're too smart. Promise me when you become some big, fancy scientist that you'll remember the girl from your sex-periment?" Scarlett's voice was too hopeful, too pleading, and she hated how pathetic she sounded.

"I'd never forget you, Red. But I think we need to make a few more memories that I won't forget."

"Oh yeah?" She gave her voice a flirtatious edge, the pads of her fingertips digging a little harder into the backs of his arms, an overt show of desperation.

"Yeah." Colin was staring at her mouth as his tongue ran over his bottom lip. "We have some time left before your family is home, and I need to make good on a promise to myself that you'd come today." Every nerve in her body seemed to come alive with his attention. A shiver ran down her spine at the feeling of his hot breath against the shell of her ear. "Can I make you come, Scarlett?"

"Yes," she breathed. There was suddenly nothing she wanted more than to lie on her back and spread her legs for him. Except for maybe his mouth, which landed on hers without any wasted time after her enthusiastic response.

"Get on the bed," Colin demanded. She practically threw herself backward as he climbed after her up to the headboard, sliding his hand under her shirt and over one sensitive breast. "All of your clothes need to come off this time, Scarlett. No hiding from me. I want to see everything."

It all happened faster than before. This time Colin flicked at her bra with ease, the cups falling away from her body as his mouth left hot, open-mouthed kisses down to her nipples before latching on and swiping his tongue over a peaked bud. The moan that left her mouth sounded distant in her ears, foreign to her body when all she could feel was Colin. He left all of his own clothing on, but she had no time to fret over it because his hands were everywhere all at once and yet not touching her enough. Her body thrummed with anticipation, and the impatient pulsing between her legs was begging to be experimented on.

"Colin," Scarlett cried out. "I need more."

Another swirl of his tongue on her nipple made her want to scream in agony over the torture. "I want to taste between your legs like this." He dragged his tongue across the other pebbled nipple, giving each of her breasts equal attention. Her brain short-circuited as he started traveling downward, and she had just enough mental forethought to panic about what he'd just said.

"What if it tastes really bad?" she asked nervously as he almost reached his destination.

"Then we get your pH checked." Colin did not seem to give a single fuck about her pH as he dragged his fingers across her clit, making her hips jerk into them. "No lube necessary this time. And I think my tongue will help."

"Oh God." It was said as both a precursor to what she assumed would be a mortifying experience once he did start eating her out, and a whine of pleasure at how good his fingers felt rubbing in slow circles. He was using everything he had learned from her small venture into voyeurism, and she shouldn't have been shocked. They had already established that Colin was a quick study. Each swirl of his fingers was backed by more pressure than she could have made on her own. Enough to distract her as his tongue replaced them with a quick drag and then a more deliberate flick. "Holy shit." Her back arched off the bed, shamelessly riding against his mouth for a second before the sensation left and restarted again, causing her to thrash under his grip. Embarrassment was now the last thing on her mind.

"I keep losing my place. Stop moving so much," Colin ordered as he shoved two fingers deep inside her—the best sort of punishment.

Scarlett gasped and writhed against his hand. "I can't." Her body was moving of its own accord, chest rolling and hips canting toward him. "It feels too good."

"It will feel better if you stop flopping around like a fish. You're making this very difficult. Stop. Moving." Colin's voice went even darker when she purposefully disobeyed and bucked her hips off the bed, squirming around his plunging fingers. "I'll hold you down if I need to, Red." That idea set fire to her veins and made the persistent pang of her body demand his follow-through to the threat, so she bucked again, just to see what he would do. A hand came down hard on her lower stomach, pinning her against the bed harshly. The moan she let out was inhuman when Colin's warm hands pressed against her bare skin. If this was what it felt like to be pinned down, she would have to ignore his suggestions more often. "That's better," he said. She had to agree, because the pleasure from where he was pressing down on her stomach was colliding with the spot inside her where his fingers were crooked and stroking, forcing her eyes to roll into the back of her head. It was all she could do to not lose her faculties completely as he bent to take her clit into his mouth again, sucking this time.

"Yes, yes, yes," Scarlett chanted. "So close." Each word was broken up by a gasping breath, and she could barely think she was climbing so high, edging closer and closer.

"Close to what? Say the exact word," he mumbled against her thigh then dragged his tongue across her entire slit before diligently working her clit again.

Scarlett had exactly zero words and could barely remember how to breathe, let alone come up with the exact word he wanted. "C-can't think. I'm... fuck." When she was sure it couldn't rise any higher, it continued, breaking her body down into nothing but pure tension, straining muscles, and curled toes, begging to get to the end. She could barely take it anymore. Balancing on the edge had her yelling out a frustrated sort of cry that must have tipped Colin off to her predicament, because he pushed down harder on her stomach, and she was done for. An aggressive tingle zapped up her spine, her body shaking as a wave of pleasure cascaded through her. Her chest arched with each new wave until they finally subsided and she couldn't even move anymore. "Oh my God." The final words were lazy coming out of her mouth, almost as if she were drunk. She could get used to the lethargic feeling of her body in the aftermath. In this rare moment of peace, her brain was quiet. It didn't last long as her muscles started waking up again, but when it came back on, she couldn't help the whirlpool of thoughts that inundated her mind.

"Did you come?" Colin popped his head up like a jack-in-the-box from between her legs, and she almost barked out a laugh at how ridiculously proud of himself he looked.

"Yes." She nodded and looked away as she finally asked one of her burning questions. "Did it taste bad?"

Colin pulled himself up her body, crawling under her covers. "Here. Try for yourself." His mouth landed on hers, his tongue immediately dipping out as she opened to him, the essence of herself still lingering there. It wasn't bad like she thought it would be, more like a sweet sort of tang than what she assumed would be foul and pungent. The taste quickly faded as he languidly kissed her, and she slowly maneuvered under her comforter. When she slid closer, her limbs entwined with his, their legs laced together. She could feel that he was hard again, his erection gently hitting her stomach. Out of curiosity, she reached to touch him. Colin arrested her wrist and guided her hand to lay against his chest instead as he broke off their liplock. "It's too sensitive. I think I'll die if you try to get me off again."

"Oh." Scarlett bit her lip. "How long does it take before you can do things again?"

He flopped down beside her on the bed. "I got myself off three times in one day once, but it was hours apart, and it was too much. I don't think I touched myself for a week after that."

"Special occasion?" She giggled.

"You know *The Promenade*?"

"The regency movie with the hot library scene?"

"Yep," he confirmed.

She curled her lips over her teeth to hold back her grin. "It kinda seems like a rite of passage for men to get themselves off to Quinn German's tits."

"Yours are better because I get to touch them." Colin smiled up at the ceiling then frowned. "I also found out that my uncle co-ghostwrote the book adaptation of that movie, and it kind of killed my enjoyment of it."

"The uncle with all the tattoos?"

"Women usually mention his tattoos when they want to have sex with him." Colin grimaced. "Do you?"

"What?" Scarlett scoffed, anger sparking behind her eyes. Not ten seconds after her orgasms, and he was already accusing her of asinine things. "I was just trying to figure out who you were talking about. He's way older than me, or at least old enough to be your guardian. You were literally just between my legs two minutes ago. Do you really think that poorly of me? If you just want to pawn me off on someone else, just say that."

Colin sat up, startled, the bedding falling around his hips. "I —that's not—I don't think badly of you at all. I just don't ever understand anyone's subtext, and I was going off of experience. Walker is more like an older, cooler brother than an uncle. I'm used to people constantly wanting to talk to Carter, Piper, and Walker more than they want to talk to me. And this is probably why, because I say things, and then everyone looks at me like I just said I was abducted by aliens. I don't know how to fucking be normal in social situations, and I can never figure out where everyone's invisible line is. Sorry. You don't have to do this with me either, you know. If I'm just a pity fuck, I don't want that." Scarlett was about to get pissed off all over again when his voice cracked, then softened. "I like you, so it'd really suck if this was all some sort of game that I'm not in on or a joke to tell your friends about when I'm not around."

"This isn't a joke," she murmured, then braced herself for honesty. "I'm a little terrified that I'm more invested in this than you are."

"How?" Colin's brows pulled together. "I'm running on no sleep because I stayed up for half the night making charts and forms."

"I just..." As she trailed off, her mind filled in missing words. *I just want to be more than an experiment.* She didn't want to be the test subject for whoever Colin fell in love with later. Being the test subject for her dad to figure out how to have a better family than the one he already had hurt enough. But she also wanted all the things Colin was offering because of the control and safety it offered. The opportunity probably wouldn't ever happen again. It was out of the box, and she doubted any future sexual partner of hers would want to be meticulously graded the way Colin did.

"I'm invested, and I'd rather you tell me outright if or when you aren't anymore," he said, and she couldn't help but feel like the safety net she was expecting was bound to wrap her up and suffocate her unawares.

Instead of voicing her worst fears, Scarlett took a deep breath. "I'm in this."

"Great. Then I think we should fill out our charts while everything is still fresh." Colin moved to get off the bed, and her stupid heart sunk further in her chest. None of this was ever going to be real, and it would be in her best interest to remember that.

Seventeen

Scarlett
22 Years Old

"Hey!" Kashvi's voice came over the speakers in Scarlett's car.

"You're bringing wine, right? I can't get through tonight without wine." Scarlett cut right to the chase, turning on her blinker with an exasperated flick of her hand.

"Yes, I'm bringing wine. What are we trying to forget, exactly, so I know how much to bring?" The best part about having a best friend who worked at a winery was, of course, the freebies. Kashvi was Scarlett's own personal Jesus, turning everything to wine the second she needed it. The winery was just a stepping stone on Kashvi's path to art curation, but Mallory Winery had already let her choose all the art hanging up on the walls of their brand-new tasting room, so she was well on her way to building enough connections to land the perfect job.

"Let's see... you already know that Colin is back." The deep sigh Scarlett let out was a poor attempt at relaxing. "I also just dumped Braiden, and he looked like a lost puppy when I set him loose, so that was fun."

"Oh, dear." Kashvi sighed. "So, out of those two things... I'm going to assume that Braiden isn't the root cause of your desire to drink."

"Yes, he is—or, it's more that he might have mentioned that he found something in my nightstand a while back that I should have gotten rid of forever ago, and he brought it up when I was dumping him." She was treading very carefully, avoiding what the actual object was.

On cue, Kashvi asked, "And that thing is?"

"I should have burned it or something. I got out a lighter today to do just that, then I started thinking about how I could potentially catch fire to my apartment and the apartments above the studio, and I'd burn that down, too. Then I thought, well, maybe that's a good thing, and I'll get introduced to a hot firefighter in suspenders who knows his way around the female body. Then I thought that sounded more like a stripper, and the thought of dating a stripper who would know what they're doing was intriguing. But then I remembered that Braiden is a firefighter, and what if he was on shift when I burned down my apartment, then that would be mortifying, and—"

"I'm going to commit a crime if you don't tell me what was in your nightstand right this second," Kashvi scolded. Scarlett turned the steering wheel, pointing it left as she turned onto her sister's street.

"It's too embarrassing, and you're going to be mad I kept it."

"Tell me anyway," Kashvi demanded.

"I..." Scarlett cringed. "It's the book Colin lent to me. It has all his handwritten sticky notes in it."

The audible gasp on the other line wasn't surprising at all. "Scarlett Eliza Wallace!"

"I know, I know. You don't have to tell me," Scarlett groaned.

"Well, I guess it's good you got rid of it now, at least," Kashvi said.

The problem with that, however, was that the book was still

very much in her nightstand, right beside the first tiny vibrator Colin had ever bought her, which, again, was an insane thing to hold on to, but came in handy after a lackluster lay. The book, however, should have zero use for her now that she had gleaned all the information she could from it, so she wasn't sure why she hadn't tossed it and let the past rest solely in the past.

"Um... yeah," Scarlett said, hoping her hesitation to lie didn't show.

"You didn't get rid of it, did you?" Kashvi's tone made Scarlett curl in on herself as much as she could, her seatbelt smashing against her breasts.

"No," she admitted. "I didn't get rid of it."

"Why? Are you still in love with him?" Kashvi's voice was calmer now, like she was trying to soothe an irate customer in the winery tasting room. "Do you still not know where to find the clitoris?"

"No! I mean yes, I do know," Scarlett groaned. "I just... it was a part of my life, and even though it ended really, really badly, the memories are mostly good." It was only true in part, because she was pretty sure, after trying and failing to love other men, that Colin Hartrick would forever own a piece of her heart. His piece was battered and bruised, but it still beat in her chest. She had always neglected to tell anyone that, including Kashvi or Harper, for fear of looking pathetic. Now, she actually *was* pathetic. It couldn't be normal to hold on to a love you had when you were that young and naive. She was old enough now to clearly see what she *should* be able to do—forget about Colin and move on—but pushing all the pain and love to the back of her mind didn't mean it didn't exist, it meant that she could cope. She could even be happy. The world kept on spinning, and she was a part of the land of the living, no matter how damaged she was. She made something of herself without relying on Colin to turn her world on its axis. She didn't need him to tell her who she was anymore. Maybe the footprints she left behind on the world wouldn't be as deep as those of someone like her brother, but hers didn't need to last forever to make change.

All her accomplishments were born after Colin left. All her accomplishments were achieved with a broken heart. Sometimes her own broken heart was the very fuel she needed to keep going out of sheer will and spite.

"I want to keep it because it's a reminder of how far I've come. How different I am now from the person who thought her world began and ended with Colin Hartrick," Scarlett said. "I don't need him to feel special anymore."

"Because you *are* fucking special," Kashvi declared.

"Thanks for the vote of confidence," Scarlett laughed and peered out the window as she pulled up to the curb outside her sister's house. "I'll see you in a bit? I'm a little early, but I couldn't stay in my studio anymore. I'm already at Harper's." What she should have been doing was finishing her brother's painting for the gala, but after staring at the still-blank canvas for twenty minutes, she couldn't stomach the thought of it anymore. There were still several months to work on it, but all her brain wanted to do lately was hyperfixate on the fact that she couldn't even start it.

"It'll just be you, me, and Harper on the drunk train tonight. Saanvi's too busy growing a human in her stomach again," Kashvi said. "I'll be there with enough wine to knock out a horse!"

"Blessings upon your family." Scarlett giggled.

After saying goodbye, Scarlett unbuckled and pulled the carefully plated deviled eggs from the passenger seat before walking them up to Harper's front door. Harper never minded when she showed up early for girls' night. It was commonplace for either of them to barge into the other's home unannounced, so Scarlett didn't bother knocking before opening the door and slipping inside, wandering to the kitchen to set the deviled eggs in the fridge.

Scarlett only made it one foot into the kitchen before being assaulted by the scene of her sister sitting on her countertop half-naked with her husband's tongue down her throat and his pants around his ankles.

The screech Scarlett let out before she whipped around to bolt toward the nearest exit must have broken up the canoodling because she didn't make it all the way to the door before Harper appeared behind her with her dress pulled back over her body. "What the *hell*, Letti?"

"I'm only an hour early!" Scarlett shouted back over her shoulder, re-covering her eyes with her hands as if that could solve her problem after the fact. She caught a glimpse of her brother-in-law Marcos' hair through the slit in her fingers and pressed her hand over her eyes harder in case he wasn't decent.

"That's too early!' Harper yelled back.

"Clearly," Scarlett huffed out sarcastically.

"Stop being dramatic. You can put your hand down. We're both clothed now. You killed the mood."

Scarlett obeyed, slowly dropping her hand to her side and squinting open her eyes. Marcos was cringing and pointedly avoiding eye contact, which made two of them. Harper, however, looked pissed. They did not look nearly done when she had walked in on them, so that was probably why. "I can leave? Yep. I'm gonna leave."

"I think I'm going to leave, actually." Marcos raised his hand, and his eyes darted to the door.

"Oh, no." Scarlett shook her head. "You don't need to—"

"I was just dropping off dinner for all of you. I'm going to go back to the restaurant to prep some stuff for tomorrow. I just got... distracted." He winced.

"Both of you need to take a Xanax." Harper rolled her eyes. "This is payback for the time I walked in on you and Colin in the shower. It's forever burned into my memory."

Scarlett's face turned beet red, and she looked down at her feet like she was an eighteen-year-old being reprimanded by her older sister again. "We weren't even doing anything," she whined. "We technically couldn't do anything because of all the cream!"

"Yep. I'm out. I don't even kind of want to know what that means." Marcos marched toward the door and flipped his keys around on his finger. With a small smirk, he looked back over his shoulder at his wife. "First my brother, now your sister? You really need to stop seducing me out in the open where we could get caught."

"Oh, I seduced you, did I?" Harper cackled. "You're the one who knew I didn't want to cook tonight and cooked all this extra food so I didn't have to. That's practically begging for it."

The grin that stretched over Marcos' face made him look like a twitterpated teenage boy. "I don't usually do the begging, mi amor." Scarlett let out a groan of disgust, and his eyes shot over to her with a grimace. "Sorry."

"Don't be sorry. She should have called me before showing up this early," Harper said in a mock chipper tone. "We'll finish this later?"

"So you're not going to get absolutely plastered with your friends and stay up way too late eating junk food and watching telenovelas?" Marcos' eyebrows rose. Lucia, Marcos' mother, had turned their girl group on to telenovelas forever ago. The intense drama had them hooked.

"Tomorrow," Harper corrected herself. "We'll finish this tomorrow."

"I will not be here," Scarlett nervously stated.

"I'll make you all breakfast when you inevitably fall asleep on the couch." Marcos laughed. Harper crossed the distance between them and sidled up to his right, affection written so thoroughly on her face that Scarlett's heart dropped in her chest a bit—a small pang of sadness and pity for herself. She didn't enjoy walking in on her sister and brother-in-law, but she loved them both. They were practically made for each other's own little happy bubble. Marcos grinned down at Harper and pressed a not-quite-chaste kiss against her lips. "Te amo."

"I love you, too."

Still clutching her deviled eggs, Scarlett decided to give them a bit of space and darted toward the kitchen. She avoided the stretch of counter that Harper had been indecently sitting on and quickly shoved the eggs into the refrigerator. It wasn't the first time she had second-guessed the hors d'oeuvres she'd brought. The second her sister was out of her lovey-dovey haze, she would notice why Scarlett had showed up early.

"You brought dressed and depressed eggs," Harper said from the arched entrance to the kitchen the moment Scarlett shut the fridge.

"You should probably Clorox-wipe the counter, you filthy animal," Scarlett diverted the conversation.

"Marcos already did. He wants to be a chef. You think he's not anal about the kitchen being clean?" Harper asked. "What's wrong, Letti? Is it Colin?"

The fact that everyone immediately assumed her temperament had to do with Colin was almost a slap in the face. "Does my mood have to be caused by a man?" Scarlett grumbled.

"Not any man," Harper corrected. "Just Colin. I doubt Braiden could evoke this kind of emotion. He can't even make you come."

They held each other's gaze for a few long seconds before Scarlett finally gave up. "I broke up with Braiden." Harper gave no indication she was going to speak and just waited for Scarlett to continue. "And I think it's because he never made me feel the same way Colin did." She hadn't admitted this to herself or even to Kashvi, but now that she was saying it aloud, it sounded like the truest thing she had said all day.

"Which was what? Heartbroken?"

"Can you hold your judgment for two seconds? I didn't say I wanted him back." Her sister was never going to understand. There was nothing like the unique way she and Colin had been. No one had made her heart race the way he did since, but there had to be someone out there she could love who would make her feel all the things he had. There had to be someone who could do all that and follow it up by not dumping her and leaving her in ruin.

"I'm not judging you for breaking up with Braiden. He was not right for you. But I don't think it's healthy to compare everyone to your ex." Harper sat down at the island, and Scarlett followed, taking the stool beside her.

"Why not? Why is it wrong to want someone who notices me? Who cares about what I'm thinking? Who is intentional and honest when they talk to me?" Scarlett heaved out a long breath. "I just want to be myself and for someone to want the chaotic stories I tell, and dear God, I want someone to be good in bed because they asked me what I wanted."

"You can want all those things as long as you know that if Colin really did all those things, then he wouldn't have hurt you the way he did," Harper said.

"Sure. Maybe it was all one big lie to him considering how he left, but on my side, it wasn't. I felt everything." It was punctuated with a pointer finger against the island countertop, the cold granite seeping its way under Scarlett's skin. "I don't know when or how it changed for him—or if he ever really felt the same, but maybe I can find someone who actually loves me the way I thought he did. I don't want mediocre. Colin is my only frame of reference for that, so yes, it's maybe not healthy to compare everything to him, but I don't know how to separate the two, okay? It's not something I can turn off, so I'm just going to use it to my advantage."

"Hey," Harper reached her hand up and wiped at a tear, and Scarlett blinked back her confusion, only then realizing that she had started crying. "Anyone would be lucky to have all of those things with you. I want for you what I have."

"You seemed really happy banging on the counter and scarring me for life." A sniff and a small laugh reeled her back from her breakdown a bit.

"I am. On the counter and otherwise. But it's not just happiness, it's... safety." Harper smiled softly and wiped at Scarlett's face again before Scarlett waved her off.

"I'll find someone who makes me feel safe." The unspoken thought in her mind was that safety was yet another thing that Colin had redefined and then destroyed before she got a real chance to grasp it. "Someone who won't leave like Dad."

"At least Dad still sends you flowers on Tucker's birthday. How's it feel to be the chosen one?" Harper teased.

"I really don't know why he only sends them to me. Maybe he thinks I'll split them up between you and Mom or something because he's too cheap to get three bouquets? Or he feels the most guilty about leaving me because I was younger? I don't know. It's not like he's dying to speak to me, or he would." Every year since Scarlett graduated high school, it was always the same: white roses in a glass vase from Sophia's Flower Shop on Main, delivered by the shop, not her dad. She kept wanting to reject them on behalf of Harper and her mom, but it was also the only nice thing her father had done for her in forever, so she always complained to Harper and then guiltily kept them. The only reason she knew who they were from was because the first year he sent them, the card he had attached to it was Tucker's old catchphrase that was an old quote their dad often said: 'a great soul never dies.' She thought Tucker had clung to that statement to relieve himself of the fear of dying. Now the statement felt like her dad's best excuse for leaving, and it was a piss-poor one. He must have decided against the quote in later years because from the first bouquet on, he never left a card that said anything other than *For Tucker*. It took her a while to notice that the number of white roses always equaled the age Tucker would be if he were still alive. Her brother was the only person she had forgiven for leaving her. "Anyway, if a man could just actually love me, not leave, and—"

"Not suggest the use of lidocaine cream?" Harper said with a laugh.

"To be fair, I think Colin has permanently crossed that off his list. Or maybe he tried it again with someone competent enough to use it." The end of the sentence soured in her mouth, but she tried to school her features so her sister wouldn't notice her distaste for that idea. Surely Colin had had other women by now and it shouldn't be such a shock to her senses to think about, but the thought made her inconceivably pissed off. The same guy who had promised her forever was probably promising the same thing to every other girl he had dated. Life was just one giant experiment for him, and it didn't matter how many people he hurt while he hypothesized.

Eighteen

Colin
18 Years Old

"My hypothesis was correct," Colin groaned. "I love this." Every single nerve in his body was in his groin now, he was sure of it, just as he was sure that Scarlett's hand moving up and down over his cock was going to kill him. His body was wholly tuned in to her touch, like reaching orgasm was the sole purpose of his existence. He wouldn't mind so much if this was all he ever did. If Scarlett was the only person he touched ever again, then he would be satisfied.

"Am I even doing this right? Is this okay?" Scarlett's voice asked. He had been completely unaware that his eyes were closed, so he pried them back open to look at her hand working him over. And it was then that he decided he should have opened his eyes a hell of a lot sooner. Her hand looked small against his full length, but her long, slender fingers wrapped around him sure enough. The sight of it made him that much more turned on, a note he would have to write down later if he remembered.

"Yes, you're doing it right." He gritted his teeth, trying to hold on to the wave of pleasure climbing up his spine.

"Should I maybe do a better technique? Or..." She gripped him tighter—a little *too* tight—and he winced.

"Don't strangle it," Colin gasped.

"Sorry!" Scarlett let go of him entirely in a panicked flurry, and he regretted saying anything at all. He could have dealt with her suffocating the blood flow to his cock as long as she was still touching him.

"*Red.*" He almost whined the word. His body felt so useless without her. "Why'd you stop?"

"I was doing it wrong." She looked down at her hand in disappointment.

"Here." Colin reached out and folded her fingers into a curled position, bringing them back to his cock. His hand as the guide, he helped her pull up and down slowly. He held back a small moan at the returned contact. "I normally take most of the weight in two or three fingers and my thumb. You go slow until everything builds, and you move with the build—that's perfect. Just like that."

"You'll tell me when to go faster?" A stroke of her hand pulled up the edge of his head before falling over the ledge to the tip. The indecent sound he let out was followed by another edged glide of her hand.

"Go faster," he ordered. She did exactly as he directed, making his balls ache for release. Her pace quickened even more, the lube doing its job as his hips started to rock forward.

"Will you put your mouth on it?" The question practically flew through his mouth, and he again wanted to retract his statement because her hand stopped moving. "You don't have to," he added quickly.

"I want to learn," Scarlett said, leaning forward. "Do I just suck the head? Or I've heard women gag themselves a lot. Am I supposed to do that?"

"I can't tell what feels best until you're doing it," Colin said simply. "I've never done this before."

Scarlett gave a slow nod of her head and bent forward. "Here goes nothing?"

"Here goes *something*," he replied with a huff as he could feel the heat of her breath hit his head. Warmth surrounded him a second later as he watched her lips wrap around him. "Fuck, fuck, fuck."

Her mouth popped off, and she looked up with wide eyes. "Bad?"

"No! Keep going." Something primal took over, and his hand whipped out from his side to push her head back down. The surprised sound Scarlett let out made him immediately release his grip on the back of her head. "Sorry. I didn't mean to—"

"Actually... could you?"

"Push your head down?" Colin clarified, scared to make the wrong move again.

A pretty blush was spreading across her cheeks again. "Not so hard, but I like your hand there. It's comforting because then I at least know you want me to be down here still." The color in her cheeks had come and gone as they moved through foreplay earlier, and it never failed to surprise him what exactly made her blush spread. It wasn't the filthy things so much as the ones that felt more intimate. Having his tongue licking between her legs didn't flush her until the end when she was near the breaking point, but she blushed furiously when he carefully lifted her legs to plant a pillow under her backside—a trick he had unfortunately learned from one of Walker's ghostwritten romance novels. It worked well enough to get the perfect angle, so Colin opted to pretend that whoever co-wrote the novel with his uncle had written in the pillow idea.

Again Scarlett had blushed when Colin's attention caught on a strip of naked skin that glowed in a ray down her body from the crack in the curtains behind her headboard. It had hit the peak of one of her breasts and slashed down to her stomach before continuing across her thigh and disappearing over the side of her bed. He knew because he had traced the path with his lips, unable to stop himself from tasting something that beautiful that had already been kissed by the sunshine. Scarlett's body was mostly uncharted territory, and yet it felt familiar now as he started to learn what she liked, his hand moving up to cup the back of her head as she had requested.

Hand laced in her hair, Colin watched as Scarlett dropped her red lips down to his cock again and sucked him into her mouth. "Just like that," he praised. "Now bob your head up and down while sucking if you c—yes, that's perfect." So perfect that he was going to come down her throat a bit too quickly for his liking. He gripped her head a bit tighter, holding on to a bit of hair before, as slowly as he could muster, he pulled her back from his cock. "It's too good, Scarlett. I want to keep going, but I was getting there too fast. I want to draw it out a bit."

"Okay. How do I do that?" She wiped at her mouth with the back of her hand. Besides her actual mouth on him, it was the most erotic thing he had ever seen.

"Seems like everything you do is going to immediately make me come." Scarlett's shy smile hit him square in the chest. "I'm probably not supposed to admit that."

"I think you should always admit that. It makes me feel good." Her teeth grazed her bottom lip and let go.

"If you want me to, I will. But I also got something that might help." Excitement had him quickly untangling himself from her to hop off the bed. Scarlett startled away from him, and he tossed an apologetic look over his shoulder once he was trudging toward his backpack in the corner of her room. As he rummaged through it, he called back, "I got a few things, actually. One of them is for you, and the other one is to keep me from coming too quickly. The best option would be for me to masturbate before we do this, but I can't do that when we come straight from school to here." His hands finally found one small box and an even smaller tube and pulled them both out. He held up the small bullet vibrator and tossed it toward her. Scarlett looked down at it with wide eyes. "I think that it'll be easier for you to get yourself off with that when I'm not around." He held up the topical lidocaine cream he had gotten at the sex shop when he went to go buy her the vibrator. "This is for me. If I put this on, the sensation should be a bit dulled, and then you can continue on without me coming too early to learn any skill from it."

"So, we just put it on you?" Scarlett asked.

"Yes. Do you want to do it?" Colin held up the small tube.

"Sure." The shy smile she offered made him relinquish control as he climbed back on the bed and passed the tube of cream off to her. The distracting desire still pulsing between his legs was why he didn't immediately notice how much Scarlett had put in her hand before it was too late and she was lathering his cock with it like it was lube instead of a numbing agent.

"Wait—fuck." Colin's eyes went wide in alarm as she immediately went to put her mouth on him. He sucked a breath in through his teeth and tried to form a single coherent thought. He had been worried about the directions for a moment before her mouth started to work and all he could think to do was buck into her mouth. Scarlett gagged and ripped away from him.

"That tastes awful!" she coughed.

A bolt of awareness struck Colin like lightning. There were several things wrong with Scarlett's method, and he was finally lucid enough to think about anything other than her mouth on him. The more immediate problem was the amount she had used. He couldn't imagine a world where anyone would need that much to extend sexual activity. "I thought you'd use the directions. It's not sunscreen, Scarlett! You used, like, half the tube!" Frantically, he patted around the bed and found the discarded cream.

"Oh shit." Scarlett's voice went all squeaky already halfway across the room to scrub at her tongue with the baby wipes she knew he kept readily available in his backpack. Speaking with her tongue still out and raking a wipe down it repeatedly, she yelled back, "I don't know what I'm doing! You should have told me!"

"Shit, I don't think it's meant for human consumption. I

think you were supposed to put it on and wait for it to set in before oral." He flipped the tube to the backside and searched for directions, reading them aloud. "Use a pea-sized amount to—fuck. My dick is going to be comatose in ten minutes."

"What do we do?" Scarlett ran back to the bed and flung the baby wipes at him, hitting him in the face with the pouch.

"Ow!" Colin fixed the glasses she'd just knocked against his face and looked up to find Scarlett with her hand slapped over her mouth.

"S-sorry. Oh God," she said behind her palm. With an expression of disgust, Scarlett ripped her hand from her lips and looked down at it. "Fuck, it's all over my hands." She wiped her mouth on her arm while Colin sat wide-eyed and staring down at his lidocaine-slathered cock. "What do we do?"

"I... it's not good for you in large quantities." He blinked, trying to fight off his rising panic and failing miserably. "It's too much."

"Colin, tell me what to do!" Scarlett shouted.

"I don't know, just—just get it off of me!" Colin finally recalled the baby wipes she had so carefully delivered right between his eyes and yanked several from the pouch, dragging them over his cock like the worst masturbation session ever. The wipes were mostly just smearing the cream around. "It's not coming off." His breathing was erratic, and not in the exciting way Scarlett had gotten him earlier. The numbing cream was just starting to set it, dulling the sensation to his cock and making his brain go haywire with panic. "It's falling asleep!" he shouted. Not only was it entering into its slumber, but it was shrinking at a rapid pace, his arousal thrown into the pits of hell.

Scarlett gripped his wrist forcefully, enough to pull him out of his battle with his own body. "Shower," she said, then yanked him in a sprint through her bedroom door and down the hallway to the bathroom. Her warm hands pressed into his chest as she kicked the bathroom door shut behind her, pushing him toward the shower.

When Colin's brain finally kicked on, he lumbered in after Scarlett, and she closed the glass door behind him. The cold spray of water that pelted him should have woken up his dick a little bit, but every second he wasted, his body was absorbing more cream, and if he waited any longer, his irrational brain said that it might just be numb forever. Scarlett carefully pulled his glasses off his face and set them on the edge of the shower before pumping an extreme amount of body wash into her hands and scrubbing at them furiously. The scent of the soap hit his nose, and he was thankful she used something natural instead of the perfumey stuff his sister Pearl used. It always made his head foggy and gave him a headache.

"Colin," Scarlett choked on his name and grabbed the bottle, holding it out to him. He looked down at it, still feeling a little outside his own body before he finally pumped some soap into his palm and started scrubbing off of the cream.

"It's coming off," Colin said. The panic finally seemed to be subsiding now, and he could think coherent thoughts again. Some of the numbing, he now realized, had been his own brain playing tricks on him. The numbness was there, but an over-the-counter cream didn't have the same strength as surgical-grade lidocaine.

"That's good," Scarlett's voice wavered, and he looked up to see water falling down her face. She wasn't in the direct stream of water, and her hair was still mostly dry. He thought it might be his poor perception of things without his glasses until Scarlett swiped under her eyes with a finger.

"You're crying?" he asked. She looked up at the ceiling. Guilt clawed up his chest. It had to be something he said. It was always something he said. Usually, it was because he was too harsh or blunt, but at this point he couldn't remember what he had said while he was trying to shove down his anxiety before it became something akin to a full-blown breakdown. "Did I say something wrong? I'm not mad, I promise. I was freaking out for a second, but I'm okay."

Scarlett's head shook back and forth several times. "No."

"Then..." He stepped toward her. "What's wrong?"

"What's wrong?" She let out an unhappy laugh. "Everything is wrong, Colin. Am I ever going to be good at this? Because right now it seems like I'm just going to repeatedly embarrass myself till I have to change my name and move to a new country."

"I'd be really sad if you moved. And I like your name," he said sincerely.

"I'm a human disaster," she whispered.

"I should have told you how to use it. I wasn't expecting you to know."

"But you did expect me to read the directions, which I should have done. When I get too nervous, all logic flies out the window." Scarlett lifted her shoulders in a sad shrug.

Colin reached out and took her hand, pulling her toward him. "Come here." She did, and he adjusted the stream of water so it hit them both and wrapped his arms around her. "The problem was that we ignored what we already knew. You don't like to be the one directing us. I do. I should have done it myself and not suggested you do it."

"Please don't ever let me do anything like that again," she groaned against his chest.

"I won't. Promise. But you're good at handling things when I can't. Your brain shuts off when you're nervous. Mine shuts off when I panic or when everything is noisy."

"So, I'll handle the life-or-death situations, and you handle the day-to-day?"

"Perfect," he mumbled against her hair.

"How's your dick?" Scarlett looked downward.

"You could sit on it and it would still be in hibernation. I can still feel it, and I think we got most of the cream off before it soaked in, but the outside is a bit—"

"Numb?"

"Not too bad," Colin assured her. "But I guess the experiment is over for the day. And I think we should toss out the numbing cream."

Her face turned up toward him with a giggle. "I think that's for the best."

"You did really well before then. Really, really, well." His eyes wanted to roll back into his head just thinking about it.

"Really?" Her voice was upturned and hopeful, so he squeezed her tighter.

"Really." He was getting a little tired of not being able to see her fully, so he bent down to pick up his glasses, ready to swipe at the steam. Unbeknownst to him, Scarlett had reached to kiss him at the same time, and his head connected with her nose.

"Ow!" she screeched and jerked backward. He couldn't quite see her in vivid detail without his glasses, but he could tell she was holding on to the bridge of her nose.

This entire day was a bumbling hot mess, and he imagined he might be feeling a hint of what Scarlett had felt earlier. Their limbs didn't line up, and they were fumbling through sex like newborn deer trying to walk. He should have realized that sex and everything in between would be this ungraceful with him. Everything he did felt awkward. "I'm so sorry," he winced.

In all the commotion between them, Colin didn't immediately notice when the bathroom door swung open.

"What the *fuck*?" A voice shrieked from the doorway. A blurry-faced girl stood gawking at them in the bathroom doorway for only a second before she slammed the door shut.

"H, it's not what it looks like!" Scarlett yelled, still clutching her nose. "Shit, shit, shit." She reached back to turn off the water, and Colin frantically covered himself with his hands, cupping his freshly washed crotch. It must be one of Scarlett's family members, back home earlier than they had planned.

The shower door was ripped open a second later as Scarlett threw herself out and frantically started to dry off. The cold air hit Colin like a freight train as he whipped his head around in search of his glasses. He was pretty sure when he hit Scarlett in the face that they had fallen to the ground.

"Colin, get dressed," Scarlett said, her voice pure panic.

"I need my glasses. I can't see anything," he said, crouching down and patting around the shower floor.

"Here." His glasses were placed on his face a moment later, cockeyed and not properly hooked over his ears. Colin reached up to fix them, the lingering steam still obscuring his vision. Grabbing blindly for a towel on the wall rack, he pulled it down and quickly swiped it over his glasses so he could see clearly. The image of Scarlett pulling her underwear up over her ass with a series of hops made him pause.

"*Get dressed*," Scarlett hissed.

Colin blinked, coming back into himself before he sprung into motion. "Shit."

The barista from Colin's favorite coffee shop in town was sitting across from him at Scarlett's dining table, and she was glaring at him. He had dry-swallowed to uncomfortably clear the air about a thousand times since sitting down. Scarlett sat beside him with her hands covering her face, so he was left to look around the room to avoid making eye contact with whom he now realized was probably Scarlett's sister. It made sense, now that he was thinking about it. Harper had copper hair that was less vibrant than Scarlett's, but she also had the same face shape, eyes, and chin, making the resemblance obvious.

"One of you want to explain what the fuck I just walked into?" Harper demanded.

Scarlett groaned and dropped her hands away from her beet-red face. "We were... cleaning ourselves."

Harper scoffed. "Is *that* what they call that now?"

"Technically, in that exact moment, Scarlett is correct. We were just cleaning ourselves," Colin confirmed.

"Thank you." Scarlett reached out and grabbed his hand, and they tightened their fingers around each other.

"You both are kidding yourselves if you think I believe you,"

Harper said and then directed her attention only to him. "Colin Hartrick, right? Does your uncle know you're here right now?"

"No." The dread seeped into Colin's chest as he prepared to defend himself. He shouldn't be shocked in the least that Harper knew who he was beyond a coffeehouse regular. "I'm eighteen, and Walker has too much on his plate. He has to deal with Piper drinking, Carter skipping school, Cooper getting bullied, and Pearl going through puberty. I'm the one person he doesn't have to worry about, and I'd like to keep it that way."

"You didn't tell me any of that," Scarlett murmured, her voice soft as she rubbed her thumb into his hand.

"I feel bad that I keep taking Wednesdays as a break from my family because I should be helping more. Being in that house is sometimes suffocating. And I thought that once everything settled and I came of age that I'd have custody of my siblings or at least have to step in in some way, but Walker refuses to let me help, so the least I can do is make sure he's not getting calls about me doing things normal teenagers do." He looked down at his hands and mumbled, "I don't drink. I don't party. Scarlett's the first girl I've even seen naked. And being with her like that is not inherently wrong, so I don't see why we'd have to bother Walker with this."

Harper was staring down at their entwined hands with an unreadable expression before she looked up. "I won't mention it. I see how haggard he looks when he comes to get coffee in the morning. Even more than usual. He hasn't been coming in with Talia."

"They got into a fight the other day and are taking a break from each other, which is stupid considering they're both happier when they're together. I don't get why two people who clearly love each other wouldn't just say that," Colin huffed. Scarlett's hand twitched in his, and he adjusted his grip in case it was too tight.

"Where do they think you are right now?" Harper asked.

"Mathletes," he said simply.

"H," Scarlett whispered. "I'm sorry I didn't tell you. I promise we're being safe. Plus, Colin's helping me with Chemistry. I got a B on my retake of the exam."

A prideful smile lifted the corners of Colin's mouth, and he squeezed her hand again. "You didn't tell me that."

"I was going to when we were..." She nervously looked at her sister. "Done."

They still had two hours until he had to be home because Walker wasn't aware that even when Colin had been in Mathletes, practice didn't last three hours. "Are you hungry? Do you want to go out and eat somewhere? I'll buy you ice cream as a congratulations."

"Right now?" Scarlett's face lit up, her chair screeching against the linoleum floor when she slid it out from under the table.

"You're just going to leave?" Harper balked from the other end of the table.

"I mean, do you want to interrogate me more? I can barely look you in the eye right now." Scarlett gave a nervous laugh.

"I don't get to do the big sister 'don't hurt her, or I'll hurt *you*' speech?" Harper said.

Colin rose from his seat, still holding on to Scarlett's hand. "You don't have to worry about that. If I ended up hurting her, then the pain of knowing that would be enough to keep me away."

"Hmm," Harper looked him up and down until he felt sufficiently scrutinized. "All right, fine." She looked at Scarlett. "I will simply burn my retinas and forget this ever happened. Only because you two are kinda cute, and I need you to bring me back food."

"Done," Scarlett singsonged, pulling Colin toward the door and calling out "love you" back over her shoulder as they made their great escape.

Nineteen

Scarlett
18 Years Old

Everything she and Colin were doing felt like a date. The fifties-style diner they decided on made Scarlett feel like she was in a rom-com, right along with Colin's decision to sit beside her in the booth so he could still hold her hand. Her veins were vibrating with the implications of it all. It felt a bit ridiculous to be this excited about getting food with someone she had already hooked up with, but it felt like a date. The jukebox in the corner was playing "Lay All Your Love On Me" by ABBA, for God's sake. Her favorite artist, the meaning of the song—it felt kismet. Like the stars were aligning.

"What music do you listen to? Can I take a guess? You like calm, relaxing stuff. Maybe you don't even listen to music, and you just listen to one of those playlists that's, like, ocean waves for ten hours straight. Or... maybe folk music? I could actually see you liking smooth jazz, too. Have you ever been to a jazz club? Wait... of course you haven't." Scarlett shook her head at the rambling mess of questions that had come out of her mouth.

"I listen to classical music and what Piper calls 'sad boy

music,' which I guess is just folk and depression music. The tones are lower in register, and I like that. And I usually listen to rain noises when I sleep. I've always loved thunderstorms as long as I'm not outside. At one point, I was really into weather science, and I still occasionally obsess over it again. I would love to go to a jazz club as long as it's not too loud." Colin released her hand, and Scarlett was disappointed until he set it on her thigh. "What do you like?"

"You." The second she said it, she wanted to cram the word back into her mouth. Clearly, he had meant music, and her brain had skipped a step, as if she had started an art piece by painting first and then sketching afterward.

"I like you, too," Colin said. He said it so casually that she wasn't sure if he meant it in a friendly manner or something else entirely. "Sorry, I wasn't clear. What music do you like?"

And now he was apologizing to her, as if his original question hadn't been obvious. She needed to start a tally for the number of times she wished a sinkhole would swallow her up. There needed to be a punch card she could stamp for every embarrassing thing she had done since she met Colin. Twelve embarrassing moments, and she could trade it in for a brain-wiping surgery so the memories didn't taunt her when she tried to sleep.

"I like sixties and seventies music. Not rock so much, but the upbeat stuff where the singers are dramatic about living or being in love. Aretha Franklin, David Bowie, Fleetwood Mac, Stevie Wonder, Queen, ABBA, Elton John. They're my favorites, but I'll listen to just about anything that makes me flail around like one of those blow-up car dealership guys."

"I'd like to see that," Colin said. Scarlett's thigh felt like the only spot on her body that was relaxed with his hand pressed into it. Everywhere else felt as though it were swooping and churning her insides in an unsettled prick of awareness. She didn't want to be his friend. Hated the idea of only getting his body when she wanted also to look into his mind, memorize the way he thought.

Colin was all about being forthright, so Scarlett took a leap and hoped she wouldn't fall. "Why are we here right now, Colin?"

"Here as in this restaurant? Or are you asking about the philosophical meaning of life?" Only Colin would ask for clarification on a question about clarification.

"The restaurant, but I'll take your opinion on the meaning of life later."

"I thought you might be hungry," he replied. "And the book I gave you suggests that emotional intimacy goes hand in hand with a sexual relationship, and a lot of the time bad sex is associated with a lack of feeling connected to your partner."

Her heart sank, and she shifted away from him, his hand falling away from her thigh so the room temperature air felt like ice against the vacant spot. "So you think we're bad at sex stuff and the only reason you want to know me otherwise is because doing that will make the sex better?"

Colin furrowed his brow. "Did I say something wrong? I was just stating the research. Do you want to keep it more superficial? No friendship, just sex?"

"I just didn't think the only reason you want to get to know me is because it'll make the sex better." Scarlett looked away, hoping she could control her disappointment before she embarrassed herself again. "But I get it. We agreed to no strings."

"I hate that rule," Colin grumbled. The irritation lacing his voice gave her pause, and she slowly turned her head to look at him again. "I was trying to make it so you didn't have to be invested in me if you didn't want to be. I don't have any friends that aren't my siblings, so maybe there's a reason for that. Maybe there's something that makes me intrinsically unlikable. Maybe it's that I relate everything back to facts, I don't know. You don't have to be invested in me, but I am invested in you, Scarlett. I like hearing you talk. I want to know what makes you decide to paint certain things or how you choose your earrings in the morning." He reached up to curl one finger around the hot pink dangling arches she was wearing today. The pounding in her chest intensified. He wasn't looking at her head-on, but it still felt like he was speaking directly into her heart. "I like you. A lot. You're hot and interesting, and when I'm with you I feel... good."

"Honey, if you don't take him, I've got a niece that will." An older waitress wearing bright red lipstick and an apron was standing at their table, holding up a pen and pad of paper.

Scarlett's face heated as she stumbled over her words, trying to think straight. "Oh, I—um, you—"

"No thanks on the niece," Colin said simply and touched Scarlett's leg again. "Ready to order?" She wasn't even close to ready. Before they had started their conversation, she was in the middle of decision paralysis between ten different things. The menu sitting on the table stared at her in judgment. "Do you want me to order for you?"

"Please." Scarlett let out a sigh of relief.

When the waitress finally left, Scarlett felt like she was bursting at the seams with all of the things she wanted to say but couldn't quite articulate. A water glass slid closer to her, and she bit her lip as Colin spoke again. "By the end of the day, you're always massaging your head like you have a headache, and I think it's because you're dehydrated, so I think you should probably drink this one and mine, too, and that will help." He slid his glass across the table.

The glasses clinked together, and she twisted her torso to face him and blurted, "I really like you."

Colin flinched. "You already said that."

"No," Scarlett said, exasperated. "I mean I like you more than as a friend, Colin. More than our experiment. I want to know everything about you because I'm pretty certain you're going to end up changing the world someday. I wish you'd tell me every thought in your head because I like your deep dives into science and facts, even when I have no idea what you're talking about. I wish you told me more about your parents or your siblings or whatever's going on with your uncle. About what's going on with *you*. I remember when my brother died, and of course it's not the same because I was so young and Tucker was fighting cancer for a long time, but you lost two people suddenly, and I know you're not okay because you occasionally let me see tiny snippets of that, and I just want to make you feel better. I want—" Colin's mouth landed on hers, and all the tension in her body melted under his touch. His hands were cupping her cheeks, and the warm comfort came roaring back into her body. Her shoulders sagged as she leaned in and kissed him back.

Scarlett's stomach dropped when Colin pulled away. He reached across the table to his backpack and retrieved a sheet of paper and a pen. It was a scoring chart for their experiment, she noticed, and she thought he was going to immediately kill the moment by grading the kiss until he took the pen and carefully struck through one of their rules at the bottom. Rule three, no attachments or expectations, was officially voided. She thought she had never been happier in her life until he said casually, "you're a visual learner, so I thought that would help with clarification." Taking it a step further, he scribbled a little note next to the strikethrough: *dating exclusively.* He didn't even seem to realize how quickly he had understood her. She did need that visual assurance. As he started to meticulously fold the paper into rectangle after rectangle, she found his leg under the table and set her hand on his thigh because she knew him, too. Colin liked contact. Like a cat arching into a hand, Colin shifted closer to her so their sides were firmly pressed together.

"Should we get rid of the 'keep everything a secret' rule, too?" She wiggled happily in the booth.

"I still think we should keep it a secret," he said. Her face fell, and she tried to recover it before he noticed. A situationship wasn't really what she had in mind when she said she wanted to know everything about him.

"Are you embarrassed of me or something?" Scarlett forced a laugh that came out extremely ditzy and punched his shoulder. It was supposed to be playful, but she had never jokingly punched anyone before, and it felt strange from the second she lifted her fist to the moment she connected with his arm.

"I didn't like that." Colin scooted a few inches away from her and rubbed the spot she punched, and she inwardly wanted to punch herself for good measure "Talia—the girl my uncle is in love with—does that all the time to him, so I know it's supposed to be like a cute couple thing, but I don't get it. Why is violence cute? I don't think we need to do that to be cute. Can you be my girlfriend without punching me?"

She groaned and buried her face in her hands. "I actually hated that. I take it back. I was trying to be cavalier, and I'm not cool, so I don't know why I did that."

"It's weird that you're trying to be cool around me when I'm the least cool of the two of us."

"Says the guy who wants to make sure no one knows he's dating me," she muttered grumpily.

"What?" Colin flexed a perplexed brow. "I don't not want people knowing you're dating me, I just don't want the fanfare from announcing it. My family would be overwhelming with the questions, and I value the peace that I've found with you. Obviously, if we decide to go the distance, they will have to know at some point, but for now, I like how quiet our little bubble is."

It wasn't exactly what Scarlett had envisioned. Having a boyfriend for the first time since freshman year, when she had dated Robbie Lackey for one month, felt like a big deal. She wanted to be seen with Colin. Still, the thought of everyone staring at them made it feel like the acid in her stomach was rising, so she could understand where he was coming from, but even so, she wanted to be fully immersed in his life the same way that they touched each other, firmly and assuredly.

"Okay." She bit her tongue. "Can we at least talk about you for once? The issues with your uncle, your parents—"

"We should fix my uncle's problem, because that's more immediate."

Scarlett smiled softly, shoving down the feeling that he seemed too eager to avoid any discussion about his parents. "What's up with him and his not-girlfriend?"

"Every single one of my siblings knows he's in love with her, and I know because he frequently checks her out and will not stop talking about her."

"Okay, so, what's the problem?"

Colin lifted both hands in an endearing, cartoonesque shrug. "I truly don't know. They're annoying. If you like someone, then ask them out. It's that simple. I like you, I asked you if you wanted to get food, and here we are. I told you I liked you, and you returned the sentiment."

She considered that for a moment. "Not everyone is as forthcoming with that information as you are. I wouldn't be if you didn't make me be brave. It's scary to admit that kind of thing because there's a lot people can lose."

"I'd argue that there's a lot people can lose by *not* saying exactly what they want or what they feel. For instance, I'm leaving for Johns Hopkins at the end of summer. If I don't tell you now that I like you, then we'd have no opportunity to see where this goes because I won't even be in the same city."

That thought churned Scarlett's insides. Everything was new, and yet the attachment she had to Colin now felt so permanent. When he inevitably left, it was going to hurt. Like a key clicking into a lock, the fear slotted itself into the back of her mind and took up residence there.

"You're right." Scarlett swallowed. "But it's still scary. Maybe with the chaos of all your siblings and dealing with that, your uncle and his friend haven't been in enough of a romantic setting to spill their guts to each other."

She could see he was thinking about it by the way he closed his eyes for a moment, rocking front to back, the way he sometimes did when she was well into a particularly long rant. Colin paid more attention when his eyes were closed, as if he needed to eliminate one of his senses to really glean the information or think properly. Sometimes his responses were quick off the cuff, but if they required more thought, he always seemed to retreat in on himself first.

He finally opened his eyes. "So, what you're saying is we need to force them into an intimate setting. Make them go on a date, and maybe they'll end up figuring it out?"

"Force is maybe a little much. I just meant—" But Colin already had his phone pulled out and a dial tone ringing through the speaker as he set it face up on the table between them. The contact glaring up from the black screen said "Carter Hartrick" with a picture of Colin's brother grinning from ear to ear. Startled by the sudden change from Colin literally just saying he wanted to keep his family in the dark, Scarlett floundered beside him, unsure if she should speak or sit quietly.

"What's wrong?" Carter was breathing heavily when he answered after two rings. The feeling Carter implied with those two words must have been universal, because occasionally Scarlett felt like she too was only one phone call away from bad news. She wondered if the Hartrick siblings all picked up the phone like that.

"I'm going to loop in Piper. I think I have an idea for how to force Walker's hand with Talia," Colin said, then started tapping away at his phone.

"Dude, I'm at basketball practice, and Piper is with Talia right now," Carter said, then sighed. "You know what? Fuck it. I'll just tell Coach Winston I'm going to the bathroom."

"Good," Colin replied. "Hold, please."

A few minutes later, the eldest three Hartrick siblings were all on the line. Scarlett's suspicions about how each sibling would always expect the worst were confirmed when Piper's initial reaction to Colin's phone call was to immediately ask if he was okay. Food was delivered midway through the conversation, and Scarlett listened in as she stuffed her face with fries and the burger that Colin had ordered her. By the time she had silently finished her burger, the siblings had an entire rundown of tasks each of them would complete to push their uncle in the right direction.

The plan they concocted was ridiculous, and there was a small pang of sadness lodged in Scarlett's throat at the thought that she would never get to do any scheming with her own brother. The things about Tucker that always hit the hardest were the what ifs. What if he had gone into remission and she had been old enough to be his accomplice for one of his many pranks? She would be fine for months on end until she would find a sparkle on the ground from the time her brother had glitter-bombed their mom. Nora had been furious at first because sparkles were a pain in the ass to get out of anything, but then Tucker looked her dead in the eye and said that she couldn't be mad at him because he had cancer. Everyone had burst into laughter, and it was forever one of those memories that was brought up at Thanksgiving dinners. All the untapped potential of future pranks had died with him.

It seemed like the Hartrick siblings' conversation was coming to a close, so Scarlett tuned back in for the end, shoving down her aching jealousy. It was silly to be envious of them at all considering the position they had been left in. Swapping out one sad story for another wasn't anything to be jealous of. They deserved a little fun. They deserved a little peace like Colin had said he had found with her.

"Dammit," Piper muttered.

"What?" Colin's voice was tinged with panic.

"Did we forget something?" Carter asked.

"No, sorry." A long, feminine sigh on the other line echoed through the speaker. "Harden keeps texting me." Another groan from Piper. "Listen to me right now, Carter, if you ever send a girl an unsolicited dick pic, I will maim you. No girl wants that shit."

"Ew!" Scarlett screeched.

"Who is that?" Piper asked, alarmed. After finally resolving herself to stay quiet for the entire conversation, Scarlett's knee-jerk reaction to a douchey guy sending Piper a schlong picture had given her away. "Carter, are you with a girl right now?"

"That would be me," Colin said casually. "I'm with Scarlett." He picked up a fry like he was finally going to eat something, bringing it to his mouth to only take one bite before setting it down.

"Another tutoring session?" Carter asked. Scarlett could detect a hint of suspicion in Carter's voice, but Colin seemed none the wiser. That was what she had been rendered to—a girl who needed a science tutor.

"We did that earlier. Now we're just eating."

"Does Scarlett get to speak, or do you speak for her?" Piper asked.

Scarlett cackled. "Hi."

"She lives!" Carter exclaimed.

"Why would she not be alive?" Colin cinched his eyebrows together.

"Maybe she died of having to listen to you yap about chemistry," Carter said.

"Ah, a fellow science hater." Scarlett smiled and caught a reproachful look from Colin. "I-I mean, hating science is wrong because everything *is* science."

"Is Colin making you read off a teleprompter? Blink twice if you need help," Piper's tongue-and-cheek response came with a chuckle from Carter.

Scarlett's eyelashes fluttered with purpose when she noticed Colin look in her direction. "What's it mean if she blinks thirty times in a row?" he asked.

"She's having a stroke," Carter quipped.

"She's trying to create a windstorm," Piper offered.

"She's using Morse code to deliver a message to an underground operation," Colin added.

"Ooh, I like that one." Scarlett grinned. "That makes me sound like a badass. I was just going for Life Alert. Like, 'help, I've fallen and I can't get up!' I'd rather be a spy."

"As Dad used to say, you can be anything you want to be, you just have to get out of bed," Carter said in a mocking old man voice.

"He only said that to you because you are a pain in the ass to get out of bed," Colin said.

"We all have our faults," Carter droned. "Colin's is that he'll tell you right to your face what your worst flaw is. Piper's is her inability to not date bottom feeders."

Piper gasped. "Rude!"

Scarlett grimaced, remembering the original text that had launched this conversation to begin with. Every single interaction she'd ever had with Harden Rochester ended with him hitting on her in a way that made her feel like she needed to take a shower after. "You're not still dating Harden, are you?"

"Absolutely not," Colin grumbled. "She's not allowed to." The older big brother attitude he was projecting made her flush with affection, and Scarlett's hand involuntarily reached up to latch around his arm again. He moved it, and at first she figured it was because she was gripping him too tight, until his arm traveled behind her, coming to rest on her hip. She liked it way too much to not lay her head back against his chest so they were practically on top of each other, his palm partially cupping her ass.

"No, I'm not." Piper said it in a way that made it clear she was rolling her eyes.

"If you want me to deck him, I will," Carter volunteered. "Also, I'm very offended that I was the first person you thought would send unsolicited dick pics. What about Colin?"

"I doubt anyone would want mine." Colin dropped his mouth to Scarlett's ear so no one would hear. "Unless you do, Red."

A shiver traveled up Scarlett's spine. She opened her mouth to say no, but she ended up just shrugging. There might come a time where she was horny enough to suggest he send her one. Penises were weird-looking, and Colin's was intimidatingly large, so she didn't think that request would ever come into play, but she didn't want it off the table entirely.

The rest of the conversation passed in a haze. Scarlett barely paid attention. Colin's hand on her ass and his hot breath near her ear made her want to sink into his touch. To be covered up in him. By the time everyone said their goodbyes, they got their to-go order for Harper, boxed up the entirety of the meal Colin had barely touched, and were sitting in the car, Scarlett was so keyed up that a knot of pleasure was sitting in her core.

"Back to your house?" Colin buckled himself and reached back to set Harper's paper bag on the backseat.

"Mm-hmm." Scarlett's mind was preoccupied, a thousand things swirling around in her head. She couldn't decide if she wanted him to render her speechless with his mouth or if she wanted him to keep talking. Per his earlier declarations, talking would make the intimacy better. Her heart won out after a moment of silence, and she lifted Colin's hand off her thigh and held it. "It was fun scheming with your siblings, but we didn't really talk about how you were feeling."

"I told you how I was feeling. I'm annoyed he doesn't just date her already," Colin said, turning the key and beginning to back out of the parking spot.

"No." Scarlett bit her lip. "I mean in general. About your parents."

Colin pulled his hand away. "I don't want to talk about that."

"But you've talked to me a little about it before. It could be good to talk about it," she urged. She was pushing him too hard and she knew it, but she couldn't help the feeling that while she talked on and on about every facet of her life and had frequently overshared about her brother, Colin had only shared trivial things.

"I have a therapist." Colin punctuated this statement with a flick of the blinker to make a right-hand turn. She could tell he was getting irritated, but she pushed on anyway, desperate to know.

"But... I'm your friend, right? You don't have to just keep your feelings hidden away in therapy, I'm here, too, I'm right—"

"No, Scarlett!" he yelled. She snapped her mouth shut and looked down at her hands. "Sorry, I just—I don't want to talk about it. You make me feel good. You give me some sort of a purpose, and I don't feel so aimless when I'm with you. The last thing I need is you knowing how fucked up I am, because you're the one holding me together right now."

"But I don't care if you're fucked up. I just want to know you," Scarlett murmured.

"You do know me," he said. "Whatever you felt when your brother died, multiply it by two because two people died, and then add in some maturity to those feelings because you were really young and I was seventeen, and you'll reach a conclusion about how I feel."

Scarlett's mouth dropped open, and she twisted her torso to glare at him. "Grief is not a math equation, Colin. It's different for every person. The fact that you even think that way means your experience *is* way different than mine because I'd never reduce it down to two plus two equals four."

"Well, that's how I think. I don't know what to tell you." His cold demeanor wasn't something she had seen on him before. He was awkward and stiff a lot, sure, but never so rigid that the light couldn't come in. "Maybe there's an entirely different way I'm supposed to be dealing with grief, but the only way that feels good is being with you."

There was something about this conversation that she wasn't quite getting, like she had finished a painting but it felt just the slightest bit off because she didn't tone the canvas beforehand. "I feel good when I'm with you, too, but grief isn't supposed to feel good. For me it felt like someone had just smeared black paint all over something pretty. Or they'd stabbed a hole straight through the center of the canvas, and I'd repeatedly try to fix it just for the same hole to be broken open again."

"I either feel nothing at all, or I feel too much and I explode. There's barely an in-between." Colin shook his head, as if to scold himself. "I think I'm supposed to cry more and sleep more, but I just feel uncomfortable with everything. The world has always been uncomfortable, and now that they're not here, it feels even more so. I was trying to get used to one equation, and it suddenly changed on me, and now I don't really know what to do about it. I haven't been eating a lot or sleeping much, and when I eat it has to be very specific foods, or I just can't do it." A flash of Colin barely eating one bite of a french fry earlier flashed through Scarlett's mind, and she felt guilty for how easily she had scarfed down her own food. "It probably doesn't help that Walker burns half the stuff he cooks, but Piper and Talia have been cooking most of the food now, and I still... I've lost a bunch of weight since they died." She had seen him without a shirt enough times to notice how gaunt he seemed, but she didn't realize he hadn't been that way before. "I'm confused about why I don't react the same way as my siblings. Carter's in a depression where he doesn't want to get out of bed even more than normal. Piper got drunk at some parties and probably hooked up with an asshole. Pearl is crying in her room constantly. Cooper has been out of character in his silence. I saw Walker having some sort of an episode that, per Google, was likely a panic attack. But I don't do any of that. Pearl asked me once if I was even sad because while she cries the most, all of them cry way more than I do. And of course I'm fucking sad! I just don't know why the thing that bugs me the most is that the routine of my life has been fundamentally disrupted and now I can't function. Is that what you wanted to know, Scarlett? That I must be cold-hearted because I really miss my parents, but I miss the way it was easier with them around even more?"

There were tears sliding down her face, and she wiped at them frantically, because the only thing that would do was make him feel even more abnormal if she could cry but he couldn't. But it was too late. "Why can I only cry when it's an explosion? Even you can cry about this," he said, exasperated.

"No, Colin, it's—I'm sad *for* you," Scarlett insisted, trying to control herself with a hefty sniff. "I cry super easily. You're not a bad person for not crying or for wanting things to go back to being simple."

"I miss that they both knew exactly when I needed a break. I miss that my mom knew what foods I'd be able to eat right now. My dad had insomnia, too, and he'd probably stay up with me and we could watch something on TV. I just want comfort, and you're the only person I feel that with. I'm desperate to keep this going between us because it's the one time I don't feel like I'm trying to guess how I should be feeling at any moment." His speech was spiraling. From beginning to end of his monologue, his breaths had quickened, his hands around the wheel tightening so hard his knuckles turned white.

"I love being that for you," she assured him. "I promise, I do." She hadn't realized that at some point, Colin had driven in the opposite direction of her house. They were completely surrounded by woods, up a graveled path that she hadn't been focused on at all. The shaking of the car must not have been Colin's body after all, but the small rocks under the tires.

"I need to breathe for a second," he said, skirting up to a pull out in the road and throwing the car in park. The Audi wasn't yet at a complete stop, and Scarlett had to brace her hands on the dash to keep from faceplanting into it when the car jerked as if it had hit a wall and could go no farther. Colin left the engine running as he flung himself from the driver's seat and stumbled out to what she now realized was the lookout above the city. As if Colin's reaction was viral and Scarlett had caught it on the wind, her chest tightened with panic. How was she supposedly his comfort when she was completely out of her element with him? Slowly, she stepped out into the dirt and traveled the distance between them at a crawl. He was gripping the small display plaque listing off Archwood's founding information near the ledge that looked out over the city's lights. It was usually a pretty sight, but Colin wasn't even looking at it, his forehead pressed into the plaque in an almost-hug.

"Colin?" Scarlett asked, leveling out her voice as much as possible. He didn't respond, just continued shaking in a metal embrace with the plaque. "I'm going to touch you," she announced as she got closer. When her hand pressed hard into his back and started rubbing, he finally looked up at her. It looked almost painful the way he unlatched his fingers from the edge of the sign before reaching for her and yanking her into his chest. The hold was just short of too tight. Her breathing was slightly constricted, but not so much that she wouldn't do this for him. Not so much that she wasn't desperate to hold him. He was warm, and for all his talk about not being able to cry, this must have been what he considered an explosion, because he was almost hyperventilating, he was sobbing so much. She returned his hug with as much force as she could and murmured a series of apologies into his shoulder as she cried, too. For him. For herself. For a world that no longer knew Cole and Paisley Hartrick or Tucker Wallace.

For all the reasons she loved this person who just wanted a little peace. By the time Colin had regained control of his body, Scarlett had resolved herself to be just that for him. Peace.

TWENTY

Colin
22 Years Old

A slow sigh of relief left Colin's lungs as he sank into the pressure. The ropes tied around his thighs and ankles were wound tight enough to give him relief, but not so tight he lost blood flow. He had practiced enough that he'd perfected the amount of constriction needed to forget he was ever uncomfortable in his own skin. When he had first taken up shibari, everything was sloppy, and he had almost thrown out his therapist's suggestion because if there was one thing he hated, it was being bad at something. If he couldn't catch on, then he gave up. Most things had a clear measure of success. They were solvable. They could be mastered. Yes, you could technically improve at everything, but Colin was happy learning a new skill, getting it to the point it needed to be, and leaving it there, finished.

The only time that frame of mind didn't work was with Scarlett. Not even at eighteen. He was always striving for better when it came to their experiment. With his leukemia research—which he could freely admit now he had fixated on because of Scarlett— he couldn't simply stop at a job well done or a lab completed.

Unless he found a cure and it well and truly worked, he would be stuck searching for one forever. That unknown didn't scare him like the ambiguous things usually did. It strengthened him and forged a connection to his work. He should have chosen that same route with his relationship with Scarlett and just found a way to work around all the bad things, but at the time he couldn't see a way through it. Even what he was doing now, lying on the floor in his room with sensory knots entangling his legs, was a way through one of the things he had to deal with. Being able to withstand wet clothes would be a swell characteristic to have given that Oregon could turn on you at any moment, but he had accepted that he would always have to immediately change and do something to calm his nerves. Rain at a funeral, after all, made sense.

If there was ever a time to feel uncomfortable, it was while wearing black in a cemetery just a few days before Christmas. It had been five years since Colin had had to endure a funeral ceremony, but even with the painful memory of his parents, he hadn't expected to feel heartbroken over someone he didn't know. If he was going to feel something, he thought that Scarlett would be the one that drew that out of him. He hadn't seen her once since the coffee shop, and he thought the sight of her alone might bring him to his knees. He had thought about her hidden tears a million times since he'd bought Theo's painting. He wondered just how many more he might cause once he started showing up regularly to her studio with an excuse that was good, but wouldn't make his presence hurt any less.

Colin doubted that Scarlett had met Isabel Castillo, and he figured she was simply there as a support system for her sister, who was Isabel's granddaughter-in-law, but Scarlett cried easily. It was one of the things he loved about her. She displayed exactly what she was feeling. From tears to stuttering and reddened cheeks, he had memorized the way she reacted to things. He realized now that part of it was a camouflaging technique to constantly collect data on how she was feeling so he could appropriately respond, but most of it was just because he cared. He simply wanted to know what things hurt her and what things brought her joy. It was why when he had known Scarlett would be attending the funeral and the mercy meal Walker and Talia were hosting, he had gone out and bought some of her favorite things. He had researched which watercolor paints were the best and which brushes were perfect for her work.

There hadn't been a chance at the funeral to give the paint supplies to Scarlett, so he had held off for the mercy meal that would be starting soon. At the actual funeral, he had spent most of his time consoling Piper, who had shed a few tears during the ceremony when she thought no one was looking. Piper had met Isabel. Not only that, but like some fucked-up family trait she had gotten from Walker, everyone seemed to know that Piper was in love with Isabel's grandson but Piper. She and Leo had spent a good portion of high school and all of college openly despising each other, but the tides had shifted. Today Leo had spent the service standing stone-faced beside his family as Piper looked on miserably, and Colin knew what she must be thinking, because he was thinking the same thing. He wanted to be beside Scarlett.

In the end, though, it wasn't Scarlett or Piper or Leo who had made his eyes water. What socked him in the chest was Lucia Diaz, who had stood near her mother's casket, pressed a hand into the wood, and told everyone that her mother wasn't perfect, but she was kind. That Isabel Castillo was a good person who had tried her very best. And, finally, that Isabel, Lucia's own mother, was her best friend.

It was the very same thing Colin's parents had been to him. His best friends. They had failed him spectacularly, and yet it still didn't change the fact that they had tried their very best. Even flawed as they were and with all the things they had missed, they were good and kindhearted people who were also capable of making mistakes.

Colin's siblings and Walker had immortalized Cole and Paisley because they were everyone's heroes. His siblings didn't have the added struggle of wondering why they were fundamentally different, while Colin had spent his entire childhood struggling over his inability to make friends. He was left confused as to how he had managed to make his mom cry over his reaction to a Christmas present she had bought him one year. He was left to agonize over what could be said aloud and what had to be cloaked in social niceties. How long to look into someone's eyes before it could pass as a normal interaction. Why half his clothes felt sensitive and rubbed raw against his skin. Why loud sounds felt like they traveled under his skin and through his veins to make his heart beat out of time with his body while his head triggered an immediate fight-or-flight response against the onslaught of overstimulation. Through all of this, his parents had consoled him and accommodated his peculiarities. And yet, there was a very valid and real explanation for it all. Knowledge was power, and Colin had been deprived of that power.

The resentment Colin had harbored for his parents after his diagnosis felt equal parts reasonable and ridiculous. They were dead, and he would give anything for them to be alive once more, yet he couldn't understand why he wouldn't let go of his anger. The distance he placed between his family and himself when he moved to Maryland, not just in miles but in communication, was strategic. Besides his journey to self-worth, he was also terrified to talk about his parents outside of therapy, so he kept to himself, coming back only for holidays until slowly, over time, the resentment eased. It wasn't gone completely, but he found himself considerably less angry once he had examined his own faults. The distance he had created between himself and his family was a fault. The way he had left Scarlett was so reactionary he was sure that to her it had felt out of the blue, out of character, and altogether mean-spirited. In his heart of hearts, he knew it was the opposite.

A knock pulled Colin's gaze toward the door where his brother Cooper was standing. "Walker, Tal, and Amala want our help downstairs with some of the food trays." Out of anyone he had left behind, he always felt the worst about Cooper. He had been the youngest of their siblings at eight years old when their parents died, and looking back, it probably seemed that Colin had just up and abandoned him. Now Cooper was newly a teenager, and Colin had missed so much that he wasn't sure how to talk to him.

"Why are you tied up like you've been abducted?" Cooper asked.

"It helps with my sensory issues. It's called shibari," Colin explained as he began to unravel himself.

Cooper scrunched his face. "Isn't that a… sex thing?" The word 'sex' was mumbled, as if his brother could barely say it. While Colin never really had a problem saying anything aloud, he knew enough about teenagers (and Scarlett) to understand that people were often embarrassed to bring things out in the open.

"Kind of. It's a Japanese bondage tactic to display the body. I don't use it to display anything, though. I just use it to calm the fuck down." Colin held his tongue on the thought that he definitely would use it for sexual purposes if the opportunity arose. He would rather do the tying, though, because tying the knots was entertaining, and he would love to see his handiwork on someone else. "My therapist back in Maryland was progressive and really into Reddit, where apparently there's an entire community of people using it just as a self-soothing tactic." Colin had been weirded out by the idea at first, but then opted to try it after a day of feeling so touch starved that he wanted to claw his own skin off.

"I think I would just feel like I'd been abducted by a serial killer," Cooper said with a shrug.

"You watch way too many serial killer documentaries with Talia." Colin chuckled, finally getting the final knot out and wrapping the rope up.

"You say that, but do you know all the ways to get out of the trunk of a killer's car? Because I do. Dateline has prepared me for every possible outcome. Also, Roscoe let me, Jayla, and Camden practice in the trunk of his cop car." Cooper proudly set his shoulders back. His messy blond hair sprouted up in the same spot Colin had had a cowlick before he managed to get a good enough haircut. Cooper looked a lot like him, especially when Colin was younger, but he had a slight auburn tint to his hair.

"That sounds like fun?" Colin asked, unsure if that was the intent.

"It was. Cam didn't realize that he wasn't supposed to actually shut the trunk, and he was stuck in there for like five minutes yelling about how he had to pee before Roscoe had to come let him out. It was hilarious." Cooper's grin was so wide that Colin matched it with a smaller version. His brother had made good friends, which made him feel a bit less guilty for staying away.

They made their way out into the hallway and to the staircase before either of them said anything, Colin taking the first stab. "So, are you and Jayla dating? Because of that one time you kissed her?" A hand slapped against his mouth, and Colin jerked back in surprise.

"*Shhh*," Cooper hissed, his eyes blown wide. "She's my best friend, so that's not— no, we aren't dating." He released his hand from Colin's mouth and craned his neck to peek farther down the stairs. "Her mom is downstairs, and Walker has been basically stalking us lately."

Colin lowered his voice. "Why does being someone's best friend hinder you from liking them romantically? Scarlett was my best friend at the same time she was my girlfriend."

"Yeah, but you haven't known her since she was eight, and she didn't kiss you in a friendzone way," Cooper muttered, running a hand through his hair. It was the same nervous tic thing Colin, their dad, and Walker did, and it was weirdly refreshing to see Cooper doing it.

Colin's eyebrows rose. "I wasn't aware friendzoned kissing was a thing. That seems incredibly nuanced. So, you don't like her romantically, then?"

"I think you're the first person to ask me that directly. Walker asks me weird in-between questions or says things like," Cooper dropped his tone into an impression of a gruffer, manly voice, "'you and Jayla seem really close.'"

"I don't dance around anything. It's a waste of time," Colin said. "And you didn't answer the question."

"It doesn't matter because she doesn't like me like that."

Colin considered that for a moment and shrugged. "Maybe. I still like Scarlett, and she doesn't like me back, but at least I can deal with my own emotions because I know what they are. What's your answer?"

"You're very good at interrogations. Ever thought about becoming a private investigator or detective?" Cooper asked.

"Nope. I like my job," Colin said. "Answer the question."

"You drive a hard bargain, and I—" Cooper literally tried to skirt past him and flee, so Colin stuck out his arm to clothesline his little brother, his arm jabbing into Cooper's throat. Cooper coughed and gave him a look of betrayal before he wheezed out his response. "Jesus. Yes, okay? Happy? Don't tell anyone. I'm hoping that feeling just," Cooper used his hand to flick the air, "goes away."

"How long have you had this feeling?" Colin couldn't hide the amusement from his face. For once, he might be the first person to outright know something about how one of his family members was feeling.

"You are extremely nosy for someone who barely kept in touch for the last four years," Cooper grumbled. The guilty pit in Colin's stomach grew two sizes, and the levity he had been feeling in the conversation disappeared in a cloud of smoke.

"I know. I'm sorry. I should have, but I really thought all of you were better off without me and my issues." Colin looked down at the floor and shoved his hands into his pockets.

Cooper shook his head. "You knew all of us were struggling, and you made sure we lost you, too." The knife Colin hadn't realized had slipped between his ribs twisted. With an angry point down the stairs, Cooper raised his eyebrows up. "Can I go now?"

Colin swallowed, unable to say anything as he nodded and

moved to the side to let Cooper past. A hand involuntarily went to his hair, and he ran his fingers through it as he watched Cooper do the exact same thing at the bottom of the steps before disappearing around the corner. Colin was frozen to the top stair, unable to move and wanting to throw up. The best he could do was sit down, so he did just that. He hadn't realized how badly he had fucked up. There was still a large part of him that did believe everyone was better off without him, but he had told himself time and time again that that wasn't true. Now, confronted with the fact that they were not, in fact, better off without him, he hadn't realized it would hurt like this. Like years of lost time. In the same way he felt about losing Scarlett, he had lost so much time to thinking that no one would want him.

"Colin?" Walker was halfway up the staircase when Colin noticed his presence. "Is it too loud? Everyone's starting to show up. I know you don't really know anyone. If you want to put your headphones on, I'm sure people would—"

"No," Colin breathed. "I'll be present."

Walker's face softened. "Did Coop say something to you?"

"Yes," Colin admitted.

"Scoot over," Walker directed, and Colin slid to one side of the top step. "You have to remember that Cooper is thirteen. So, whatever he said, it feels ten times as big for him because of puberty."

That statement should have eased the pain in Colin's chest, but, surprisingly enough, his tendency to accept facts at face value did not toss him a life jacket this time. So Colin squeezed his eyes shut and repeated back what Cooper had said, before noting, "I think he meant it."

A slow nod of Walker's head confirmed it. "He can only see his world through a small funnel. He can't see the big picture or any of the struggles you had to get through. You were diagnosed, and you immediately went to college. I thought about telling you to take a gap year to figure everything out, but I had already told you so many times to not put your life on hold because of your parents' death, and I wasn't sure if backtracking on that was the right move. Then you kind of shut us out. I did my best to insert myself into your life as much as I could, but I was more worried that you thought we didn't want you than you not wanting us. Was I... right to be worried about that?"

Colin swallowed and nodded. The air felt suddenly thick with pressure, and the tightening at his nose indicated he might cry for the first time in a long time.

Walker sighed. "Well, you're back, so you must have figured out that that's not true. What changed?"

"It wasn't one thing in particular," Colin answered. "It was a bunch of tiny little facts that made up a whole. At some point, I couldn't take a step back to look at all those facts and not see what was obvious. No matter how hard I am to love, you all still seem to like me."

"I don't know about that." Walker shifted beside him. "I don't find it hard to love you at all. It's intentional, sure, to make an effort, but I think the way we love you is the fact itself. It's not the conclusion from all the things we do, it's the reason we do any of the things. And the reason we love you is not because of anything you did. We'd love you regardless of what you do, though I did miss all of your puns. Not so much a fan of the making me run every morning, though. Hate that."

Colin chuckled. "You were already running every day."

"Keeping up with you requires more energy, and I've basically been pulling that energy out of my ass," Walker laughed.

The urge to cry left, and Colin felt a bit lighter. He saw several people walk by the staircase, and it made him wonder if Scarlett was already here, somewhere, standing at her sister's side. Instead, he said to Walker, "It was nice of you to host this. I know I don't know the Diazes well, but they seem like good people. I liked what Lucia said about her mom. And Piper obviously likes Leo."

"Ah, that was my original reason for coming up the stairs, actually. Lucia got here a bit ago and asked where Leo was and, of course, he's in Piper's room. I get the pleasure of breaking up whatever the hell they're doing in there." Walker grimaced.

"Leo doesn't bother me the way Harden did," Colin said. Piper's high school boyfriend was the source of one very eventful night for him that he wished he could redo half of.

"Between you and me, Leo is the only one of Piper's—whatever the hell he is to her—that I actually like." Walker stood up and brushed at his black slacks. "Assuming they aren't doing something nefarious in her bedroom right now."

"Good luck." Colin rose to his feet.

"Good luck to you as well," Walker said. When Colin raised his eyebrows, Walker patted his back. "Scarlett's here."

Twenty-One

Scarlett
22 Years Old

The Hartricks' house was just as Scarlett remembered it. The front door stuck a little more from the old paint, but she had spent so much time there during the summer that she knew which drawer the utensils were in when someone was looking for a serving spoon for one of the dishes. In the same way she knew that Paisley Hartrick had designed everything in the house, she knew that Piper had chosen the blue color for the kitchen cabinets. Knowing her way around should have made her feel less anxious, but all it did was make her confront all the wasted space in her head filled with knowledge of this family.

"You really didn't have to come to this." Harper gave her a solemn smile when Scarlett returned with the serving spoon. "I know this isn't exactly comfortable for you."

"Are funerals supposed to be comfortable?"

"You know what I mean."

"I'm fine," Scarlett assured her with a hand on her shoulder. It wasn't true, but out of the two of them, reliving the ghost of ex-boyfriends past wasn't on par with her sister losing yet another person to cancer. Scarlett knew exactly where she needed to be today, and it was beside Harper, no matter how strange it was to be inside this house. She was bound to run into Colin at some point—they could only travel in the same circles for so long before the Venn diagram overlapped—but death was the absolute worst reason for their paths to cross again.

Scarlett had only met her brother-in-law's grandmother once at Marcos' birthday party, but it was plain as day from all the downcast faces wandering around with plates of appetizers that everyone loved Isabel Castillo. No amount of her own loss could prepare Scarlett for how to react to all the ways people dealt with grief. She had learned a long time ago that she often said the wrong thing. What worked for her often didn't translate to other people—Colin, mainly. Occasionally when she'd go on a camping trip with her sister, they'd travel up the Trenton Creek Pass and stop at the lookout on the way to their camping spot, and Scarlett would remember the day she had pushed Colin a little too hard and they had spent an hour in one of the most beautiful spots just outside the city, crying and holding on to each other in the cold. He had hugged her then as if she were the only thing keeping him afloat. She would remember every time after that they spent in that exact spot, kissing and touching each other in all the ways that were burned into her memory.

"I can see that far-off look in your eye, Letti. I know you think you have to be here because of Tucker, but really, I can handle it," Harper's voice cracked, a sure indicator that despite what she was saying, she really didn't want Scarlett to leave.

Scarlett smiled and squeezed her sister's side. "I will always show up for you, H. I'm going to go get you some wine."

Harper sniffed and wiped at her eyes, clearly trying to hold it together, but she nodded. "Thank you."

In the dining room, Scarlett found Amala pouring wine and passing out glasses to Isabel's family, all looking worse for wear, and she got in line to grab one. It was her first time in this room today, and her eyes immediately landed on the gallery wall of family photos that had a few more frames than she remembered. Her old favorite was always the one of Colin's dad holding a baby Colin in the air in a lunge position like he was in *The Lion King* while Colin's mom stood beside him with her head thrown back in laughter. This was the kind of love Colin grew up with. There were a few staged family portraits, but the majority of the photos were pure chaos. A younger version of Colin with a toad in his hands standing beside a large white bucket next to a little version of Piper with a look of disgust on her face. The newer pictures were all from the last five years. Walker bending Talia backward on their wedding day in a kiss, Piper and Carter's respective graduation days, and one Scarlett remembered like it was yesterday. She hadn't expected to see herself on the wall, but there she was on her high school graduation day wearing a white cap and gown and holding on to Colin, in a navy cap and gown. His arm was tossed over her shoulder, and instead of looking at the camera, he was looking down at the top of her head with a soft expression. Like he loved her.

"Wine?" Amala waved a wine glass in front of her face, weaving her head from side to side to get Scarlett's attention, knotless braids swaying across her shoulders. Scarlett cleared her throat to bring herself back to the present, embarrassed she had been caught staring at the wall.

"Can I get two? I'm going to bring them to Marcos and Harper," Scarlett explained.

Amala nodded and started to pour one of the glasses. "He requested that picture to be hung up instead of his solo one." She tipped her head in the direction of the graduation picture Scarlett had been staring at.

"Oh." Scarlett swallowed and carefully secured the two wine stems Amala handed to her in each hand.

"Little weird to see yourself hanging up on your ex-boyfriend's wall?"

"Yeah, I wasn't expecting..." Scarlett's voice trailed off.

Saving her from having to finish the end of that sentence,

Amala shrugged and said, "The Hartricks are weird as hell," before leaning forward as if to tell her a secret. "But that's why I like them. That, and because they're the kind of people to throw someone else's wake so they don't have to worry about hosting a billion people when they're grieving."

"You seem like you're that kind of person, too," Scarlett said kindly.

"Of course I am." Amala grinned. "I'm also the kind to warn you that Colin is walking over here. I love him, but I'm also a girls' girl."

"Shit," Scarlett squeaked, looking over her shoulder to see a flash of blond hair headed right for her. Both sides of the dining room were open archways, so she turned her back to Colin and tried to escape out the other way, only to be blocked by several people stopping to chat under the entryway. Her body stiffened as if she could feel Colin somewhere behind her, and she squinted her eyes shut, muttering an incantation of "please go away, please go away, please go away," to herself as if she could wish the request into existence.

"Okay," Colin's voice said from behind her. She jumped, not realizing that he had gotten so close. "I was just letting Amala know that Talia needed her in the kitchen, but I can go outside or something." Scarlett winced, back still turned to him and double-fisting wine glasses as if being in his presence required her to get sloppy drunk. When she turned around to backtrack, to let him know that this was his house and it would be silly of her to demand he sit outside the whole time she was there, he had vanished. Except now it didn't feel so great that he had done exactly what she asked.

"Yikes." Amala flashed her teeth in a cringe, and Scarlett let her face fold in on itself, eyes shut and properly mortified.

"Fuck my life," she whined, gesturing for Amala to leave the dining room first to heed Colin's request for help in the kitchen. "Would you care to also go away?"

Amala let out a laugh through her nose and grinned back at

her as they both paced toward the archway. "*He* at least got a 'please.'"

"I like to preface all of my requests for people to leave their own home with a please. You don't live here, so." Scarlett gave a casual shrug.

"I'm sure he's unfazed."

"Sounds about right," Scarlett groaned. "He'll forget about it, and I will remember it fondly when I'm awake at night, staring up at the ceiling."

"Enjoy the lifelong anxiety!" Amala singsonged as she made her way into the kitchen.

It was going to be a very long night.

Harper was several drinks in by the time Scarlett finally gained courage enough to clear the air with Colin. However, when she peeked out on the back porch, Piper and Leo were the only ones outside. She checked out the front as well to no avail. After searching for half an hour, she was starting to think Colin had taken his job of disappearing so seriously that he had created a machine to slip into another dimension. When she finally found him in the living room, he was talking to Lucia Diaz and holding a gift bag in one hand. Not wanting to interrupt, she hovered nearby, clinging to the wall.

"I appreciated what you said about your mother at the funeral," Colin told Lucia. "That she wasn't perfect, but she did her best. That was my parents as well." He seemed to harp the most on the part about imperfection, which read as odd to Scarlett considering he had only ever put his parents on a pedestal when they talked. She remembered wondering multiple times how he had gotten so lucky with two perfect parents while she had a broken but present mother and a father who hadn't bothered to stick around. She knew from experience with Tucker that loving and losing was better than never having love at all.

Lucia nodded and offered Colin a small smile in return, her eyes watery. "We can only ever do our best. My mother was very stubborn, and sometimes that made me want to pull my hair out." She laughed lightly, but a tear slipped down her face. Scarlett always had a hard time watching other people cry. The waterworks were never far behind, and she could feel the sting of salt in her nose from listening in on the conversation. "But she was also full of life and loved every person she met with her whole heart. I met your parents once. They were both very kind to me, even as a stranger."

Colin bobbed his head and slowly held up the small, wrapped gift. "Admittedly, I got this for someone else. Leo tried to convince me to still give it to her, but I don't think it will be received well, so." Colin stretched out his hand, offering the bag to Lucia. Lucia gingerly took it, confusion creasing her face. "It's watercolor paints and brushes." Scarlett stilled. Even the tear rolling down her face seemed to slow. "Someone once told me they preferred this to acrylics or oils because the way the colors mixed with water reminded them of faded memories. Maybe you could use it to paint some."

That *someone* was herself, Scarlett concluded, and like the photo hanging on the wall in the dining room, it made her heart ache in her chest. In her younger years, she didn't think anything she said was worth remembering. Even now, all her friends knew her as someone who could talk for ages and never get to the point. When she had something of note to say, it often felt like it got lost in the middle of the unimportant details and side stories, but Colin had always had a superpower when it came to gleaning the most important bits from her stories. He soaked up the information like a sponge and relayed it with perfect clarity. She had assumed that he'd mostly forgotten all the details of their long pillow talk conversations, and it felt strangely gratifying to know that she had made some sort of a mark on him, no matter how small, because he had definitely left his mark on her.

In the haze of her thoughts, Scarlett missed the end of Colin and Lucia's conversation and was woefully underprepared when Colin turned around. His eyes traced her from head to foot as he stepped aside, lifting up both hands in a show of surrender.

"I'm just going to hide in my room. It's a little cold outside now," he said, moving to shuffle past her. "I promise you won't run into me again."

"You don't have to do that." Scarlett reached a hand out to halt him. They both froze, anchored by the contact, and she watched his head drop to the spot she was gripping on his forearm. It was wider than she remembered, less lean like it had been from the difficulty he had with eating back then. "You weren't supposed to hear me when I said I wanted you to go away. I'm sorry. I was mostly mumbling to myself, and I feel bad that you took me seriously. This is your house, Colin. It'd be insane of me to dictate where you get to be in your own home. *I'm* the intruder here."

The Adam's apple dipped in Colin's throat. "You are always welcome here. You aren't intruding."

She wanted to argue with him, demand to know why he thought she could ever be comfortable here again, but shoved down the feeling and let go of his arm. "Thanks. I'm just here for my sister."

"I know. I'm here for my family, too." He was still standing so close to her that she could feel the warmth from his body and could remember every time she had wrapped herself up in him. "That, and I have nowhere else to go. Finding an apartment during a housing crisis is not easy. I'm mostly looking in Merrick, so once I find one, the likelihood you'll accidentally run into me in Archwood will be a lot lower."

"I lucked out with mine. The building is really old, and sometimes the plugs don't work when I need them to, but I'm a pro at flipping the breaker since my landlord is like eighty years old and gave me a good deal to begin with. Plus I got the grant for the shop at the bottom for my art program—that's the one where that painting I sold you was made. Thank you for the donation, by the way. It wasn't necessary, but Theo's going to be thrilled when he graduates and has some extra funds, I'm sure. And—" She stopped mid-sentence, noticing when Colin's eyes shut. He always used to do that when she was rambling so he could focus on what she was saying. *Keep talking to me*, he had told her the first time he had done it. *I listen better like this.* She had fallen right back into old habits and already forgotten that they were nothing and no one to each other anymore. The reason he knew none of what she was rambling about now was because he hadn't been there for it.

The sound of clapping saved her from having to think of a segue out of the conversation. Colin's eyes flew open, and they both pivoted to find Leo, Piper, and two other college-aged students at the front of the living room holding massive bowls and a few grocery bags.

"Thank you all so much for coming," Leo called out. "And thanks to the Hartricks for hosting." He looked fondly down at Piper, who was holding a large bouquet of mini sunflowers, and Scarlett could see the affection in his eyes so clearly that it was safe to assume Harper would soon stop suggesting Leo as a viable partner for her from now on. "As much as all of us are sad, Abuelita would absolutely hate all this moping around, so we're going to change that. This is officially a tamalada and a card game party."

"Mutiny!" The tall blond man beside Leo shouted with a raised fist.

"Mariana, can you help people make the tamales in the kitchen?" Leo raised his grocery bag in the direction of his sister.

"Are you really designating the kitchen job to your sister right now?" Piper tsked.

Leo rolled his eyes. "She's the second best at making them. Marcos is already in the kitchen, and I can't ask Varo or Antonio because they suck."

"You gonna ask me and your mom to help next?" Piper asked cheekily.

"Not you. I don't really want all the tamales to end up on the floor when you inevitably trip over nothing." Leo grinned down at her and received a shove to his shoulder. They both seemed to use the excuse to touch each other for longer, and if it hadn't been obvious before, Scarlett was now sure they were fucking.

"I'm going to set up a few tables for cards and Monopoly," Talia called out, already starting to shuffle some furniture out of the way with Walker's help. Colin always had near perfect posture, but he seemed to straighten even more at the mention of Monopoly, and Scarlett had lost so many times to him at that exact game that she knew he was prepared to show exactly zero mercy.

"Fair warning," Carter joined in on the chaos, throwing his arm over Colin's shoulder as he addressed the crowd that had formed in the living room, "if you're planning on playing Monopoly, be prepared to lose because Colin is ruthless and will win every time."

"You're no fun," Colin huffed. "I need new victims. I get tired of beating you over and over and over again."

"You did lose once," Carter noted.

"Doesn't count when I purposely forfeited," Colin said.

"Why would you ever lose on purpose?" Leo demanded.

If the heat traveling up her neck was any indication, Scarlett knew exactly why he had forfeited, and she wished she could go back in time to spray herself with water. If Kashvi were here, Scarlett would thump her on the forehead for ever giving her the idea. Especially because, from the look on Carter's face and the way he briefly glanced in her direction, he knew everything.

She whirled on Colin angrily, jabbing a finger in Carter's direction. "You showed him?"

"What?" Colin's eyes widened. "Showed him what?"

"I guessed," Carter jumped in somewhat frantically.

"Colin was just easy to read," Piper added. "He didn't show us anything, I promise. He wouldn't do that."

"Piper and I had to help him escape out the window later

because we were all on house arrest, and I figured he had to have a really good reason to escape." Carter kept the same urgency in his voice, but Scarlett was already as mortified as she could get. Nothing was going to make this better.

A mixture of "You did *what?*" and "The window?" was shouted from across the room by Walker and Talia.

Head smarting, Scarlett scrunched her eyes shut and whispered in Colin's direction, "Do they know about the charts, too?"

"They've seen one, but I didn't show them," Colin pleaded, touching her arm. She flinched away from his touch and looked to his sister, hoping that Piper would look clueless as to what they were talking about. But she didn't look clueless in the slightest.

"Carter's just really nosy," Piper said. "I'm sorry."

At one point, Scarlett would have given anything to be a part of this family. During the period where no one knew about their relationship, she'd had to stop herself from begging Colin to claim her in front of his family. It was highly apparent now why he was so reluctant to do so back then. "I need to get out of here," she said before shooting Harper an apologetic look and booking it to the front door. She could vaguely hear an argument starting up as Walker's faded parental voice echoed behind her. The sound of footsteps chasing her was the more immediate fear, though, and it propelled her faster.

Outrunning her past and all the mistakes she had made as a stupid, lovesick teenager felt like a never-ending marathon she just could not escape.

"Scarlett," Colin called after her when she made it to her car. He was standing on the perfectly manicured front lawn by one of the hanging lanterns, both hands held to his head like he was trying to keep it from rolling off his body.

She didn't look in his direction for long, catching her own red and tear-stained face in the rearview mirror before she started her engine and peeled away from the curb with a jerk of the wheel, leaving Colin in the dust.

Twenty-Two

Scarlett
18 Years Old

Cupcakes made everything better. Unfortunately, Scarlett could usually only bake them when Kashvi was present because the number of times she had set the tray in the oven only to immediately forget to set a timer had resulted in one too many burnt batches. Sometimes, in addition to needing a map of her sexuality, she wanted a map of her brain so she could point to whatever part made her so forgetful and easily distractible. It shouldn't take her a decade to clean her room because she suddenly felt the deep desire to organize her entire closet when she hadn't even picked up her laundry off the floor. That particular predicament was how she had decided body doubling was her best way to get out of being found dead days later under the pile of clothes she was still deciding on whether she wanted to keep or donate. Kashvi was easily bribed by the prospect of cupcakes like any true friend would be.

"Oh my God." Kashvi moaned dramatically as she adjusted the horrendous denim beret they had found in the far reaches of Scarlett's closet and proceeded to giggle about for a solid ten minutes. It was incredibly small and didn't properly fit on Kashvi's head, making the sight even more ridiculous.

"You sound like you're fucking your cupcake," Scarlett cackled.

"If this cupcake was interested in me like that, it could put its babies inside me." Kashvi plopped the remainder of her red velvet cupcake on her tongue and slapped the carpeted floor like the cupcake was legitimately giving her an out-of-body experience.

"Would the babies just be mini cupcakes?" The full-sized ones were good, but they had literally just bought boxed cake mix at Lydia's grocery and thrown it in the cart with a travesty of spray cheese and crackers, so it wasn't a revelation or anything. Granted, Kashvi had snuck a bottle of wine from her sister's stash, and while Scarlett was still working on her first glass, Kashvi had already downed hers in a few gulps. Not only that, but compared to Scarlett's five feet eight inches, Kashvi's pint-sized body always got drunk way faster.

"I think maybe at first they'd just be a little sprinkle until they grew into a full-sized cupcake," Kashvi declared. "You should know way more about baby-making than me, though. How's it going with Milo Thatch from Atlantis? Still super in love with him?"

"I'm not—I'm only a *little* in love with him," Scarlett argued. "Plus we haven't exactly been doing the part that makes babies."

"What have you been doing for the last month if not hooking up with your boyfriend constantly? What happened to the sex-periment?"

That was still very much happening. Foreplay had become somewhat of a sport to them now. Colin was so good at going down on her that she kept giving him fives across the board on their chart. This last time, she had only docked him one point because she'd orgasmed too quickly, and she wanted to enjoy his tongue for just a little longer. With the numbing cream idea nixed, they'd usually get him off as quickly as possible so after she had her own round, they'd both be ready for round two.

"I think he's worried that I won't like it—or, actually, I know he's worried about that because he straight-up told me." Scarlett let out a long sigh that could have blown down the brick house in the Three Little Pigs fable. "He's read way too many books on the female body and has convinced himself that I might not like it no matter how hard he tries. He's a bit obsessive about being good at things. I keep telling him that I want to try it again and I don't mind if it's bad because we'll figure it out like everything else, and he just keeps saying 'soon' and then checking out another book from the library about vaginal sex. I'm going to beat my head against a wall with all this waiting."

"Then what are you doing here? Shouldn't you be out trying to seduce him or something?" Kashvi took a cheese-whizzed cracker from the wood cutting board they had taken from the kitchen to be classy.

"Colin's at that school auction thing tonight scheming with his siblings." In all honesty, Scarlett would have loved to witness the entire debacle with their uncle, but Colin hadn't invited her. It was probably for the best since Scarlett had a feeling the Hartrick siblings were severely underestimating how pissed Walker and Talia were going to be the second they realized what was happening. Auctioning off a date with Talia was one thing, but not getting her permission to do so and then making sure Walker sat front row for the show to force him into bidding was... well, it was fucking bonkers. But desperate people did desperate things.

"You could still seduce him. The auction is probably over by now," Kashvi said through a mouthful of cracker.

"What, like, go to his house?" Scarlett balked.

"No, dummy. Sext him!"

"And... how would I do that, exactly? I've never sent anyone anything like that." As evidenced by the way Scarlett's face turned pink, the thought of sending something salacious by text felt even more risky than actually doing it live in person.

"You start off with a little flirting and then hit them with something more sexual. Usually guys take the hint."

The idea that Colin would casually flirt with her over text was laughable. "Colin doesn't know when I'm flirting with him, Kashvi. I literally have to hit him with 'I am flirting with you,' or he thinks I'm just stating facts. One time I told him I thought he looked better without clothes on and batted my eyelashes at him, and he said, and I quote, 'I have to wear clothes outside of the bedroom or I'll get arrested.'"

"Okay, so, he doesn't do subtle." Kashvi hummed. "What if you tell him you're going to masturbate? Surely the image of that in his head will make him crazy, right?"

"This conversation is mortifying." Scarlett groaned and threw herself on the floor, pressing her face into the carpet. "But I might be buzzed enough to do it."

"Yessss!" Kashvi clapped her hands together. "There are friends that tell you to make better choices, and then there's me, who highly encourages you to send something absolutely filthy to your boyfriend."

"I have no idea why my mom thinks you're a good influence." Scarlett rolled over and pulled out her phone.

"Easy. I present as a sweet little Indian girl with perfect grades. Parents adore me. I'm going to Yale. They, and *my* parents, just don't know yet that I'm majoring in art history. There's still time to be a massive disappointment, I assure you." Kashvi flashed her classic innocent smile. That one was going to be a shock for Kashvi's parents when it inevitably came out that she had zero plans to go into pre-law, but as far as Scarlett was concerned, she and Kashvi were a match made in platonic heaven, a future art curator and a hopeful artist.

"A *major* disappointment, some might say." Scarlett grinned at her own pun.

"You're starting to sound like Colin." Kashvi laughed and pointed toward Scarlett's phone. "Get to texting."

"Okay, okay." Scarlett dutifully pulled up the text thread she had with Colin, which was usually just an exchange of times and locations to meet up and the frequent "did you drink any water today?" text from Colin. The answer was always a no. She typed out a few different things, settling on the most obvious of them all. Kashvi hummed in approval when she moved to read over Scarlett's shoulder. "Here goes nothing." Scarlett held her breath and pressed send.

SCARLETT 9:23 PM

I think I'm going to test out that vibrator you bought me tonight. What are you doing right now?

The three little bubbles indicating Colin was texting popped up immediately, and Scarlett met Kashvi's eyes with excitement. "He's typing!" she screeched. The anticipation only lasted a moment before his text came through, and her face fell.

COLIN 9:23 PM

Cool. Hopefully it works okay. I'm playing Monopoly.

"Wow." Kashvi gave a low whistle. "Man cannot take a hint to save his life."

"I knew this was a bad idea," Scarlett groaned.

"No, no. Listen, your first attempt, I'll admit, did not exactly work, but you need to double down. Like... send him a hot picture or something."

"I don't have any good pictures of myself. I look like I have crazy eyes in every picture."

Kashvi mumbled something under her breath and shook her head. "Well, I can see why you're together because I apparently have to spell everything out for you. I meant like a tasteful boudoir picture."

"What?" Scarlett's voice cracked on a high note. "I can't do that... can I?"

"It was just a suggestion. You don't have to do it," Kashvi

backtracked. "If you don't want to, that's a completely different story. Or if you're worried he'll share the picture, then I wouldn't suggest it, but he's already seen you naked, has he not? And from my own conversations with him, I can't imagine he's the douchey type to post it anywhere. I mean, when we all went out to lunch the other day, he gave me a list of all the gross things Rick said about me when he was his lab partner. They were listed in order of severity."

"I can't believe you were ever interested in that guy." Scarlett made a grotesque face. She had been there for the making of the list after Colin had asked her whether Kashvi would want to know that information.

In all her life, the riskiest thing Scarlett had ever done was hook up with Colin, and so far, every step of the way, she had felt safe. She was frequently embarrassed, and they had floundered their way through plenty of things, but never once had she felt unsafe. Confidence was the thing she lacked most, and the idea of having sexy pictures—not even for Colin, but to remind herself that she was desirable with or without him—was enticing.

"Let's do it." Scarlett slapped her thighs in decision. "I think I have the perfect thing to wear. He's really into red. You think you can pose me right? Because these are going to be awful if I try it myself."

Kashvi grinned. "I'm obsessed with paintings and statues of naked people. Of course I can pose you! You're going to look like you belong in the Louvre."

Twenty-Three

Colin
18 Years Old

Walker was pissed. He had been sitting rigid in his seat at the dining table, aggressively slapping his train token down on the Monopoly board every single turn he took. Colin's battleship token was dominating the board as usual. He had bought up all the orange and red properties on either side of the free parking space, which were statistically the most likely spots to land on, giving him the edge. Every single time Walker landed on one, everyone at the table seemed to simultaneously wince. There weren't many times in his life that Colin knew, without a shadow of a doubt, that he had fucked up, but the live auction was definitely a fuck-up.

The second Colin had gotten up on stage at their high school fundraiser, the combination of the lights and people in the crowd shouting their bids at him had been a recipe for disaster. His siblings had done a good enough job of taking over when they did, but even in his semi-panicked state, Colin could see that the entire thing was a shit show. Not because it didn't go exactly the way he had planned it, but because Walker and Talia were much more angry about being meddled with than he had anticipated. He had never seen that murderous look on Talia's face before, and when a creepy, balding man in the back row of the theater started heavily bidding for a date with her, Colin realized he had severely miscalculated how much money Walker would have to drop to bail her out. It was a price tag Walker was now demanding that Colin, Piper, and Carter pay him back for. They were all set to start working for Talia at Lydia's Grocery on Monday so they couldn't just use their parents' funds to pay for it. On top of that, Walker gave all the household chores to them, including Pearl's and Cooper's, and threw in cleaning Talia's and the Winstons' houses because he had decided halfway through his rant that one house was simply not enough. The massive argument that ensued when Walker put them all on house arrest and took Colin's keys had lasted for over an hour, because while Colin didn't mind working off his punishment, he *did* mind not getting to see Scarlett. No one in the room knew she was the real reason Colin was so vehemently against the second half of the punishment, but Walker wouldn't let up.

"Uh, you don't have to pay him for that," Piper squeaked when Walker again landed on the space to the right of free parking.

Carter shifted in his chair. "Yeah, I don't think—"

"Yes, he does," Colin interrupted, shoulders held back with confidence. "Those are the rules."

Walker said nothing, just bitterly slid a couple of bills across the table. They had both been in a sort of stand-off since punishments had been doled out. Once Pearl and Cooper were asleep, Talia had suggested a game to ease the tension, but it had had the exact opposite effect. Colin was public enemy number one in Walker's eyes, and Piper and Carter were his two evil henchmen. Too pissed off about losing his car keys and not being able to see Scarlett for the foreseeable future, Colin played the villain. Monopoly was his strong suit, and he was planning on petulantly cleaning Walker out of all his paper cash like he always did.

"Maybe we should take a break," Talia suggested.

"No," Walker and Colin answered at the same time.

"Clearly, this isn't going well, and everyone's a little on edge." Talia sighed.

"It's going great for *me*," Colin said, lifting up the wad of fake cash.

Walker took Colin's keys out of his pocket and jingled them in the air. "Same."

"You're treating me like a child," Colin snapped.

"If the shoe fits." Walker shrugged.

"You're not my dad. You're only nine years older than me, Walker. I'm an adult."

"I know I'm not your dad," Walker said. "But your dad definitely would have been pissed about this. It was morally wrong and childish behavior. So, if you want to be an adult so bad, you should have acted like one."

Colin scrunched his nose furiously. "And you should have sucked it up and talked to Talia so we didn't have to force you to do it. Pearl and Cooper need routine and for you two to be solid, not fighting and avoiding each other."

"That was my fault," Talia chimed in.

"No, it wasn't," Walker silenced her. "And I honestly don't care what you have to say, Colin, because out of anyone, I would have expected you to take the direct route, not the scheming and conniving route. You could have talked to me. You could have talked to Talia. You didn't have to sell her at a live auction to me like cattle. Do you realize how fucking insane that is?"

The plan hadn't seemed so wrong when Colin had thought of it to begin with, but now that it was over, the alarm bells rang loud and clear. "It was... for charity," he said lamely. Walker barked out a laugh, shaking his head. "I just thought if I could get you two to sit down in a more intimate setting like a restaurant, you'd have to talk to each other."

"We're really sorry," Piper chirped from her seat, covering her face with her hands.

Carter nodded aggressively. "Very sorry."

"Colin?" Walker prodded.

"I'm sorry that it was the wrong way to do it," Colin stated and then gestured between Talia and Walker. "I'm not sorry that my plan worked and you're talking again."

"Jesus Christ," Walker muttered.

"We would have started talking again on our own, without the insane parent-trapping," Talia said. "We will consider giving you your keys back, but for now, let us be pissed off that you gave a bunch of people permission to ogle me on stage."

"For the record," Colin grimaced, "I didn't really think about that because I don't think of you as a sexual being. You're more like a friend or an aunt."

"That's... nice," Talia said, the ending coming out as more of a question.

"I mean, you're fine, I guess. You're not my type. You're too old, and I'm more into redheads." Colin shrugged.

"Redheads?" Walker asked. "That's an interesting development."

Given the wide-eyed look on Carter's face, Colin ventured that he had said way too much. There was only one redhead he frequently saw, and Carter knew that. Fear crept into Colin's throat, and he knew he was only a few seconds away from being found out, especially if Carter opened his mouth to say something about Scarlett. Before he got a chance to divert the conversation, his phone pinged. His family all watched him as he pulled it from his pocket to see he had gotten a text from Scarlett, as if he had summoned her. It had been a while since she'd texted him back, and he assumed she was probably letting him know if the vibrator worked.

SCARLETT 9:57 PM

If I was a space on a Monopoly board, would you land on me?

Confused, he went to reply that he would have to roll to land on her when an image loaded that she must have sent with the original text. His knee connected with the underside of the table. "Ow, shit!" he cursed, holding the phone's screen against his chest to block anyone from seeing it.

"You okay?" Walker asked, all anger gone from his voice.

Okay was relative. Especially when the image Scarlett had sent him was making his head swim. She was on her knees with her thighs spread atop her bed in his favorite red bra and underwear. Back arched and hands holding her wavy copper hair up, he could clearly see the tops of her breasts pushing up against the cups. The picture was taken at an angle so the mirror hanging on her far wall caught her backside. The band to her underwear was higher up on her hips than usual, and her round ass was on full display in the reflection.

"I um, I—" Colin sputtered for a response but came up short. All he wanted to do was look at the picture again. "I'm fine."

"Okay, well, it's your turn to roll." Walker pointed at the Monopoly board Colin no longer had any interest in.

"Oh." He nodded.

"You're looking a little sick," Carter said, head cocked to the side.

"Yeah, your face is super red," Piper noted.

"Do you need some water?" Talia asked, concern creasing her forehead.

"It's been a long night. I'm too tired to play now. I forfeit," Colin declared, taking his battleship from the board and tipping it sideways like he had just sunk the Titanic.

"What?" Walker gaped. "You've never forfeited in your life!"

"I'm not feeling well!" Colin practically shouted. He wanted to glue his eyes to that picture for the rest of the night, and every second at this blasted table felt like a waste.

"Okay, well, good night, then," Walker said slowly.

"Night!" Colin yelled, already launching out of his seat and jogging for the stairs to his bedroom. As soon as he hit the safety of the top stair, he pulled his phone screen away from his chest and looked intently at Scarlett's body the entire way to his room.

Once he had locked the door, gotten in bed, and committed the photo to memory, he finally typed out a response.

COLIN 10:01 PM

I don't cheat at board games, but I'd cheat to land on you every time.

Scarlett responded immediately, only giving him a second to look at the picture again.

SCARLETT 10:02 PM

What would you do once you landed on me?

COLIN 10:03 PM

Are you a one-dimensional rectangle when I land on you?

SCARLETT 10:03 PM

Colin, I'm sexting you. Please get with the program. What would you do with me right now if you could?

"Fuck," Colin groaned, pulling the photo back up. His cock was thickening in his pants, and he responded without much thought at all.

COLIN 10:04 PM

Sorry. Commencing sexting. Are you with anyone or are you alone?

SCARLETT 10:04 PM

Kashvi just left. I'm laying in bed alone and thinking about you.

His breathing had turned erratic, his hand going to his belt to unclasp it.

COLIN 10:05 PM

Have you used the vibrator yet?

SCARLETT 10:06 PM

It's between my legs right now. I wish it was
you, though.

Fisting his cock, he flipped back to the picture and gave himself a few slow strokes. It wasn't as good as her hand or even as good as watching her get herself off. He needed more. He needed to hear all the sounds she made when she was using it. The glowing phone icon at the top of her contact didn't have to taunt him long before he clicked it and pressed the phone to his ear.

"Hi," Scarlett answered on the first ring. Her voice was low and breathy, just like he thought it would be. "You're not sitting at a table playing Monopoly anymore, are you?"

"I quit. I'm in my room," Colin said. "And I don't think I'm any good at sexting, so I figured I'd just call you."

She let out a twinkling laugh. "You did just say 'commencing sexting' like you were on a top secret mission or something."

"Am I not? I'm hiding out from my family, and my one objective is to listen to you come, Agent Red."

Another laugh, and he was grinning like an idiot. Her laugh loosened the pressure in his chest the same way her touch did. "I have no idea why I'm into this, but I am. What are you doing right now, Agent..."

"Cox," Colin deadpanned. It was a very literal choice, but perfect nonetheless.

"No," Scarlett giggled. "Agent Cox sounds like a porn star name."

"I keep looking at the pornographic picture you sent me, and I'm getting myself off, so I think it's fitting." Colin stroked himself twice as if to punctuate his argument.

Scarlett blew out a slow breath. "So, you like the picture?"

"'Like' is an understatement. Are you wearing that bra and underwear now?"

"Yes."

Colin pressed the back of his head harder into the pillow, closing his eyes to imagine it. "God, I wish I was with you."

"You never told me what you'd do if you were." Scarlett's voice cracked like it did when he went down on her or fingered her, so he knew she was back to touching herself if she had ever stopped.

"I'd want to watch you use the vibrator. I'd help you with it." He groaned, his hand moving faster over his cock.

"And then you'd fuck me?" she asked. "Because I need you to."

"I want to." He panted, his hand flying over his erection now.

"Good," Scarlett gasped, and Colin could faintly hear the buzzing of what he assumed was her vibrator, like she had turned it up. "I'm tired of waiting."

"What position do you want to be in?"

"All of them," she whispered. "I don't care as long as you're inside me soon." Her voice was almost a whine, and he could practically picture the way her back would be arching off the bed. "It's going to feel so good."

"I need to see you tonight." Colin sat up, phone pressed hard to his ear so he didn't miss a single one of her sounds. Listening to her labored breathing wasn't enough. He could come like this, but it wouldn't be as good as burying himself in her heat. At this point, putting off sex felt ridiculous, and he didn't know why he had been so scared to do it again. All of the worry paled in comparison to how desperate he was to finally rock into Scarlett like he had wanted to do so many times before.

"How?" The vibration stopped abruptly. "We don't have anywhere to go. You can't sneak into my bedroom."

"And Walker took my keys," Colin huffed, shoving his angry cock back into his pants in frustration. In all the commotion, he had completely forgotten about the auction debacle. "I'm on house arrest. They were really pissed about us meddling with them."

"Oh." Scarlett's disappointed sigh on the other end of the phone drove him crazy. "That's too bad."

Colin could feel the goal of being with her slipping through his fingers like sand, so for the second time that day, he decided to execute an insane plan. "I'll steal my keys. Then I'll sneak out and come pick you up. We'll go to the lookout. I can put the seats down so we have more room." He hadn't envisioned their second time being in the back of his Audi, but in that moment, he didn't really give a flying fuck where he had Scarlett as long as it was as soon as possible. Blame the hormones and his sudden lack of self control, but he was going to hook up with his girlfriend under the stars. He was going to find a little peace.

Tonight.

Twenty-Four

Scarlett
22 Years Old

The wood backing of the canvas felt sturdy in Scarlett's hands as she transferred it to the last easel in the corner of the room, away from the others that faced the front. Normally, there was a potted snake plant in that corner because it was by far her neediest plant with its thirst for direct sunlight, but she had to move it every Monday after her evening paint and sip class to make more room. Last night, however, she had moved it earlier than planned because Lucia Diaz had showed up to the paint and sip class with Harper, Saanvi, and a slew of other people. The unusual turnout had Scarlett scrapping for extra space and supplies, dodging her cat skittishly hugging her legs in fear of company. Lucia had brought her own supplies, of course, still packed in the gift bag that Colin had given her. Like always, Colin must have done his research because the supplies were the brands Scarlett splurged on when it was her birthday or a special occasion. In a way, the paints and brushes ended up as a gift for her after all, because watching Lucia smile as she painted, sipped wine, and swayed to an ABBA record was what made teaching so special. Painting had brought

Scarlett back to life after the loss of her brother all those years ago, and watching Lucia work through her own grief was a gift. Something about breathing life into a blank canvas made living feel all the more special. The paintings made in today's class were going to be on the more abstract side, given the developing hand-eye coordination of children, but nonetheless, they would be beautiful.

The color theory lesson Scarlett had planned was prepped, complete with laminated copies of a few different color wheels throughout history dating back to 1704 alongside the bright-colored images she had printed of flowers found in the woods during a search for inspiration. Some of the ones she had taken photos of matched tattoos coloring her right arm: all flowers that could be found in Oregon wildlife. A small thrill settled in her bones as she finished setting out the last of the brushes. Every art class day was a good day. She loved working for the foundation, but there was something special about watching young minds create and express themselves. It was a high like no other.

The station Scarlett created for herself at the front of the class had its own canvas at the ready that she had already toned with a burnt tan color. It was fully dry and the perfect size to finally start her portrait of Tucker. And yet, she had looked at it all morning hoping that excitement would blossom and propel her forward, and all she felt was anxiety. Knowing her, she would probably get within a scary amount of time to finish the project before the gala and kick it out in a hyperfixated deadline trance.

It was twenty minutes before class was supposed to begin when Scarlett heard the studio door open from her office. Her cat, a white Turkish Angora, hopped out of her lap to greet the guest before she could even move her chair out from under her desk. No one usually showed up this early, but occasionally she would get a new student who would come in with their parent or guardian ahead of time to meet her. It was either that or a random walk-in for a commission piece. When she caught sight of sandy blond hair and a tan knitted sweater, she realized it was neither of those options and instead a secret third option that was much worse.

"Colin?" Scarlett almost choked on his name, coming to a grinding halt when she saw him. For the most part, Colin had kept his word to stay out of her life, so she couldn't imagine why he was showing up to her art studio before a flock of kids was due to come in. The funeral had taken place nearly a month ago, and she hadn't spoken to him since. Harper had seen him once when the whole Diaz side of her family traveled up to Fletcher University to watch the musical that Leo had directed, the very same play Colin's sister Piper had starred in. Harper had mostly been quiet about any interactions she had had with Colin other than to make note that she and Saanvi had given him a few more withering looks than normal.

"Hi." Colin waved stiffly and adjusted the leather tote bag on his shoulder. "Who's this?" He smiled slightly and pointed down at the heap of white fur rubbing up against his legs like the little traitor she was.

"Pepto," Scarlett said shortly, bending down to pick up her cat. Pepto squirmed in her hold, no doubt annoyed that Scarlett had prevented her from getting her head scratched by the new love of her life, Colin Hartrick. Typical. "She's my studio cat."

"You named your cat Pepto?" Colin asked. "Like peptide bonds and pink Play-Doh?"

"What are you doing here?" The question came out angry, but Scarlett couldn't help it any more than she could help that her heartbeat was suddenly in her ears. It was her own damn fault for seeing the cat's cute pink nose and ears three years ago at a shelter and—as Colin had so easily deduced—naming her Pepto after her and Colin's first-ever chemistry lesson.

Colin's head swiveled around the room, and Scarlett was suddenly very self-conscious of where she had placed every object in the space, right down to the colorful rug beneath her feet and the abundance of plants lining every available surface, some of which had dead leaves she hadn't gotten around to removing yet.

"I joined the mentorship program you asked me to join, and they paired me with Theodore Whitlock." Colin pulled a stack of papers out of his bag and held them up as proof. "I'm supposed to meet him today. His foster mom and I agreed that I should come early so that when he arrives, I'm already a part of the environment."

"They paired you with Theo?" She loosened her grip on Pepto, and the cat happily plopped to the floor and started figure-eighting between hers and Colin's legs. Scarlett's heart felt like it was stuck in her throat. She hadn't realized that Theo was in the program at all, but it made sense. A lot of the after-school programs coincided. A bunch of the kids from her class also attended the Boys and Girls Club and a gardening program run by none other than their old high school chemistry teacher, Ms. Matthews.

"I know you said that you wanted me to stay away, but your aunt seemed to think you might change your mind if it was for Theo. They haven't been able to get him a mentor yet." Colin bent down to pet Pepto, and it took Scarlett a second to reboot her brain from the shock of seeing him, let alone him getting along with her cat like he had been here a thousand times. Colin being partnered with Theo meant that not only would she see him today, she'd see him twice a week for however long the mentorship program lasted.

"Okay," she managed to get out, fighting back tears already. There should be no reason she should have this reaction to Colin still, but at one point, he had been the person to whom she had laid her entire heart bare, and seeing him everywhere was starting to create an ache in her chest that wouldn't go away. Something must have shown on her face because Colin's features pinched, and he rose from his crouched position, taking a step toward her.

"Maybe this is a bad idea. I can tell Eden to pair me with someone else. Your aunt just thought I would understand him well," Colin said, sticking his hands in his pockets only to pull them back out a moment later.

"Why would you understand him well?" Scarlett's shaky voice asked. He was too close to her. Not quite close enough to touch, but enough to make her head dizzy.

"He's autistic," Colin replied simply.

"I'm aware," Scarlett said. "I don't even really teach him. He paints to self-soothe in the corner away from the other students with noise-canceling headphones because sometimes the other kids can be a bit overwhelming. Fair warning, you probably won't like the noise, either." Colin swallowed, his Adam's apple dipping in his throat, and Scarlett unnecessarily followed the motion of it down his neck.

"That's partially why they thought we would work well together." Colin looked even more uncomfortable than he normally did, and she had the sudden urge to fold him in her arms like she used to. A lingering muscle memory she wished would leave. "And... other things."

"Other things," Scarlett parroted blankly, then watched Colin tap his leg repeatedly with his fingers like his own form of self-soothing from this uncomfortable conversation. It hit her as if she had been looking at a painting upside down for years and trying to figure it out just for someone to flip it right-side-up and reveal what had been obvious all along. Honestly, she felt a bit stupid for not seeing it earlier. "You're autistic?"

Colin nodded. "Yes."

"Oh." Scarlett blinked and then bobbed her head resolutely. "Then I guess you would be the best mentor for Theo."

"I really can ask for a new kid if you need me to."

"No." Scarlett shook her head. "Of course not. Theo deserves this." Somehow, the second Colin said he was partnered with Theo, she knew she would have no objection. Despite the heartache it would cause her, if she was going to sacrifice her mental peace so Theo would have a trusted adult in his life, then so be it. Colin, despite their falling out, was a good person. The fact that he was a good person was what had made everything that much harder when he left.

"Your aunt said that you would say that." Colin gave her a soft smile that unfortunately did wonders to set her at ease. "I figured you would, too, but I thought I should ask first given that I have a habit of making choices on behalf of both of us."

"I appreciate the heads-up." She let out a slow breath, mind whirring. The new information made her want to impulsively backtrack on their entire relationship and see it through the new right-side-up angle, but in the end, it wasn't as if the outcome would have changed. In every scenario she had ever workshopped, Colin never stayed. She had closed that door a long time ago, and opening it now would be a mistake. "I'll show you where he normally paints." She gestured for Colin to follow and showed him to the spot in the corner she had set up earlier by the open window. The art studio tended to start smelling like chemicals if she didn't air it out every now and then. It was freezing in the studio now, the January chill icing over the window and the tiny flowers she had painted around the edges. She quickly shut the window and turned to face Colin. "I have a space heater I'll turn on in a second," she explained. "But this is it. I let Theo do his own thing. I showed him how to start and the proper technique for what he's doing, but after that, he surpassed me and has become more skilled than I could ever teach him to be."

"I doubt that," Colin said. "The head scientist at my job didn't know about the new study on nano-robots they used in Sweden to kill cancer cells in mice, and he is way more advanced than I am. There's always something to learn regardless of how good you are."

"I guess so." Scarlett shrugged. She wasn't sure what cancer research had to do with the geology job he must have now, but she figured he must have been trying to make some connection to her so it didn't go in one ear and out the other.

"May I ask you questions about him? I know a bit from your aunt and his current foster mom, but he hasn't been there long, so they don't seem to know much. I know he's a level two autistic and he's verbal. What else should I know?"

"He is verbal," Scarlett confirmed. "But he doesn't speak much. It's only out of necessity, and I think he prefers not to speak. He has noise sensitivity like you, so his last foster parent got him noise-canceling headphones, and he usually wears those while he paints. I let him stay an hour past when everyone else is here because he gets hyperfixated on painting, and I can tell he loves it. I usually work it out with whoever his foster parent is at the time to let him stay longer. Since my aunt is his social worker, it's been a lot easier to connect with the parents. Jessie is still his foster mom, I assume?" Colin bobbed his head yes. "Then she definitely won't be back to get him till an hour after. She usually has four foster kids at one time, and if they're all in my class. I let them all stay an hour past to give her a break."

"She has two others right now, but they're toddlers, so I think it'll just be Theo," Colin informed.

"That's probably not so great for Theo's noise issues." Scarlett grimaced.

"I'm going to find another place to take him, too, so he has somewhere else to go for a break on days he's not here," Colin said. "The lookout, maybe."

"Great." She nodded. "I positioned him to face the clock so he knows how much time he has left and it's not a shock when he has to leave."

"Smart."

"I hope someday he has his own art studio and he never has to leave. I feel like I'm always watching the clock, too, hoping time slows down or something so he can stay longer. He's incredible." It was strange how excited she was to share Theo with someone. Unless they had an extensive background check, no one was allowed to watch classes. The community outreach after-school program was state-funded from a grant, so everything had to follow strict safety guidelines. Even parents tended not to come around because the bus would take most of the kids home after the program anyway. Theo was the exception to that rule. Finally being able to show someone what she did on a daily basis was exciting, and that feeling warred with the one that knew Colin Hartrick was the last person she should confide in.

"Do you feel like you never want to stop painting, too?" The question was spoken in the same way Colin always used to ask her things. His eyes weren't on her face, but she could tell he was listening intently because his body was rocking a bit. Stimming, she now realized. What she didn't know was why, considering Theo always did that when he was excited or engrossed in his art piece. Sporadically, he would have more urgent stim movements when he was stressed to calm himself down, but Theo usually wasn't stressed in this environment if she could help it. Colin wasn't visibly panicking, and she couldn't imagine he was excited to talk to her.

"Sometimes I get carried away when I paint, sure." Scarlett cleared her throat. "Anyway, I guess the other thing you need to know is that he doesn't like to be touched."

"Doesn't like it at all, or doesn't like soft physical touch or touch without a warning?" Colin asked, his hand fingering the corduroy elbow patches on the tan blazer he was wearing over his sweater.

"I guess I don't know," she admitted. Colin's preference had always been firm physical touch, and he always used to say if she was going to touch him to be sure about it. So much of him made sense now, but she supposed it always made sense to her. She had been shocked to find that other men liked lighter touch at all. "I suppose it might just be lighter touch, but I'm not positive. One of the kids touched his arm once to get his attention, and he didn't like it. He also had an incident once with the tag of his shirt rubbing him wrong."

Colin shivered. "I hate that. I always remove all my tags or get clothes with the tag printed on them. Seamless clothes are always better, too, because then you don't have this raw edge chafing you all day till you slowly start losing your sanity. What else?"

"He really hates fire," Scarlett noted.

Colin cinched his eyebrows together and looked around the studio. "Are you expecting to light things on fire?"

"Not presently."

"Good, it's hot enough in here as it is," Colin said off-handedly.

She blinked at him for a moment because the statement made no sense at all. She hadn't yet turned the heater on, and it was probably a brisk sixty-five in the room. "Was that a joke? Or is it really too hot in here?"

Colin looked down at his feet and brushed his hands against his thighs. "It was a joke about temperature and finding you attractive. I'm now realizing I probably shouldn't have made the joke, considering..."

Scarlett fought the urge to adjust her hair in its loose French braids. Compliments used to flow so freely between them. Now she couldn't tell if she wanted to impress Colin, or if she wished that he thought she was ugly. The fear that it was the first of those two options was what made her voice come out harsher than she expected. "Considering you never actually wanted me." Colin flinched, and his mouth dropped open as if he were going to say something, but she cut him off before he could. "I think that's all you need to know about Theo. Should be a pretty quiet time. I doubt he'll speak to you, so you'll probably just keep him company."

"Okay." Colin nodded. The rocking from ball to heel had stopped, and he instead fidgeted with the bottom of his blazer, yanking on the fabric. It was strange how much had changed, and yet nothing had changed at all. He was still Colin, but she now had the added benefit of knowing he could easily crush her heart and the knowledge that some or all of their relationship had been a lie. An experiment. "Scarlett, can I ask—"

"Supplies are by the metal sink in the corner. I usually help Theo get those because he can't reach the top shelf. But you are clearly capable of doing that. He uses the oil paints because he only does pointillism, and oils have the thickest consistency and don't easily run." Scarlett gestured to the lined shelves of paint and turned on her heel to all but sprint across the room to her canvas. She could feel his eyes on her, the way they never were when she was looking directly at him. A gaze that was probably picking apart everything about her. Her choice to wear rainbow pinwheel earrings was suddenly the thing her brain wanted to harp on. The daisy overalls she was wearing with paint splotches everywhere seemed juvenile when paired with her earrings, but they had seemed like a good fit when she had decided on the color theory lesson plan for today.

"I think we need to talk before Theo arrives so this isn't awkward," Colin called from across the room.

Scarlett hesitantly turned to face him again. "What is there to talk about?"

"I need clarity on a few things, and I don't want to avoid asking anymore because it will be all I can think about when I'm here." Colin took a seat on the stool in front of the easel. "I need to focus on Theo, and I can't do that if I'm thinking about you the whole time. We can talk from this distance if it makes you more comfortable." He gestured to the expanse of her studio she had placed between them.

"Fine," Scarlett released a sigh. She didn't want to talk about it, but that in and of itself was the childish way to go about this, so she knew she should suck it up. "I guess I have a few questions, too."

"Do you want to go first?"

"No, because I'll then be wondering what your questions are the whole time. Just ask what you need to ask." She brandished a hand in his direction.

"Do you really believe that we weren't dating?"

The first question slapped her in the face. "What?"

"At the coffee shop, the first time I saw you again, you said that we didn't even date and it was all just an experiment. That was not my understanding of what happened at all. I thought you were my girlfriend that I was doing an experiment *with*. I know it started as just an experiment, but I thought we were *together* together."

Scarlett's mouth parted, then closed a few times before she settled on an answer that ultimately was the truth. "We were dating, Colin. We were going to move in together, of course we were dating. You said what you said when you ended things, and I took that to mean you wished the entire thing didn't happen."

"I'd never wish that," he stated evenly. "So, then, you would consider me an ex-boyfriend?"

The title was so lacking for what he really was to her, but she answered with "yes" anyway. "Any other questions?"

"You know I never showed Carter, Piper, or any other family member that picture you sent me, right?" Colin kept setting his feet on the bottom rung of the stool and then on the floor as if he couldn't quite get comfortable enough until Pepto happily jumped into his lap, and he relaxed, stroking her back.

"Carter and Piper said as much. How many of the charts have they seen?" She wasn't sure if she wanted to know, but the thought had been plaguing her since she left the Hartrick house in December. The entire Christmas break, she had been haunted by the question, so she might as well free it from her mind so she could move on. Or continue to think about it when she was trying to sleep.

"Just one. Carter found it in my bedside drawer. I should have hidden it better. I'm sorry."

"Which one?" she asked, walking to the space heater to finally plug it in and to avoid watching her cat bask in her ex-boyfriend's company.

"The candle wax one," Colin called out.

Scarlett froze, cord halfway to the outlet. "So, the worst possible one?" her voice cracked.

"I mean, besides the obvious, the rest of the chart from that day wasn't bad."

"Why did it have to be that one?" She huffed, jamming the

prongs into the outlet, and hit a few buttons on the heater with more aggression than necessary.

The question was rhetorical, but Colin took her question literally. "It was on top of the stack because I was studying it. They found it right before I left for college, so it was after we were already broken up."

Her mind whirred and sputtered, finally landing on a new question. "Why would you study it after we broke up? For future girlfriends?"

"No, to figure out where I went wrong. I haven't dated anyone since you, Scarlett. I went on one date with a girl from my math class once, but I didn't know it was a date, or I wouldn't have shown up."

"How do you not know you're on a date? Was it not obvious?" She knew she shouldn't ask at all, but her curiosity was piqued.

"She asked me to get food, and I was hungry. She tried to kiss me, and I said 'no thanks,' then I think she was angry about that for the rest of the semester. I don't know where I went wrong there, either, because I shouldn't have to kiss someone when I don't want to kiss them. I thought we were just going to eat fries and talk about calculus."

Scarlett tried to hold back her smile, but it was to no avail. "I agree that you don't have to kiss anyone you don't want to kiss. For future reference, though, if a girl is doing things for you constantly or she asks you out to food alone, most of the time it's because she's interested in you."

"Noted. So, the girl in my organic chemistry class my freshman year who offered to help give my wardrobe a makeover?"

"I can't say for certain, but probably. Did you take her up on that offer?" Scarlett knew exactly what she was doing, and it was insane that she even cared what little dating history Colin had, especially when he had already said he hadn't dated anyone. It wasn't as though she needed to compete for his attention.

"No," he said. "I didn't really like the way she dressed and didn't want her to pick out a bunch of black and gray clothes." The relief Scarlett felt was instant, and she hated the way her body reacted to this news, her shoulders slackening from their hiked position around her ears and her frown subsiding. If there was one thing she didn't do, it was wear drab colors. "I did think it was a good idea, though, so I hired a stylist I found online. Min still has my measurements, and she knows I'm autistic, so she makes sure to only suggest clothes that won't bug me. She had most of my jackets and blazers sent to a seamstress to put corduroy patches on the elbows so I have something to touch when I need it."

Scarlett thought he must need it a lot by the way he was petting Pepto's back in the sort of rhythmic way he did everything. "That's nice," she said. "I wonder if Theo would like that."

"If he talks to me, I'll ask him." Colin nodded. "I'm not going to expect much, though. I'm not a part of his routine yet, so I won't force it."

It was simultaneously the worst and best thing ever that Colin was here. He was going to be the perfect person for Theo. That nurturing part of Scarlett that begged for the kids she taught and the ones the foundation sponsored to succeed lit up like the fireworks on New Year's Day. In the same way he had given new light to Lucia Diaz, he would have the same effect on Theo.

"Hello?" a voice called from the front door, and Scarlett and Colin's heads both swiveled to the front where Jessie and Theo walked in, two twin girls toddling in alongside them. If Scarlett had to guess, Jessie was only a few years older than her at most, but her sleek black hair was the antithesis of Scarlett's burnt sienna, and her figure was more that of a yoga instructor with tight black workout pants to contrast Scarlett's overalls, large hips, and full bosom. They both had similarly charitable hearts, though. Since Scarlett had known Jessie, her home had always been open to foster kids. The twin girls she had today thankfully seemed quiet, but Theo already had his noise-canceling headphones on, so that must not have been the case on the drive over.

"Hi, Jessie." Scarlett waved and offered a smile to the brown-haired boy who was already making a beeline to his corner spot.

Colin slowly stood up from the stool, Pepto bailing from his lap. Theo barely gave him a glance as he took over the spot and reached out to touch his special paintbrushes, running his hands along the handle and metal ferrules. Colin watched with a curious expression, then made his way over to Jessie and stuck his hand out. "Hi, I'm Colin."

"Sorry about him." Jessie shook Colin's hand, looking a bit rattled, then gestured to the twins holding on to both her legs. "They were both screaming in the car, and there wasn't anything I could do about it until we were parked."

"No need to apologize," Colin said. "I have some paperwork for you with all my contact information and a list of activities I think would be a good fit for the days we meet outside of this class. I have a copy for Theo so he can choose, but if he can't, I'll need you to choose one so we can get it on a schedule to prepare him in advance. I also printed out some resources and information on autism I've found helpful. Some people take it as an insult when I try to give them information they already know, so you can just toss it if it's unhelpful."

"Oh," Jessie said, taking the stack of papers from his hands.

"Scarlett?" Colin turned back over his shoulder. "Your aunt said you'd need a copy of my background check and mentorship program paperwork to be here. I printed you a copy." He pulled a manila folder from his tote and stretched it out to her. As usual, Colin was prepared. The spark of familiarity lodged in her chest like an anvil as she moved toward him.

"Thank you." She took the folder and sifted through the papers inside, unsurprised when everything was ordered, binder-clipped together, and three-hole punched in case she kept this kind of documentation in a three-ring binder. Colin had always despised staples.

"You two know each other?" Jessie gestured with the paperwork in her hand to the two of them.

"She's my ex-girlfriend," Colin said with zero hesitancy. Scarlett bit her lip, unsure if that information should have been shared with Jessie. She didn't want Theo's foster mom to think that she and Colin couldn't exist in the same space with Theo.

"You've... dated?" Jessie's tone left something to be desired. She wasn't directing the question to Scarlett at all, but to Colin, as if he were incapable of having a love life.

"Yes," Colin said simply. He didn't seem to get what Jessie was really implying, and Scarlett felt a pang of anger in her gut. He might not have loved her, but it didn't bar him from having loving relationships.

"He wouldn't be here if he was incapable of connecting with people," Scarlett said in irritation. "He's very close with his family and universally liked."

Jessie's mouth dropped open, finally catching on to how narrow-minded she was. "I didn't mean to suggest he wasn't."

"Universally liked is a bit of a stretch," Colin chimed in. "But yes, autism doesn't bar me from having relationships with people."

"Of course." Jessie cringed. "I'm thrilled you're going to be working with Theo."

"I'm very excited," Colin said, glancing over in Theo's direction. "I'm mostly just going to introduce myself and sit in his general vicinity." One of the twins at Jessie's feet took this opportune time to make a break for it, running toward Theo. Colin backtracked and stepped in between them, blocking the toddler's path. "I think he wants to be left alone," he said to the little girl. She looked up at him with wide eyes as Jessie scooped the girl up with one arm and set her on her hip.

"Sorry," Jessie said. "I—really, you have no idea how much I appreciate this. Both of you." She turned her head to address Scarlett, too.

"No problem, I'll try to make it twice a week besides paint days so you have a break," Colin said kindly.

"God, thank you." Jessie let out a long breath and adjusted the squirming child on her hip. "I'll be back an hour past, as long as that's still the plan?" She turned to Scarlett with a hesitant but hopeful expression.

"Of course." Scarlett offered her a smile. "We'll see you then."

By the time Jessie had left, Theo was already at the supply station, snatching tubes of oil paint in various hues of blue off the wooden shelves. When he couldn't reach a yellow color he wanted, Colin pulled it down from the shelf and handed it to him wordlessly. He hadn't yet introduced himself, but Theo seemed at ease in his presence, so Colin's plan seemed to be working well enough.

The best part of Theo's pointillist paintings besides the finished product was that Scarlett never knew what the painting was going to be until he had gotten close to finishing it. The last painting he finished of a forest scene was on the wall in Roaster's Republic, ready to be sold, so that meant he was starting fresh today, and she had zero idea what he would paint next. It was something of a game to her to guess in her head what his next masterpiece would be, and all the blues he had chosen made her think it might be an ocean setting this time.

When the other students started to arrive, Scarlett lost herself in her work, helping kids choose from one of the printed photos she had prepared and gather their acrylic paints from the cube storage at the front of the classroom. But even in her work trance, she was all too aware of Colin and Theo in the corner, slowly making their silent introduction.

Twenty-Five

Colin
22 Years Old

Scarlett had been right about Theo, for the most part. Non-verbal was his preferred form of communication, and Colin was happy to comply, leaning against the wall and waiting for a proper introduction. Occasionally Theo would make his way over to the supply station and point to a tube of paint he needed that was just out of reach, but for the most part, he didn't speak or even acknowledge Colin's presence. Colin didn't mind the silence, too intrigued by the way Theo set out his colors in order of shade in the plastic tray on the little side table by his easel. Everything had its place, and even the brushes he used were perfectly separated with an inch of space between them, the handles arranged in a straight line. The orderly way he went about everything scratched an itch in Colin's brain.

While Theo started in on the outer edge of his canvas, rocking back and forth yet making dots with such precision it was clear he had done this a thousand times before, Colin took a moment to observe the room. He hadn't had a chance to focus on much, and he could finally take in the commotion of Scarlett's class with

Pepto curled up in his arms. She was soft, and the warmth under his hand coupled with the subtle vibration of her purring when he pet her made him think that he needed a cat of his own. That would undoubtedly make his already difficult apartment search even harder, though, so he discarded that idea quickly.

The plants scattered around Scarlett's studio were the most surprising. Colin had seen pictures of the space on her social media before, and there had been a few plants in those, but the wide shot of the whole thing was a sight. Vines hung from hooks off the ceiling, and there were stands in every available space, with overgrown plants climbing up the walls. Scarlett had once told him that she always wanted to be a crazy plant lady but could never keep plants alive. She must have figured it out, though, because the plants in the room were thriving. He could almost imagine what this room would look like in the spring when flowers were in bloom—like Scarlett's tattooed sleeve she had unveiled from her cardigan once the room had heated up enough.

In the front of the classroom, once the students, who were mostly middle school aged, were set up in front of their canvases, Scarlett began her lesson. Colin listened in while he surveyed all the various paintings Scarlett had hung up like a never-ending gallery wall, some of which he could tell were her own: watercolor pictures of buildings, a sunset, and his favorite one of all, the lookout up the Trenton Creek Pass. It was the place his parents had gotten engaged and the place his dad had taken him a thousand times growing up after he'd had a bad meltdown and needed a place to decompress for a few hours. There was something so calming about that spot. The harsh lights in the city weren't as bad when he looked at it from a bird's eye view. It was one of the locations that was listed on the sheet he had given to Theo's foster mom, and he was secretly hoping Theo would choose that one off the list.

When the class ended and the chaos of pickups got a little too loud for Colin's liking, he pulled his headphones from his tote bag and slid them over his ears. Theo, who he thought hadn't paid him much attention, surprised him by turning toward him and pointing at Colin's ears, then his own, a question written on his face that was so clear, Colin knew exactly what he was asking.

"I need them, too." Colin pointed to himself and made an explosion motion with his hands near his ears in case Theo couldn't hear him through his headphones. "It's too loud."

Theo bobbed his head and returned to his painting with no further communication. Colin smiled to himself, counting the interaction as a win. He would have put the headphones on a long time ago if he knew they would interest Theo, but he also enjoyed watching Scarlett's lesson on color theory. Her voice was like a soothing balm, and he missed the long-winded stories she used to tell him.

"Why don't you paint, too?" Theo's voice was quiet, muffled by the headphones pressed to Colin's ears, but he heard the small voice well enough. It was the first thing Theo had said all evening, so Colin figured the question must have been important enough for him to ask. That, and Theo had clicked the side button on the right of his headphones, which meant he could hear the response.

"I'm not very good, and I don't like doing things I'm not good at," Colin said. Theo nodded, taking his answer at face value. Colin pointed to the painting Theo was working on. "You're very good. I own the DNA painting you made."

"I like that one," Theo stated.

"Me, too," Colin agreed. Sensing that the conversation was over and not wanting to push too hard, Colin added, "I'll leave you to it. I'm going to help Ms. Wallace clean up." The button on the side of Theo's headphones was pressed once more, and just as Colin had suspected, Theo seemed relieved by the silence. Colin wasn't offended by it. People were tiring, and trying to keep up a conversation with someone he didn't know had to be all the more exhausting for Theo.

"What did he say to you?" Scarlett asked eagerly when he approached her.

"He wanted to know why I was wearing these." Colin lifted

the headphones that were now resting around his neck. "I told him it was too loud, and then he asked why I wasn't painting."

"What'd you say?" Scarlett's eyebrows rose.

"In layman's terms: I suck at painting." Scarlett laughed, covering her mouth with her hand, and Colin shrugged. "You know I do. You have all the artistic talent between the two of us."

"Mmm." She nodded. "And you have all the math and science knowledge."

"Carter always says 'different strokes for different folks,' but it was usually to explain why he'd skip class in high school, and both my parents and Walker didn't think that was very funny."

"Makes sense." She picked up some paintbrushes that had been left out by a student who hadn't cleaned their station very well, and Colin took the cue to start wandering around to pick things up.

"You know a lot about the science of art, though. I didn't know Issac Newton made the first color wheel," Colin called out as he grabbed a spray bottle and a rag from the counter beside the metal sink in the corner of the room.

"I think you're probably the only person who found that interesting," Scarlett said. "The kids barely pay attention when I lecture them, and it usually ends up being a free-for-all, but I figure if one of them ever listens, it's worth it."

"Theo was listening." Colin sprayed a spot on the ground that must have been the byproduct of a messy painter, and he started to scrub.

"He had his headphones on the whole time." Scarlett scoffed.

"Yeah, but there are different settings on our headphones, and he clicked off noise cancellation during your lesson." Colin had noticed it immediately because the button was located in the same spot as his.

Scarlett stalled at the sink, the water running over the brushes in her hands. "Oh... I didn't know he did that."

"Your lessons are worth listening to."

"Thanks," she murmured. "They're a bit more put together than the rambling side note stories I used to annoy you with."

Colin hummed and shook his head. "Did I make it seem like those stories ever annoyed me?"

"No, but I annoy myself sometimes."

"I like your stories." He stood up beside her untouched canvas at the front of the classroom. "What story is this one going to tell?" He had thought she was going to paint earlier, and he had been somewhat disappointed that he didn't get to watch her do it. It had been forever since he'd seen her create anything.

"Something I've been putting off." Scarlett walked over to the canvas and stared at the rich brown color she had washed over the whole thing.

"Why are you putting it off?" He was sure he seemed entirely too eager to get her to keep talking, but he couldn't help himself. Every interaction with her left him wanting more, hoping maybe he might just be satisfied with one more story. One more moment with her to make up for all the ones that he had lost all those years ago.

"It's a portrait of my brother for the foundation's annual gala. It'll be a silent auction item."

"From experience, silent auctions are definitely the way to go. Definitely don't do a live auction where you auction off a date with your aunt to the highest bidder," Colin jested and added with an off-handed shrug, "in case that was ever on your radar."

Scarlett barked out a laugh. "I still can't believe you did that."

"I do recall you telling us it was a bad idea. As usual, you were right."

"Not always," she said. "Were they mad when they found out that you snuck out the window that night?"

"Only a little mad." He sighed. "Talia actually found it hilarious, which I think helped Walker be less pissed until your sister told him what happened after I snuck out."

Scarlett winced. "Sorry. She really hates you. I'll try to get her to stop holding a vendetta on my behalf."

"Don't worry about it." Harper's ire felt like his inner thoughts personified, the punishment he felt like he deserved. "She didn't say anything that wasn't true."

"But she doesn't need to stir things up," Scarlett argued. "I was the reason you snuck out. I was the reason you broke that window. We were both young and stupid."

Colin thought about it for a moment, then frowned. "Young and reckless, maybe, but I don't think we were stupid. I don't regret any of it. I'd endure the bad parts all over again for a chance to relive the good parts."

Scarlett's posture visibly stiffened beside him. "You don't have to lie to make me feel better, Colin. I'm over it. It was a long time ago."

"I'm not telling you to make you feel better. I'm just stating a fact." Before he turned loose every emotion he had in the last four years on an unsuspecting Scarlett, he took a few deep breaths and refocused his attention on the reason he was there to begin with. "I need to find a way to communicate to Theo that I want to take him to the lookout tomorrow. Can I take down your painting of it so I can show him? I'm more of a list person, but I think he's more like you and will respond better with pictures."

"You're going to take him to the lookout?"

"It's still my favorite spot in the city. I have no bad memories there." The implication of his statement was that every second they had spent together there was a good memory. Scarlett didn't seem to react, though, as she walked over to the painting on the wall and slowly pulled it down from the shelf it was sitting on, nodding her head for him to follow her over to Theo.

Engrossed in his painting, Theo didn't immediately look up when they came to his side until Colin stood in his line of sight, tapped the mode button on his own headphones, and pointed at Theo's right ear for him to do the same. Theo complied, but continued dotting his painting.

"The picture Ms. Wallace is holding is a real place. My favorite place," Colin said. Theo glanced at the picture, then did a double take. His brown doe eyes stared with interest the second time around, and he pushed his shaggy hair out of his face to see better. "It's very quiet up there. I never even need my headphones. My dad used to take me there to read sometimes. Maybe you'd like that, too?"

"I like comic books," Theo said.

"Any particular comic?" Colin asked. Theo tilted his head to the side as if to consider the question before making the universal sign for Spider-Man with his middle and ring fingers bent into his palm and his wrist up, ready to shoot webs. "Ah, good choice. I can bring you a few of those. Do you want to go to the lookout with me tomorrow, then?" Colin pointed at the painting in Scarlett's hands again. Theo bobbed his head somewhat excitedly. "Great. I'll pick you up at six." He gestured to the clock, then held up six fingers for good measure. "The lights are prettier when it's dark, but I'll bring you a book light so you can still see the comics. Sound good?" Colin held two thumbs up, and Theo returned one in confirmation. It was a good start. Theo might not talk much, but he clearly understood the things going on around him.

"You have about twenty minutes until Miss Jessie comes to get you, which means you need to start cleaning up," Scarlett added.

Theo grabbed a few brushes covered in paint with his left hand, holding them out to Colin. He gestured wildly to his painting with the one brush in his right hand, his eyebrows bent in concentration.

"You want me to clean up so you can paint a little longer?" Colin inquired. Theo vigorously nodded his head. "You have to learn to clean up after yourself, but I'll do it this one time because I want you to like me." Scarlett laughed beside him as he held out his hands, palms up, for Theo to drop the brushes into so they didn't accidentally make contact.

"I'll paint Miss Wallace or Pepto for you when I'm done." As if that were answer enough, Theo turned back toward his painting before Colin worked out what he meant. The two things in the room Colin had paid a keen interest in other than Theo himself were Scarlett and her cat. Naturally, the way Theo thought to prove that he liked Colin was to paint one of those two things. Colin briefly glanced at Scarlett to see if she understood the meaning as well, only to find that her face was bright pink, the way it got when she was embarrassed.

"Pepto is fine." Colin chuckled. "I don't think Miss Wallace wants me to have any more pictures of her."

Twenty-Six

Colin
18 Years Old

"Shhh." Piper slapped her hand over Carter's mouth as she waved him and Colin into her room. Colin had half a mind to tell Carter he couldn't help with his grand escape at all if he didn't stop laughing. In hindsight, Colin should have asked Piper first since he knew her window would be the easiest to get down from, but he was trying to keep the number of people who knew about Scarlett a secret, and despite his loud mouth, Carter could be a steel trap when he wanted to. "What is going on?" Piper hissed, rubbing the sleep from her eyes. "You all scared of the dark or something?" She pointed to the stack of blankets and pillows Colin was holding.

"I need to climb out your window," Colin started in immediately. "Carter's is too far away from the edge of the roof. I'm sure I could jump it, but he was worried I'd fall and break my neck."

"We don't have a whole lot of luck when it comes to death," Carter said.

"Not that I'm not on board with you sneaking out, but why?" Piper asked.

"Why does anyone sneak out?" Carter scoffed.

Piper's eyes widened a fraction of an inch, and she smirked. "You're going to see Scarlett?"

"You know?" Colin asked, surprised.

"You're way too touchy with her at school for her to just be the girl you're tutoring." Piper shrugged. "So..."

"She's my girlfriend," Colin said. "Please don't tell anyone, and please don't ask me any questions."

"What?" Piper balked. "You finally get a girlfriend, and I don't get to ask any questions? Did he get to ask questions?" She jabbed a finger in Carter's direction.

"Nope," Carter popped the P. "Colin won't tell me shit."

"She's the one thing I look forward to every day, and I don't want to ruin it." Colin sighed. "I don't want a thousand questions. I want to keep her to myself for a little while without the added stress of Walker and you and everyone else in my business. Can this just be for me? Please?"

"Okay." Piper nodded.

"Okay," Carter mimicked.

Shocked that there wasn't more pushback, Colin looked between his siblings with caution. "That's it? You're not going to fight me on it?"

"No. You found someone that makes you happy right now, and that's more than I have, so I don't want to ruin it for you." Piper swallowed.

"Agreed," Carter said. "There isn't a whole lot of happy to go around, and you deserve some."

"So do both of you," Colin said.

"Yeah, well, when we find it, we'll tell you to stay the fuck out of our business." Carter grinned.

"You all can stay the fuck out of my business regardless," Piper chirped and flashed them a smile.

"Great. It's settled. We all have a 'fuck off' sibling pact," Colin reiterated. "Can I climb out the window now?"

They moved over to the window, and Piper carefully slid it

open so it wouldn't make a sound, then grabbed a thin flathead screwdriver from the top of her nightstand. Like she was a seasoned pro, she slotted it into the corner of the window. "This is the loudest part," she whispered, popping the screen off with a series of snaps on one side. When she had a good handle on it, she unsnapped it from the other side, and the window was open to the one a.m. night breeze. All three of them stilled, waiting for Walker to inevitably come up the stairs to catch them in the act. There was nothing but silence, and Colin figured that Walker and Talia were just as he had left them: passed out on the couch in the living room watching a movie. When he had stolen his car keys from where Walker had haphazardly left them on the coffee table, he'd thrown a blanket over the both of them, and they had gravitated toward each other in a cuddling heap the way he and Scarlett often did. Once again, Colin was left to think Talia and Walker would both be better off if they stopped beating around the bush. If they figured their whole situation out beforehand, he wouldn't have to sneak out, and if both the front door and the sliding glass door to the backyard weren't so close to the living room, he wouldn't have to go to such extreme lengths to see Scarlett.

"So, getting on the roof looks easy enough," Carter whispered as Colin reached through the window to set the bedding down. "What does he do after that?"

"I usually go to the back corner and climb down the trellis to the back deck." Piper pointed. "You have to be careful, though. There's a broken slat near the bottom you can't step on, or you'll fall. Luckily, it's not a very big fall, or I probably would have broken something the last time."

"We should be more concerned that the world's biggest klutz frequently roof-hops," Carter said to Colin.

"I'll worry about it later," Colin said, lifting his foot to the window ledge.

"Be careful," Piper and Carter whispered at the same time.

"Go to sleep," Colin told them. "I'll be back in the morning."

The window was cramped, but he made it through to the other side and easily balanced on the slanted roof with his supplies in tow. He had worn his best traction shoes for the occasion and effortlessly made it to where the trellis waited like the perfect ladder for his escape.

By the time Colin had reached his car, the excitement of everything had him vibrating. He rocked in the driver's seat a few times, trying to get control of his body before he had to perform. The blankets and pillows were secured in the backseat along with a strip of condoms he had pulled from his pocket. Everything was ready. *He* was ready. The engine started with a roar he hoped wasn't audible from inside the house, and he was off.

Scarlett's house sat in darkness. Even her window, which was visible from the street where he had parked, didn't have a light on. Fifteen minutes with no response to his text had him a bit worried, so Colin finally bit the bullet and walked up to the house. Hundreds of romance novels and movies alike had one thing in common, and as Colin stood beneath Scarlett's window, tracing over the smooth surface of the rock in his hand with his thumb, he thought there couldn't possibly be a more romantic way to get her attention. The first rock he threw missed the window entirely. The second hit dead on, but nothing happened. The third rock, he should have realized, was too pointy. He shouldn't have thrown it so hard.

The sound of breaking glass shattered all his hopes of romance and sex under the stars. The blood-curdling scream from Scarlett's room had him sprinting for her front door.

Twenty-Seven

Scarlett
18 Years Old

Sitting at the dining room table with Colin should have sparked fond memories for Scarlett. Memories of chemistry lessons and early moments in their relationship. But when her mother, sister, uncle, and aunt, with a sleeping Lindy curled into the crook of her elbow, were sitting across from them in the dead of night, it was unpleasant, to say the least. The silence after her uncle got everyone to sit down was so loud, Scarlett was sure she was going to drop dead in front of everyone. Dying would be better than facing the ramifications of her and Colin's failed attempt to sneak out.

"You want to take it away, Nora? She's your daughter." Uncle Marty gestured to his sister, who made a screeching sound with her chair when she scooted out from the table a bit.

"Give me a second. I'm barely awake, Marty," Nora snapped and ran a heavy hand over her face. Eventually, she looked over to Scarlett's partner in crime. "Colin Hartrick, I presume?"

"Yes, ma'am. Nice to meet you." Colin stuck out his hand, but still didn't make eye contact with her mother. Scarlett covered her face with both hands and peeked between her fingers as her mom and boyfriend traded introductions at the worst possible time.

"I thought you were her chemistry tutor," Marty grumbled.

"He is," Scarlett squeaked out.

"Chemistry and statistics. I tutor her every Tuesday and Thursday. She's been doing really well on her exams. Her grades should reflect that," Colin said, his hand finding hers under the table and squeezing. If her grades were their one saving grace in this reckoning, she was going to cling to that.

"He's so helpful!" she pleaded. "Ask me about the laws of thermodynamics."

"Don't ask her about that," Colin butted in. Scarlett turned to glare at him, and he shrugged. "You got that question wrong on the quiz. I was going to go over it again in our next session."

"It's safe to assume there won't be a next session," Marty said coldly.

"Not necessarily." Nora shook her head. "They're right. Scarlett's grades in those two classes are much better now."

"Well, he's clearly not just her tutor, or he wouldn't be pulling a Romeo in the middle of the night," Aunt Eden sighed.

Marty pressed his hand down on the table as if to assert his dominance in the conversation. "No one is playing Romeo." The glare in Colin's direction made it clear that his statement was directed at a party of one.

"She's not exactly a child, Uncle Marty," Harper said. "She's allowed to have a boyfriend. She's eighteen." If there was ever a moment Scarlett wanted to throw her sister a parade in her honor, now was that time.

"He probably means the general sneaking around and breaking the window more than the me being her boyfriend part of it," Colin said.

"Yes, thank you—no, wait, no thank you!" Marty pointed at Colin aggressively. "You're the problem here. And none of us even knew you were her boyfriend."

"I did." Harper raised her hand.

"I did, too." Nora nodded.

Scarlett's mouth dropped open. "I didn't tell you he was my boyfriend!"

"I know my daughter," Nora said. "I might not have known it was official, but for the last two months your interest in AP Chemistry skyrocketed, and you brought up Colin every possible chance you could. You asked me to re-up your birth control that you barely kept track of before. I wasn't born yesterday."

"To be fair, hun," Eden patted Marty on the back, his face stuck in permanent disgust from the birth control comment, "you and Lindy are the only ones who didn't know." She smiled down at Lindy, who was still out cold in her arms.

Scarlett groaned. "Oh my God." Colin was still staring at his lap, but there was a slight smile on his face, and his thumb started to massage the back of her hand.

"Well, that's just great." Marty huffed and looked at Scarlett. "You've been in my house since you were twelve, and I apparently don't know you as well as I thought I did."

"My uncle doesn't know either, if that helps," Colin murmured.

"Your uncle?" Marty questioned before his eyes slowly widened. "Colin Hartrick." He pronounced every syllable like each new sound he formed with his mouth was another lock to unpick. "You're Cole and Paisley Hartrick's oldest son." Scarlett saw the exact moment the realization set in because a sad expression crossed her uncle's face, and his voice softened. It wasn't a question anymore. It was a statement, and everyone in the room knew what that meant.

"The very same," Colin confirmed.

"How long have you been dating Scarlett?" Marty cocked his head.

"One month, one week, three days." Everyone, including Scarlett, was taken aback by his quick-off-the-tongue calculation. "As of midnight," Colin added.

"And what were your intentions to come here tonight *past* midnight?" Marty raised his eyebrows.

"You don't have to answer that," Scarlett said quickly. She was somewhat fearful that Colin would straight up tell her uncle that he was planning on taking her up to the woods for sex, which had definitely been the plan before she started her period and got stuck in the bathroom with nausea and the worst cramps imaginable. When she had finally walked back into her room to grab her phone and call the whole thing off, her window shattered all over her bedroom floor. More than anything, it had scared the shit out of her, which in turn woke up the entire house. All their plans had been thwarted by something she could have known was coming if she had paid attention when she was taking her birth control pills.

"Are you okay?" Colin unlaced his hand from hers and placed it on her back, rubbing up and down as she hunched over. She had been trying to suck it up the whole time. The urgency of the situation didn't seem like the right time to cry out in pain.

"Fine," Scarlett squeaked out, shutting her eyes for a moment and squinting them hard. At the beginning of the conversation, she really had been fine, but she couldn't help the new wave of nausea and the tearing feeling inside her that made her think she was either going to shit herself or sweat to death.

"Do you have Midol or something?" Colin asked the room. Scarlett's head snapped up in surprise. "And water? I'm willing to make a large bet that she hasn't drunk the amount of water she should have today." The face Nora made was somewhere between pleased and shocked. Scarlett would be shocked, too, but she had lost track of the number of times Colin had surprised her by just knowing things about her. "My sisters always like heating pads if you have that, too?" And therein lay the explanation for this particular knowledge: his sisters and mother.

"We've got all three. I'll grab them," Harper offered, quickly moving toward the stairs.

"I think I'm gonna put Lindy back down and go to sleep," Eden yawned. "Before she wakes up again in two hours."

"I'm so sorry for waking her up," Colin said sincerely.

"Sorry," Scarlett chirped, gripping her middle even harder as another cramp made her entire body shake. She would always forget just how bad they were in the beginning by the time they rolled around again, and this time she had wanted to see Colin so badly that she had missed all the warning signs until it was too late. The underwear Colin liked so much were a casualty of that awful gushing feeling, and she doubted he would think they were sexy now.

"He's a nice kid, honey. Don't interrogate him too much," Eden kissed her husband's forehead, and off she went. All Scarlett wanted to do was lie curled up next to Colin in bed with his body acting as her personal heating pad. Instead, she knew her bed was covered in glass, and there was no way Marty was going to let Colin stay over.

"Nora? What are you going to do about this?" Marty asked.

"Scarlett and I will figure out a way to pay for the window, and—"

"I'll pay for the window," Colin interrupted. "I broke it, and I can pay to get it fixed. I'll come by tomorrow, and I'll clean the glass up myself."

"Are we supposed to keep this from Walker?" Harper asked, coming back into the kitchen and setting Scarlett's necessities down. Scarlett took the water glass first and downed the pills while Colin continued talking and unwinding the power cord from around the heating pad.

"I'm not planning on telling him anything. He's no longer my legal guardian, and he only ever was for less than a year. He's not my parent. He's barely old enough to be my little brother's parent. I've been doing my best to help him, not add to his stress, and I went a little too far yesterday trying to help him, so I think it's best if I just stay out of his business and he stays out of mine" Colin said resolutely. He held up the pronged end of the power cord and looked around for an outlet.

Scarlett pointed to the one behind her chair. With such care it was making her a little dizzy, he plugged in the heating pad, turned it up to the highest setting, and adjusted it across her stomach, pressing a hand on top of it to keep it in place until she pulled her shirt down to hold it there. It was the worst possible time to decide she was in love with someone, but mixed in with the period cramps from hell, the feeling tapped her brain like a fact. It wasn't sexual in the way she wanted him earlier—with her womb wanting to part like cells during mitosis, sex was the furthest thing from her mind. This was more consuming than that. She wanted to be his. She wanted the number Colin recited earlier of months and weeks and days they had been together to become years that turned into decades of stories shared under a blanket and wrapped up in each other. Memories made while experiencing life together. She wanted every chart they made during their sexual awakening to be her own cheat sheet to his body. She wanted more of this: more of Colin noticing she was in pain and doing something about it. She wanted to hold her hands over his ears like she had done earlier when Eden and Marty couldn't get Lindy to settle down. She was so sure that her life's purpose shouldn't revolve around a man, and yet every second she spent with Colin made her feel like she was special because there was no doubt in her mind that he was.

"This whole thing is my fault anyway," Scarlett said, finding comfort in Colin's hand sliding up and down her spine again, his free hand laced in hers once more. "If you want to punish me, that's fine, but I'd rather be treated as an adult because I am one."

"Nora?" Marty asked, somewhat resigned.

"I remember being young and in love once," Nora said, a wistful smile on her face that Scarlett wished weren't there. Even after everything, her mom held no ill will toward her dad, even though she should. She should hate him for leaving the way Scarlett did. "They're both adults, and I think whatever decisions or mistakes they make are theirs to make at this point. They're going to do what they want to do whether we think it's a good idea or not, and currently the only wrong thing these two have done was accidentally break a window. I'd rather them both know that they have people to confide in instead of people they have to hide things from."

"But don't you regret that our parents didn't stop you from doing things when you were her age?" Marty demanded.

"No." Nora shrugged. "It wasn't all bad. Even the bad moments, when I look back at them, weren't all bad. I got two beautiful daughters and one beautiful angel out of it." A wistful expression crossed her face, and she reached over to pat Scarlett's hand. "I'd endure the bad parts all over again for a chance to relive the good parts."

TWENTY-EIGHT

Colin
22 Years Old

The car was dead silent on the way up to the lookout. The only sounds from the backseat were Theo adjusting in his booster seat and pulling at the seatbelt that was slashing across his neck. Twice Colin had had to tell Theo that he couldn't put the strap behind his back, no matter how uncomfortable it was. He hated that some of the only words he had spoken to Theo were a reprimand for something that was clearly irritating the kid, but safety came first, and Colin knew all too well the dangers of car accidents, even when the proper safety equipment was used. The cheap booster seat Jessie sent him with looked hard in all the wrong places, and Colin had probably gained a few frown lines when he put it in his car, knowing Theo would be uncomfortable. It all made sense; the comfortable ones were expensive, and foster kids never got the expensive stuff. Autistic kids in foster care weren't always going to get the resources that they needed to succeed, and that fact was depressing.

"I'll have a different booster seat and a seatbelt pillow next time," Colin called to the backseat, where Theo was rocking back and forth and had one hand fisted in a ball as he bounced it off his leg in a repeated motion. "You can choose which one you want when we get there."

It took a moment for Theo to respond, and Colin wasn't exactly expecting him to, given that what he had said was a statement, not a question, but when he finally did, it was almost inaudible. "Seatbelt pillow?"

"Yes." Colin nodded as they finally hit the dirt path to the lookout. "It's a padded piece that goes over your seatbelt, so it won't bug you as much. My parents got me one when I was little, and I used to take naps on it in the car." There was no response from Theo, but again, Colin didn't expect one, so he focused all his attention on the dirt path ahead and the gravel pit at the end of it. The Trenton Point Lookout didn't usually look like much in the light of day, just an informational placard in the makeshift parking area that Colin had all but memorized when he was little and wanted to be a geologist when he grew up. The second you got past the small line of trees, though, the large igneous rock formation had a semi-flat top to it, making the area perfect for chairs to look out over the city at sunrise, sunset, or, his personal favorite, right now, in the dark of night, because the city was glowing below like the firefly sanctuary he once went to see when he lived in Maryland.

Once they had parked and Theo had all but bailed out of the car, Colin scooped up his supply of two chairs and his leather tote containing the Spider-Man comic books Theo had requested, a thirty-page printout of the National Cancer Institute's *Milestones* highlight magazine from this past year, some black pens, yellow highlighters, trail mix, and a blanket shoved on top. Wordlessly Colin handed Theo the one flashlight he had packed, and they headed past the tree line and out to the main landing. He had explained all of this in advance so nothing would be a shock to Theo, but it was helpful that there was no one here, and the woods were quiet except for the crackling of a few branches in the breeze and the occasional squirrel skittering up a tree. Theo worked the flashlight like an eight-year-old, which meant Colin couldn't see shit as he bumbled toward the spot he usually sat at when he came up there. Luckily, it was only a few yards away from the parking area, and he had been up there so many times before, his muscle memory wasn't likely to let him fall off the cliff's edge.

When they made it, the gasp and hopping sequence Theo did as he pointed out into the city below was worth every single inconvenience to get there. Scarlett's painting had been a beautiful rendering of it, but there was nothing compared to the real thing and being surrounded by fresh air and the kind of silence that only spoke in the woods. Once they were seated and Colin had gotten Theo set up with the blanket, a comic, and a book light, they settled into a comfortable silence.

This place held fragments of Colin's past the same way his childhood home did. Depending on the company, the memories ranged from chaotic to peaceful, loving to sad. When he had come with his dad, it was a comfort after turmoil, or occasionally, when they would come 'just because,' they would talk for hours about all the things that interested them. With his mom, it had always been more emotionally charged. She would ask him questions about friendships and girls that he could never quite understand, or, like right now, they would just sit in silence and breathe. With his siblings, Piper would usually end up injuring herself, Carter would pretend that he was going to jump off the edge to scare the shit out of their parents, Pearl would request a retelling or reenactment of their parents' engagement at that exact spot, and Cooper was so young that he was usually playing with the sticks and dirt until he was filthy.

And then there were the times he had come here with Scarlett. Listening to her stories, sharing his own, kissing every chance they could get, and falling in love without a clue they would break each other's hearts.

TWENTY-NINE

Colin
18 Years Old

"This rock is made of andesite," Colin said, lifting himself up on his elbows to glance at the rock ledge past their makeshift bed of blankets and pillows. The sun was starting to set, and vibrant pinks and oranges were beginning to form in the sky beyond the far mountain range.

"Andesite," Scarlett repeated back to him. "I thought it was igneous. Isn't it volcanic?"

"Andesite *is* igneous, it's just a type of igneous rock. It's the remains of basaltic magma that crystallized certain minerals when they were removed from the melt. That's why it kind of has a salt-and-pepper speckled look about it. They think this specific rock formation is late-stage magma that cooled in the throat of a volcano," Colin explained.

"The throat?" Scarlett asked, shimmying up to his side and placing her hot mouth on the column of his neck. He found her lips with his a moment later and slowly traversed down to her throat, planting a kiss there in confirmation before continuing his geology lesson.

"It's the upper part of the main vent in a volcano, Red," Colin breathed into her skin.

"Mmm," Scarlett hummed introspectively. "If this was in a volcano, how'd it get here?"

"Easy," he murmured, one hand traveling downward across her ribs and then her hip, dragging across her stomach and under the hem of the color-blocked dress she was wearing. Scarlett's breathing slowed as he slid his fingertips along the inside of her thigh. "The volcano erupted," he announced before deciding to demonstrate with a firm press of his fingertips into her clit. Her hips bucked toward him, seeking more friction, and he obliged. "Basically, it chaotically tossed a bunch of earth everywhere, and the outer pebbly layer of cooled magma crumbled away." He moved her underwear to the side. "And what we were left with was the core." Two fingers speared her as if that were explanation enough, and it was, or at least it was for him because the noise Scarlett made in response made him want to erupt.

"I think I love geology," Scarlett said breathlessly.

A deep-throated chuckle left Colin's mouth. "I already told you that you loved science, you just didn't *know* you loved science. Even this is science." He kissed her, fingers still pumping in and out of her while his thumb massaged her now swollen clit.

"Okay, so, I love geology, and I love sexy science," she groaned.

"And chemistry." When she didn't respond, he punished her with a harsher thrust of his fingers.

Scarlett gasped, shaking her head. "If I say yes, can I come?"

"You still don't like chemistry?" Colin asked, surprised. She had been doing so well in the class that he assumed he had converted her.

"No," she sighed. "But I would have lied if I knew saying that was going to turn you off."

He hadn't realized he'd stopped moving his hand entirely. "Shit. Sorry, I can—"

"It's fine." Her laugh was light and airy, like they were floating on a cloud together. "I just came up here to hang out with you, anyway. You're the one who turned rocks into foreplay."

"You're distracting. All I want to do all the time is touch you," Colin admitted.

"And talk about earth science," Scarlett noted.

"True."

"What do you think you'll do once you get your bachelor's? Become the next great geologist?"

"I'll probably get my PhD and then hopefully get a job as a research geologist. What about you? What are you doing once we graduate high school?" He knew from prior conversations that she didn't seem like she was college-bound anytime soon, not because she wasn't smart or couldn't get in, but because the future was a big question mark in her book, and dumping money into something she wasn't certain of felt like a waste. He couldn't imagine not knowing what his exact next step was. The mere thought of having to figure it all out along the way would make him break out in hives.

"It sounds so stupid, but I just want to paint." Scarlett shrugged.

"Why would that be stupid?" Colin asked.

"It just sounds so vapid compared to whatever mysteries you'll uncover about Earth's creation. I have this thing where I feel like I need to do something important, but working for the foundation and painting is all I can think to do."

"Funding cancer research with the foundation isn't good enough? That's probably more important than what I'll be doing."

"Sure, but that's not my passion, that's the thing I do because I'm honoring my brother. I just wish my passion and my heart wanted the same thing, if that makes sense." Sitting up, Scarlett faced the sunset, her eyes focused on the colored sky beyond. "I love the part where I get to meet and support families the most. I wish I loved fundraising and networking so I could put my entire soul into the foundation to make a greater difference. Hell, I wish

I loved science as much as you do so that I could search for the cure to cancer myself."

In the last few months of being with Scarlett, Colin had been reading up on the latest cancer research as if he could belatedly fix her grief, so he could understand the need to be helpful, the desire to change the world even if it was just one person's world. The bleeding heart in her chest was probably why she had paid him any attention at all, why being with her was the only place where his own grief didn't feel so insurmountable.

"Why do you like painting?"

"It started as a sort of outlet, I guess, after Tucker died. I like that my mind goes quiet when I paint. That I can finally focus on one thing and only one thing for hours on end when I'd usually struggle to stay on task. I love watercolors specifically because the way the paint and water mix together and fade into a canvas makes me think of old memories. Like a vintage photo, but better, because it's not just capturing the moment in a still, it feels like it's moving."

"Like water." Colin grinned.

"Exactly. I can even completely reinvent a memory if I didn't like it. It was a bad rendering because I wasn't very good at that age, but one of the first things I painted was Tucker in the hospital the day that he died. I gave him hair and balloons and a smiling face simply because I could and I didn't want to remember the way he looked pale and sickly that day when he should have enjoyed his last day." She was still looking at the sunset, but her eyes were watery.

"Maybe that's why my uncle writes," Colin considered. "He can rewrite any story he wants. My parents were happy when they died, I think. They were on a date night, and my mom got all dressed up for it. My dad even bought her flowers. I was in charge of watching my siblings, so I don't think Walker would need to change that, but I think if he was going to rewrite it, I'd want him to change the ending."

"I could do that, too. Paint something that doesn't even exist if I wanted. Paint our future so we have more time together. Paint the past and make it so we were friends in elementary school," Scarlett said, lying back down beside him and curling into his side. "I could paint this exact moment if I wanted to. And the thing about paintings is that they last longer than a lifespan. Van Gogh is still alive and well in his paintings." She tipped her head to the side as if a contradiction were on the tip of her tongue. "Okay, maybe not him, because he wasn't exactly *well*, but you get the point."

"I think all of that sounds world-changing, even if it's just that you make a moment permanent," Colin said, and wrapped both arms around her in a tight embrace. "I want this exact moment to be immortalized forever." Truthfully, he never wanted to leave this spot. He could grow old right on the surface of this rock, holding Scarlett forever in the peaceful bubble they had created together. He thought this feeling must have been what his parents were feeling the night they died and every other day they spent together. It felt good to just *be* with someone. Whether or not life and grief were weighing down his normal routine, he had Scarlett to get lost in, to feel peace in. He had Scarlett to love. And maybe it was that simple. All the internet searches and online quizzes he took to find out if he was in love hadn't explained it in such simple terms, but he was now certain that he loved her beyond comprehension. He never really believed in 'the one,' but he also couldn't imagine any universe or alternate timeline where he didn't want Scarlett, so soulmates must be a thing.

"We could immortalize it now," Scarlett whispered, her fingers toying with his sweater. "We still haven't tried to have sex again."

"I know, but I think we need to wait for—"

Scarlett groaned. "For what? Are you still scared I won't like it?"

"No, but I want it to be something you don't have to reinvent with a painting so it's good. I want it to be romantic and planned out and everything we want it to be."

"And I think you're putting too much pressure on it," she said. "You can't be perfect at everything, Colin."

"I can try, though, can't I?" Her response was a burst of laughter through her nose and a nod against his chest. "Prom night, then. I'll get you a corsage. We'll both be dressed to the nines. We'll slow dance. Then we'll spend an entire night in bed."

"Perfect, if a bit cliché."

"Too cliché?"

Scarlett's chin tipped up, and she brought her mouth down against his in a slow press before smiling and saying, "The right amount of cliché."

"Sometimes all I want is to be cliché," Colin said. "I want something to just be so stereotypically normal that for once I feel normal."

"For the record, I like you weird, but I get that." Scarlett sighed. "I wish I had one of those cookie-cutter, cliché families with two parents who are still deeply in love, siblings who are never sick, and a big, happy house. Instead, my dad ditched us after my brother died, and we had to move in with my uncle because my mom couldn't afford a place with one income and the mountain of medical debt from my brother. She tells me not to worry about it, but I saw one of the bills one time, and it's bad. It's so stupid she has to keep paying for it because no medicine actually fixed him. He still died so, like, what the fuck was the point, you know? My brother used to say 'a great soul never dies,' and I guess he was right because he lives on through the insane debt." Colin closed his eyes, anticipating that Scarlett was about to go on for much, much longer, and he wanted to hear every word. "It's a partial Maya Angelou quote, in case you were wondering. My dad taught it to Tucker before he even got sick, but after he was diagnosed, he used to recite that quote and tell me and Harper that he was going to come back as a ghost and haunt the shit out of us. One time I could have sworn—" At her abrupt stop mid-sentence, Colin slowly opened his eyes and looked over at her curiously. "Sorry, I'm rambling again. Are you falling asleep, or just bored?"

"Neither," he answered easily. "I listen better like this. Keep talking. I love your stories, Red."

"Well, now I don't even know where I was at." Scarlett giggled.

"Your brother was haunting the shit out of you, I think," Colin regurgitated.

"Oh, right." Scarlett settled in as he once again closed his eyes. And for the next hour, until the sun went to sleep and they were surrounded by darkness other than the city lights below, Scarlett weaved stories with elaborate details, side quests that sometimes started entirely new stories, and so much heart that he wondered how he had ever gotten lucky enough to be the one who got to listen to her.

THIRTY

Scarlett
23 Years Old

> DAD 3:48 PM
>
> Happy birthday, kid.

The message Scarlett had both been dreading and hoping for came at the exact wrong time. Her students were going to show up for class any minute, and she had no time to respond. She promptly locked her phone and stashed it in her pocket out of sight. It probably would have only taken a moment to respond. A simple "thanks" would do because Lord knows her dad didn't deserve much more than that. Even his use of the word "kid" felt like an insult. After all, the last time he had seen her, she *was* a kid. If she scrolled back through her messages with her dad, every single one was some sort of a holiday requirement. "Happy Thanksgiving." "Merry Christmas, Letti." "Happy New Year! Wishing you all the best." That last one she hadn't responded to at all because he clearly wasn't actually wishing her the best. He was wishing for distance with a cordial text for the holidays that sounded like a Hallmark card. The wildest part about all of it was that Tucker got a grander gesture on his birthday, the roses that would undoubtedly show up later this year like clockwork.

As Scarlett set out the rest of the materials for her students, she did her best to forget about the message. It was her birthday, after all, and it was a special year because it had fallen on a Thursday. She got to do what she loved: work with students and observe Theo as he created his next masterpiece. After a few months of working on a rainy street scene, he was on to something else that required a lot of dark colors. Colin, who had dutifully accompanied Theo to every class, knew what the painting was going to be, because in the shocker of the century, Theo had told him. Scarlett was both extremely jealous that her favorite student was latching onto her ex-boyfriend and so thrilled they were getting on well that she frequently found her eyes watering when she looked over to see their matching noise-canceling headphones and their mostly silent conversations with wild hand gestures.

"Happy birthday." Colin's voice and the familiar sound of a waxed paper bag crinkling called out from the doorway just as she finished setting up. The memory of that first day back in chemistry class sliced through her heart when she saw the matching donut bags suspended in Colin's hand. He was early again, as was his routine.

"Happy birthday to you, too. I think that's the only time I've ever said that and it wasn't an accident, like when the server at a restaurant tells you to enjoy your food and you go 'you too,'" Scarlett said, taking the maple bar from his hand as Pepto sprinted to Colin's side to greet him.

"I don't think I've ever done that."

"How does it feel to be the chosen one?" Scarlett scoffed.

"Chosen for what exactly? And who's choosing me? You?" Colin's eyebrows rose.

"Chosen by God for the great honor of not being an embarrassment at restaurants."

"Considering he made me awkward in every other social situation, it's nice that he skipped one." He took a giant bite of his maple bar and crouched down to scratch behind Pepto's ears. "Lucky me."

"I mean, he might have made you socially unaware, but he also made you..." Trailing off, Scarlett could feel her cheeks go hot. This conversation was a trap of her own making.

Colin swallowed, and she watched the dip of his throat closely. "Made me what?"

Along with spring, lately her libido was blossoming, except it wasn't elegant like the flowers lining her shelves. She was more like a feral raccoon, and she was starting to think Colin's constant presence over the last few months was the root cause. "Nothing," she said, not allowing herself to look him up and down like she wanted to.

"He made me nothing?" If he didn't seem genuinely confused by this, then she wouldn't have said anything further, but he did, and she was nothing if not a rambler.

"No, I meant 'nothing' like 'never mind' because I didn't actually want to say what I was going to say out loud." Her mouth was its own truth serum as well, apparently.

He downed another bite of his donut before responding slowly. "So, it's something embarrassing about me, then?"

Scarlett groaned. "I don't even know what the original question was anymore. You're conventionally attractive. That's all I meant. Let's move on from this conversation forever."

"Okay." Colin straightened. "How's your brother's painting going?"

Her face fell, and she threw up her hands in frustration. "Out of all the questions, that's the one you chose? I'd rather talk about you being hot! The gala is in two months, and I have sketched and erased like fifty times. I've had six months to paint this. The foundation is prepping for my brother's birthday 5K now, and I'm still stuck thinking about the gala because I can't finish up the auction pieces. I'm starting to think I don't know how to paint at all.

What even is art? Some people just glue a bunch of trash together and display it. Maybe I should start doing that? The piece will be called 'I give up.'"

Ignoring her catastrophizing, Colin walked past her to the toned but blank canvas at the front of her classroom and picked up the photo of her brother leaning against it. "This is what you're trying to copy?"

"I'm not even trying at this point, I'm just failing," she grumbled, taking a large bite of her maple bar before tossing it on top of the cube storage behind her easel.

"You have like five portraits of people hanging up on your wall." He peered around the room. "I'm going to assume that skill is not the problem here. Am I right in thinking that it's more of a mental hang-up?"

"I just..." Scarlett's voice cracked. "I don't think I can do him justice. It's never going to be exactly right. I thought maybe I'd wake up this morning and have the sudden inspiration to finish it because that picture was taken on my birthday, but I woke up and I feel the same way I did yesterday. I was really banking on my motivation to be through the roof today because I'm pretty much out of time."

"Hmm." Colin looked down at Tucker's picture, up to the canvas, and back down again. "The project I'm working on right now at work has many variables, but my team is only testing one of them repetitively until we have sufficient data. Like how our chemistry teacher would have us run three trials, except we're running hundreds, changing one tiny thing and running it again. I don't have a problem with repetition, but sometimes my lab partner, Warren, gets bored of doing the same thing for weeks on end. Maybe you should... change the variable?"

"What, like, choose a different picture?" Scarlett asked. She was almost certain now after a few scattered comments Colin had made that he was working in a lab of some sort. And given the random commentary he had on medical science, she was starting to think he wasn't a research geologist like he had planned.

"No, change what you're doing entirely. Do you enjoy painting portraits?"

"Sometimes. I don't like doing people I'm close to much because I feel like I can't get it exactly right." She used to paint people she knew all the time, but at some point, she had found she was trying too hard and was never satisfied with the result.

"So, don't make it perfect." He shrugged. "Maybe you need to make it your own. Change all the things you want to change. You once said you loved repainting memories and fixing all the details you wished were different, so put your own spin on it. Add things. Get rid of things. Make it an expression instead of a portrait."

The heartbeat in Scarlett's chest quickened as she took the photo from Colin's hand, looking down at it. This particular memory, captured in a still, was all wrong. She had seen this picture a billion times, but it wasn't how she recalled that day. Her mind had remembered things that the camera had missed and filled in things that were never there. But even so, she wished there was a way to make the picture real somehow. If there was some way she could incorporate all the things her brother had missed since he passed, *that* would make this picture special. Not a portrait dwelling on the past, but a painting looking forward to the future. That elusive spark she didn't have that morning ignited under her skin, and she smiled down at the photo for the first time since she had started this project.

In an outward expression of the joy brewing inside her, Scarlett set the picture back down on the easel and whipped around to fling her arms around Colin's middle. "Thank you." Since the day in January Colin had shown up to meet Theo for the first time, they had mostly been able to avoid touching. There had only been two or three instances of their hands brushing when cleaning up or grabbing supplies. The wall she had carefully crafted to avoid him was blown to pieces with one embrace. Colin's warm arms tightened around her, their fronts pressing together in a way that didn't feel at all platonic. His fingertips were digging into her shoulders like the hug was too gentle and he needed more pressure, but she had been pretty forceful to begin with.

"You're welcome," Colin's low voice brushed against her ear, painting her body in warmth from head to toe. She could feel the way his mouth wasn't far away from hers, and if she just tilted her head, she could make a huge mistake.

"Oh." Scarlett panicked, pushing off his chest and jumping away from him. "Sorry. I didn't—that wasn't—I don't know."

Colin straightened easily, as if it hadn't affected him at all. "It was just a hug." That statement alone was enough to reel her back in. Whatever her body was feeling and reacting to was one-sided. He didn't want her then, and he didn't want her now. Nothing had changed, and she didn't even want it to, so the disappointed ache in her chest shouldn't be there at all.

"Right." With a concise nod of her head, Scarlett swallowed.

"I think Theo's here," Colin noted as the door opened at the front.

Looking for anything to do, Scarlett announced boldly that she was going to plug in the heater despite the fact that she felt entirely too hot. Jessie and Colin did their usual hand-off with Theo, which mostly involved Theo bolting to his station and Colin walking Jessie through the next few days so she could enforce the schedule. Scarlett wrestled the heater out of her office, forgetting that that was the last place she had used it, and regretted deciding to turn it on at all when the studio didn't feel remotely cold. By the time Jessie left, she had managed to wheel it into the spot by her painting with considerable force.

She peeked over her shoulder as she lifted the cord to the outlet, noticing that Theo wasn't wearing his headphones yet. "Other kids are showing up soon," she called out. "They're never quiet, so you both might want to—" A pop followed by a whooshing sound grabbed her attention again, and she turned back to the outlet with alarm. Orange flames were climbing up the plastic cover where she had plugged the heater into the wall.

"Shit." Throwing herself back on her ass and dropping the cord, she did a quick scoot and crab walk backwards. "Fire!" she yelled.

"Fuck," Colin's hissed behind her. Theo started wailing.

All hell broke loose.

"I need something to put it out." Scarlett scrambled to her feet as the orange flames spread higher and smoke started to billow from the spot on the wall. One side of her studio was made of brick, but, of course, the fire had chosen a sheetrock wall as its victim and was consuming everything in its wake. A canvas fell from low on the wall as she started to sprint to the office for the fire extinguisher.

Colin arrested her on the spot and all but threw her in Theo's direction. "Get him out of here, now!" he yelled before covering his ears. She redirected, running over to Theo and putting him in a bear hug to lift him up off the floor, where he was now huddled in a fetal position. He writhed in her grip, but she held on to him well enough as her adrenaline kicked in. Colin, she realized once she was already near the door, had thrown his long, heavy jacket onto the fire, effectively smothering some of it.

"The fire extinguisher is on the wall in my office!" Scarlett called out. By the time Colin had run back to grab it, she was through the door and pulling Theo to safety. When they were a safe distance away, she sat Theo on the curb and ripped her phone from her pocket.

The mayhem of nine kids showing up for art class while fire trucks sped down the street had taken a moment to die down. The bus driver, bless his heart, had taken Scarlett's frantic directions to heart and hauled all the kids but Theo back into the bus, driving them back to the middle school, where they could call their parents to pick them up early. Theo, finally settled down after nearly twenty minutes of screaming and flailing, was sitting in the back of an ambulance with his headphones on, eerily quiet in comparison to a moment ago. Unlike the tiny flame art she had done in her class once, this was different. Theo hadn't just panicked, he had completely shut down, and in his panic, he had triggered Colin's sensitivity to noise.

"All right." Braiden, decked out in all his fire protection gear, came to stand beside where Scarlett was sitting on the curb. Out of all the people to be called out to this incident, it seemed par for the course that it would be her ex-boyfriend. "The fire was out completely by the time we got in there, and we turned off your electricity. You're going to need to—"

"Where's Colin?" Scarlett shot up from her seat. "Is he okay? What about my cat?"

"I probably should have led with that. He's fine. He's—"

"Right here," Colin's voice said from behind her. Her chest collapsed in relief as she whirled around, ready to throw caution to the wind and throw herself at him again. She stopped dead in her tracks once she saw that he was both not wearing a shirt, holding Pepto in his arms, and suspending one wrist out to the side like he was anticipating her overzealous embrace to hurt him.

"Are you injured?" Scarlett's eyes bounced across his body, finding first his wrapped wrist, then something that must have been blocked by Pepto's head when she had first looked at him. Now it was the only thing she could look at.

"He has a second-degree burn on his wrist, but it's not too bad," Braiden answered for him. "I assume you're *the* Colin, then?" With her brain running a million miles a minute, she almost didn't catch Braiden's comment—she was too focused on the black tattoo adorning Colin's chest.

"I don't know what that means, but sure," Colin replied.

"You're Scarlett's ex," Braiden said simply. If he outed the fact that she still had the book Colin had given her back in high school, she was going to scream. Everything was too much all at once, and she could understand why Theo's body had just given out on him completely.

"Yeah," Colin confirmed and stuck out his right hand before

switching to his unburnt left, shifting Pepto to the opposite arm. The sweater he was previously wearing swayed on the crook of his elbow. "You know Scarlett?"

Braiden wasn't much of a posturing asshole usually, but apparently meeting the guy who he must have determined was the reason they had broken up had changed that. Not only did he not shake Colin's hand, he seemed to find great enjoyment from the fact that he knew things that Colin didn't. Out of anyone standing there, however, Scarlett felt like the one who was not in the know. "I'm also her ex-boyfriend," Braiden answered wryly.

Colin's outstretched hand dropped to his side, and he frowned. "Nice to meet you."

"Can't say the same, given the fire we had to put out," Braiden said coldly, gesturing to the fire trucks.

"I'm the one who put the fire out," Colin corrected matter-of-factly. Scarlett didn't know whether to laugh out loud or cry. With Braiden desperately trying to make some kind of a statement and Colin clearly missing the entire fight to nuance while he stood in all his shirtless, cat-wielding glory, she wanted to crawl into a hole and never come out. She wanted to say something to end this ridiculous display, but she couldn't take her eyes off Colin's chest, where the sketch she had given him when they had met on this exact day all those years ago was inked onto his left pec.

"Right." Braiden clicked his tongue obnoxiously. "You put it out with all your clothes."

"Not all of them. Just my jacket and a fire extinguisher," Colin again corrected. "The paramedic told me to take my shirt off because they wanted to put ointment on my wrist. The material is really scratchy where it's burned now, so I wouldn't be able to wear it anyway."

"You can't handle a tiny little burn on a shirt?" Braiden asked, the undertone making it clear that he had decided the most unmanly thing Colin could do was not wear a crispy shirt. Scarlett was over it. Over Braiden's attitude and over staring at the fucking cum face tattoo she had drawn in high school.

"He's autistic, so no, he's not going to wear the fucking shirt that's going to irritate him," Scarlett snapped at Braiden.

Braiden winced. "Oh, I didn't—"

"I don't think he even noticed that you were trying to puff out your chest and do some sort of dick-measuring contest anyway, so you might as well quit while you're behind."

"For the record, I did know what he was doing, because he didn't shake my hand. I just thought it was stupid, so I didn't participate." Colin shrugged and scanned Braiden from head to foot. "I have no clue who you are because she's never mentioned you, so you can't be that important. You clearly know who I am, though, so I'm still important."

Braiden's mouth dropped open. For all of Colin's declarations that he wasn't playing Braiden's game, he was in fact playing it perfectly. It only made Scarlett more pissed. "Okay, at least I didn't dump her and come crawling back."

"Both of you need to shut up," Scarlett scolded. "Braiden, I didn't break up with you because of Colin." It wasn't entirely the truth, but it was at least partially true, and if it hurt Braiden's fragile feelings less to lie, then she simply didn't care if it was morally wrong. "Colin, what the hell is this?" Her pointer finger jabbed into his chest, connecting with the forehead of the half-floral-faced woman.

"A tattoo." Sweet. Succinct. To the point. Not at all what she was asking.

"No shit!" She should keep her voice down so that Theo couldn't hear, but she was hoping his headphones were on the noise-canceling setting. "Why on earth would you get my art tattooed on your body?"

"Because I like it," Colin said, voice unwavering.

"I—" Scarlett raised her hands to her head, breathing deeply. "I can't deal with this right now. I just want to go home."

"Unfortunately," Braiden cringed, "that was what I was going to tell you when you interrupted to check on the well-being of your friend."

"We aren't friends," Colin stated evenly.

"Someone sedate me," Scarlett grumbled.

"Anyway," Braiden drew out the word. "We turned your electricity off. To prevent any future fires, we suggest leaving it off until repairs and an inspection are done. You need to find somewhere else to stay."

There were only a few options, but given that Harper was frequently in the throes of trying to make a baby, Scarlett decided her uncle's house was the best option. Because, after all of this, what she really needed was to sleep in her childhood bedroom where she had repeatedly hooked up with Colin.

"I'll go stay with my mom and uncle," Scarlett sighed, admitting defeat.

"I still can't find an apartment, or I'd let you stay with me," Colin said.

"I would offer, but... that's weird." Braiden smiled awkwardly.

"Oh, it's probably weird for me to offer that, too, then, huh?" Colin backtracked.

Braiden bobbed his head. "It's also weird to get a tattoo of your ex-girlfriend's artwork, man."

Colin's shoulders lifted, unbothered. "I don't regret it."

"Between that and the book she keeps in her nightstand, I'd say all of this is weird," Braiden said. And there it was. A new wrench thrown into this strange meeting, because she couldn't just get by with having any secrets. They needed to come to light on her birthday in a strange pissing match between her ex-boyfriends. Before Colin could wrap his head around the idea of her also keeping something of his, Scarlett turned on her heel and made her way over to Theo. Avoidance was a bad coping mechanism, but she felt like she had been bled and wrung out to dry, so Theo would be her best company right now. Once she sat down beside him in the ambulance, she took a few deep breaths to recenter herself and peered over at her ex-boyfriends, unsure if she should have left them to their own devices. For the most part, the penis-measuring seemed to be over, and they were casually chatting. Again she couldn't tell if that was good or bad.

"I'm sorry," Theo's small voice said beside her. Her head whipped in his direction to see his eyes closed and face in anguish.

"Oh, Theo," Scarlett said sadly. "You don't have to apologize. You did nothing wrong. You were just scared."

"Colin helped?" Theo asked.

Scarlett nodded. "He did."

Theo clicked the button he must have turned off to listen to her response, which in turn meant he wasn't expecting any further communication. Before he moved on, he got in one last sucker punch. "I like Colin."

"Me, too, bud." Scarlett sighed. "Me, too."

THIRTY-ONE

Colin
23 Years Old

"What if I meet someone tonight?" Pearl wiggled excitedly in the passenger seat and Colin glanced in her direction for only a second as he seamlessly parallel parked outside of the community center.

"Like a guy?" Colin asked cautiously.

"Yes!" Pearl squealed. "What if I have this incredible love at first sight moment with someone and we dance all night? You said there would be dancing, right?"

"There will be dancing, but it's a charity gala. It's mostly going to be adults. Also, I promised Walker that I wouldn't let you dance with random strangers, so the likelihood that you'll dance all night with someone you just met is zero," he said simply. "You're sixteen, so the likelihood that you'd fall in love is even lower."

Pearl pouted and crossed her arms over her chest. "You fell in love when you were eighteen. Most people say that's young, too."

Colin shifted the car into park and killed the engine before turning toward his sister. "Yes, I was young, and it didn't work out because I made a dumb decision based purely off an emotion that didn't stick. Don't do what I did. You have plenty of time left. Just be lucky that I talked Walker into letting you leave the house in that dress."

"Okay, one, you're too hard on yourself, and two, this dress isn't even scandalous." She looked down at her princess line dress with a frown.

"It makes you look older than you are, which is why Walker is not a fan, but it's a nice dress."

"I'm almost an adult," Pearl protested. "I should get to dress like one."

"I wouldn't have bought you the dress if I knew that was your reasoning. I agree with Walker. You don't need to grow up any faster, and you don't need to be dancing with boys or falling in love anytime soon." Colin unbuckled his seatbelt, and Pearl followed suit, huffing as she stepped out of the car and followed him around the front.

"What's with the big brother act? You're gone for years, and now you want to come in and pretend to protect me?" A shiver ran through her little body, and she brushed her hands over her arms a few times as they stepped onto the cobblestone path that led up to the grand entrance. "I should have brought a coat," she muttered. Colin paused and yanked off his jacket to drape it over her shoulders.

After his other jacket perished in the fire last month, he had ordered the same exact one from his stylist, Min, back in Maryland, and she had shipped it to him already customized with his corduroy elbow patches. The brown slacks and gray-brown blazer he was wearing now had come in the same shipment, and he had finally ordered some clothes for Theo as well. Theo's jackets and sweaters were customized with micro suede elbow patches, because while Colin loved the ridges of corduroy, Theo detested it and had looked at that fabric sample like it had personally offended him. In an attempted show of good faith toward Pearl and Cooper, Colin had also offered to get them things, too. Pearl had opted for the silky blush pink dress she was wearing now, and Cooper had readily declined, still angry and unwilling to accept any gifts if Colin was the one giving them.

"I'm sorry I didn't come back or talk to you all as often as I should have." Colin sighed, getting back to Pearl's comment. He had been getting the cold shoulder from Cooper for months now, and he was desperate to work his way back into his little brother's world again, but Pearl was more direct with her disdain over his absence. She was old enough to talk about more mature topics, at least the dumbed-down version, and he knew he was overdue for an explanation. "I was not well, Pearl."

"Not well," Pearl repeated before prodding further. "Not well as in sick, or not well as in not okay?"

"Mentally sick," Colin replied. "I got diagnosed, and I made some terrible choices based off a feeling I felt at the time, and that feeling didn't go away for years." He knew he was being vague, and that usually wasn't his style, but he had spoken to Walker and his therapist about it a few times, and they had both confirmed that he was allowed to share however much he wanted to share with whomever he wanted to share it with. "I wanted to come back, but I thought everyone was better off without me, especially in that state."

"That's not true." Pearl all but stomped her foot on the ground, outraged at the idea.

"I know that now, but even when I came back for holidays, if I stayed too long thinking about Archwood, I'd think about Scarlett, and my... feelings would get even worse."

Pearl smiled softly, and he dropped his eyes to the ground. "Are you still in love with her?"

"Yes." There was no use in lying about it. "I've tried not to be, but I can't help it." The breeze kicked up, and Colin could feel the chill now through his blazer and pinstripe dress shirt.

"You should dance with her tonight. If I don't get to, then at least one of us should get to dance with someone they love." Pearl pulled at the lapels of his jacket, hugging it around herself as they got closer to the large brick building.

"I *am* going to dance with someone I love. You." The only response he got was an eye roll as they reached the top of the stone staircase and a tall man wearing a catering outfit held open the door for them. Colin let Pearl enter first, waving her forward before he trailed behind her and jogged to catch up. Pearl was tiny, but she always moved at the speed of light, outpacing even his long legs. "Should I be offended that you don't want to dance with me?

"I love you, and of course I'll dance with you, but I also want to dance with someone who's not my brother. You're going to be really technical about it," she said.

Colin furrowed his brow. "Dancing is technical."

"It's also supposed to be fun," Pearl said.

They followed the line of guests dressed to the nines down the hall as they filed into the ballroom. Colin adjusted his shirt and nervously patted his pants downward over his thighs. "I think practicality and control are fun. Knowing the right steps makes it so you don't have to worry about doing the wrong thing. If it's choreographed and not left open to chance, then there won't be any awkward lags."

Pearl took his elbow as they moved through the large doorway into the heart of the gala. "I get that." She nodded and then tipped her head to the side. "But getting swept up in the excitement of not knowing what comes next is half the fun. Like... a kiss."

"A kiss?" Colin furrowed his brow and guided her to a table in the back corner.

"Yeah. Like that butterfly feeling you get when you aren't sure if it's going to happen, and then the relief when it does mixed with an explosion of feeling." Pearl pulled out a cushioned chair and sat down at the white-linened table.

"But I knew when I was going to kiss Scarlett because we agreed to it, or I just wanted to, so I did." He sat down beside

Pearl and shifted the plate and silverware so that everything was perfectly parallel. "Do you think that's where I'm going wrong? I'm not good with spontaneity. It makes me panic. I did put out a fire in her studio. That's spontaneous, right?"

"Um, sure," Pearl said slowly. Her face fell a moment later when she shrugged. "But I think where you went wrong is thinking she and all of us were better off without you to begin with. I know you were sad, but we could have helped you."

"Pearl." Colin swallowed and looked briefly at his sister before dropping his eyes to his hands. He thought they had moved past this line of questioning, but given the dejected look on her face, he was wrong. "I'm sorry."

"Don't be sorry, be better."

He shifted uncomfortably in his seat, trying to think of something that would better explain why he had made himself so scarce without featuring the worst parts. "Do you remember the night Walker and Roscoe told us about our parents' accident?"

"If I'm being honest, no." She turned toward him and gave him a flat smile. "I think I blocked it out."

"Well, I remember it vividly. I had a full-blown meltdown at the thought of any change at all, let alone the loss of our parents." Colin drummed his fingers on the table, fighting against the pang of sorrow and regret in his chest. "Walker was moving in, and I screamed at him that he wasn't allowed to because I didn't want him to disrupt the routine. I scared the shit out of you and Cooper. You were sobbing in the corner the whole time, and I couldn't pull myself together for long enough to see that I was making everything so much worse, no matter how much Walker, Piper, and Carter tried to calm me down. Change, especially the bad kind, makes me feel like my nerves are on fire and trying to crawl their way out from under my skin like a million little bugs writhing around just under the surface. I wasn't in control of my own body. After everything that happened with Scarlett, I truly thought that everyone would be better off if I made a new routine. College was a lot of change all at once, and the only reason I got through it was because of my hyperfixation on my studies. But I did it. I did it without hurting anyone because I wasn't around to hurt anyone."

"We missed you, Col," Pearl murmured. "None of us were thinking about the times when you can't control yourself. We were thinking about how you weren't around to make a stupid pun or beat us at Monopoly. I was thinking about how no one cared as much as you did about my questions. No one ran off to research my thoughts and came back with a dissertation as an answer. No one is like you, Colin."

"I guess that's true. No one has my exact DNA."

"No one has your exact personality, either." Pearl smiled. "You know, the personality of someone who takes my extremely heartfelt declaration about how much your family loves and misses you being around and turns it into something about science."

Colin let a smile spread across his face. "I love science." He shrugged. "I think it's safe to say that my original hypothesis was wrong, though. No one was better off without me."

"Very wrong. For that massive brain of yours, you're really very stupid sometimes."

Colin scoffed, shaking his head. "I might purposely step on your toes later."

"I'd like to see you try." She smirked. "I think you'll be too distracted all night, anyway."

"Why?" He pulled his eyebrows together and followed Pearl's responding nod toward the stage. Scarlett was always easy to pick out of a crowd due to her bright copper hair, but Colin was pretty certain he would be able to find her in complete darkness. The dandelion yellow floor-length dress she was wearing dipped at her cleavage, revealing even more as she bent to fix a microphone stand. He swallowed involuntarily and looked away. "Do you think she needs help with any of the setup?"

"Hmm," Pearl hummed. "Why don't you go ask, lover boy?"

"I hate that nickname." He grimaced. "I'm not a boy."

"Lover manchild, then."

He got up from his seat and brushed his hands against his thighs again, patting down the fabric. He had only washed this new set of clothes once, and they still felt a bit starchy. "The odds of me stepping on your toes just increased."

"I'll have to find a new dance partner, then," Pearl challenged.

"No." Colin pointed at her. "Walker would kill me."

"Walker doesn't have to know."

"The answer is still no, Pearl." He gave her a stern look, and she slumped in her seat, looking like a sad puppy.

"Piper did so much worse than me when she was my age."

"She did. She made poor choices and dated guys I hated so much that I punched one in the face. Don't make me punch anyone, Pearl. Pay attention to the way she is now with Leo, not the way that she was when she was your age. Now, stay put while I check in with Scarlett."

"Fine," Pearl grumbled.

Before he had a chance to think twice about it, Colin strode over to the other side of the ballroom all while fidgeting with his shirt. Scarlett's hair was down today, waves of smooth curls jerking back and forth as she wrestled with a mic stand. Even in a fight with an inanimate object she looked beautiful. The last few steps he took to get to her were careful and quiet, scared to startle her with his presence. In the months leading up to the gala, he had been a bit of a coward every time she mentioned the fundraiser, electing not to inform her that he would be in attendance. He couldn't figure out where the line was. Sometimes he thought she didn't mind his company at all, maybe even enjoyed it. The tight hug she had given him the day of the fire felt like it had scorched his skin more than the actual fire had. But if her unhappy reaction to his tattoo was any indication, she would no doubt feel like he was inserting himself into her life without her permission or without coincidence.

Trying to gauge what her reaction might be was exhausting, and due to the ongoing renovations at the studio, art classes had been postponed, so he didn't get a chance to tell her closer to the event like he had been planning. The last time he had seen her was the day after the fire, and it was only briefly to let him into the studio so he could collect some art supplies for Theo to continue to paint while everyone waited for the studio to open back up. He had been without her for long periods of time before, but after spending so much time with her in the studio, two months away made him feel like he was in a desert, waiting for a sip of water. And seeing her again wasn't just a sip, but an oasis.

Just as Colin suspected, when Scarlett's gaze flitted up from her vise grip on the stand, she clocked his presence, and her green-speckled eyes widened. "Do you want any help?" Colin asked tentatively.

"W-what are you doing here?" Scarlett stuttered.

"Your charity is sponsoring my work. Most of my coworkers are here." When her mouth parted in what looked like confusion, he continued, "If you mean what am I doing standing in front of you, I saw you messing with the microphone and thought I could help."

"You work for Sloan CRO?" She stopped maneuvering the stand for a moment, and Colin nodded. "What happened to Earth science?"

"I changed my mind long ago." He spoke carefully, unsure of how far he should take this conversation given that his special interest in his occupation had everything to do with her.

"Do you work for the lab or the clinic?"

He evaded her gaze and shifted his stance. "The lab. My bedside manner isn't great. Best to not be around people, or at least be with a bunch of other nerds." He pointed to her hands to avoid further questions that he knew he would answer if she asked. "Do you want help?"

Scarlett lifted her chin and set her shoulders back. "I can do it myself. I'm capable."

"I didn't say you weren't," Colin said. "I asked if you wanted help, not if you needed it. I know you don't need me."

Scarlett paused in the way she used to do, getting that distant look in her eyes. It didn't mean she wasn't listening or thinking about it, it was the exact opposite. The same way he was listening best when he wasn't making eye contact at all. Scarlett always retreated into her head for a moment before any outward response. He could tell the moment she decided because she stepped back from the mic stand and gestured for him to go ahead. "The clasp is really tight, and I forgot the last time we held an event here I had to hit it with something so I could adjust it."

It only took Colin a few seconds to lift himself up onto the stage, eager to do anything Scarlett asked. This was the closest she had really let him into her world outside of Theo and their conversation about the painting, and he felt tingly with excitement. He had to tell himself repeatedly that it didn't mean anything, but if he could just be her friend for a minute, then he would consider it a success.

The clasp was just as tight as Scarlett said it was, but Colin managed well enough, prying it free from the main rod and looking to Scarlett to tell him how high she wanted it. To his utter delight, she stepped closer, so close he could feel the heat of her skin just inches away from touching him. He thought she might close the gap, but she didn't, leaving him so unfulfilled that he thought about doing something rash, like pulling her in. Maybe he could do spontaneity if it meant he could touch her one more time. Her hands moved the extension piece up to her desired location, and she looked up at him, their faces only a breath away. His body hated it, both the near touch and the prolonged look she gave him that made him feel entirely too perceived before his gaze snapped away.

"This is good," she murmured.

"Hmm?" Colin hummed, distracted by how good it would feel to grip her body and drag her over to him.

"The stand?" Her voice was solid and confused. He wasn't exactly sure how he had managed to forget what he was doing in the span of ten seconds, but his brain finally caught on and bent the clasp back to hold the extension in place. "Thanks." There was no lingering like he wished there would be. Scarlett pulled away from his side and started toward the side stairs, seemingly nonplussed. If there was any tension at all between them other than her general distaste for his presence, then he couldn't tell. Then again, it wasn't like he could read people well. It was times like this when he wished Carter and Piper were present to extend their knowledge on social cues to him.

Frustrated with himself, Colin returned to Pearl at their round table and slumped into the seat.

"That was interesting," Pearl noted.

"Me failing at talking to Scarlett? I know." Colin ran his fingers through his hair then nervously combed the top of his head to fall over his cowlick.

"Failing?" Pearl cackled. "I don't think you failed. That was not a two-person job, nor did it require you both to stand unnecessarily close together."

Colin abruptly sat up straighter in his seat, his interest piqued. "That was good? I thought she was just making sure I was doing it right."

Pearl shrugged, looking amused. "I doubt it."

As much as Colin wanted his sister's assessment to be true, he also knew that Pearl had a habit of romanticizing anything and everything. In Pearl's world, no one just looked to look at something. Everything had a hidden meaning of love and affection, even when it didn't. "I think she was just doing her job."

"And I think you don't go out of your way to touch someone like that, especially someone you have history with. If she hates you as much as you seem to think she hates you, then I would think she'd keep her distance. I would think she wouldn't have even entertained a conversation with you at all." Pearl punctuated her statement by grabbing her glass from the table and taking a large sip of water. Colin drummed his fingers nervously on the table, a feeling seeping under his skin and making him rock forward and backward. Hope wasn't something he had wanted to hold on to, because he had all but convinced himself that Scarlett would never, ever consider being anything other than an acquaintance to him again. Their encounters at her art studio were becoming more friendly, but it still felt like there was a wall between them.

"I want to believe that," he finally said. He looked back over his shoulder, seeking out Scarlett in the crowd. He found her sitting at a table near the front, speaking animatedly to her mother and sister with a glass full of ice in her hand.

"Why don't you just tell her?" Pearl suggested. "Get her to dance with you, and tell her you're in love with her."

"Because I don't think she wants that," Colin said simply, reaching for his own glass and taking a sip before he looked over at Scarlett again, unable to help himself.

"Okay, so, you're trying to get her to like you again first?" Pearl asked.

"I'm not strategic about it. I'm not manipulating her into liking me again, I just do things to help her out because she deserves it, and I want her to be happy." Hand raised to a passing waiter, Colin leaned toward the man as he came to stop in front of him. "Can you please refill the waters at that table over there?" He gestured toward Scarlett's table, and the man nodded before beelining toward her with a pitcher of ice water. A lot had changed about Scarlett since they were eighteen—her confidence, for one—but some things hadn't changed at all. She never drank enough water. Sometimes at the studio, he would watch her go hours without it, and he would try to gently remind her that water was necessary to survival, especially when she started to massage her temples like she was about to get a headache.

"Thank God, people I know." The table jolted a bit as someone sat down to Colin's right. Colin shifted his attention to the kid and lifted his eyebrows in surprise to find his brother Cooper's best friend, Camden, wearing dress clothes and a bow tie. It was a massive change from the Crocs and gaming T-shirt Colin had seen him wear earlier that week. "My mom has been talking to sponsors for over an hour now, and I think I'm starting to get gray hairs," Camden said.

"You're thirteen," Pearl scoffed.

Camden raised a finger. "Thirteen and three quarters."

The shock of Camden's presence wore off in time for Colin to remember an important piece of information. "Your mom works for the foundation."

"Yep. She's in charge of the donations. She keeps telling old women that I'll dance with them, and people keep pinching my cheeks like I'm a child. I'm both bored and humiliated." Camden's head swiveled to look at Pearl as he grinned. "How much do I have to pay you to dance with me the whole night so I don't have to dance with any of them? I'll warn you right now that I only have five bucks."

Pearl laughed and shook her head. "Walker said I'm not allowed to dance with anyone but Colin."

Colin considered that for a moment before butting in. "He said you weren't allowed to dance with strangers."

Camden, who had previously deflated, sat bolt upright in his chair. "And I am not a stranger."

"True." Pearl leaned over the table toward Colin. "Dancing with him will be like dancing with a brother, anyway. Can I?"

"We aren't related," Camden grumbled.

While Colin was generally clueless about this kind of thing, he was not oblivious to the massive crush he knew Camden had on Pearl. Between Carter blatantly telling him about it and Walker watching Camden like a hawk every time he came over, there wasn't much Colin *could* miss. But, in the end, Camden Fortran was harmless. "You can dance with him and only him," Colin decided.

"Better than nothing," Pearl said, brightening a bit.

Camden lifted his chin. "I'm going to spin you so much that you throw up."

"Charming." Pearl rolled her eyes.

"If you want me to be charming, I can be charming."

Reaching across the table, Camden snatched a white rose from the centerpiece, and Colin watched in mild amusement as he held the stem out to Pearl. "For you. I would have brought you a whole bouquet of flowers, but I didn't know you were going to be here."

"And because you only have five dollars," Pearl said, taking the rose. Colin's attention was mostly focused on Camden now. Despite the childish way he went about things, the kid was surprisingly smooth. Within just a few seconds, he already had his crush agreeing to dance with him.

"I don't have a job yet, but I'll steal flowers for you." Camden's voice cracked a bit, as if he was trying to lower it into something more manly.

"I don't know if I can dance with a criminal," Pearl said.

"Too late. You took the rose. We're both criminals now, so we might as well dance until they catch us."

"I will dance with you *once*." Pearl pointed a stern finger at him.

"We'll see about that," Camden challenged.

"How do you do that?" Colin interrupted whatever thing Pearl was going to say next.

"Do what?" Pearl and Camden answered in unison.

"I can barely get Scarlett to talk to me, let alone dance with me. You," Colin gestured at Camden, "clearly like my sister, and you got her to agree to dance with you in less than a few minutes."

Camden's eyes widened comically as he jerked his head from side to side. "What? Me? No, I don't!"

"Ew," Pearl giggled. "I'm not into thirteen-year-olds. He's like my brother."

"Thirteen and three quarters!" Camden practically shouted. "And I am *not* like your brother. Not at all. We don't share any blood."

"I'm adopted. I don't share any blood with my brothers, either," Pearl pointed out. "Your name even starts with a C, and you're at my house so much you might as well live there. Like my brother."

A frustrated groan slipped from Camden's mouth before he turned fully to Colin, who had been doing his absolute best not to laugh at the whole encounter and had finally gotten his smile under control. "To answer your question, I guess I picked up some of my charm from my asshole dad. I got a front row seat to him flirting with countless women." Camden shrugged and then quickly added, "not that that's what I was doing."

"I unfortunately only have a dead dad," Colin said.

"Dad was also a huge dork, so I don't think he'd help you with getting Scarlett to dance with you," Pearl chimed in.

"He used to dance with Mom all the time," Colin reminded her.

"Oh. I guess I don't remember that." Pearl blinked slowly and cleared her throat before shaking her head and standing up quickly, rattling her silverware atop the table. "I'm going to use the restroom." The second Pearl was out of earshot, Camden broke Colin out of his longing gaze at the table across the room with newly filled water glasses.

"Is she okay?" Camden asked.

Colin peered across the room just as Pearl exited the double doors that led toward the restrooms. "She's just using the bathroom."

"No, she got up after you talked about your parents dancing. I don't think she actually has to use the bathroom."

"I didn't realize that was why she got up." That small voice Colin had pushed away so many times told him once again that everyone was better without him. Not five minutes into the gala, and he had already made Pearl leave the table. Worse, he didn't even know what he had done wrong. "Did I upset her?"

"I don't think it was you. I've forgotten a lot of things about my dad from when he was around, but it doesn't hit me hard because my dad was a jerk. I think if he wasn't a jerk, I'd be sad to forget any memories of him." Camden swallowed and reached for a water glass on the table, taking a swig. It was frustrating that no matter how hard he paid attention, Colin would never understand the same subtleties that Camden had picked up on with ease. He would never catch when Scarlett was upset without a verbal confirmation. If he couldn't tell when his own sister was unhappy, then it would be the same with Scarlett if he ever got another chance with her.

"Shit," Colin said glumly. "I wouldn't have known if you didn't notice."

"Catching on to other people's emotions isn't your thing." Camden shrugged. "But action is. I bet now that you know, you'll do something about it."

He was right. Colin was already calculating ways he could cheer Pearl up. Someone in their family had to have a video of their parents dancing to show her so she didn't have to remember. It was hard to speak about their parents, but maybe not speaking at all wasn't the best option, either. The memories needed to be kept alive. Just like Scarlett's brother's memory needed to be kept alive. "Action," Colin murmured.

"That's the key for how I got Pearl to agree to dance with me, too. And how I'll get her to cheer up as soon as she's back." Camden took another rose from the centerpiece and held it out to Colin. "Sometimes being bold is the answer. Sometimes it's not, but my dad's one good quote was that 'you miss one hundred percent of the shots you don't take.'"

"That's actually a Wayne Gretzky quote," Colin corrected.

"I'm not surprised he took someone else's quote and used it to hit on hot younger women, but that's not the point." Camden shook the stem a bit, the flower still outstretched to Colin. Colin finally took it, a curious expression crossing his face. "Her dad left, didn't he?" Camden asked.

"He did."

"If I were her, I'd want someone to stay," Camden said simply.

Colin felt his face lose all its color as he peered across the room at Scarlett again, a knot in his stomach. "And I left exactly like her dad did."

Camden cringed. "Yeah, that's probably why she's not giving you a second shot so easily."

"So, then, what do I do?" Nausea roiled in Colin's stomach, and he thought he might throw up. He knew that Scarlett would be upset when he broke things off, but he hadn't realized that she would take it as yet another person who had left like her dad, or even her brother, who didn't exactly have a choice but to go.

"That seems like a pretty obvious answer to me," Camden said. "You stay."

With a resolute nod, Colin agreed. "I stay."

Thirty-Two

Scarlett
23 Years Old

The moment the keynote speaker started droning on about the latest scientific discoveries, Scarlett tuned him out like she had that catalytic AP Chemistry class from back in high school. She knew she should be paying attention, especially because those scientific discoveries were of great importance to her brother's foundation, but she was fairly certain that Colin and his coworkers were the only people at the gala who could understand a word of what Dr. Seymour Bishop was saying. She thought at one point she had heard the word "covalent," and that was about as far as she could pinpoint what he was talking about. The only thing that she could focus on was Colin, both the past and present versions of him. Any mention of science had her thinking of sex performance charts, which meant she thought of them with the slightest provocation (as Colin had once told her: everything is science). What she now knew he was hiding under his shirt thanks to an electrical fire—undoubtedly science.

With her routine up in the air and her mind untethered by the studio, Scarlett's imagination had run completely rampant. Lately, she felt like she was always on the brink of doing something reckless.

She had peeked at Colin's table enough times to know that he had brought his sister to the gala with him, and the fundraising coordinator's son seemed to know Colin well enough to sit at the table animatedly chatting with him for the majority of the dinner and introductory speeches. A small pang of sadness pricked her heart at the thought that she no longer knew what they could be talking about. The dynamic he had with his family was still the same, though, familiar in all the ways that she used to enjoy and find comfort in.

A cleared throat beside Scarlett made her pull her attention away from Colin's table. Harper was staring at her with wide, expectant eyes and nodding her head toward the stage. There was something Scarlett was supposed to be doing, and given the blank stares in the crowd and the emptiness of the stage, she had clearly missed whatever was going on. When had Dr. Bishop even finished his speech? It must have been sometime between her reminiscing on her first chemistry lesson and her prom night.

"Beautiful painting!" a voice shouted from somewhere behind her. She whipped around to find Colin looking in her direction with raised eyebrows and a lift of his program sheet.

"Amazing!" The fundraising coordinator's son echoed the sentiment.

"I definitely want to know more about it!" Pearl agreed in a loud voice, making all three of them sound like hecklers at a comedy show. Harper had her hand pressed into her mouth to stop a laugh from escaping, and in all the commotion, Scarlett finally found the one brain cell in her head dedicated to remembering things, picked up her clipboard with her speech, and jumped up from her seat to bolt toward the stage.

The microphone made a loud feedback noise when Scarlett tapped it to check it was working, and the entire crowd winced. "Everything is going so swimmingly," she said with a nervous edge. Chuckling from the audience made her loosen her shoulders a bit. "I guess I'm supposed to talk about the painting I made for one of the auction pieces." She twisted a bit to gaze at the displayed canvas sitting on the corner of the stage in its large ornate frame before peeking at her notes. "Originally, it was supposed to be a basic portrait, but I spent months dragging my feet and staring blankly at an old photo of my brother smiling up at a camera like he didn't have a care in the world, and I could not bring myself to—" She swallowed and choked back her emotion as she held up the photo she was supposed to copy and knew that the same photo must be projected on the screen behind her as planned.

"I didn't want to paint him because he seemed so perfect on his own. I remember when this picture was taken, because it was my birthday. I remember being so jealous of all the attention he was getting at my party because it was just a few days after he was formally diagnosed. I was so young and didn't really realize the severity of what was going on at the time. I just knew it was my birthday, and everyone was sad but Tucker. Now I wish I could give my brother a hundred more of my birthdays." She wiped at the tears starting to streak down her face and shook her head to clear it. "Someone I know suggested that I didn't need to make his portrait perfect, I just needed to make it my own, and I think Tucker would have agreed."

Scarlett found Colin at his table with his eyes closed, slowly rocking in his chair, and she felt the corners of her mouth tip up. It was like she could see him absorbing every word. To someone who didn't know him, it might look like he wasn't paying attention, but she knew he was.

"So, I made it my own. Despite having photo evidence, I actually remember his shirt being blue that day, not red, so I rewrote history a bit and gave him a blue shirt." A small laugh escaped Scarlett's mouth, and she found Pearl's smiling face in the crowd, then Harper's, giving her a tear-filled and encouraging nod. "The florals splitting his face and taking over half of the frame represent the life my brother brought to every room. The life he still brings to a room, even in his passing. The legacy he left behind and all the change he's making. There's a white rose for each of the birthdays he's missed, and a carnation for every child this foundation has sponsored since we were founded. Eighty-three children. Some of whom are no longer with us. All lives we've changed from the donations received from people like you. For every ten thousand dollars we've raised for Sloan CRO to find a cure, I've painted a daisy, which doesn't have a huge significance except that 'daisy' kind of sounds like 'day,' and I hope the funding is getting us one day closer to a cure."

The room was so quiet, but all eyes were focused on her, except for Colin, still swaying in his seat. His eyes were no longer closed, but he was staring intently off to the side. He and everyone else were hanging on her every word.

"I think my brother would be proud of what we've accomplished. I think he would also tell me I'm gross for getting all sappy." The audience laughed, and Scarlett finally let herself smile all the way. "This painting represents everything important to this foundation and everything wonderful about my brother all in one. As we carry on with the music and dancing portion of the evening, there are several silent auction pieces lining the room for you to bid on, among them, this painting. I hope you'll consider donating tonight. If there's one thing I've learned, it's that sometimes changing the world is as simple as changing one person's life. That, and changing the world often requires a lot of money." The crowd laughed, and she beamed across the ballroom. "And as we round out the speaking portion of the evening, I wish you all an open-bar-filled night to loosen you up as you dance and network. Thank you all for coming."

The DJ immediately started up the music from the booth on the corner of the stage, and Scarlett was grateful that it took away some of the pressure of her walking down the steps. Chatter and the usually nervous energy of a room reluctant to dance followed her back to her seat. Dancing had been removed and added back to the event list multiple times, but she had gotten the board to agree with it by insisting that unlike other galas, this one would be fun. The set list would milk the generational bond between old and millennial music to keep people drifting down nostalgia lane. Like a wedding, minus the songs that had people screaming about sweat dripping down their balls. All of this coupled with the biggest donation of the evening—the alcohol—would keep the checkbooks opened. Or, at least, she hoped it would. The dance floor was still empty.

"Harper," Scarlett whispered to her sister. "Go dance with your husband."

"Do I have to?" Harper whined. "I've been here since noon. I'm exhausted."

"It's a slow song, and I don't have a partner, so yes. Someone has to start this off."

"I can be your partner." The deep tenor of Colin's voice beside her chair made Scarlett's face instantly heat. Her body continued to react to him no matter how much she begged it not to, and it was beyond frustrating. Earlier, when she had brushed against him while he fixed the mic stand, she thought she might combust. No words formed on her lips as she stared up at him. He was looking down at his hands and fidgeting with them, and she wondered if his body had the same reaction to hers as she had to him. Touch starved and all the while knowing that it would be a terrible choice to go back down that road. "I'm asking you to dance if that was not clear. I figured I'd ask because I want to, but obviously you don't have to say yes."

Scarlett looked at the empty dance floor, back at Colin, and then back at the dance floor once more, fighting with herself on her answer. If she had an ounce of self-preservation, she would say no, but the voice telling her that Colin could help her get the party started was making a strong case. "Okay," Scarlett finally decided, slowly getting out of her chair. She didn't dare look at her sister, who she imagined was shooting daggers at Colin.

"Really?" A smile bloomed across Colin's face, and he held

out a hand to her. She took it gingerly and stepped away from her table.

"Just one song," Scarlett said, grimacing as they made their way onto the wide-open dance floor. "Or at least until other people start dancing, too. I thought people would be into this, and it looks like I was wrong."

Colin dropped her hand, and the whiplash had her wanting to turn right back around to go sit at her table again. "I'll get people to dance," he declared. He jogged back over to his table, stranded in the middle of the floor alone. Not two seconds after agreeing to dance with him, she was already regretting saying yes. She pinched the bridge of her nose and let out a slow breath, steeling herself against the abandonment. "Did you drink enough water?" Scarlett's hand fell away from her face, and she looked over to find Colin beside her again. "Do you need to drink some before we dance?"

"We're still dancing?"

"Yes? Did you change your mind?" The confusion was clear as day on his face.

"You asked me to dance, then immediately left," Scarlett clarified.

Colin shook his head. "No, you said you needed people to dance, so I just told my sister and Camden to dance." He gestured to where Pearl was being spun around by the fundraising coordinator's son in the very center of the floor. "I'm not going to leave, I promise."

Scarlett watched as Pearl giggled on a particularly aggressive spin. A slow breath released from Scarlett's lungs. "One dance," she decided. Colin held his hand out again. Folding her fingers in his felt equal parts natural and like a precursor to something terrible. She had to remind herself that no matter how charming Colin could be, he would eventually leave, and the best thing for her to do was to never go far enough with him that she would be disappointed when he inevitably left her high and dry.

But when Colin pulled her in, his free hand finding her waist with a firm touch, Scarlett found herself responding in kind, her palm resting on his shoulder and her stiff fingers relaxing into his warmth. "I only know how to waltz."

"Uh... I don't know how to do that." Scarlett bit her lip. "I didn't know we were going to do an actual dance, I thought we were just going to freestyle."

"I don't freestyle," Colin said simply. "I'll lead. Follow me?"

"I'm going to have to because I don't know what's happening."

"It's a box step in a one, two, three, one, two, three count. I practiced a bit with a YouTube video before we got here." Colin looked down at his feet and lifted one foot, holding it in the air. "You'll do the opposite. Step back."

After several box steps, Scarlett started to move without direction. Colin's hand somehow ended up at the small of her back, and she let their bodies move closer together with the music. Once she was confident enough, Colin added exactly two variations to their box step, one spinning her under his arm and the other rolling her out and back in. He wasn't bad at dancing, albeit extremely technical, but the last time she had danced with him was at their senior prom, and dancing was the least important thing that had happened that night.

THIRTY-THREE

Colin
18 Years Old

"You, Colin Hartrick, are going to the prom?"

Colin looked at his perplexed uncle at the bottom of the stairs, suddenly nervous that Walker could see right through him. Walker had missed one hundred percent of the things Colin didn't outwardly tell him, but that was the beauty of being the sibling who rarely hid anything from anyone. When he did need to hide things, no one was the wiser. Dishonesty wasn't his favorite pastime, so Colin carefully walked the line, only giving out truthful bits of information.

"I am." Colin nodded. He was, in fact, going to the prom.

"I think that's great!" Talia beamed from beside Walker. After their brief spat—and a makeout session that Carter had accidentally interrupted—Walker and Talia were back on friendly terms, yet still inconceivably not together. Colin just didn't get it. They were clearly in love with each other, a fact every single one of his siblings had pointed out to them, but Walker insisted he needed to attend therapy before starting anything with Talia. Colin couldn't imagine a world where he was in love with someone and didn't tell them outright that that was the case. What was the point of dancing around the subject when you could declare it and either move on from rejection or move forward with acceptance? That was why he had plans that very night to tell his girlfriend exactly how he felt.

All of the research had been done to back up the conclusion Colin had come to: he was in love with Scarlett. While most articles were wishy-washy in their determination of what exactly love was, there was a science behind it that he found most intriguing. The articles he'd printed off in case Scarlett wanted proof and the typed summary he had created with pictures and diagrams wrapped in the text to give her something visual to look at explained it all. Beyond the obvious release of hormones such as dopamine, serotonin, and oxytocin, there were three basic components to love. He had had a sexual desire for Scarlett from minute one, so that was an easy enough box to check. Infatuation came next. He could almost replay in his head how he had fallen for her like it was his favorite movie. He had become obsessed with the way her brain worked. The way she dressed. The way she talked and rambled and stuttered. God, even the way she breathed was interesting to him, especially when they were in bed and her breathing picked up speed with her heart rate. He couldn't get enough.

The final nail on the proverbial coffin was attachment. Similar to the way he was attached to his family members, Colin found himself attached to Scarlett. The loss of his parents had upended a routine that had been in place for years. The loss of that comfort and companionship had felt like a gaping wound, a puzzle that was missing a single piece to complete it and therefore would be unfinished forever. Scarlett didn't fix that particular puzzle, but maybe she would become an edge piece, a foundational part of him that he needed to hold up the rest of the puzzle and even the gap where his parents were missing.

Colin was in love. There was no denying it, and he would never deprive Scarlett of any of his thoughts. He had promised her as much. So, he endeavored to tell her that, and hoped that it would end with them tangled together and naked until morning. A proper prom, if the movies and books were correct. He had researched that as well, needing this night to be as normal and stereotypical after he kept going down rabbit holes with his search history every time he had a therapy session.

Dr. Thomlinson's questions had started to grate on Colin enough for him to do his own research to counteract them. Sure, he thought that eye contact felt aggressive, but he could do it. He could hold someone's gaze if he tried—it wasn't as if he was incapable. And if he often didn't understand the emotion or underlying meaning behind someone's words, that didn't mean there was something wrong with him, it just meant that he needed to pay more attention to someone's body language so he could know that if their face twitched a certain way, they were angry. Everyone had fabrics and materials they didn't like. He knew for a fact his mom had despised the feeling and sound of Styrofoam. Once, when it was raining, his dad had complained about the chafing of his cargo shorts. It was common knowledge that certain things were a sensory nightmare, right down to the idiom of nails on a chalkboard, so if his reaction to certain textures was a bit over the top, he could tone it down. Loud noises were the hardest of all, but maybe his parents had done him a disservice by not exposing him to them more frequently. He could control himself, and he would tonight. He would dance with Scarlett to loud music on a crowded dance floor, and he would tell his psychiatrist that he'd had no problems. Mind over matter.

The declaration Colin was ready to proclaim to Scarlett was hard-won. He had practiced a hundred times in the mirror while looking into his own eyes. It was a bit easier knowing that the reflection was himself, but it was still uncomfortable. It felt forced coming out of his mouth because he was so focused on not screwing up the eye contact, but he had gotten good at reciting the verbiage he had heard in movies and read in books. There was a lack of feeling behind it because he had scripted it and written it down to memorize, but he could manage to not count in his head while holding eye contact after several rounds. The entire thing had made him irrationally angry at himself before he got it down, and at one point he'd had to take a break, using that time to perfect his attire for the night. He had found he was talented at tying a tie and lost himself in several YouTube tutorials on harder knots.

"Is that a Double Windsor?" Walker asked, squinting at Colin's tie.

"It is. Does it look okay?" Colin dipped his chin down but couldn't quite see the knot from that angle.

"Looks great. Is... there a reason it needs to?"

"It would be annoying if it was crooked," Colin replied.

"He means are you trying to impress a girl," Talia chimed in.

"A redhead, maybe, since you said that was your type." Walker pumped his eyebrows suggestively.

Colin swallowed. "Oh. As far as the tie goes, I was mostly just practicing different knots." Another partial truth that skirted around the real truth.

"As far as the tie goes?" Walker said slowly, narrowing his eyes at Colin. The discomfort of his gaze made Colin shift on his feet. "Well, I hope you get to dance with whoever you want to dance with." There was really only one person Colin would ever dance with, and he was about to say as much until he was saved by his sister coming down the steps behind him. "Piper, what the hell is that dress?" Walker huffed.

"A normal one for a high school girl." Talia smacked Walker's arm, making him flinch. Colin swiveled to see Piper stomping down the steps in a floor-length, blush pink dress with a slit high up on her thigh.

"I thought you went shopping with her for the dress," Walker grumbled

"She did," Piper said sweetly. "I know you insist that I dress like a nun, but I'm not a child."

"Let it be known that I think your dad would despise that dress," Walker said.

"You aren't going to get me to change by playing the dead dad card." Piper folded her arms over her chest.

"Fine," Walker grumbled. "No dancing with boys."

"Isn't that hypocritical?" Colin cut in. "You just told me you hope I dance with whoever I want to dance with."

A few steps behind him, Piper grabbed on to Colin's shoulders and squeezed. "You are absolutely right. Super hypocritical."

"I'm usually right." Colin shrugged.

"The difference is that Piper has experience with lying to me and sneaking behind my back. You do not," Walker said. Colin looked down at the floor, fighting back the urge to correct his uncle. Sneaking behind Walker's back was his forte now. Even Piper knew that, but their sibling pact was still well intact, and he knew both she and Carter would never rat him out. "I will concede that Piper's allowed to dance with people as long as it's not Dickwit or anyone associated with him."

"Who is Dickwit?" Colin inquired.

"Harden," Piper answered before responding to Walker, "I don't want to dance with him, so that shouldn't be a problem." As Piper descended the last few steps, one of her heels slipped off. A squeak escaped her mouth as she flailed before Colin stepped out and caught her arm, righting her.

Colin looked at her feet and frowned. "Why did you wear stilettos when you can't walk in them?"

"Because I look hot in them. Why are you going to Prom when you won't be able to stand the noise?" Piper shot back. She knew exactly why he was going, so he responded for Walker's sake.

"Because I think our parents would want me to experience it at least once." It was part of the reason, to be sure. His mother had routinely expressed how badly she wanted him to have friends and a love life. Piper's face fell, and she gave him a quick bob of her head, her black-tipped blond hair swaying. It wouldn't normally be obvious to him that she was upset, but these days he could hear her crying in her room late at night. He never knew what to do about it and figured she was hiding it from everyone on purpose.

"Speaking of your parents," Walker murmured, holding up his phone, "your mom would roll over in her grave if I didn't get a few pictures. Act like you like each other and stand a bit closer."

"She's my sister. I *do* like her." Colin furrowed his brow and stepped closer to Piper. "I don't have to act like it."

"Thanks, Col." Piper set her hands on her hips in a pose beside him. Once again, Colin considered that he was reading too much into her reaction to a mention of their parents. She didn't look the least bit upset, smiling from ear to ear. He folded his hands in front of himself, always unsure what he should be doing with them in a picture or otherwise, and offered a tight smile in Walker's direction.

"I think I got one. Colin looks like I pulled his teeth to be there, but Piper looks nice," Walker noted.

"You both look great." Talia beamed. Colin made his way toward the door, and a hand on his arm stopped him in his tracks. He turned to find Piper biting her lip.

"I meant to ask you, can you drive me there?"

"I already told you, you can take the van," Walker called out, jangling his keys in the air. "I'm not going anywhere, and both Pearl and Coop are spending the night at a friend's house. Carter is at the movies, most likely with a girl he didn't tell me about. Plus, Tal is here, so she can drive me if I need to go somewhere."

"Um..." Piper looked over her shoulder and then up at Colin with an expression he couldn't read at all and stared for an uncomfortable amount of time before dropping her voice into a low whisper. "Please drive me."

"Why?" Colin wrinkled his forehead.

"I'll explain in the car. *Please*," Piper begged. Colin let loose a long sigh and nodded resolutely, turning to peer back at Walker, who was looking confusedly in their direction. "Actually, we want to drive together, but thanks for offering," Piper called back and whipped open the front door, stumbling onto the porch. Colin followed after her and shut the door behind them as he pulled his keys from his pocket.

It took all of three seconds after they had gotten settled in his Audi for him to ask, "Why am I driving you? We're going to have to make several pit stops before the prom because I had a bunch of plans, so I hope you're okay with that."

"That's fine." Piper nodded. "Sorry. I just don't like driving."

"You don't like driving," Colin repeated. She had driven plenty of times, so he didn't see why it was suddenly a problem.

"Okay, fine. I'm *scared* of driving," she mumbled and looked out the window. Now that he thought about it, he couldn't think of a single time Piper had driven anywhere since their parents had died. It was on both of his parents' list to buy her a car before they had died, and they'd gone so far as to visit several dealerships. Colin figured the reason she hadn't been driving was because Walker hadn't yet gotten around to getting her a car himself and she hadn't really needed to drive anywhere. Before, Piper had taken the car to do mundane tasks all the time, so it maybe should have occurred to him that she hadn't in a long while, but he had been almost entirely focused on Scarlett lately.

"Why are you scared?" he asked.

Piper scowled. "I think that's pretty obvious."

"It's not obvious to me. Is it because of the statistics?"

"No, it's because our parents died in a fucking car crash, Colin," Piper snapped.

He turned the ignition, and warm air started blowing through the vents. "Don't raise your voice at me." He didn't often have to pull rank on his sister, but he would pull it out when she was being unreasonable. "I get your fear, and I'll drive you, but don't snipe at me when the root cause of that accident was alcohol, Piper. Something you apparently had no problem dabbling in earlier this year, so sorry if I didn't immediately understand your reservations about driving."

"It was someone else drinking that caused it, so it's valid to be afraid of other people driving on the same roads as me. And how many times are you going to make me apologize for drinking? I'm sorry, okay? Don't you ever just want the grief to stop?" Piper's voice cracked. "Of course you wouldn't get it. You're just stoic, and nothing about our parents' death seems to bother you. How are you okay all the time?"

"I'm not fucking okay, Piper!" Colin yelled. He didn't often get angry, but when he did, it felt like it came out of nowhere. He took a deep breath and steadied himself before he broke down completely and she'd see the difference between their grieving styles to its full extent. His grief felt like it was on a delayed timer, bottling up and exploding in what felt like random spurts that he couldn't control. "Everyone thinks I'm okay, but it's just that I don't react to it the same way as all of you. My therapist is running this assessment on me, and I'm starting to think—"

"Assessment?" Piper straightened. "What kind of assessment?"

"It's nothing. He's wrong, so it doesn't matter. It can't be what he's thinking." Colin shook his head and let out a slow breath. "Look, I'm sorry for bringing up the drinking again. I'm just worried about you, and I think if something happened to you, too, I would lose my damn mind. I only feel okay when I'm with Scarlett. She's good with me when I'm struggling."

"Are we going to pick her up right now?" Piper broke out into a smile.

Colin felt himself smile as he put the car in reverse and started to pull away from the curb. "First, I have to drop by Julie's Flower Shop to pick up her corsage, and *then* we're going to pick up Scarlett." He pulled out onto the street, his insides vibrating with nerves. "While you're here, you're good at lying, right? How do I lie about where I'm going after Prom tonight so Walker doesn't know I'm in a hotel room with Scarlett?"

"Jesus." Piper gasped. "Going straight for the jugular with the questions. Um, I'd probably just tell them that you're spending the night at a friend's."

"I don't have any friends."

"Yes, you do. Scarlett is your friend, right? And you're always hanging out with Kashvi, too. I guess you can't use either of them, though, because that would be suspicious. Maybe just make up someone random? You might run into some trouble if he asks about them later and they don't actually exist, but you could give it a shot. Walker would question me, but I don't think he'll question you. You're eighteen, and you never lie."

"I've been lying for months," Colin said proudly.

Piper whipped her head in his direction. "So not just when we snuck you out of the window?"

"Nope. I don't have Mathletes on Wednesdays. I didn't even sign up for the team this year," he boasted.

"Scandalous." Piper laughed. "You must really like her, then."

"I love her," Colin said. The words came out a lot stronger than when he had said them in the mirror before, and he figured that was a good sign. It was also the first time he had said it out loud to anyone, and for some reason, it made sense that it would be Piper who he would tell first. She was always the most in tune with other people's emotions, while Carter caught on to a joke or social cues quickest.

Piper stayed silent for a long moment before she finally spoke. "I'm really happy for you. Is this scary for you?"

"I mean, I'm scared she won't love me back," Colin considered.

"I don't think you have to worry about that. When we're at school, she looks at you the way Mom looked at Dad." Colin perked up at that, and a smile returned to his face again. "I meant more like... you aren't worried about losing her like our parents?"

"Not really." Colin said. He had thought about this before and had already asked the proper questions and calculated the outcomes. "I have the same chance of losing her to sudden death as I do you or Carter or Pearl or Cooper. Granted, there are a ton of factors that go into it, but I already know that Scarlett doesn't have the RUNX1 gene mutation that her brother had, so I can most likely cross Acute Myeloid Leukemia off the list. She was tested for it forever ago."

"I have no idea what that means."

"If she had familial platelet disorder from that gene, she'd have a twenty to fifty percent lifetime risk of getting a blood cancer," Colin replied. It had always been his norm to research every little thing, but his research on Tucker was starting to rival for his attention the most.

"Okay, but what about the saying 'when it rains, it pours'?" Piper asked. "Wasn't it already unlikely for us to lose both our parents? Who's to say the odds will ever be in our favor again?"

"I think that saying has more to do with people's ability to recognize the bad when they're already in a negative spot. Or, I guess, people can put themselves in a situation where the odds are higher. That's why I don't have a problem with driving or with the idea that Scarlett will die, because those are all risks that I can't control much. I *do* have a fear that you'll drink and something will happen to you because of choices you made that you could have mitigated risk for." Colin pulled around a corner on Main Street and saw the flower shop in the distance.

"That's a very sweet way to say you're worried about me and think I'm irresponsible." Piper let out a small scoff.

"You aren't usually irresponsible." He found a parking spot right outside the shop and meticulously started to parallel park.

"Thanks."

"You should choose a corsage. I think they have some premade ones you could get. Maybe a sunflower one."

"It's weird to get a corsage from your brother," Piper protested as she was getting out of the car.

"You could always take your own advice and tell everyone you got it from someone made-up."

"Clearly, they have to be tall, dark, and handsome, with the temperament of a golden retriever," Piper said.

"You can't date someone with a similar personality. It'd be like hanging out with yourself. Scarlett, for example, is an artist who hates chemistry, loves to dress in bright colors, and frequently forgets to take her birth control pills," Colin said, holding up a finger for each of his bullet points. "I suck at painting. I love chemistry. I dress in cool or neutral colors. And I'm the one who reminds her to take her birth control pills." He reached for the door and held it open for Piper, who walked under his arm into the flower shop.

She looked back over her shoulder. "How do you remind her?"

"I have a reminder set on my phone, and I call her to take it and stay on the phone till she does." Colin shrugged.

Piper scrunched her eyebrows together in confusion. "She can't just put a reminder on her phone to do it herself?"

"She has one," he explained. "But it's like her brain runs at a billion beats per second unless she's focused on a project. So the alarm will go off on her phone, and when she's halfway to the sink to get a glass of water to take the pill, she'll have moved on to something else."

"Chaotic," Piper giggled.

"I like her chaos. She fills in all the gaps in conversation so I don't have to worry about what I should be doing or if I should be talking more or less. And she laughs at my jokes." Colin couldn't help but feel prideful about how much Scarlett loved his brand of humor.

"She likes your really terrible puns?" Piper teased. "She's a keeper."

THIRTY-FOUR

Colin
18 Years Old

Prom was a terrible idea.

The music was too loud. The crowd was too loud. Everything was so fucking *loud*. Colin could barely think, let alone remember his own name. Even the slow song he had all but suffered through to dance with Scarlett had felt like a ticking time bomb for the out-of-control feeling taking over his body. He had sworn to himself he would last at least an hour so Scarlett could have the night she deserved. It had only been fifteen minutes, and he had gone completely nonverbal in the first five minutes under the harsh flashing lights, loud voices, and uncomfortable amount of bodies touching him even on the outskirts of the mob of dancing high schoolers.

"Are you okay?" Scarlett's voice called out to him, but he kept trying to piece her words together to make any sense and couldn't come up with anything remotely coherent. It felt like he was hearing the auditory form of hieroglyphics, shapes and symbols and emotions and *noise* dancing around in his head and never letting up. He was pretty sure his body was shutting down. A lesser version of going into shock. "Colin?"

Again, Colin couldn't respond, so he let his shaking hands wrap around himself, as if he were trying to hold in all the broken pieces of his consciousness. Warm hands cupped over his ears, creating a sort of echo chamber around the muffled sound of someone speaking. The loud sound came back a second later when a new warmth on his arm yanked him off his feet. He stumbled off in the direction he was being pulled. His heartbeat was everywhere all at once, in his ears, bouncing around in his skull, and wreaking havoc on his stomach.

The sound was finally gone a few seconds later, but nothing about his body's reaction had changed. His still-spiking heart rate and the tightness in his chest made him feel like peeling his skin off.

"Close your eyes," Scarlett's voice whispered. "Breathe in and out." Her hands found his ears again and blocked out any remaining sound. He wasn't sure if he had heard her at all or if his body just always responded to hers the way it should, but he shut his eyes. Slow breaths loosened the vise grip on his chest until it didn't feel like he was having a heart attack anymore. Then again, maybe that was what it was. He reached up and prodded at his face on both sides to verify there was no loss of feeling. This wasn't the first time this had happened to him. Noise hadn't been the cause of every one of these meltdowns, either, but he always felt the need to check if he was dying of a stroke. His eyes slowly squinted open.

"I-I," he stammered. "Shit. Sorry."

"It's okay." Scarlett's soft, soothing voice floated into his ears, and he could now feel her hands clinging to his arm. He had no idea how they had ended up in the hallway sitting on the floor, or how he had ended up half lying on her, but his body was starting to come back into its own.

"I'm sorry," Colin murmured again. "I can't do it. I thought I could handle it."

"It's really okay," she said. "We came. I got to wear a pretty dress, and you bought me a corsage. We danced."

Colin covered his face with his hands, groaning. "We danced for one song."

"That counts. It was loud in there, even for me."

He peeked out from behind his hands. "Your dress *is* really pretty, Red." She was wearing a shimmering emerald green number with a ribbed bodice that dipped at her cleavage. That was what he should have been focused on. Maybe if he had just stared at the soft pillows of her chest in the ballroom, then they wouldn't have had to leave.

"Thinking of me naked?" Scarlett bumped her shoulder against his.

"Yes." He nodded. "Since the second I picked you up." Barring the interlude of sensory overload, that was true. He had thought about unzipping her dress and sucking one of her breasts into his mouth so many times in the car that he felt like he should have gotten an award for even making it to the dance after he dropped Piper off at the front and they went to park.

"What do we think about the shoes?" Her foot kicked out from under her dress, and Colin smiled down at her white Converse.

"Practical. My sister is wearing crazy heels that she can't walk in. I like that you're sensible."

"No one can really see my feet under the dress, so I didn't think it was necessary to wear heels. Someday I want to get customized ones with the little embroidered flowers." She leaned into him a little more, a comfort he freely accepted, his hand finding hers and slotting their fingers together. Normally, Scarlett would start to tell a long story, but there was an occasional moment after orgasm or times when he was mentally spent that they would just sit in silence. Colin could stay like that, huddled together with her for hours, ignoring anything outside the comfort of her touch, and disappearing into a quiet peace.

They must have been near the bathroom because as they sat in silence, a few people meandered in and out of the ballroom and around the corner before returning to the dance floor. Colin barely paid them any mind until a loud couple of boys stumbled out of the doors, laughing loudly. His old chemistry lab partner Rick, whom Kashvi had read to filth, and Piper's douchebag of an ex-boyfriend were shoving each other and clearly drunk. Scarlett scrambled to her feet, adjusting her dress to cover herself more when both drunks looked in her direction. Colin followed suit, rising beside her and internally hoping the intruders would leave the hallway sometime soon so he could have his quiet peace back.

"I'm gonna take a whiz," Rick said, sauntering off to the bathrooms.

Harden pulled a metal flask from the inside pocket of his black suit and started to screw the cap off. "This where the freaks hang out?" If the chaperones were smart, Colin thought, they would have done pat-downs of the attendees before they entered the hotel where the dance was being held. Neither he nor Scarlett answered the slurred question. "Oh, you're still mute? I thought now that you're hanging around the redhead you'd be more talkative. Tell me, does the carpet match the drapes?"

Colin furrowed his brow and looked around. "Where? My bedroom doesn't have carpeting. Scarlett's does, but the curtains don't match. They're just white lace."

"Colin." Scarlett shook her head and clutched his arm tighter. "That's not what he's talking about. Let's go."

She pulled on Colin's arm to get him to move, but he was a statue, watching as Harden started to laugh at him. With no context, the anger heating up in Colin's body was quick to take over. He fucking hated it when he didn't understand the underlying meaning of something or the tone in which it was said, and he flat-out refused to leave until he knew why some asshole thought he had a right to laugh in his face. Not only an asshole, but one who had gotten his sister drunk when she was clearly grieving. The same guy who had then tried to get in his car and drive drunk, leaving Piper to fend for herself.

"Scarlett, tell me what he means," Colin demanded.

"It's nothing." Scarlett evaded his gaze.

Harden swayed as he chuckled and set one hand on Colin's shoulder, most likely to stop himself from seeing double. "In this scenario, the drapes would be the hair on top of her head." Colin jerked away from the touch, almost shivering in disgust. He liked it when Scarlett touched him, but unexpected touching made his skin crawl. Harden slapped his palm against the wall beside him instead, balancing his drunken self against it. "The carpet would then be the hair..." A low whistle left his mouth as he dragged a pointer finger down his chest and pointed to his crotch.

There were moments in Colin's life where his impulse control was nonexistent, usually brought on by a burst of emotion. The white-hot rage that bubbled up inside him now felt inescapable and desperate to explode from his chest.

So he detonated and swung.

There was a low crack of sound when his fist connected with Harden's face, and a jolt of nerves lanced up his arm. Scarlett let out a noise somewhere between a gasp and a shout of alarm beside him as Harden crumpled to the floor.

"Ow, shit!" Colin's mouth dropped open in pain as he cradled his throbbing hand, shaking it out a bit to see if that would help. It actually made it much worse, so he stopped attempting to flick the pain away.

"Colin!" Scarlett all but shrieked his name, her hand pressed over her mouth. Harden groaned and rolled over on the ground, clutching at the side of his face.

"I assume he deserved that?" a low voice asked. Colin jerked his head up to peer down the hallway. Leo Diaz, a junior from Piper's Spanish class whom she despised, stalked down the hallway toward their altercation.

Colin was slowly coming back into his own body, deeply exhausted from all the exertion. "I don't know," he answered honestly. "Punching him might have been an overreaction."

"Doubt it." Leo ran his fingers through his curly black hair and looked down at Harden with his nose wrinkling in disgust. "What'd he do?"

"Nothing," Harden moaned from the floor and tried to get up. "He assaulted me!'

"I didn't ask you, pendejo," Leo spat. "Stay down, or I'll make you."

"He's technically right." Colin grimaced. "I did assault him."

"Is your hand okay?" Scarlett's worried tone caught Colin off guard, and he leaned into her a bit, seeking out the comfort of her touch. She obliged and wrapped her arm around his back, and he did his best to not fall on her or make her carry too much of his weight, but his limbs felt so tired, his brain barely capable of stringing two thoughts together.

"It hurts," Colin managed to say and winced as he lifted his arm to show her. Scarlett took his hand and gingerly started to examine his skinned knuckles.

"You're going to need to put some ice on it," Leo told him. "Someone want to clue me in on what the hell happened? I need to assess whether to ruin Harden's life or not."

"He wanted to know the color of my girlfriend's pubic hair," Colin said flatly. Scarlett froze beside him, and he realized that this might be one of those scenarios she wanted to keep between them. Leo didn't need to know all the details.

"I would have punched him, too." Leo shrugged. Harden groaned something under his breath and moved to get up again, but Leo glared at him, and he stalled his progress.

"I don't think he was asking to learn about melanin levels in hair growth on different parts of the body," Colin noted. "He was just being crude."

The corner of Leo's mouth quirked up. "Astute observation."

"Thank you."

"I'll take care of this. It doesn't look like there are cameras in this hallway, so I'm willing to say that he fell and hit his face on the ground. It helps that he's clearly drunk." Leo smiled down at Harden. "You should really be more careful."

"Colin," Scarlett whispered. "We should go before someone comes out here."

"I have a hotel room upstairs," Colin said. "I was going to tell you before it got too loud in the ballroom. You brought all your stuff, right?" She nodded. "Can you pretend you're at Kashvi's?"

A shy smile formed on Scarlett's face, and she nodded. "I'll text her."

"I have to call my uncle and make up a reason why I'm not coming home. Piper told me to say I was with a friend or make someone up."

"Your uncle knows who I am," Leo butted in. "Tell him you're with me. I'll vouch for you."

"Piper really hates you, so I don't think that's a good idea," Colin said.

"Oh, I know." Leo smirked. "That's why I suggested it. I take out the trash," he pointed to Harden, "and you piss off your sister for me. An even trade."

"Why do you want to piss off Piper?" Scarlett narrowed her eyes at Leo.

"It'll give her a personality other than the sugar plum fairies and butterflies for once," Leo said. "Basically, I think she's annoying, and I want to get a rise out of her."

"She *is* annoying sometimes," Colin agreed.

Leo grinned. "Then it's a deal."

THIRTY-FIVE

Scarlett
23 Years Old

The hand pressed against Scarlett's waist felt like a brand through the thin silk layer of her dress. Five years had done nothing to make her forget the way Colin's bare skin felt dragging and pressing against hers. Even through clothing, she could feel the whisper of what once had been an imprint. Colin's fingers were stiff, digging into her side in a way that was just shy of too much, as if he thought she might disappear if he didn't keep her grounded. But it was the same pressure. The same feeling that flipped in her chest. The same far-off look on his face she knew too well that meant he was concentrating. It was almost painful now not knowing all of his thoughts. To know the shape his face made when he was focused, but to not know why. Their time together all those years ago had been like a crash course on knowing every facet of someone's being just for them to become a stranger months later. The scars he had left behind were still on her skin—faded in color, but permanent.

Other couples had finally made their way onto the dance floor after a few rounds at the open bar, and it made the night seem significantly more successful. There hadn't been a chance for Scarlett to examine the auction sheets, but she had been watching donors circle the room with pens in hand. She wasn't the only one who had put this event on, yet she felt solely responsible for the outcome nonetheless. Dancing with Colin felt like more of an indulgence now than a calculated plan to entice people out onto the dance floor. She had done that already. She had gotten the ball rolling. Yet there she was, still holding on to Colin and swaying to the music when she should be making rounds.

"What are you thinking about?" Colin asked, like the game they used to play when they were younger.

"I'm thinking about how I might have put the wrong color pens down for everyone to use. What if black was the way to go? You always used to prefer black ink. And what if we spent more money on this event than what was donated? What if everyone gets food poisoning? We served salad, and I'm always hearing about recalls on lettuce and random strains of E. coli in stuff like that. Could you imagine the headlines saying that the cancer foundation gave everyone cancer?" She paused only to suck in another breath to keep talking. "I don't even know if E. coli and cancer have anything to do with each other, but probably giving anyone an illness or a disease is a bad rap for the foundation. Maybe I was seeing things earlier on stage and no one is really enjoying themselves right now. Maybe I should have laid the guilt on more? I don't really like going about it that way, but donations tend to happen when people have a guilty conscience, right? I don't know. Maybe this dress is too tight, and I'm overreacting. Maybe this dress is too dressy in general. I said this was a formal event on the invite, but I think there's a man wearing cargo pants in the corner. Then again, I haven't seen him in a while, so maybe he was just in the wrong place. Or he's our biggest donor, and he left because he hates everything about this event." She jerked her head around, trying to find the long-lost guest again.

"Are you done?" The low tenor of Colin's voice had a lifted edge to it, and the strange sound of it made her decide to fully look at him for the first time in several minutes. The bastard was actually smiling.

"I'm done," Scarlett grumbled. She shouldn't have been speaking all the thoughts that came into her mind like she used to when she was lying in bed naked with Colin anyway, but he brought out this uncomfortable truth in her that she still couldn't shake. "Sorry."

"I always like hearing your thoughts, Scarlett. I'm the one that asked, and I'm glad that you told me. I miss you telling me things," he said. The already spiraling thoughts in her head changed course and curled around her heart. The last part of his response, he had said so softly, almost like he didn't want to tell her that information but couldn't help himself. Her emotions warred between wanting to scream into the ether that he didn't get to miss her like that and begging for him to let her tell him every single tragic thought she'd had since the start of the gala. "I only asked if you were done because I wanted to know if you want me to solve any of those problems or if you want me to just listen."

That was new. Usually, Colin jumped into an immediate response, categorizing her thoughts into smaller, more manageable pieces. The implausible or completely illogical were debunked with a statistic or two on why they were a non-issue. Most of which she already knew were not logical in the slightest. Then he would parse out the rational bits and find solutions to each one. The eager look on his face made it seem like he wanted to do what he used to do but was holding back for her sake.

"I do know the E. coli bit seems unlikely," she said. "And maybe if someone is that particular about blue or black ink, then they should probably carry their own pen."

Colin bobbed his head. "I keep a black pen with me because I like black ink, so if someone wasn't prepared, I think that's on them. I like that you run the charity off of integrity and real experiences. You're honest, and you don't intentionally make people feel guilty. The cargo pants man is a plus-one for one of the lab assistants from my lab. They met on a dating app, and since my coworker is still here and the cargo pants man seems to no longer be in attendance, I don't think the date went well. Probably because he showed up to a formal event in cargo pants. Your dress..." He paused and looked down past her face. His eyes drank in her body in a way that felt all too much like the way he used to peruse her outfits when she would self-consciously ask. It wasn't the usual way men would casually glance up from their phones and give women placating answers. Colin *looked*, and he never paid a compliment he didn't mean. "You're the most beautiful person here."

"So the dress is bad?" She raised her eyebrows.

"On the contrary. It accentuates your best features."

"Which are?" Scarlett egged him on, and she had no idea why she was goading him. It wasn't like Colin had ever faked being physically attracted to her, but for some reason she felt like playing with fire tonight.

"Your breasts, obviously. They've always been fantastic, but they've only gotten bigger, so that's a nice surprise." The way that he said it with a completely straight face made Scarlett let out a loud cackle that she quickly muffled with her hand to her mouth and her forehead to Colin's shoulder. When she finally peeked back up at him, there was a smile pulling on his lips, making his frustratingly handsome face look even more so.

"I probably should have guessed that," she said through another laugh. "I don't suppose you stopped being a boob man."

"Do you want to hear the rest of my list?" Colin asked.

"Do I want you to continue to compliment me?" Scarlett pretended to consider it. "That would be a huge hardship for me."

"Oh, okay," Colin said quickly.

"Sarcasm," she explained. "Please, tell me. Did Johns Hopkins bring out your inner foot fetish?"

He shook his head. "I am still not into feet. I think my newest favorite is this." His hand left its spot on her waist and traveled up her left arm, where the watercolor flowers stretched across her skin. Every place he touched felt like a fire scorching her. "Walker's tattoos are all dark and black. I like that yours are colorful and bright."

"Yours is also black," Scarlett noted. She hadn't seen him much since the fire and the shirtless cat incident, but the image was burned into her retinas. It wasn't exactly an unwelcome image anymore, either. The more she thought about it, the more she liked the idea of Colin marking himself with her, because if she was going to have permanent mental scars from him, the least he could do was ink their time together onto his body.

"My dad said that when he and my mom were dating and he was too poor to buy her flowers, he'd pick wildflowers. That's what this reminds me of." Colin held her arm and turned it from side to side to look at all the flowers.

"That's a lovely thought." She wasn't sure when it had happened, but her voice had transitioned into something softer and more intimate. Their positioning and hushed tones would seem like a lovers' conversation to any outsider. They were still swaying to the music, but Colin had stepped closer to her, pulling her in so her head was right beside his shoulder, and she could smell the light, sweet, honey scent of his skin. It wasn't overly fragrant, but a calming smell she always loved. She had never asked him what kind of shampoo or soap he used when they were together, and the urge to ask him now felt dangerous. Too risky. There should be no good reason for her to want to know that information.

"Your eyes are also very pretty," he finally murmured into the shell of her ear.

"You never look at my eyes," she argued.

Colin hummed introspectively, "I don't like eye contact, but it doesn't mean I don't look at your eyes when you're not looking at me. They're green, with a ring of copper around your pupils." He reached up and swiped his fingers over her forehead, adjusting her hair and sweeping a long strand out of her face. "Your bangs are cute, too. They frame your face well."

"Hm." Scarlett bit her lip. She knew all too well she should stop this conversation in its tracks, but Colin ended up doing that for her.

"What's left of your worries? Donations outweighing the costs and people enjoying themselves?"

After where the conversation had ended up, Scarlett had completely forgotten about her list of anxieties. She had forgotten about anything other than Colin and was almost surprised to find they were still on the dance floor and there were other people dancing around them. Pulling back a bit to right herself from what must have been a too-intimate embrace with her ex, she cleared her throat and gave a jerk of her head. "Yes."

"I'm a donor, and I'm enjoying myself," Colin said.

"I don't think you dancing with me counts as fun."

"I never got to dance with you at prom. This is quieter than that, and I get to be close to you, so I think it counts as fun." The thumb he had pressed into her side started making sweeping circular movements.

"We did dance at prom," Scarlett carefully side-stepped his comment.

"Barely. It was too loud, remember?" he asked, as if she could ever forget that night. The night that he had lied. The night that he had told her everything she wanted to hear, and she had fallen for it hook, line, and sinker.

"Yeah." She swallowed. "I remember. Do you remember how you punched Piper's ex in the face, and then we..."

"The hotel room," Colin murmured, eyes sparkling when she looked up at him. "I remember everything, Scarlett."

Thirty-Six

Scarlett
18 Years Old

'A hotel room' was what Colin had said. Instead, what they walked into wasn't just a hotel room, but clearly the honeymoon suite. It looked as though Valentine's Day had thrown up everywhere. The bed was a massive, pillowy heart shape spread with white linens. The wood console table against the wall had a bucket filled with ice and sparkling cider. Rose petals scattered across every inch of space.

So much to look at, and Scarlett could not pay attention to any of it as she shouted the same word in her head with varying tones to test its viability. *Sex.* They were finally back where they had started. She could finally give all of herself to Colin, and she wanted nothing more. After everything, she thought she couldn't love him more, and then he had to go and defend her honor in the hallway, and she had fallen a little harder. Veins vibrating with excitement, she glanced around the room Colin had prepared for them, smiling at how far he had leaned into the cliché of it all. It was perfect.

"I don't really get the point of rose petals," Colin said,

standing at the foot of the bed and frowning down at the torn-apart roses. "Do people just have sex on top of them, or do they have to break out of foreplay to then remove them all so they can lay down?" He adjusted the bag of ice they had gotten at the ice machine down the hallway on his knuckles.

"I think red is just a sexy color, and it looks pretty. It's also the universal sign for 'I want to have sex with you.'" Scarlett smiled nervously.

He reached out and picked up a handful of rose petals, letting them fall through his fingers as he nodded. "I guess it's good they're here, then, because that is true. I do want to have sex with you."

"Great." She picked up one of the petals and smoothed her thumb over it, trying to get a handle on her nerves that had skyrocketed since they had entered this room.

"After your bedroom window, paying Walker back for the auction, this hotel room, and all the added romantic flare, I'm going to have to get a job when I get to Maryland," he said. "If you like it, though, it was worth it."

"You did all this just for me, even though you don't see the point?"

Colin nodded and sat down on the edge of the bed. He patted the spot next to him for her to sit, and Scarlett obeyed, plopping down with an overeager bounce. "I've done extensive research on this, and I confirmed a suspicion I've had for a long time despite the research on it being shaky at best. You'd think with it being one of the most important things in life that there would be more data and a more defined definition."

"What?" Her eyebrows bunched together in confusion. "On sex? I imagine there's quite a lot of research on that."

"There could still be more on sex, but I'm not talking about that."

"I'm really confused. What are we talking about, then?"

"The research on love," Colin said simply, tossing his ice bag onto the nightstand. The words didn't quite register in her head until he reached out and grabbed her hand, his body starting to sway. The excited rocking motion that was always her favorite confirmation that he was happy to be there with her.

"The research on love?" Her voice cracked as she repeated his words back with uncertainty.

Colin's hand let go of hers and slid up to cup her cheek, his eyes meeting hers head-on. She blinked back at him, alarmed by the sudden eye contact that felt both strange and forced.

"I... uh." Colin's thick eyelashes fluttered once before he locked his gaze on her yet again. She squirmed this time, discomfort rolling up her spine.

"What is it? You're kind of scaring me. Are you okay? Are you sick?" Scarlett pulled away from his touch and scanned his body for possible injury, taking special note of his hand to make sure it hadn't swelled up too much. "Are you hurt?"

"No," he replied adamantly. "I was just trying to look into your eyes and tell you I—" He met her eyes again and stalled.

"You... what?" Scarlett's brain felt like it had rebooted ten times since the start of the conversation.

"I can't think when I'm looking straight into your eyes like a deranged serial killer," Colin said. "And I don't get how that's romantic and the best way to tell you I love you."

She rebooted again. "W-what are you—do you?"

"You're really cute when you stutter." He shifted closer to her, and her breathing started to pick up. "I know I'm supposed to talk about love while looking deep into your eyes, but it feels so wrong. Can I please do it the way I want to do it?"

"Colin, I don't know what the hell you're even talking about." Scarlett let out an exasperated breath. "You keep mentioning love, and I think I'm going to have a heart attack if you don't tell me what you mean right now."

Without a word, Colin folded her in his arms and pulled her head down to rest against his chest. He lowered them to the bed and scooted until her body was flush against his with only the burden of clothes between them. "This is better," Colin murmured and kissed the top of her head. Affection flooded her system, and she had no choice but to lean into him even more, hear his heartbeat in his chest and smell the scent of his clean skin. "What I meant to say was that I love you. I have an entire packet of research and a typed summary with pictures if you want proof."

A small sigh of relief exited her nose, and she closed her eyes, burying her nose into the warmth of his chest as she asked, "You love me?"

"I do. I think I have for a while, but I'm really sure I do now," Colin said.

Every tight limb in her body relaxed, muscles she didn't even know were stiff going slack as she whispered, "I love you, too, Colin. So much."

His arms squeezed her tighter. "I was hoping you did."

She giggled. "Do you want me to sign a contract as proof?"

"I didn't think of that. Maybe I should have drawn one up."

"No." She tried to hold back another laugh. "I don't need that." If there had ever been a moment in her life that she had been happier, she couldn't think of it. To finally know for certain that Colin felt the same way she did made her feel electric, her body buzzing with energy.

"Good." He let out a long sigh and pressed his cheek into her hair. "I'm so tired." The contrast of this statement and how she felt were so at odds that this, out of everything, felt like the most shocking thing he had said all night. When she thought about it a bit longer, though, she could see why. The loud noise had all but drained Colin of his energy, and the fight in the hallway had to have sucked even more life out of him. Emotions always seemed to hit Colin harder. He felt everything all at once, like the night at the lookout. Then, for a few days after, he pulled back a bit from conversation.

"Don't go quiet on me, okay?" Scarlett begged. "You can't tell me you love me and then ghost me."

"What?" Colin's tone held a sharp edge of confusion.

"You just... every time something emotional happens, you tend to shut down."

"I just physically can't be present sometimes, Scarlett." The edge to his voice was gone, replaced with resignation. A bone-deep exhaustion. "It's fatiguing to try to be normal constantly. It seems so easy for people to make conversation or share what they're feeling, or look people in the eyes when they're speaking, and for me, it's like I don't even know how I'm feeling until it explodes out. It's a mess of confusing shit, and then I'm punching Harden in the face. I didn't really realize I was that pissed off about it, but the way he was talking about you, and knowing everything he did to Piper? Harden doesn't deserve to breathe the same air as my family. He doesn't deserve to look at someone as beautiful as you or think about you like that, because he doesn't care about you. I just fucking lost it. I'm sorry I can't be normal. I'm—" His voice choked a bit, and he sucked in a breath of air. "I wanted to dance with you at the prom. I promised myself I would, and I couldn't. I wanted to tell you that I love you with a big romantic gesture like they do in the movies, and then I wanted to make love to you, but I couldn't, and right now I'm so tired that I can barely keep my eyes open, let alone perform anything sexual. My hand is throbbing, and I just want to sleep and hug you."

"I don't want you to be normal," Scarlett soothed. "I just want you to tell me when you need to retreat so I don't worry about you. It's okay if you need to decompress."

"I need to retreat," Colin whispered.

"Retreat, then." A secret smile snuck onto Scarlett's face as she sat up. Colin didn't move with her, his lean body spread out against the mattress and limbs haphazardly laying exactly where she had left them. She scooted toward the edge of the bed and pulled his foot into her lap from where it was dangling over the side. There was no movement from Colin, so she continued, unlacing his shoe and sliding it off. The process was repeated until she had his socks off, leaving both his feet bare. She moved up to his waist and unclasped his belt, unbuttoned his pants, and pulled down the zipper.

"I know you're half asleep already, but I'm going to need you to lift your hips," Scarlett said, keeping her tone calm and even. Without a word from him otherwise, Colin's hips rose from the bed, and she slipped his pants and underwear down over his ass and proceeded to peel them from his legs. His shirt was next, and Colin put in a minimal amount of effort to lift his arms at the right times to help her. When he was fully undressed, she undressed herself, set her corsage on the nightstand, plucked all the rose petals off the bed, and folded their clothes the way she had seen him do before. When she pulled back the covers, Colin limply flopped around until he was under the sheets, and she crawled in bed next to him naked after shutting the lights off. She removed his glasses last, kissing his forehead and gently unhooking them from his ears before folding them and setting them with his clothes.

"I love you." Colin's voice was barely audible as his arm folded around her, her backside resting in a spoon against his crotch, his bare skin warm to the touch. She could feel it now, how tired her body felt. It had to only be around nine-thirty, but for once her brain felt unusually calm. There was always something to worry about, but at that very moment, her brain was quiet because she simply didn't care about anything other than the here and now. Wrapped up with the boy she was in love with, who loved her back. The comfort from knowing that there was someone amongst the billions of people in the world whose heart was hers and hers alone, and he was sleeping right beside her, curled up with an adorable scrunch to his nose and one weighted arm draped across her stomach.

"I love you, too."

"Scarlett?" Colin's groggy voice pulled Scarlett out of her newest spiral since she had silenced her six a.m. alarm an hour ago. Usually, when that alarm went off, she would hit snooze so many times her finger got sore, but there were too many thoughts swirling around in her head to curl back into Colin and go to sleep again. Light was pouring in from a crack in the window, reminiscent of a spotlight that was ready to expose all her feelings.

She rolled onto her side and propped her head up on her hand. "Colin?"

"I've been watching you stare at the ceiling and toss yourself around for the last ten minutes," he said. "What are you thinking about?"

"I'm thinking that I really, really love you, and I'm terrified," Scarlett admitted.

"Why are you terrified? Did I do something to scare you?"

"No, but you're leaving," she said miserably. "We don't have very long before you go to Maryland. What are we going to do? You really think we'll be okay with long distance? You don't even like it when I gently touch you. How are you going to be okay with that?"

Colin scooted closer and set his chin on the top of her head. "Come with me."

Scarlett jerked her head back and looked up at him in surprise. "Come with you to Maryland?"

"Yes."

"We've been dating for like three months, Colin. I assume you'll be in a dorm room for at least your first year. What am I supposed to do? And what am I even going to do in Maryland?" A million questions sparked in her head with their own subcategories of worry.

"We'll get you an apartment." He sat up with a wide grin like he was imagining it, too. "If you want to enroll in community college, I'm sure you could do that. We'll get you a place with a spare room that you can paint in. You can help me study for all my exams, and we'll cuddle every night till we fall asleep, and my roommate will have the dorm mostly to himself."

The hope of a future with Colin seemed more important than every other aspiration Scarlett had at that moment. It was all she really wanted. "This is... insane," she whispered with an incredulous shake of her head.

"Is that a no?" Colin asked, the light dying behind his eyes. She lurched forward and kissed him deeply before pulling back and laughing.

Out of every question in her head about logistics or her fears, the most basic of all the questions seemed the most important. *Did she want to go?* The answer came so quickly to her mind that there was no other option but to accept.

"Okay." She nodded. "I'll move to Maryland with you."

Colin pounced on her, his mouth descending in a million peppered kisses across her face as she giggled and squirmed under him until his lips found hers in a more indulgent press. She breathed him in, her fingers lacing into his hair and gripping.

"Red," Colin murmured into her mouth. "Can we brush our teeth?" The heat developing in her core drained from her body in a flash, and she bolted up from the bed. Looking alarmed, Colin rolled off after her, frantically grabbing at his folded underwear on the nightstand and pulling them on. "What's happening?" He jerked his head from side to side, searching for the problem as if the room were going to burst into flame.

Scarlett covered her mouth with her hand, mortification sinking in. "You basically told me my breath is bad."

"So?" He pulled his eyebrows together. "It is bad. Mine probably is, too, considering the weird taste in my mouth. I wanted to brush my teeth immediately when I woke up, but I didn't because you were doing that thinking and staring at the ceiling thing you do, and I thought I should check on you first."

The heat in her cheeks lessened, and she let her shoulders sag a bit. "We were kissing, and it felt like we were going to go further when you said it, so it was embarrassing."

"Oh." Colin grimaced, rocking back on his heels. "Can you tell me *how* it's embarrassing? I just thought we'd get out of bed, we'd brush our teeth, I'd throw some deodorant on, and then we'd have extremely passionate sex after we both smell and taste good."

"Oh." Scarlett bit her lip and looked down at her feet. "Yeah, that sounds nice."

"What did I do wrong?"

"You weren't really wrong, I guess," Scarlett considered. "I just don't like being told negative things about myself while we're actively making out."

"Okay, so how do I...?"

"You probably just could have stopped kissing me, gotten out of bed, and told me exactly what you just said. The 'extremely passionate sex' part was a nice touch."

"That will definitely be happening." Colin's eyes flicked over her, and Scarlett realized she was standing in the middle of their hotel room in the morning light, completely naked.

A slow grin spread across her face. "I guess we should get to scrubbing our mouths raw, then."

"More than just your mouth will be raw." The comment was delivered in Colin's usual dry tone, so Scarlett almost missed it until she replayed it back in her head, and she laughed out loud. The victory smile she got from Colin as they raced to the bathroom was like a reward. It was one of the things she loved about him. He didn't smile often, but when he did, it was almost always in response to someone else laughing or smiling from something he'd said. Every time she got one of his elusive smiles, it felt like she, too, had accomplished something.

They silently brushed their teeth side by side in the mirror, and never had dental hygiene felt so sensual before. With the anticipation of what they were about to do hanging between them, every stroke of the bristles Scarlett used to scrape her tongue felt like a premonition for how she wanted to drag her tongue down Colin's torso or over his cock. She could see Colin get repeatedly distracted by her breasts as she brushed and they bounced with her movements. His electric toothbrush vibrating the way she wanted her vibrator to between her legs. After a couple minutes, they quickly spat into the sink and moved through the remaining motions in a hurry.

By the time they made it to the bed, Scarlett was already so keyed up that she couldn't imagine needing anything but Colin inside her immediately. "Passionate sex?" she asked, turning to Colin, who was already stripping off his underwear again and folding them.

"Tell me how you want it. I don't care how we do it as long as you come and you like it this time."

She inhaled before releasing everything she had learned about herself since the beginning of their experiment. "I want you to pin me down. I want you to use your hand on me first while you kiss me. I don't want to come from your hand alone, though, just work me up until I beg you to go further. I want you to tell me what you're doing or what you want to do to me while you're doing it, and order me around. I like it when you're direct and you tell me how it feels or what you see. Then, when you fuck me, I want it to be so deep it almost hurts. I'll use my hand to help me finish when we're getting close. And I want you to make it clear you love me when we're finished."

"Done," Colin said, a condom perched between two fingers that he must have pulled out during her speech. His cock was already hard between his legs, and she watched him rip open the condom wrapper and slide the rubber over himself before he pointed to the mattress. "Get on the bed and lie down on your back with your knees up and spread apart." Need blooming in her core like a dull ache, Scarlett crawled to the headboard and did exactly what he said, letting her legs fall open in a blatant display of herself. "Look at that, Red. You're wet already. I brought lube, but I think I'll have no problem this time. Even with how tight you are, I'll be able to slide right in."

"Fuck," she said, the desperation in her voice already showing. "Tell me what *you* want."

"I need to know I'm doing it right. I don't want to guess if you're enjoying it." Colin dropped to his knees on top of the bed and maneuvered between her legs, his fingers sliding down the inside of her thigh. "I need you to like it this time, yeah?"

"Okay." Scarlett bobbed her head fervently, arching toward his hand.

"But if you don't, please tell me. Don't try to push through."

"I'm gonna like it, Colin. Please just—" She wiggled a bit. "Touch me."

He did, his fingers finding her clit first and pressing in slow, sweeping circles. "Make some noise, Red." Her eyes scrunched shut, and her mouth fell open on a moan as he slid his fingers down in a wet line from her clit. The push into her was slow at first, a tantalizing press as his long fingers bottomed out inside her. Then his thumb went back to work.

"Oh, God," Scarlett panted, bucking her hips off the bed. Colin caught on to her usual antics and quickly pressed the broad expanse of his forearm down against her stomach, holding her in place and heightening the torture. She squirmed under his touch, moaning with each press and rub of his fingers.

"You remember the safe word?" Colin asked.

"Isn't it just 'stop?'" she managed to squeak out.

"Yeah." He nodded. "You tell me to stop if you—"

"Colin!" Scarlett practically yelled. "If you stop, I'll die."

Still carefully working her over, he said, "You can't actually die from this unless you have a heart attack or there's a freak accident."

"It's a hyperbole," she gasped. "Colin. Please—I need—fill me."

"Give me your wrists," he ordered. The hands previously playing with and rubbing her own breasts snapped together as she held them out, exposed wrists up as an offering. She watched with rapt attention as he sat back on his heels, slowly pulled his fingers out of her, and lifted them to his lips to suck them into his mouth before using the same hand to lock her wrists together with his fingers digging into her skin. She liked the pressure, which wasn't respectful in the slightest. He wasn't gentle about pinning her wrists above her head, and she liked the minuscule amount of pain he caused. She didn't think she could handle much more than what he was giving her, but riding the line between pain and pleasure was exactly what she wanted. His hips pinned the rest of her body down as he lined himself up, the head of his cock knocking against her entrance. "Breathe, Red." She did just as he pushed in. There was no pain this time, just a fire between her legs that made her want to rock into him, but she couldn't with his restraints. "Holy fuck," Colin groaned. "Please tell me this feels good to you."

"So good," Scarlett confirmed, her voice shaky with pent-up desire. He started to thrust, and it was all she could do not to move against him. The strokes became more deliberate and deep as Colin got more confident and unhinged above her, the hold on her wrists loosening as they kept going. When his eyes slid shut and his mouth was left permanently ajar, she matched his energy by hooking her legs under his ass. He went even deeper, and her toes curled under the intense pressure.

"Are you going to touch yourself?" Colin panted.

"I don't need to." She shook her head. "I can get there like this. Keep going as deep as you—" Her words were cut off by a loud moan when he shoved so far into her that she could feel him in her stomach. "*Yes*."

With surprising tenderness, one of the hands at her side grasping at the bedding was met with Colin's, his fingers lacing with hers as he rocked relentlessly into her. And it was maybe that contact more than anything else that set her off.

"I'm going to come," Scarlett said in between quick breaths.

"Me too," Colin rasped. His eyes were still closed, and each stroke felt deliberate, his face scrunching with the push and pull like he might break at any moment. His fingers curled against her knuckle in a massage-like press and released while he pulled back and dipped forward. "I need you to come on my cock, Red. Right now."

"*Colin.*" She jerked under him, palming her breast as the intense, building pressure came to a peak of ecstasy. Her body rode the line between agony and satisfaction for an unbearable amount of time before the tightening of her muscles and watching Colin's face clench with his own orgasm finally sent her careening over the ledge. Every muscle spasmed as waves of a pulsating heat twisted and spread from her core. And when the most intense orgasm of her life finally ceased, she collapsed against the mattress, chest heaving.

They both winced when Colin removed himself, her intimate parts too sensitive to withstand the touch she had been begging for just moments ago. Colin flopped to her side on the bed, his own breaths ragged and uneven as he pulled off the used condom.

"You okay?" Scarlett finally asked.

Every other word he responded with was broken up by a deep breath. "That was amazing. Holy shit."

"Yeah?"

"Oh, I forgot!" he exclaimed suddenly. His lips pecked at hers in a quick kiss before he delivered a casual, "I love you."

"I love you, too."

"We are going to have so much sex in Maryland." Colin sighed happily.

"Our experiment will just continue on forever." Scarlett grinned.

"We're still grading our performance?" he inquired, and she could tell instantly that he was delighted by that thought. Combining sex and science was one of Colin's favorite things.

With one fist raised in the air, she called out with a giggle, "Grab the comprehensive chart!"

THIRTY-SEVEN

Scarlett
23 Years Old

Remembering her past with Colin was one thing, but rehashing it was another altogether. She didn't want the song and dance of why it didn't work out, despite the literal song and dance she was in the middle of with Colin's hands on her hips. The conversation was moving into dangerous territory, one that would definitely leave her crying and doubting her ability to trust anyone. Their breakup hurt bad enough the first time. There was simply no point in reminiscing on the details of what she used to think was the best night of her life.

"As it turns out, Maryland was actually devoid of sex," Colin said, bringing her back to the present.

She shouldn't have been shocked that *that* was the commentary he was going with to remember their time on prom night and the morning after. While she was thinking of how naive her younger self had been to believe that she would get to brush her teeth beside the love of her life every morning, Colin was reminiscing on how they didn't have sex in Maryland as planned. It shouldn't have made her bitter, but she had had enough, so she pulled away from his arms.

"I'm going to check on the silent auction forms." When Colin moved to follow her, she pressed a hand to his chest to stop him, the barest prick of a tear starting to form in her waterline. "*Alone.*"

He froze in his spot and flicked his eyes over her face. "Scarlett?" he asked, incomprehension written so clearly into the groove between his eyebrows. "What did I do? I thought we were having fun remembering."

"It's never going to be fun for me to remember a lie, Colin," Scarlett snapped, her voice a little louder than she would have liked. Her head jerked around the room to see a few faces looking in their direction, and her cheeks heated. "I just need... a moment." The word she landed on felt underwhelming compared to all the moments she wanted back. All the moments she wanted to forget, to not care about any longer. All the moments she didn't get to have because nothing had ever been real. She managed to make it to the exit on quick feet before her vision was truly blurred from the tears, calling out a quick "I'm fine" to Harper and shooing her away as she made a break for it.

It was raining when Scarlett made her way outside, racing down the stairs to the cobblestone path leading up to the community center. Tears streaked down her face as she mentally berated herself. When would the ache in her chest finally stop? Even when it was manageable, it was still there, ready to hurt her all over again. She wiped at her face in irritation, sniffing and looking up at the sky as if to shout at it for making this night worse. If there was ever a time the weather deserved a "fuck you," it was now. Well, now and also during every natural disaster that had ever happened, but she was the natural disaster this time around. She knew full well that she shouldn't have accepted a dance with an ex-boyfriend she had never fully gotten over. An ex-boyfriend who had looked at her when she was crumbling and taken a hammer to her heart anyway.

"Scarlett." She almost thought she had imagined Colin's voice, she was so in her own thoughts, until she saw him at the other end of the cobblestone path. Standing there, his hands in the pockets of his long coat.

"What?" Her voice was exasperated and raw as she wiped at her face. "What more could you possibly want from me, Colin?"

"Want from you?" he asked incredulously. "I-I just want to fix whatever I did, Scarlett! I want to know how the fuck I made you cry again so I can figure out how to stop doing that."

"Well." Scarlett sniffed. "You had no problem making me cry five years ago."

Colin ran a hand through his hair and closed his eyes, misery washing over his features. "I didn't like it then, either."

"It's fine. I shouldn't be crying, anyway." She turned away from him as the rain picked up.

"Let me give you my jacket," he urged, stepping forward and pulling his arms out of the sleeves. All she responded with was a petulant shake of her head. "It's cold, Scarlett. Your dress is beautiful, but it doesn't even cover your shoulders."

"You're the one who doesn't like wet clothes," she reminded him. "Put it over your head like an umbrella, and maybe you won't get wet."

The fight on Colin's face lasted longer than she thought it would given the discomfort forming in his features. Wet clothing irritated his skin, and he couldn't control that any more than he could control his reaction to loud sounds. For some reason, watching him give in and hold the jacket above his head gave her a small bit of relief. The relief didn't show, however, because a shiver wracked her body, a clear tell that she was cold. It wasn't at all warm out, and she should have thought twice about leaving the gala with her jacket still on the back of her chair. She would deserve an award if she could make it home with her jacket instead of absentmindedly leaving it here.

"Stand with me, at least. Your teeth are chattering." Colin

stepped toward her, and she let him, already feeling his body heat. "I'm sorry," he whispered.

"You're sorry," Scarlett repeated, as if the words had no meaning at all. If she was being honest, coming from Colin, she wasn't sure they did.

"I upset you. I don't know how, but it doesn't matter, because I did."

"I'll get over it."

Colin shifted the jacket to better cover her. "Get over what? What did you mean when you said you don't like remembering a lie? What part of that memory was a lie to you?"

"All of it," Scarlett whispered, shaking her head.

"Was it because you didn't come with me to Maryland?"

"It was because you never loved me." Her voice was barely a murmur at this point, scared to be near him and scared to move away. A violent shiver zapped up her spine when Colin stepped in so close his face was only a few inches from hers.

His eyelashes fluttered shut and fanned out over his cheeks as his face wrinkled with a pained expression. "Is that really what you think?"

"I don't want to think about it at all." She was putting up a hard boundary, and she set her hand on his chest in a stop position to make it clear.

Colin's eyes flew open, ripping down to where her hand was. Scarlett swallowed and went to pull it away, only for Colin to drop one side of his jacket in favor of grabbing her wrist and placing her hand back on his chest. Inside the community center ballroom, she was safe, and she didn't have to worry about touching that went beyond dancing. Now that she was alone with him, the line felt blurred, and touching him felt terrifyingly personal. His heartbeat felt familiar under her fingertips.

Colin readjusted the jacket, still holding it over his head. "I like it when you touch me. I feel less unsettled."

It was typical that while he could feel comfort from her touch, what she felt was more complicated, confusing, and definitely unsettling. There shouldn't be a flip in her chest where there once was, and she felt almost guilty at its presence, like it was a betrayal to her younger self, who had gone through torture to get over him. The years of agony she had endured before she knew she didn't need him to make her place in the world. But having him here now felt electric. To feel so loved despite knowing that Colin would never love her and never did. With his gaze on her lips in the present, she decided what he must have been feeling was pure lust, and they had had plenty of memories to fuel those thoughts.

"Tell me I can't kiss you, Red." She must have stepped even closer to him, because his lips were so close that his breath was dancing across her nose. His eyes were closed again, but he had clearly bent down a bit to reach her. She wasn't short, but he still had height on her.

"You can't kiss me." The words came out low and sultry, the antithesis of what they meant, but Colin nodded and opened his eyes again, straightening his spine to pull back just as Scarlett rose to her tiptoes. "But I can kiss you." Her face tilted up in time to catch the surprise on Colin's face before her lips crashed into his.

He swayed into her, the heat of his body molding to hers and his mouth slanting harder against her lips. It was everything at once. A roiling fear in her bones that said she shouldn't be kissing him. A fire licking up her spine and combating the chill, telling her to keep going, to take anything she could from him.

The warmth of his tongue slid along the seam of her lips, and she opened to him, gasping into his mouth and begging for every kiss with her body. It had been so long since she had had this— not just a good kiss, but that indescribable feeling that felt like freefalling while rooted to the ground. Their first-ever kiss five years ago had that feeling, despite it being awkward and hesitant. There was no hesitation now, though, as Colin dropped his hands so his jacket cocooned them together in darkness. His mouth was greedy, biting and sucking on her bottom lip as she frustratedly kissed him back. She wanted it to be awful. She wanted her hands to not know to grip his arms tighter because he liked the pressure.

She wanted that dull ache in her core to stop spreading for him. It shouldn't be this good. It shouldn't make her feel alive. His fingers tangled in her hair and splayed across her back shouldn't feel so right when everything about this was wrong.

A soft beeping noise Scarlett at first thought she had imagined was what finally pulled her free from him for a moment. "Ignore it," Colin said, kissing her again.

"What—"

"My watch," he mumbled against her neck, dragging his lips down her throat.

"Your... watch?" she asked breathlessly, the feeling of his lips against her skin further distracting her.

"Mm-hmm," Colin hummed, muffled by her collar bone. One of his hands moved to cup her breast, and she leaned into it, gasping in desperation. When she finally looked down to see the glowing face of the watch on his groping wrist, she giggled at the illuminated message there: a high heart rate notification, alerting Colin that his pulse had unexpectedly spiked. The spark of joy she got from seeing that felt juvenile, maybe because the last time she had felt this way was when she was eighteen.

Sometimes her past felt like a faded sepia-toned memory she could never replicate on canvas. But now, as her past and present collided, everything was in screaming color. Red: her nickname and her underwear once folded neatly on a nightstand. Blue: eyes that slid over her body like the rainwater. Pink: the heat sprouting across her cheeks as he leaned harder into her just as he had done every time before. Green: the ivy climbing up the brick wall behind them and the color of her chemistry binder back in high school. Black: the darkness behind her eyelids and the depression she had slipped into when he left. Gold: the dress she was wearing now and the joy she had to find without him.

"How are you better than I remember?" Colin groaned. "God, I missed this."

And that was all it took. *I missed this.* This, not *her.* Sex was still the driving force for him, and she had deluded herself into thinking that she was more than that, even for just a moment. Not just something to put his hands on. Not just someone to warm his bed when he was bored or sad.

She shoved him off her and untangled herself from his jacket. "I can't do this."

Colin came out from under the cocoon, too, letting it fall to the cobblestone below. "Red?" he asked, his confusion evident in the disoriented way he looked around for an answer.

"Don't call me that," Scarlett practically shouted.

"I'm sorry." Both hands raised in surrender, he stepped forward, a worried expression replacing the confused one. "Did I hurt you?"

It was a loaded question, because if he meant physically, of course the answer was no, but in every other way, he had practically broken her.

"I can't be your little experiment again." Her voice cracked.

Colin's jaw dropped open slightly, working with an inward thought. "We don't need to do the experiment again. We know what we like."

Tears came in full force again. "What I *like* is when the person I'm sleeping with actually likes me back. I want to be in love, Colin. I deserve that, and you aren't going to give it to me."

"Why not?" Something resembling a flash of anger passed through his eyes, and his voice rose. "I'm not allowed to love you because I'm autistic? Is that it? I'm not good enough for you?"

"You aren't allowed to love me because you *don't!*" Scarlett shouted.

His arms flexed at his sides, nose scrunching in clear frustration. "I loved you then, and I love you now. Not a single thing has changed."

The fat tears rolling down her face picked up speed as her dress started to soak through in the rain. "No, you don't."

"Yes, I do." Colin's voice was all sincerity, but it didn't matter how true it sounded when she knew the real truth and had witnessed it firsthand. "I never said I didn't love you, Scarlett."

"In all the ways that mattered, you did," she whispered.

"No." He adamantly shook his head as if he could erase everything he had said back then. She wished he could so she could forget, too. "You know me. I say exactly what I mean. I know what I feel and what I've felt since I told you on Prom night five years ago. I love you."

Righting her dress and sniffing back more tears, Scarlett straightened her spine and willed herself to be stronger than the eighteen-year-old girl who had fallen in love so hard and fast that she didn't ask any questions or expect anything in return. In the strongest voice she could muster, she responded with what she should have said on Prom night and every other time he had ever said those three little words. "I don't believe you."

Feet moving her down the cobblestone and back to the gala, Scarlett found what little will she had not to turn around when Colin called after her.

"You will, because I'm staying."

Thirty-Eight

Scarlett
23 Years Old

"Red alert! I made out with Colin." The front door to Harper's house swung too wide with Scarlett's grand entrance and hit the wall with a loud smack. She winced, both because of the noise and the company she hadn't realized would be at her sister's house for their weekly wine and telenovela night. The information had been bubbling up inside of her for days, and she needed to debrief with all her favorite people. As expected, her sister was sitting on the couch, but so was Piper Hartrick.

"What the fuck?" Harper gasped. "Why would you do that? Was this why you left the gala early?"

Kashvi and Saanvi poked their heads out from the kitchen, eyebrows arched in matching sisterly interest. "Finally!" Kashvi exclaimed and walked out with a tray full of charcuterie, setting it on the ottoman in the middle of the room. "How was it?"

"Uh... I..." Scarlett bit her lip and deflated a bit, looking nervously at Piper.

"I already know," Piper said casually, sipping water from a glass.

"He told you?" Scarlett's cheeks flushed. She felt an undercurrent of satisfaction as well as something else she couldn't quite put her finger on. It wasn't quite joy, but there was a certain thrill from knowing that Colin had gone straight home to tell everyone that he had kissed her.

"Pearl told me." Piper paused, the corners of her mouth hitching up while she was clearly trying to hold back a smile or laugh. "Then Carter... then Colin." The breath Scarlett had been holding while Piper was speaking finally released. "Via text," Piper tacked on, holding out her phone to Scarlett.

Gingerly, Scarlett took the phone and stared down at the text message Colin had sent just this morning to the sibling group chat appropriately labeled "The Hartrick Orphans."

COLIN 6:23 AM

Pearl told me I need to share more, so I'm informing you that Scarlett and I made out outside the charity gala last night. 10/10 would kiss again. I also told her I still love her and she said she didn't believe me, so that part sucked, but the physical part was great. I will work on the rest.

The text was so Colin-coded it made her want to laugh out loud. The ending, however, had her intrigued, so she read on.

CARTER 6:25 AM

Dude, you woke me up. It's too fucking early for you to be blowing up this gc with that kind of information.

COLIN 6:28 AM

Oh, sorry.

PIPER 6:30 AM

Carter is in a depressed post break-up funk. Don't worry about him. The rest of us are up and out of bed.

COOPER 6:32 AM

I think I heard him crying last night.

PEARL 6:33 AM

Definitely crying

CARTER 6:33 AM

My life is a deep, dark pit of despair.

COLIN 6:34 AM

Would it help if we told you that your girlfriend sucked? I don't usually make unilateral decisions about people's character, but I feel confident that Stella was a bad person. If Scarlett was like Stella, she'd be easy to get over.

COOPER 6:35 AM

Colin's decisions are usually wrong, but he's right this time.

PEARL 6:36 AM

Coop, give Colin a break. We get it, you're an angsty teen who can hold a grudge for way too long.

PIPER 6:37 AM

Coop, if I can forgive you for tattling on me to Walker when I tried to sneak out the window in high school, you can forgive Colin.

COOPER 6:38 AM

Shouldn't you be thanking me? Your klutz ass would have fallen off the roof.

Scarlett held back a laugh. The windows were frequent fliers in the Hartrick household, apparently. She wasn't sure what Cooper was holding a grudge over, but her urge to defend Colin was a surprising and unwelcome thought.

CARTER 6:39 AM

Everyone shut up, I'm trying to wallow.

PEARL 6:41 AM

Turn your phone on dnd, old man.

PIPER 6:42 AM

Coop, I'm gonna tell Walker you said "ass."

COLIN 6:43 AM

Cooper, will you just tell me exactly what I need to do to get you to forgive me? I've already run through a list of suggestions from Google

COOPER 6:45 AM

Make a time traveling machine.

Scarlett went to scroll on, and Piper quickly grabbed the phone before she could. "I shouldn't let you see the whole conversation," Piper said sheepishly.

"Why? What did he say?" Harper demanded.

"It's just a bunch of personal stuff that I think he'd rather say in person," Piper said.

"Probably should have said it years ago," Harper grumbled, unknowingly mimicking Cooper's thoughts. Piper, for all her bubbliness, turned toward Harper and delivered the most venomous look Scarlett had ever seen.

"If you expected an eighteen-year-old autistic boy who just lost his parents to be able to articulate all his feelings perfectly, then that seems like more of a you problem," she said contritely.

Harper blanched but met Piper's gaze directly, and it felt like a trainwreck Scarlett couldn't look away from. Except the trainwreck was her life, and she was just watching from the sidelines. "I never said I expected that. I just expected him to not destroy my sister on his path to well-being."

"Stop it," Scarlett cut in, tone sharp and directed at her sister. "He did not destroy me. I'm fine."

"You are *now*." Harper pursed her lips. "And that's why I'm worried. You're finally over it, and you're just going to fall right back into it."

"I was never fucking over it, okay?" Scarlett snapped, her voice way louder than she intended. The room went dead silent, and she caught Kashvi's brief look of shock before she squinted her eyes shut. "Look, I can appreciate that you want to protect me, H. And I know I made several stupid decisions when I was eighteen, but I don't regret any of those mistakes. I also know that I went a little off the deep end back then, but it felt like the person I was in love with had just died, so I think that warranted a bit of a depression. I'm so grateful for you." She gestured to her sister then looked up to toss a glance between Kashvi and Saanvi. "All three of you. But if I want to fuck up my own life, I'm going to. I make my own decisions, and I'll learn from them. I get to come here hoping to have a girls' night and freak out over accidentally making out with my ex in the rain until his fitness watch lit up like a Christmas tree because I made his heart rate spike."

"Oh my God!" Kashvi gasped and wiggled in her seat. Out of everyone, Scarlett could always count on her best friend to have an appropriate reaction. Saanvi glared at her sister, either for interrupting Scarlett's long-winded rant or because she thought this wasn't a cause to be cheering for. "What? You have to admit, that's romantic as hell."

Scarlett bit her bottom lip and straightened her shoulders, blushing slightly. "It's the best thing that's happened to me all week. All year, maybe."

Piper was clearly feigning disinterest, looking up at the ceiling and awkwardly fingering a string on the couch that had come loose. The strange part was that Scarlett didn't even care. If Piper wanted to immediately text Colin after this and tell him everything she had said, it might be a bit embarrassing, but it was still true. Finally, when Scarlett braved a glance at her sister, she was surprised to find that Harper was no longer maintaining a harsh facial expression. It had softened significantly, her eyes sincere as she gave her a microscopic nod.

"And then," Scarlett's voice cracked, her face falling. "I get to tell you that he told me he loved me, and I didn't cave. I didn't accept it at face value, because I learned my lesson the first time. I don't believe him, and I'm not sure I ever will."

"Oh, Letti," Harper said glumly. She waved her arms toward herself, beckoning a hug. Scarlett obliged, letting herself fall into her little sister role where Harper would tuck her under her chin and stroke her hair. "I don't think not believing that someone loves you is the win you're thinking it is."

"It is," Scarlett argued, sniffing back the tears starting to form in her waterline. "I fell for it the first time, and I'm not doing that again. He may believe he's in love with me, but just like last time, he's not."

"Can I just—" Piper raised her hand politely. "I don't know if you want my opinion or if it matters to you, but for what it's worth, I know my brother, and he's so in love with you he barely talks about anything else other than his job, and even that is—" She cut herself off with a shake of her head. "I promise, he loves you."

It took Scarlett a moment to respond, weighing her options. Nothing Piper said had swayed her, but putting it into words was hard. "Maybe I'm a hyperfixation of his right now, but I wasn't for five years. My dad taught me everything I need to know about leaving, and even if my dad thinks he loves us, it's not real love because you don't give up on people you love."

Piper nodded and swallowed, her eyes going glassy. "I, um, I have this thing I'm working on where I purposely don't get attached to people and I don't let people in because I get scared that the more I love them, the more it'll hurt when they leave. When Harper invited me over today, I had the thought that we were maybe getting too close and that was a bad idea since she'd eventually leave or die."

"Wow... that's fucked," Kashvi said. She and her sister were sitting on the ottoman now, leaning forward in interest.

"So, are you saying Colin is the same?" Saanvi asked.

"I'm saying all of us are a little fucked up, and he fell in love with Scarlett right after our parents died. Not to mention he was undiagnosed." Piper turned to face Scarlett. "I think he was really confused and dealing with a lot, and you were his comfort person. He didn't really talk to Walker or any of us about his grief. He talked to Carter, but it was mostly about you. I'm not trying to give him an excuse for hurting you, because he clearly did, but, from the outside looking in, it felt like you two were in this happy little bubble, and then Colin's bubble popped before yours did. He hit reality with the force of a brick wall while you were still in that happy place."

"He was cruel about it," Scarlett whispered.

"He knows." Piper gave her a solemn smile. "I think you should talk about what really happened that day, because I know your stories are very different."

"And in the meantime..." Kashvi pumped her eyebrows. "You could go back to banging him because you two were clearly good at that."

"Ugh," Piper gagged.

"What is wrong with you, seriously?" Saanvi chastised her sister.

"I wouldn't suggest it if I didn't like Colin. I was his friend, too. I know what he did, but I also know how happy Scarlett was when she was with him. Maybe I'm just into red flags." Kashvi shrugged before adding, "I also haven't gotten laid in like," she held up her hands as if to count then sighed dramatically. "Eight months, maybe?"

"Have you considered sleeping with Varo?" Piper suggested. All eyes swiveled to her, scandalized, and she let out a puff of laughter. "What? You two married Diaz men." She pointed at Harper and Saanvi. "And I'm with Leo, so it seems like..."

"We all have fantastic sex lives?" Saanvi asked, patting her pregnant belly.

"I mean, I do." Harper grinned.

"Exactly." Piper looked at Scarlett. "I think my brother would agree that our small case study on Diaz men would conclude that the fourth Diaz brother must also be…" She trailed off suggestively.

"Colin would say it's a hypothesis that has to be tested." Scarlett laughed. "So, I guess it's a good thing one of us *has*, in fact, tested it."

Harper gasped. "Letti?"

"Not her." Kashvi waved them off. "That would have been my eight months ago."

"Was it bad?" Piper's eyes widened.

"No, it was great. He's just an aimless floater who's never around. Plus he's in the middle of a bus conversion to replace his van conversion."

"Ah, I guess it's settled, then." Piper gripped the sunflower necklace at her neck before she swiveled her finger around the room. "No one tell Leo that I mentioned his brother."

"Oh, you don't have to worry about that." Harper tossed a hand in the air. "Saanvi and I are aware that the Diaz men are the jealous type."

"I wish Colin was the jealous type. He met Braiden and seemed like he could care less." Scarlett blew out a breath.

"I kept telling you to date Leo or Varo. If you did, then you'd get a big heap of jealousy," Harper said.

"Just to be clear, I am also the jealous type." Piper straightened her shoulders.

"You'll be happy to know she was uninterested." Harper chuckled.

"Now I'm kinda offended on behalf of Leo. Why were you uninterested? Because you're secretly still in love with my brother?" Piper leaned forward with a mischievous twinkle in her eye, and Scarlett avoided the question about Colin entirely.

"Varo is more Kashvi's type. And Leo... is terrifying." Piper had started to take a sip of water when she choked on it and started a coughing fit, waving her hand in front of her face as laughter bubbled up intermittently between coughs. "Be honest, how many times have you had to use a safe word?" Scarlett egged her on, happy to draw focus to Piper's love life instead of her own.

The entire room was in fits of giggles now as Piper wheezed into a tissue she had ripped out of the box on the end table beside the couch. "I've never had to use a safe word." She paused and tilted her head to one side with a smirk. "Leo's used it once, though." The room erupted again. "Listen," Piper giggled. "I really don't think Scarlett, out of all of us, has any room to talk about kinks. I wish I could burn my retinas after seeing one of your weird-ass sex experiment charts."

Scarlett flipped over and pressed her face into the carpeted floor with a groan.

"She wouldn't even let *me* read them!" Kashvi huffed.

"You can blame Carter, actually. He was snooping after you and Colin apparently stole all his condoms," Piper said. "I didn't know what I was reading until it was too late, and Carter's an asshole."

"I had just managed to forget that you've seen one." Scarlett whined, voice muffled by the ground. "I think I'm going to hide forever. I've made a home here on the floor, and if I can't see you, I'm convinced you all can't see me. If I need sustenance, you can just throw charcuterie at me like a blindfolded petting zoo."

"But we're blindfolding the animals?" Kashvi cackled.

"Sure." Scarlett nodded, the carpet making a burning friction against her nose. "Kashvi, would you still love me if I was a worm?"

"Always, babe."

"At least you didn't walk in on them in the shower," Harper said to Piper

"*No,*" Piper gasped before letting out a long, drawn-out "*ewwww.*"

It took an extreme amount of self control to not shout about how the scales had definitely evened between Scarlett and her sister given her accidental run-in with Harper, Marcos, and their kitchen counter.

"I'm scared to ask." Scarlett shyly looked over at Piper, wincing. "Colin told me which chart you saw, but... how far did you get? Because that particular day was not my shining moment."

"I looked at it for the least amount of time possible so I didn't actually see a lot. I read a sentence about your tongue that was revolting and then something about candle wax being a no-go, but I don't even know what that means?"

Scarlett had vowed to herself to not look back on her and Colin's time together so she wouldn't end up rewriting it, but this particular incident had been the exception to that rule. It was so clear now how badly she had fucked up by inadvertently crossing one of Colin's unspoken boundaries while he had crossed over hers at the same time. The lack of communication on her part had backed them both into a corner.

"What the hell were you doing with candle wax?" Harper squeaked.

"Something really sexy, I imagine." Kashvi grinned.

"I worry about you sometimes." Saanvi looked in disapproval toward her sister.

Instead of answering the what of the question, Scarlett buried her face back into the carpet, shaking her head in misery. "It wasn't sexy. It was something we never should have tried."

Thirty-Nine

Colin
18 Years Old

"Do you ever just lie on the floor?" Colin peeked up from where he was sprawled out on the carpet in Scarlett's bedroom. Scarlett fastened the hooks to her bra and shimmied it back into place. He indulgently watched her breasts jiggle before they were trapped again by fabric.

"I used to when I was younger," Scarlett said, reaching to pull her shirt over her head. "But why not just lie on the bed instead?"

"It's not the same. The ground is nice because it's hard. Sometimes I don't want things to be so soft," he said and scooted closer to her when she came to lie down beside him. "Also, your bed currently smells like sex."

"It does." She giggled.

"There is one soft thing that I always like, though." He wiggled along the floor so his head lined up with her chest and leaned his cheek into her breasts with a sigh as she played with his hair, massaging his scalp and drawing a groan from low in his throat. He could have sworn he wouldn't like physical touch so much with a sexual partner, but Scarlett had proven that wrong time and time again. As long as she was touching him with solid and ungentle hands, everything she did felt like his version of heaven.

"This is nice." Scarlett hummed.

Colin lifted his hand, and she tangled her fingers with his. "I feel like we opened up a can of worms."

Her chest stopped expanding and retracting under his head. "What do you mean?"

"I mean I'm insatiable now. All I can think about is sex," he explained. Her chest resumed breathing with a laugh, only to stop again when he started his speech. "I want to fuck you on every surface in this room. I think about skipping class and dragging you out into the parking lot to fuck you in my car when we're at school. When I'm at home I just want to sext you or pull up the pictures you sent me last time so I can pretend I'm fucking you. I can't stop. I know it's hormones and whatnot, but it's becoming a problem. How on Earth am I ever going to do anything else when all I want is to see you naked? Even now." He briefly looked down at her body and licked his bottom lip. She couldn't see his face, but her fingers in his hair gripped him harder, and her body tightened against him. It didn't take much to get him going, even ten minutes after their first round. He had memorized the way Scarlett looked naked at this point, and if he wanted—and he pretty much always did—he could conjure up an image of her without a stitch of clothing on with his mind alone. "Even now, I'm thinking about what new thing we could try next for our experiment."

"I feel the same." Her breathing was shallow as he turned his head a bit, angling his face toward her chest. "I'll be in class, and the seam of my jeans will hit just right, and then I'll be stuck thinking about how badly I want you." Untangling her hand from his, he palmed one of her breasts, stretching his fingers to get more. His hands were large, but never big enough to hold her completely in one hand. "Colin, I just put my clothes back on," Scarlett chastised.

"I can take them back off for you." He dragged his hand down her stomach, and she arched into him. "Do you want to try something new? I've read a few new romance novels, and I have a few ideas." His fingers deftly flicked at the button holding the top of her jeans together.

"What time is it?" Scarlett gasped, wiggling under him and angling her hips toward his hand. The small laugh she let out when he burrowed his face into her breasts was infectious, and he smiled against her chest, feeling the vibrations of sound in her body.

"Twenty minutes till."

"That's cutting it a bit close to when my family will be home," she breathed as his hand traveled under the band of her underwear.

"I can accomplish a lot in twenty minutes," Colin promised. The tips of his fingers found her clit and started to circle and press just the way he knew she liked it.

"What were you thinking?" Her body responded with a flutter of eyelashes, her hands in his hair circling and massaging at the same pace.

"You know that time I went so deep that you said it hurt a bit? But like a good kind of pain?" The question came out hoarse, he was already so hard again. He wanted to go that deep now. Rut into her from behind and pin her down the way she always wanted.

Scarlett's head bobbed in acknowledgment above him. "I have a belt you can whip me with if you want to try the pain route."

Colin's head popped up from the floor in alarm. "What? No, I was going to suggest something gradual, and if we end up liking it, we can move on to whips."

"Oh." She blinked. "That makes sense." He was always a little shocked by how willing she was to try new things with him. As far as he knew, there hadn't been a single time she didn't want to try something from a book or online forum, which felt like a home run given that, at some point, everyone was uncomfortable around him. "What'd you have in mind?"

On their way into her bedroom, he thought he had spotted a candle on the dresser in the back corner, but his memory was a bit foggy as he was busy with peeling all of Scarlett's clothes from her body and backing her toward the bed. They barely had the front door to her house open this time before they were making out and trying to make it up the stairs. His memory was confirmed, however, when he rose to his feet and found it, plucking it off her dresser. A delicate sniff of the candle confirmed that he really hated overly fragrant things, but the smell wasn't what he was after this time, and he would suck up his distaste for the smell for Scarlett's sake.

"I read a romance novel the other day where the guy dripped candle wax on his girlfriend. and apparently that's really erotic? I hadn't thought to try that, and I was curious, so—"

"You researched it," Scarlett finished his sentence with a smile as she got up off the floor.

"Of course I did," Colin confirmed. "I read a few Reddit threads on wax play, and it seems people like it because the hot wax is a bit of a painful sting, but then it cools pretty quickly, so it's a good way of testing out if you like pain during sex. What do you think?" Colin held the candle up. He was sure he would hate this if the wax was being dripped on him, so if she declined, he could move on pretty easily. Scarlett stared at it for a moment before slowly nodding her head once.

"Okay, let's try it. There's a lighter on my dresser." She pointed, and Colin found it easily enough, lighting the wick and scrunching his nose at the floral smell that immediately wafted into the air.

"Get undressed," he directed. She always liked it when he was a bit more demanding during sex, so he opted to get right to the point this time. The pink coloring her cheeks like her watercolor paintings flushed into a deeper red as she did as told, pulling her underwear and jeans down her legs and kicking them off while she removed the rest. The urge he always had to pick up her clothes came back, but he batted those thoughts away, trying not to ruin the moment. Everything he read on the internet about testing pain said to be connected with your partner and to make sure you were watching their face for any discomfort beyond what they could tolerate. He made a point to meet her eyes and count to five in his head for an appropriate amount of eye contact, then had to drag his gaze over her body to focus on something more comfortable. By the time she was naked and lying on the bed and he had prepped her by rubbing her clit until she was grinding against his palm, the wax in the top of the candle had melted into a pool of hot liquid, ready to use. "Open your legs more. I'm going to drip it on your thighs." Again she took his direction and parted her thighs like the red sea—red in the literal sense of the word because the tuft of ginger hair between her legs was his favorite fireplace. Her knees tipped out, and the pads of her feet pressed into the mattress. Carefully, he brought the candle toward her and sat back on his heels between her legs.

"Colin..." Her voice was faraway-sounding, so he figured it was the same as the way she said his name during sex. Like a prayer or a plea for him to continue. He tipped the candle toward her and let the hot wax drip over the edge. Her body tensed when the wax made contact, muscles contracting as Scarlett let out a small sound he had never quite heard before. He tipped the candle over on the other side and was met with the same sound again. The wax still drying on her thighs, he moved the candle over her entrance, toying with the idea of dropping wax there, too. "Colin," she said again as she squirmed back toward the headboard. He followed, chasing her in the playful way they always did, grimacing a bit from the awful scent he had now painted her thighs with.

When he aimed the hot wax right where he wanted it, he watched in devout interest as her body went rigid and shrunk away from him, pulling away so forcefully he glanced up, expecting to find Scarlett giggling or beckoning him forward, to tell him to take his clothes off, too. He wasn't sure he wanted sex after he had ruined his favorite place with a painfully fragrant smell, but he was doubly sure he no longer wanted to when he saw Scarlet's face.

Hypothesis and predictions normally came easy to Colin because facts led somewhere concrete. Scarlett had said his name, she had writhed below him like she did every time before when he pinned her down. Except this time, he had never been more wrong about an outcome in his life.

Everything changed in an instant, and his heart dropped into his stomach. Tears were rolling down over Scarlett's face, and she was shaking her head repeatedly in the universal sign for 'no.'

"Scarlett? What happened?" Colin's eyes widened in alarm. Her hand shot up from the comforter and waved around, pressing on the glass candle jar and jerking upright so her knees were tucked into her chest in a sort of fetal position. "What—"

"I don't like it," she whispered. Colin backed away from her in bewilderment and set the candle on the nightstand.

"You didn't like it?" He was still so confused. Everything she outwardly said confirmed she did like it. She hadn't said to stop, and yet the fat tears rolling down her face immediately made him feel guilty.

Her voice cracked with her responding, "No, I didn't. You didn't see that I was trying to back away from you?"

Colin's mouth opened and shut several times. Surely that should have been something he should have noticed, but he had been so focused on the words. The breathless way she had said his name. The new sound he elicited from the new experiment. A sound he now realized must have not been one of pleasure like he had assumed. "You... you didn't say the safe word."

"I..." Scarlett sat up and wiped at the tears before hugging herself a bit tighter. "Sorry."

"Sorry?" All he could think to do was repeat everything back as a question because he simply could not wrap his mind around it. "Why didn't you? If you don't like something, you need to tell me to stop."

"I don't know why I didn't. I just... my brain short-circuited, and I figured if you looked up for two seconds instead of being so focused on my body, you'd see that I was uncomfortable." Her face was twisted in a new way he hadn't seen before, and there was a pressure rising in his chest that he knew all too well.

"We agreed, Scarlett!" Voice bitter, he pulled himself angrily off the bed and found her clothes on the floor. "You have to use the word 'stop' when you don't fucking want to do something."

"*You're* mad at *me?*" she shouted back.

"Of course I'm mad," Colin fumed, angrily tossing her clothes onto the bed.

"*Wow.*" Scarlett snatched her underwear from where they had landed on the mattress and started to aggressively wipe herself down with a baby wipe from the nightstand, peeling off the remnants of the wax as he paced the room, unable to watch her wince through it. She was making a lot of noise, huffing and puffing as she aggressively shoved all her clothes back on. Colin ran a hand through his hair, trying to calm himself, but to no avail. Before he knew it, his body started to shake from emotion just in time for Scarlett to land another blow. "I never thought you'd be someone who was mad I didn't have sex with you."

"Are you serious right now?" He whirled on her. "I'm not mad we didn't have sex. I'm mad you didn't fucking say anything when you didn't like it!"

"I said your name twice and tried to get away from you, what more did you want?"

"The fucking safe word, Scarlett! Tell me to stop!" Colin snapped. The angry way he started to list off the appropriate ways to reject advances ramped him up even more. "The word 'no,' 'please stop doing that,' 'ouch, I hate this,' literally any one of those would have worked. I'm not a damn mind reader. I can't clock your facial expressions. I have no idea what you're thinking. You say my name all the time when we're having sex."

"I don't say it like *that*," Scarlett argued.

"Like what?" He didn't know what to do with his body anymore. All of his limbs felt like they wanted to fly off in different directions, and he could feel his heartbeat thrumming in his ears. "Please enlighten me, because I can't tell the fucking difference between you begging for me to touch you and you telling me to stop when you use the exact same word."

"I said it like I was scared you were going to hurt me. You just wouldn't look at me because all you care about is sex." Her voice cracked, and more tears spilled down her face.

Colin's breathing was so heavy now that he was starting to hyperventilate. What exactly was he supposed to tell her? That he didn't like staring lovingly into her eyes? That it made him deeply uncomfortable? Every time he forced himself to look directly, it felt so aggressive. But that was what couples did, right? They stared into each other's souls and got lost there. In every romance novel he had ever read, including the one that had provided this stupid candle wax idea, the couples always looked at each other. Really *looked*. They *wanted* to look. There had to be something deeply wrong with him to have to focus so hard to make eye contact with someone he loved. Scarlett's eyes were beautiful, and yet he felt like his skin was crawling when she looked back at him at the same time. All of that would prove what she said, that all he cared about was sex, when that didn't feel true in the slightest. What he hated was feeling innately perceived by *anyone's* eyes.

"I don't—I—" His chest heaved, and he sat abruptly on the edge of the bed, sucking in short breaths that didn't give him nearly enough oxygen.

"Colin?" Scarlett's voice felt distant again, and when she reached out to touch him, he jerked away from her hand, fearing it was yet another way she said his name that meant something he didn't understand.

"I'm sorry." A panicked huff of air was all it took to tip him over the edge of lost control, and he started shaking his head repeatedly.

"No, *I'm* sorry. I didn't mean that." Scarlett came closer to his side, and he practically jumped away from her. "Shh, shh, shh," she soothed, grabbing his hand and pulling him down to the floor with her. He followed until they were both lying back in their original position, her hands firmly stroking his hair and his cheek pressed into her breasts. It took a few minutes for his heart rate to slow and his speaking ability to return.

"I can't tell the difference," he murmured. "I don't know when my name means stop or go. And I want to know, I really do. I want to be able to look at you and tell when you're uncomfortable. I should be able to. But I can't. I'm scared I'll hurt you if you can't say what you mean."

"Okay." She nodded. "I'm sorry. It was burning, and I could barely think of your name, let alone anything else. I'll try harder next time."

Colin wrapped his arm around her. "There won't be a next time for that."

"I guess it's a good thing we didn't start with whips." Scarlett huffed out a laugh.

"This isn't funny." The world still felt like it was spinning a bit. He had crossed some sort of a boundary, and he didn't know where to go from there.

Scarlett sighed. "I know. Sorry, I was just trying to deflect because I'm uncomfortable." He appreciated how much she had been able to say things out loud to him lately, but the time for that would have been a few moments before when he was unknowingly hurting her.

"We're not going near masochism again," Colin said resolutely. "And I don't just care about sex."

"I know." Her fingertips paused in his hair.

"But is that what you think?"

"Sometimes." She shifted against him. "Everything you tell me and your actions say you love me, but your body doesn't always say that. You never really look at me except on Prom night, and when you did, it was like you were staring through me. Maybe I'm just overthinking it."

"No, you're not. The eye contact, it..." Colin trailed off and restarted, frustrated that she had noticed that about him when he had tried so hard to fix it. "I don't know why, but I can't focus or pay attention to anything if I'm looking into anyone's eyes. It feels unnatural and really aggressive, and I always have to do this thing where I count to two Mississippi so people think that I've really looked at them, when really I've just been counting in my head and staring off into space."

"You do that with me?" Her voice was so sweet that he wanted to promise her it took no effort at all to look at her, that she was the one exception to the rule, that he could stare into her eyes all day long. The truth was a harder pill to swallow, but he said it anyway.

"I changed it to five seconds with you because everything I've read suggests that I should want to look into your eyes for longer."

"Oh." Her voice was so small, and he had the sickening feeling that he should have kept that to himself.

"You know I love you, right?"

"Yeah," she murmured, kissing the top of his head. "And you know I love you?"

"Yeah," Colin confirmed and swallowed down the rock in his throat. "I should be able to tell when you're uncomfortable." His mind was whirring and replaying everything his therapist had said recently. In the beginning, he had put hardly any stock into it, because there was no way that the people that loved him would miss that. The more he researched it, though, and the more his therapist requested that he stop pretending to look at him, the more he was starting to think that everyone was in the know but him. Everyone knew there was something wrong with him, and he was the only one in the dark.

Scarlett cupped the sides of Colin's head and tipped his face up toward her. He attempted to look her in the eyes again, but she brought her hand up and brushed it down over his face, effectively closing his eyelids. The relief was instant, and he relaxed into her touch. "We don't have to do everything the way it's normally done. We get to make the rules. I love you because you're exactly the way you are and you let me be who I am. I don't have to be embarrassed when I go on a long rant or when I tell you exactly what I want."

"I like your stories. I get a whole bunch of little pieces of your life that I wouldn't know otherwise," Colin said. "I like that I get to be the one to remind you to drink water. Speaking of which, when's the last time you drank water?"

"Um..." she stalled. His eyes flickered open, and he rolled away from her, rising to his feet and holding out his hand. He needed to be useful again, and taking action with Scarlett's water consumption was the best way he knew how to do that. It was proof that he loved her, because he didn't like seeing her in pain from a headache or from something he did.

Scarlett took his hand, and the firmness of her grip settled the uprising in his chest.

"Water," he directed. "Now."

FORTY

Colin
23 Years Old

Colin's morning routine was underway. He had already run three miles before the sun rose with Walker, drunk coffee, and taken a shower in his new, mostly empty apartment. He didn't have to go to work on a Sunday, but he swung by anyway to finish one of his reports and use the database to read up on what he hoped his research project would be on when he started his doctorate program. The best part of his routine was that he barely had to think about it. He could move through the motions because they were expected. He could get in a bit more work because work, while it challenged his mind, wasn't mentally taxing in the way emotions and masking were. Unfortunately, nothing would stop his brain from hyperfixating on the night before—the best night he'd had in a long time before it had crashed and burned epically.

I don't believe you. He had never had someone blatantly tell him that before, because no one ever had cause to think he'd be lying. Walker, maybe, given the things Colin had lied about his senior year, but even then, Walker seemed to wholeheartedly believe everything that came out of Colin's mouth. His word was infallible. Even back then, if Walker had called Colin out, he would have told the truth. Most of his lies had been lies of omission, anyway. Most had been because he was in love and wanted to see Scarlett. In truth, he knew why she would think he didn't love her. It was the same reason Cooper had told him he needed a time machine that morning, and if he didn't love his job so much, he would consider going back to school to become a physicist. Neither of them knew the war with his mind he'd had to fight just to come back, let alone admit that people wanted him around.

When Colin made it back to his apartment after finding a good stopping point with his research that evening, he took one look at his mostly empty living room—apart from Theo's easel and art supplies—and turned to head back out the door. He didn't know how to make this place look like a home, but the emptiness was starting to grate on him, and if he ever wanted it to feel like a home and a place he and Theo felt comfortable in, he needed furniture other than the simple bed frame he had picked out. Theo's DNA painting was the only piece of artwork on his walls, and he had hung that haphazardly over his bed. If he ever had a hope for Scarlett to come over, he knew it was time to ask a professional because she would no doubt be appalled by the lack of color and bare walls.

After Piper graduated, she had taken over their parents' interior design business and found a place in Archwood to rent with Leo when the two had finally locked each other down. Colin already knew Piper would be the best person to fix his space into something livable and homey, but he hadn't gotten around to asking her yet. Between that and knowing she had finally worked past some of her relationship issues, he could kill two birds with one stone. Everyone's protests about Piper being the worst person to talk to when it came to romantic exploits must no longer be valid given her hard-fought relationship with Leo. Carter had been the self-proclaimed relationship expert before, but given his recent break-up with a girl Colin thought was the textbook definition of controlling, Piper was his best option. He liked Leo, and

Leo didn't send off alarm bells in his head, unlike Piper's previous boyfriends.

When he arrived, Piper's Mini Cooper wasn't in the driveway, but that didn't mean much considering Leo often took her car to run errands when his own car was broken down. The hood to Leo's clunker was propped open where it was parked in the gravel to the side of the driveway, so Colin figured it was still likely that Piper was home and Leo's car was acting up again. It was a wonder how they had managed to get the car down to Archwood at all.

Colin knocked on the door and waited only a moment before Leo pulled it open with a phone pressed to his ear and raised a finger to silence him.

"That won't work. We need at least ten gallons of corn syrup. It's the most important shot of the movie, and we're going to keep flashing back to it, so I need there to be enough blood. Get more," Leo demanded, presumably to whoever was on the phone since Colin had zero plans to buy more corn syrup. Without any sort of goodbye, Leo ended the call and looked up at Colin, swiping at the black curls on his head. "Piper should be back later, if you're looking for her. She's hanging out with my sisters-in-law."

"Ah." Colin bobbed his head awkwardly. The only sisters-in-law Leo had were Harper and Saanvi. He had only briefly met Kashvi's sister once at Piper and Leo's musical production of *Guys and Dolls* a few months back, and it was safe to assume that she and Harper were both on the same page about disliking him.

"Do you want to wait for her? Sam is here, and he's being annoying as shit, so it would be nice to have another voice of reason in the group," Leo said.

"You asshole, I am as cool as a cucumber!" Leo's friend popped his head from around the door and waved. Colin had met Sam a few times: at the funeral for Leo's grandmother, starring opposite Piper in the musical, and the occasional time Sam was at the house with Leo for a script meeting with Walker. The indie film Leo was directing and producing was an adaptation of one of Walker's novels, a romantic psychological thriller with apparently enough fake blood to be sponsored by corn syrup. "Good to see you again."

For all of Leo's gruffness, he continually surrounded himself with the chipperest of people. Colin didn't mind it. Sam minorly reminded Colin of Scarlett in the way he got excited about small things and laughed often. On the other hand, he was as tall as Colin, with blond hair brighter than his own and a face built for the big screen if Colin had ever seen one—all chiseled lines and perfectly straight teeth. Scarlett was round in all the right places, soft and squishy like his favorite pillow. Leo was the antithesis of both of them, tall, dark, and handsome, except he was five-eight at most and had the countenance of a Rottweiler rather than the golden retriever Piper had proclaimed she once wanted. At some point, Colin would have to remind Piper that he was right about his 'opposites attract' theory.

"Good to see you, too." Colin gave Sam a nod of acknowledgment before dropping his eyes to Leo again, looking slightly past him. "You might be able to answer some other questions I have, actually."

"Sure." Leo opened the door and stepped to the side to let him in. They all wandered into the living room, where several green swatches were painted on the wall, no doubt a display of Piper's indecision. Leo caught where his gaze had landed and said, "She could choose any of them, but she's been agonizing over it for a week, like if she chooses the wrong shade of the same color, walking into this room will make us all fall into depression."

"They're all different," Sam scolded.

"I'm sure they have different color codes, but they look pretty much the same to me," Colin noted. The swatch on the far left had more of a beige hue to it, maybe, but even that was a stretch.

Leo gave a wry smile and gestured to Colin, who had just taken a seat on the sofa. "Like I said, voice of reason." Besides the paint, everything else about the room was finished with warm colors and sensible furniture. He thought the leather couch would be uncomfortable when he sat down, but he found it was the opposite, and he sunk into the cushions, relaxing. Piper was shaping up to have the exact same taste as their mother, who valued both fashion and practicality in her approach to interior design, which was a good sign if he needed his apartment to be both comfortable for his and Theo's sake and aesthetically pleasing for Scarlett's sake.

"I'm on pins and needles," Sam cooed. "What are you going to ask him? Are you going to fight him in a duel for your sister's honor?"

Colin looked to Leo. "Why? Did you do something to her?"

"Depends what you mean by that." Leo smirked.

"I mean did you hurt her or something else that would require me to hit you," Colin explained.

"Shit, I forgot that you'd take me literally. Sorry, I was just making a joke." Leo waved a hand in the air in dismissal "No, I'd never do anything to hurt her like that. The most I'll do is needle her about how all the paint swatches she's deciding between look exactly the same. And that's more because I find it fun to get a rise out of her. She's very cute when she's pissed off."

"As someone who has argued with her plenty, I disagree," Colin said.

Sam cackled and motioned to Leo. "Well, Lover Boy here is mostly heart eyes around Piper, even when she's yelling at him."

"I told you to stop calling me that," Leo grumbled.

Sam barreled ahead, addressing Colin. "Can't imagine you would hurt a fly, anyway."

"I've punched someone in the face before, so I would definitely hurt more than a fly," Colin recounted.

"I completely forgot that was you." Leo sat up straighter and turned to Sam conversationally. "Colin's the one who punched Piper's ex in the face back in high school."

It had been a long time since Colin had thought about what happened that night, other than telling Scarlett for the first time he was in love with her and falling asleep with her naked and curled into him. It was still the best night and best morning of his life, to this day. At the time, he didn't even know why he had been so angry to the point of violence with Harden, but now he knew exactly why. Harden deserved it, but Colin's emotional dysregulation had also come into play. Between the loss of his parents that caused a well of pent-up and confusing emotion and the loud music that had made his brain go into fight or flight, one more thing had pushed him over the edge, and he simply couldn't take it anymore.

"I met that guy once," Sam said. "If there was ever a person that needed to be punched in the face, it's that guy."

"I'll offer up my services for his next reckoning," Leo said, casually cracking his knuckles before flipping the subject. "What'd you want to ask Piper?"

"I was going to hire her to make my apartment not look like a serial killer's apartment."

Leo's smile was so wide and genuine as he jumped up from the couch that Colin wasn't sure what exactly he had said to warrant such a reaction until Leo jogged into the office he and Piper shared and came back out with a file folder of papers. "Here. She's already worked up several design options for you and printed off pictures of furniture options for you to choose from. I think there's even a corduroy accent couch in there." Colin probably should have guessed that Piper would have already prepared for this, given that they both had the same organizational obsession they had gotten from their mother. In addition to that, they both had gotten their father's mathematical brain, and it was evidenced by the pricing breakdown Piper had provided within a spreadsheet.

"This is perfect." Colin nodded and closed the folder. He would look at it in depth later.

"But you said you had a question for Leo, too, right?" Sam interjected.

"Yes," Colin folded and unfolded his hands. "I was going to

ask you how to prove you love someone, because you're clearly into my sister and you got her to go from despising you to living with you in the span of a few months."

Leo blinked, a startled look about him before he cocked his head to the side. "Scarlett, I assume?"

"You assume correctly," Colin confirmed. "Does that mean I'm transparent about it?"

"I'd say you're pretty damn obvious," Leo said.

"I'm confused. Are you trying to figure out if you love someone?" Sam asked.

"I don't have to figure it out. I know I do. Scarlett doesn't know that I do," Colin explained.

Sam scoffed and shot a look at Leo that Colin couldn't place. "Why don't you just say 'hey, I'm in love with you'?"

"Sometimes it's more complicated than that," Leo muttered.

"I don't think it is more complicated than that at all—that's my problem," Colin said. "I told her I love her."

"Ooh." Sam cringed. "Did she not reciprocate?"

"She said she didn't believe me." Colin swallowed, his mouth feeling dry and sticky. "It hadn't occurred to me that she'd think I was lying. But, given our history, I guess it makes sense."

"Right, Piper told me about the sex chart. She followed it up with a bunch of gagging, but I thought it was very crafty of you." Leo chuckled.

"Scarlett now thinks that that experiment is all I want when I couldn't give two fucks about finding out what I like in bed. I already know what I like, and it's *her*. How do I prove that?"

Leo hummed, leaning his forearms against his thighs. "You weren't around for five years of her life. A lot has happened since you left. That last time you told her you were in love with her, you were both young and stupid."

"She was never stupid." Colin glared at Leo.

"That was more of a turn of phrase, like young, dumb, and broke," Leo clarified and then, with an added smirk, said, "I like that you defended her, though. I know she's not stupid. Harper kept trying to set me up with her a while back, and no one would ever suggest I date someone dumb."

Colin's spine straightened, an acidic feeling churning in his gut. "You dated Scarlett?"

"No, but I can see that you hate the idea of that. I was always six hours out, so I barely even interacted with her." Leo cocked his head. "Didn't picture you as the jealous type."

"I'm not jealous. It makes sense that she's dated other people. It makes sense that one of them was an attractive firefighter who was actually very helpful in getting my mentor kid some information. I took him on a trip to the fire department, and Braiden showed him around so he wouldn't be so scared. He's a nice guy, I just don't like the idea of Scarlett in bed with someone else or holding hands with someone else or telling long stories to someone else while cuddling. That makes me want to pull my hair out, and I hope I was better in bed than all of them combined."

"Friend, that's jealousy." Sam laughed.

"Is it?" Colin asked. "Even if I have no right to feel that way?"

"Yep," Leo confirmed. "I have no right to be annoyed when men look at your sister, but she's mine, so everyone else can fuck off. Your sister feels the same when anyone looks at me, too. The best part is I'm not at all interested in other women, but I really like how she resembles an angry Tinker Bell when she's jealous."

Maybe that would explain how Colin's mood had soured so stupendously after the night of the fire. When Scarlett's ex had mentioned the book Scarlett still had in her nightstand, all Colin could think about was how Braiden had seen the inside of her nightstand and he hadn't. He had survived his apparent jealousy by deciding that Scarlett had to frequently read the book because all her ex-boyfriends—besides himself—were inadequate in bed.

"If I could interject and get us back on track as the person here who's been in a relationship the longest—" Sam raised his sharp chin to the ceiling and smoothed his hair over. "This is a simple answer to me. With Wes, it didn't take a bunch of dicking around to—"

"You're gay, right?" Colin interrupted. Sam nodded. "Then you quite literally dicked around."

Sam grinned wide and cleared his throat. "I did not *pussyfoot* around with Wes," he corrected himself. "I said what I said, and I proved it by showing an interest in him. Maybe instead of trying to prove that you've always loved her—"

"You learn who she is now and love *that* person," Leo tag-teamed, pointing a finger in the air as if to punctuate the 'aha!' moment. "I think she'll be more inclined to believe you if you show her that."

It didn't take any deliberation on Colin's part before he was out of his seat and standing at his full height. "So, I tell her I want to hang out with her, strictly because I like the version of her that she is now."

"And don't bring up anything physical," Sam agreed.

"Shouldn't be too hard considering I've been running on the memory of her for five years." Colin adjusted his glasses. "I'll just masturbate before I hang out with her so I can think about anything other than her breasts."

"That's... so much information." Leo grimaced.

"A solid plan," Sam said.

"At least it's not a liquid plan," Colin retorted, then reconsidered. "Or maybe it is more of a liquid plan."

Sam barked out a laugh and shoved Leo's shoulder. "My God, where have you been hiding this guy?"

"I don't get out much," Colin explained.

"I know you just went to the gala, but maybe go to the 5K for the foundation next week as a show of good faith?" Leo suggested. "Piper and I were planning on going."

"Same." Sam raised his hand.

"Okay, good plan." Colin started to pace with excitement. The tightness in his chest he'd had since the night before lessened. This was feasible. He could show her how much he loved the current version of her. It wouldn't be hard because he had watched her for months, listened to her animated art lessons, and shown up earlier than necessary to every one of her art classes as an excuse to see her. Soon, the art studio would be open again, and he would be back in her company. The 5K was yet another perfect excuse to see her. "I'll get my entire family to go and get sponsors for all of us."

Leo opened his mouth to say something but was interrupted by his phone ringing in his pocket. Colin peeked at the caller ID displaying the name "Princesa" with a sunflower emoji and a picture of Piper flipping the camera off just before Leo answered it. "Hey, when are you—" The alarming way Leo catapulted from the couch with his eyes wide made Colin's heart drop in his chest, his stance going completely rigid. "Where are you?" The tone was all panic, and Colin gritted his teeth, waiting for Leo to get off the phone and tell him what had happened. Sam had risen to his feet as well, eagerly standing beside Leo. "It's okay, mi vida. Your brother's here, so I'll have him drop me at the hospital. Do you want me to stay on the phone with you?" A pause. "Okay, I love you. I'll be there in just a minute."

The second Leo ended the call, a single word shot out of Colin's mouth. His brain had latched on to it, and the fear had wrapped around his head, pulling taut. "Hospital?"

"Piper broke her arm tripping over Harper's end table." Leo, who was already sprinting toward the front door, called back over his shoulder, "I need you to drive me to the ER, and we need to roll your sister in fucking bubble wrap."

Forty-One

Scarlett
23 Years Old

Hospital waiting rooms were the most bland-looking place to get life-altering news. It made sense that none of the surgery wing waiting rooms were particularly colorful, and neither was the emergency room. That was reserved for the pediatric and maternity wings, the former which Scarlett had been to a thousand times with her brother and for the foundation. The walls in the OR waiting room were white, the accents a cool blue that she assumed were painted that way to calm the surgical patients' loved ones. Given the way that Leo and Colin both stormed into the waiting room, it did nothing to alleviate anyone's worries.

"She's in surgery," Harper said, meeting a near-frantic Leo in the center of the room.

"It's a spiral fracture because she fell on it weird," Saanvi added, rising to her feet.

"Goddammit, Piper," Leo grumbled under his breath.

"Which bone did she break?" Colin asked, but he wasn't asking Harper or Saanvi, or even Kashvi, who had risen to her feet to join everyone, he was asking *her*, as if Scarlett's opinion and recollection was the only one that mattered in the room.

"It was—" Harper started, only to get cut off by Colin, raising his hand in a stop position.

"Let Scarlett tell it. She'll give us the entire story with the most detail," Colin said. Leo's hopeful eyes turned to her, and Scarlett found herself moving toward them, officially tasked with informing the group of Piper's condition.

"First and foremost," Scarlett lifted a finger, "she's okay, and the surgery is expected to go well. It will be over in two hours at most." Leo still looked like he was about to throw up, so she continued talking, reassuring him about the procedure and the entire story of Piper's fall that felt incredibly anticlimactic for how gross her arm sounded when she had hit the floor and how panicked their entire group had been at the time they had hauled her into Saanvi's car and driven to the hospital like someone had lit a fire under their asses. Like Colin, Piper didn't drink, so her lack of balance was all her and not a byproduct of their wine and telenovela night. On the way to the ER, between worried statements about how Leo was going to take the news, Piper had passed out exactly once, and they were able to rouse her easily. Throughout the story, Scarlett maintained that Piper was okay, even while in pain. By the end, she got a resolute nod from everyone but Leo, who was clearly determined to wear a path into the floor for the next two hours. She took a seat just in time for the rest of the Hartricks to show up, Walker shaking like a leaf and Talia trying to calm him down.

So, with a pleading look from Colin, Scarlett started her story over, relaying everything once more.

Thirty minutes into the surgery, a silence had fallen over the room. People were still talking, but everything was hushed, as if any sudden noise would disturb the surgeons behind several walls. The nervous energy in the room coupled with the wait had Scarlett wanting to pace with Leo, but she knew that wouldn't help matters. She was sure Leo's pacing was making Walker's (and the entire room's) anxiety much worse, but she needed to get up and move soon, or she would get too antsy to be helpful.

When she stood, Colin followed suit, raising his eyebrows at her from across the room. "Where are you going?" Everyone swiveled their heads from their various places in the room to watch their conversation, and Scarlett was suddenly very aware that everyone there must know about their falling out at the gala.

"The pediatrics wing." She swallowed, avoiding everyone's gaze. "There's a kid the foundation is sponsoring there, and I figured I could go visit her while I wait for Piper."

"Can I come with you?" Colin's back was ramrod straight, his hands fumbling with each other as he nervously glanced around. A few people averted their gazes because they must have noticed his discomfort with everyone looking at him, but she could tell how much he wanted to escape. Scarlett nodded, taking pity on him, because she too could no longer stand the prying eyes. When they made it around the corner, Colin breathed out a sigh of relief. "Thank you."

"You could have just left on your own, you know," Scarlett said.

"I wasn't sure what was appropriate. Everyone seems content to sit and wait, but the chairs are really uncomfortable, and even the material they used for the cushion part was scratchy. Now, I have an excuse."

"The children's wing is a lot better. It's colorful and warm, and mostly everything was donated so they could pay for the nicer stuff," Scarlett explained, pointing left as she glanced at the curved mirror up on the wall to watch for anyone turning the corner.

"I'd love to see the kinds of people you help. I've seen you in the studio with kids, and I know what kind of research you fund, so it'll be nice to see the other part of your job," Colin said, walking swiftly beside her. She had forgotten how long his legs were when they walked side by side, and picked up her pace to match him so he didn't have to walk with an unnatural rhythm.

"Liliana is twelve years old, and she has the same type of cancer Tucker had. Last I heard, she was doing really well and responding to chemo, but she caught a fairly high fever, so her parents took her in last night," Scarlett informed Colin as they stepped around another corner. The sign for the pediatric wing was embossed on the wall with the colorful handprints of children. She hit the call button when they reached the door.

"Hi, Scarlett." The woman at the counter smiled and waved at her through the glass. Marcia was one of her favorite people here, and Scarlett knew Marcia liked her back because in the years she had been coming here, she and Kashvi had brought dozens of cupcakes to this floor for a little morale boost, and Marcia had begged for the recipe.

"Hi, Marcia," Scarlett cooed back. "We're here to see Liliana. This is Colin." She gestured to Colin, and he raised a hand in an awkward wave. "He'll be joining me today." From the look on Marcia's face, Scarlett hoped to God that the woman wouldn't say anything about her companion. She hadn't ever brought a man with her apart from her Uncle Marty, so she could already tell this was going to be the hot gossip on this floor for who knew how long. Marcia smirked but stayed silent as she pressed the button to let them in. Scurrying inside, Scarlett latched on to Colin's arm to drag him along, hoping that more people wouldn't see them together and start talking. The move felt so intimate that she was about to force herself to let go just in time for Colin—damn him —to reach for her hand instead, lacing their fingers in a tight-gripped hold. She could extract her hand, but the feeling of it left her warmed on the inside, and she figured Colin might need the show of support while he waited for his sister.

When they got to Liliana's door, Scarlett disentangled their fingers and knocked on the open door. "Hello?" she singsonged.

"Scarlett." Cora, Liliana's mom, beamed and waved her

inside. Liliana was in a deep sleep on the hospital bed, a few strands of sweat-soaked hair clinging to her forehead when they entered the room.

"How's she doing?" Scarlett asked.

"Good, just resting. They got her on some fluid, and her fever broke, so now I think she's just exhausted. They're keeping her for another day just in case." Cora's eyes roved up to where Colin towered over everyone. "And who's this?"

"Colin." He stuck out his hand, and Cora shook it and introduced herself.

"He's a friend," Scarlett said, and then, needing a reason other than that for him to be there, she quickly added, "Colin works in the research lab for Sloan CRO, so he's well-versed in all of this."

"Just the research side," Colin corrected.

"What are you researching?" Cora asked, sounding interested.

"Blood and bone cancers," he answered. Scarlett swiveled her head to look up at him. As usual, he didn't meet her gaze, but she watched his hand twitch at his side. "I have an idea for my doctorate, so I'm also researching for that so that I can submit a research proposal and garner some support for it when I'm ready."

"Lilliana's dad is a professor at Fletcher University and working on his doctorate." Cora nodded. "What's your expertise going to be in?"

Colin shifted on his feet, and if they weren't in a hospital room, Scarlett thought he might be bashfully kicking rocks. "My dissertation would be on Acute Myeloid Leukemia, specifically in children." Scarlett froze, all the muscles in her body suddenly locking up. "Oddly enough, Scarlett's cat gave me the idea for my research project."

"Pepto?" Scarlett's voice cracked, eyes wide with the onslaught of new information. She should have asked what he was researching at the gala. Should have known already that he was studying the exact form of cancer her brother had. A slew of questions spiraled in her head as Colin continued.

"Yes. It's going to take a while to come up with specifics, but a novel d-peptide has been used in differentiation therapy with leukemia before, and I'd love to further that research."

Cora was looking at Colin like he was a hero, completely unaware that Scarlett's head was swimming. "I have no idea what that means." Cora smiled. "But I'm so happy that people like you exist." It was similar to what Scarlett had told Colin all those years ago. She wasn't the kind of person who could solve this problem and other problems like it. She had told him back then that she thought he was the type to change the world, and she was right. She just didn't have a clue that this was how he planned to do it.

"I need to use the bathroom," Scarlett announced, motioning toward the doorway and escaping to the hallway quickly before the salt burning her nose manifested and tears started visibly falling down her face. Escape was the only thing she could think to do, because if Colin didn't love her like she knew he didn't, then she couldn't fathom why he would choose this occupation over geology. When had he changed his mind? Did it mean anything, or was she a random influence that became a stepping stone in his career?

By the time Scarlett returned from the bathroom, she had adopted an unperturbed attitude as she worked through her list of questions with Cora on whether their family had any immediate needs, jotting down a few things in her phone and texting them to her mom to get the ball rolling. Liliana stayed fast asleep the entire time they were there, and after a half hour of listening to Colin and Cora discuss all the things his job entailed, Scarlett was so unsettled that she thought the OR waiting room might actually be less anxiety-inducing.

The stark silence between them as they moved down the pediatric wing hallway was so loud that Scarlett thought she might combust. Colin stopped suddenly and gestured at the wall. "Did you paint this?" He pointed to the framed watercolor of brightly colored flowers she had painted three years ago, and Scarlett nodded. "It's beautiful."

She sucked in a deep breath, steeling herself. "Thank you."

"Can I ask you a question?" Colin asked, eyes still looking over her painting.

"As long as I get to ask one, too." It was time to stop hiding from the elephant in the hallway.

"All right," he agreed. "Me first?" Scarlett nodded. "I'm wondering if it's too much to ask you to come over and teach Theo while he's painting? I appreciate that you let me come pick up some supplies so he could continue his piece, but I know nothing about art, and I tried once to play a YouTube lesson, and Theo hated it. It's not quite the same without you."

"Where would we go?" She was certain she already knew the answer, but was waiting for it not to be what she secretly hoped it was.

"My apartment," Colin replied.

"Okay," Scarlett murmured. After kissing him last night, her heart fluttered at the idea of being at his place. The same way it did when she thought she was moving to Maryland to be with him. And just like it had been back then, it was a terrible idea to accept. "I could do that."

"I'll text you my address, and you could come over?"

"Tuesday?"

"I would say Tuesday, but I made plans to go to an art museum with Theo in Merrick because I figured that'd be better than YouTube again. He doesn't usually like outings much unless it's the lookout, but he seemed excited about this one. Can we do Thursday at the usual class time or even a little before? Theo's off school for the summer, and he ends up hanging out with me for most of the day when I have him."

"Sure," she said, solidifying her fate. "When you go to the museum, they have a watercolor exhibit and a pointillism exhibit, so you'll have to show him both for me." Colin opened his mouth like he was planning on inviting her to the museum as well, and she didn't think she could handle watching him dote on an eight-year-old unless she had some purpose to be there. Teaching Theo was a good reason to be around Colin, but she couldn't find enough of an excuse for a museum visit as well, and she needed to guard her heart before Colin inevitably sucked her under his spell again. "Just let me know what time you want me over on Thursday," she said.

Colin closed his mouth, nodding, before pulling out his phone, tapping out a message, and pocketing it just as hers dinged in her pocket. "You still have the same number," he noted.

"I do." The words she left unspoken hung between them. *You could have reached out any time.* Kashvi had been able to keep in touch when she was away at college. It wasn't hard to pick up a phone or make time to visit during the holidays. They had FaceTimed almost every day. It could have been the same with Colin, too, even just as a friend, but he hadn't even tried to reconcile.

"Your turn to ask a question," he said, turning to look at her painting once more.

Scarlett's voice was strained when she finally choked out, "When did you decide to study Acute Myeloid Leukemia?"

"Right after we broke up."

"Why?"

"The long answer is that I don't like the idea of anyone going through what you did," Colin replied, still staring at her painting. "I wanted to fix one of your problems, and I found I liked studying cellular biology."

"What's the short answer?"

"You already know that," he said. "You just don't believe me."

I loved you then, and I love you now. Not a single thing has changed.

"I..." Scarlett swallowed. "I don't know." She knew what he was referring to, but it didn't quite prove what she wanted it to. He had kept his distance for five years and hadn't contacted her a single time. Her number hadn't changed. She hadn't blocked him. So even if he had chosen his career because of her, it had to be residual guilt from the way he had left things, or he had simply happened upon something he loved because of her.

"It's okay, Red. I'm certain you'll understand eventually.

When you do, I'll explain more." Colin gave her a sad smile and inclined his head toward the door. "Walker texted me that Piper's out of surgery. Let's head back."

She didn't notice he had used her nickname until it was too late and he was holding her hand again.

Forty-Two

Scarlett
18 Years Old

"You can't move in with him. You barely know him!" Uncle Marty sighed. The ongoing fight with Scarlett's uncle was underway yet again when she had brought home boxes to start packing for Maryland. For what felt like the hundredth time, she was staring across the table at her mom, aunt, and uncle, fighting for what she wanted.

"I can, and I'm going to." Scarlett folded her arms over her chest in defiance. "I'm an adult, and I can make my own decisions. And I *do* know him. I'm with him every single day. I'm over at his house so much that Walker has put my schedule up on the big family whiteboard calendar. You all said you liked Colin, so I don't see what the problem is."

"Liking him is way different than thinking you should bank your entire life on him!" Marty exclaimed, throwing up aggravated hands. "Nora, talk to your daughter."

"She doesn't think the same thing as you. She knows I can make my own choices," Scarlett stated definitively. The flat line of her mom's mouth turned downward, and Scarlett raised her eyebrows. "Mom?"

"I don't think it's a good idea, honey. You know we love Colin and Colin's family loves you, but this is… can't you just do long distance?" Nora asked, pleading.

"No," Scarlett snapped. "We don't want to be away from each other for that long."

"So you're going to move clear across the country to be with a guy you just started dating not that long ago?" Aunt Eden pried.

It wasn't as if Scarlett didn't know that on paper it sounded like an insane plan, but she didn't care. Her heart wanted to go. She could figure out the logistics of a job and the rest once she made it to the East Coast. Colin would start school, and she would have plenty of time to find out what she wanted to do. "You are acting like I haven't thought this through at all."

Marty scoffed. "You haven't."

"Marty." Nora sighed and touched her brother's arm. "Let me."

"Let you what?" Scarlett demanded. "You're not going to convince me of anything. I want to go with Colin. It'd be the same thing as me moving away for college. What's the difference?"

"The difference is you're moving for a boy!" Marty shouted. "Are you just hoping he'll decide for you what to do with your life?"

"Marty!" Eden chastised. "Let Nora talk to her daughter. You are not helping."

"Letti, listen to me." Nora leaned over the table and grabbed her hand. Scarlett reluctantly let her. "I know you're in love, and I know you want to be with Colin, but you are so young. You have your whole life ahead of you, and I'm worried if you focus so much on what Colin wants and what he's doing, then you'll lose yourself along the way."

Scarlett snatched her hand back angrily. "We aren't you and Dad. Colin won't leave me."

Nora sighed and pinched the bridge of her nose. "I know that, honey. But if he won't leave in Maryland, then he won't leave you if you aren't there, either."

"Why are none of you considering what I want? You're acting like he's forcing me to go when I *want* to go!" Scarlett shouted. This was not how she wanted to spend the morning of her graduation. She could feel her eyes prick with tears, and she worried it might ruin the makeup she had spent forever on to look good in all the photos they were bound to take today. "I have a plan," she croaked. "I love him."

"Loving someone is not a plan," Eden said softly. "We all want you to be happy and in love. Of course we do. We just think that you need to think about what you want outside of Colin."

A tear rolled down Scarlett's face, and she shook her head. "I want to paint. I can paint anywhere. I can paint in Maryland."

"Sure you can, but you're not going to Maryland to paint," Nora said. "You're going because you're following someone else's dream. You won't have the same support as you do here, because if you're in Maryland, you'll be Colin's support, not your own."

"Colin can be my support. You just want me to work for the foundation, and now you're disappointed that I'm not doing that. Is that it?" It was the one thing about moving to Maryland Scarlett didn't like. She loved doing things for the foundation, loved elevating her brother's legacy, but in the end, she would only be gone for four years, and everyone was acting like it was the end of the world.

"No." Nora shook her head. "If you didn't want to do anything for the foundation ever again, that would be okay with me. It's not your cross to bear. I'm disappointed that you're getting your self worth from a boy and you're planning the rest of your life off his career and his needs. What about yours?"

"But I don't know what I want to do with my life, so why can't I figure it out in Maryland?" This conversation felt like a perpetual circle or a revolving door that she couldn't escape from. No one was listening to her. She could figure out who she was in Maryland. Everything that she could do here, she could do with

Colin at her side. She might not have her family to rely on, but Colin would be enough.

"A lot can happen in a relationship over four years..." Nora trailed off.

Scarlett nodded her head slowly, understanding seeping into her resolve. She knew exactly why everyone hated this idea. They didn't believe she could do it. "You don't think Colin and I will stay together."

"It's not that." Eden sighed. "We just know how hard relationships are. Even Marty and I have our moments. I couldn't imagine having those moments at eighteen."

"You have a kid." Scarlett rolled her eyes. "We aren't having kids, and we're careful."

"I really don't need to know anything about that," Marty grumbled.

"You will have to heavily rely on each other to get through a bunch of hard stuff," Nora said. "He's still grieving. You'll both be new in town. Your schedules are going to be chaotic with him at school and you finding a job. All of that is going to be very hard, Letti. I don't want you to just make a decision based on love alone."

"We've been relying on each other for months, Mom. I know he's grieving. I can help with that. He can help with my dreams, too. He makes me feel special and like I can do something important with my life, too."

"You don't need a man to make you feel special. You are special," Nora said sternly. "I love that he makes you feel like that, but you don't need him to do what you want to do, Letti."

"Yes, I do!" Scarlett pushed her chair out from the table furiously. "You may not need Dad, but I don't want to just survive on my own. I want love, and I have it, so I'm going."

Storming away from the table, she pulled out her phone and called Colin. When he picked up immediately, she breathed a sigh of relief, stomping out the front door and slamming it shut behind her. "Can you pick me up early?'

"We're going to be late for line-up." Scarlett sucked in a breath of too-thin air and groaned as she felt the head of Colin's condom-wrapped cock knock against her.

"We'll make it. But we have to be quick," he panted, hands lifting her hips up. "Breathe, Red." She did, and he shoved her back down, his cock spearing her in one thrust. Knowing that they didn't have much time to get her prepped, Colin had swiped a travel packet of lube over and inside her. They both closed their eyes and groaned at the connection, pressing their foreheads together.

They would have been over an hour early to line up for graduation if Scarlett hadn't started impulsively rubbing Colin through his slacks on the drive over. She knew exactly what he had meant when he said he was insatiable, because she felt it, too. The dire need to have him inside her any chance she could felt like a monster she constantly needed to feed. So when they started making out heavily at red lights and feeling each other up beyond the scope of safety during a drive, they took a detour up to the lookout, parked in the makeshift gravel parking area, and were quick to scramble into the backseat. It wasn't the first time they had fucked in Colin's car. They had skipped a few classes to do the exact same thing, and Scarlett had spent a few evenings with Colin's cock down her throat in the front seat and one with Colin's head between her legs as the sun went down on the lookout rock. Sunsets were especially beautiful when her vision was fuzzy from orgasm. Anywhere and anytime they could, they were getting each other off, because they were good at it now. Their charts were starting to look like nothing but five stars and the smiley faces Colin kept drawing on hers. Instead of venturing into more experimentation, they did what they knew worked.

"Colin," Scarlett whimpered.

"Is that a good or bad 'Colin'?" he asked, lifting his ass off the seat to meet every drop of her hips with a slap.

"Good. So good."

"Oh, fuck, Red. Just like that." He pulled the bodice of her graduation dress down so her breasts spilled out, bobbing with her as she bounced in his lap.

"I'm gonna come so quick if you keep this up," Scarlett praised. His fingers massaged her clit with the perfect amount of pressure, as always.

"You're certainly keeping me up," Colin quipped, his voice breathy.

Scarlett threw her head back with a laugh as she started to jerk with her orgasm. "Come with me."

He did until they were folded in around each other and trying to catch their breath. They only took one moment to themselves with a quick kiss before they hopped out of the backseat, Colin disposing of the used condom in the mini trash can he had dangling from his headrest and offering Scarlett baby wipes as they righted their clothes.

"Shit, where's my cap?" Colin dipped his head, looking around the back of the car.

"Got it!" Scarlett chirped, finding where it had fallen on the floorboard and tossing it to him.

"Thank you." Colin slapped the square hat on his head, adjusted his valedictorian tassel, and swung the driver's side door open as Scarlett clambered into the passenger seat, giggling. He smiled when she got fully situated and scanned her over, fixing the sleeve of her gown by pulling it back up her shoulder.

"Are you nervous about your 'I'm a four-point-oh genius' speech?"

"I'm feeling very relaxed, thanks to you." Colin ducked down to give her a chaste kiss on the lips. "I love you."

Scarlet sighed happily as he started the engine. Her mood had drastically changed for the better after the discussion with her mom. This was how she was supposed to feel, and she refused to listen to anyone but Colin any longer. "I love you, too."

FORTY-THREE

Colin
23 Years Old

Theo was humming. Colin had frankly never seen him happier. Even when they frequently went to the lookout and sat in peace together, he was never this happy. Even in the studio, he had never been as obvious with his joy as he was right then, making tiny little dots as he rocked from toe to heel in Colin's living room. Scarlett had finished her meticulously planned lesson on the history of pointillism and was standing beside Colin with the same enthused look in Theo's direction, no doubt finding something wistful in the way he painted.

"Has he ever hummed like this with you?" Colin murmured to Scarlett.

"Never," she whispered back. Both their eyes trained on Theo again as they leaned against Colin's kitchen counter, listening. Scarlett drank from the mug of Earl Grey tea Colin had made for her, and he drank the coffee he had been self-medicating with all day. The caffeine felt like it hit his veins extra hard today when he got a few sips in. It was either that or the close proximity to Scarlett that had him so focused. He wished he would have suggested this arrangement forever ago. After Scarlett had given Theo her lesson, she had spent the last several hours chatting with Colin and had even gone on a few of her long-winded tangents. It felt so natural for her to be there that he couldn't help but hope that she'd keep coming back.

A knock on the door announced that Jessie was back to pick Theo up, and Colin sheepishly looked at his shoes, anticipating what Scarlett would say. "When did she say she was coming?" she asked, right on cue.

"Now." Colin cringed.

"But Theo hasn't cleaned up yet." Scarlett, for all her whimsy and fun with her art students, was a stickler for making the kids pick up after themselves. He knew as well as the next person that it was a good skill to teach kids, but he was a bit of a pushover when it came to Theo.

"I usually pick up after him. It's not a big deal," he added as an afterthought.

"Colin." Scarlett rolled her eyes, making her way to the door. "You can't let him do that every time."

"But he was humming," he protested, enjoying the fact that she seemed comfortable enough to answer his front door.

"Hi, Jessie." Scarlett waved her in with a bright smile, and Jessie and two bored-looking teenagers stepped into Colin's still-furnitureless living room. The twin toddlers had gone back to their parents as ordered by the court, and ever since, Jessie had had a revolving door of other kids passing through. He admired her capabilities because Theo was really the only kid Colin felt like he could handle. Jessie seemed to have the opposite problem; she was out of her depth with Theo but could handle pretty much any other kid. She knew well enough that what Theo needed most was routine, though, and because he had been to so many homes since his parents had given him up at four years old, the constant change was setting him back years. Colin had confirmed with Jessie many times that she wasn't planning on letting Theo go, and told her if she needed him to show up more so that she could handle Theo staying there for longer, he would do that. So far, their current routine seemed to be working.

"Oh, you're still here." Jessie smiled back at Scarlett.

"Yep," Scarlett replied. The tone was a bit unusual, but Colin paid it no mind as he made his way over to Theo and squatted down to his eye level, tapping his ear.

Theo removed his headphones. "I did a lot more that time," he said. He had been speaking more frequently lately despite his preferred communication still being silence, and it was confirmation to Colin that Theo must be getting more comfortable in their arrangement.

"You did, bud." Colin bobbed his head and finally looked at what he was painting. Theo's little body had mostly been blocking his view, so he didn't realize what he had started. It wasn't nearly done yet, but the one green eye he had finished today was unmistakable. "Are you painting Ms. Wallace?"

Theo nodded and handed over his paintbrush, and Colin quirked a brow.

"Do you have a crush on her?"

Theo scrunched his face in disgust and shook his head. "You stare at her a lot. You can put it up on your wall." Theo pointed to one of the several undecorated walls in Colin's living room.

"Okay." Colin blew out a breath and looked over his shoulder, happy to find that Scarlett, Jessie, and the emo teenagers were far enough away to not hear Theo's commentary. "You are correct. But," Colin lifted a finger, "that's not usually something we say out loud, because it embarrasses everyone involved, and embarrassing people is not very kind."

Theo handed another paintbrush to him and pointed to Colin's chest.

"No, I'm not embarrassed. Ms. Wallace might be if you told her that, though," Colin said.

Theo seemed to consider this and stared at his painting for a second before frowning and pointing to himself, then the painting, and making a flicking hand motion like he was tossing something in the trash.

Colin shook his head. "No, there's no need for that. She'll love your painting. Keep working on it. I meant she would be embarrassed to know that I stare at her when she's not looking."

Theo bobbed his head and wandered around Colin to go meet Jessie, conversation over.

"Thanks so much for taking him for a while," Jessie said when Colin joined the group. She reached out to touch his arm, and he stepped a bit out of her reach. He was sure it was supposed to be a comforting gesture, but he didn't really like the light touch she tried to give him. "It was really good to see you again."

"Four days a week, as per usual." Colin nodded, confused. She was acting like he hadn't literally seen her yesterday when he picked Theo up to go to the lookout.

"Right." Jessie sighed. "I guess I'll see you on Sunday, then?"

"That is the schedule," Colin said.

"I should have the studio up and running by Saturday again, so we'll be back to the normal summer classes next Tuesday and Thursday," Scarlett chimed in.

"Great. But then it'll just be you on Monday?" Jessie asked Colin, hovering near his shoulder but not touching him. She was still a little too in his personal space for his liking, though, so he took yet another small step away from her.

"Another lookout day," he confirmed. They had had the same schedule for months, and Jessie hadn't had any problems with it before. He wasn't sure why she was rehashing it now, but she had done the same thing last week, so he wondered if picking Theo up on Mondays was now an inconvenience for her. "Did you have something planned for that day?"

"No, I'm free. Did *you* want to plan something for that day?"

"Yes?" Colin scrunched his face. "The lookout?"

"Right, duh." Jessie smacked her palm against her forehead. "Anyway, I gotta get going." Colin left it at that, waiting for her and the kids to leave so he could clean up Theo's paint mess. Once they were gone, he waited for Scarlett to do the same, but she lingered.

"You don't have to help me clean up. It doesn't take very long," Colin said, in case that was her reason for staying.

"Colin, you know she's into you, right?" The words exploded out of Scarlett's mouth like a bomb, and he froze on his way to the sink.

"What?" He turned to face her, blinking.

"Jessie," Scarlett huffed. "She's into you. She's acting all weird. Trying to touch you? Mentioning dates she's available?"

"Oh." Colin made his way to the sink, set his watch off to the side, and turned the faucet on. Scarlett was behind him and seemed to want more of an answer than that, so he squirted some cleaning solvent onto the two brushes and shrugged. "I'm not interested."

"Not at all?" Scarlett came up to his side, leaning against the counter.

"Scarlett, please," Colin said, exasperated. His eyes shut for a moment in agony. "I'm really trying here. What are you not getting? I don't want Jessie. She's very nice, and I appreciate everything she's willing to do for Theo, but I want *you*. I don't ask to hang out with Jessie because I don't want to. If I did, I'd ask her to come watch Theo paint for a few hours and make her tea."

Scarlett looked down at the mug she was holding and bit her lip. "Okay. That kind of makes me feel better."

"Why?"

"Because I—" Scarlett scrunched her eyes shut and set her tea on the counter. "This is going to sound so stupid to you because you don't get jealous. You met my ex and barely cared, but I care that Jessie clearly likes you. I don't particularly enjoy knowing that, which is confusing because we aren't together, and you're free to do what you want."

"I do get jealous." Colin dabbed the clean paintbrushes on a paper towel and set them on his drying rack, turning to face her. "Or so I was recently informed."

"You were informed? What does that even mean?"

"I told Leo and Sam that Braiden is a very good guy and I have no appropriate reason to dislike him, but I despise the idea of you being with anyone but me. They said that's jealousy, regardless of whether I agree with my own mind. I don't like that he's seen inside your nightstand because that means he's been in your bedroom. I hate that he's seen you naked. The current version of you. I hate the idea that he might have—" He cut himself off with a shiver and dried his hands a bit too aggressively on a hand towel.

"That he might have what, Colin?" Scarlett stepped closer to him, and unlike Jessie, he didn't want to back away. He wanted her to snap to him like a magnet.

"Cuddled with you," he whispered, his eyes dropping to her lips.

"That's what bugs you the most?" She laughed. "Not that we've had sex, but that we cuddled?"

"So, you did cuddle?" Colin felt like he had been punched in the face.

Scarlett scoffed. "That's normal behavior for a couple, Colin. Yes, I cuddled with him."

"Did you like it?" He braced for the answer and still felt sucker-punched when it came.

"Sometimes."

He bitterly folded his arms over his chest and gave her a curt nod.

"You're really jealous that I cuddled with someone else?"

Colin tipped his head to the side. "Well, the sex part also really bothers me."

"Good," Scarlett replied shortly.

"Good? How is that good? Logically, none of that should be a problem to me, and I know that." He ran a hand through his hair, getting more frustrated by the second. "I know I shouldn't care at all. I know I'm the one that broke things off, but I fucking hate it, Scarlett. I really do. You were supposed to be mine."

"You left. Was I supposed to just wait around for you and fall right back into your arms like nothing happened?"

"Of course not." But that was exactly what he had done. He had waited. He had gone to years of therapy. He had worked so hard to believe that he deserved her and everyone else in his life. Eyes closed, he could feel her quick breaths dancing across his lips. If he hadn't slipped his watch off when he'd gone to wash the paintbrushes, he was sure it would be alerting him of a high heart rate again. "I'm sorry." His eyelashes fluttered, and he confirmed how close she really was. It wouldn't take any effort at all to kiss her. Slowly, he reached up to remove his glasses and arched backward to set them on the counter beside his watch, resigned to the war waging in his head. "And I'm sorry for what I'm about to do."

"What are you—" she began to ask, but it was already too late. He crashed into her, damning all his no physicality rules in an instant. He wasn't one to not follow a plan he had come up with, especially a good one, but the way Scarlett was kissing him back had him wanting to throw out every plan he ever had where she was concerned. Her hand flew to the back of his head, her fingers digging into his scalp. She arched her spine and craned her neck to slant against him harder, taking his desperate kiss and giving him more by dragging her tongue along his bottom lip. He was gone. Finding the nearest wall, he pressed her into it, caging her with his legs and cupping both sides of her face to kiss her like he couldn't breathe unless she gave him the air to do it. Her body and her mouth were pliable under his, and the way she folded around him felt like finally coming home, a warm pressure he had been searching for for years. When her leg hitched up on his side and their fronts aligned better, he rocked forward with a greedy thrust of his hips. She moaned into his mouth, and he couldn't help but do it again.

"Red," Colin panted. His mind was screaming at him to stop. This was a bad idea. This wasn't the way he wanted her to finally want him again. Breaking free from her a bit, he kissed down her throat and collarbone, trying to regain his composure. When he found a sliver of sanity, he pushed off the wall and took a step away from her with her with his hands raised up in defense. "We shouldn't."

Scarlett sagged against the wall and fixed her bangs, smoothing them down and letting out a frustrated breath. "You're giving me fucking whiplash. I'm so confused. You say you want me, and then I finally decide I want to, and you don't want me anymore?"

Colin laughed humorlessly, the thought was so ridiculous. Even his body had made sure to declare that he wanted her, his erection pressing against his zipper painfully. He snatched his glasses off the counter and shoved them back on his face in frustration. "I've been telling you that I want you for weeks. Months. *Years*, Scarlett. I want you like every other time I've wanted you—desperately. Like there's an itch under my skin, and it'll only be satiated once I touch you. The same way I did when we were two minutes late for graduation because we couldn't control ourselves enough to not fuck in the backseat of my car."

"Then why did you stop?" Her voice cracked as she looked down at her hands and curled in on herself.

"I don't want you to think that this is an experiment or that I just want sex." He heaved out a sigh.

"Maybe that's what *I* want," Scarlett said harshly, her nose turning up at him in a telltale sign of her anger. "Ever thought that it's not just about you? Maybe I just want to get laid by someone who knows what I want for once."

He swallowed, his Adam's apple feeling like a lead rock in his throat. "If I do that, you have to stay the night. This isn't a game to me."

"I have to feed Pepto," Scarlett argued.

"You live at your uncle's right now. Text your mom to feed her," Colin shot back. "If we're having sex, you're staying the night, and I'm going to spoon you when we're done with aftercare. You're going to tell me one of your long stories, and I'm going to catch up on everything I've missed in the last five years while I play with your hair. Then I'm going to make us both breakfast in the morning. That's how this is going to work, Scarlett, or I'm not doing it."

"Fine." She stepped toward him, and he was dangerously close to throwing her up against the wall and taking her right there in the kitchen. "But if we're hooking up, then I need this to be the most erotic night of my life so I don't regret it. Make up for the five years you left me alone, Colin. I want fantasy and experimentation. I want to come so hard I can't see straight."

"Music to my goddamn ears." Colin grabbed her wrist. "Come with me." He knew exactly what he was going to do, and it was going be pure torture until he finally got to push inside her.

When they got to his bedroom, he flicked the lights on to reveal the sparsely furnished room and looked down to gauge Scarlett's reaction. Piper would start his project as soon as she recovered a bit more from her fall, and in the meantime, he had been tasked with deciding on what design he wanted. He had already apologized when Scarlett had shown up to his apartment and there was nowhere to sit, so he figured there was no reason to apologize now. The boxes of stuff he had collected were half unpacked and lining the outskirts of the room, and he kicked one to the side when they got to the foot of the bed. He couldn't quite hear her, but he thought she had mumbled something in the realm of "familiar."

"Do you want me to take over like I used to?" Colin asked, setting his hands on her shoulders. "And are you on birth control?"

"Yes to both." Scarlett nodded. "I have an IUD. The pill got a little hard to remember to take when you weren't calling me to take it."

"Do you have a condom?" he asked. "Because I don't. I wasn't expecting this, but I can go out and get one if—"

"No, I'm fine without it if you are. I got tested after Braiden."

"More than fine," he murmured, his mouth dipping forward. He pressed a slow kiss to her neck, avoiding her dangly red trapezoid earrings that had hit him in the face when he had aggressively kissed her the first time. "No more talking about Braiden." His hands slid down her arms, fingers folding under her daisy-printed T-shirt. She obeyed his unspoken command and lifted her arms so he could slide her shirt over her head. Her skin was just as he remembered, pale and dotted with freckles he could spend hours tracing. And her bra—damn his spiraling heart—was ruby red like their first time and the picture she had once sent him. He folded her shirt and set it on his nightstand. "I need you to tell me to stop when you need to."

"I understand." Scarlett nodded. "I get it now."

"And I'm going to check in with you verbally, too, in case you freeze up instead of telling me to stop, okay?" He unbuttoned her bell bottom pants and slid them down her legs, indulgently digging his fingertips into her thick thighs.

Scarlett sucked in a sharp breath. "Okay."

"Don't get annoyed when I ask too much." He gently shoved her backward so she fell on the edge of the bed.

She let out a breathy laugh. "I won't."

There was a spark of happiness in Colin's chest when he bent down to take her shoes off and realized they were the same floral embroidered yellow converse she had once wanted. And when he realized the simple cotton underwear concealing her more intimate parts matched her bra, he wanted to hook her legs over his shoulders and pull them to the side to taste her again. But he could wait. He had already waited five years.

In his crouched position, Scarlett gripped his shirt and peeled it over his head, his glasses catching for a moment before he fixed them. It was all the awkwardness of taking someone to bed—the fumbling of clothing removal, the adjustments he had to make to accommodate the height difference—but unlike when they were younger, he felt no discomfort from it, and Scarlett didn't seem embarrassed by it either because they knew now. The imperfection of some moments was part of intimacy, and sharing them with her felt like he had stepped back in time to when they were lost with what to do with each other's bodies.

Scarlett dragged her hand with a firm pressure up his torso to the tattoo over his heart. "I can't believe you got the cum face tattooed on your body."

"It's a very discreet cum face," he said. "It makes me smile sometimes when I look in the mirror and remember how much you laughed when I made that joke."

"When did you get it?"

"It was a college graduation gift to myself."

"That long after we broke up?" Scarlett sat up straighter, looking shocked.

"You have got to stop being surprised by the amount I thought of you in the last five years." He shook his head and kissed the inside of her thigh before rising to his full height, offering her a hand to stand up.

"You never called or said hi when you came back for holidays, so it is surprising to me."

"I really didn't think you'd want to see me." Colin unbuttoned his pants and pulled them down his legs, leaving his underwear on but removing his socks and tennis shoes. He folded the rest of their clothes and neatly set them on the nightstand with her shirt. Scarlett didn't respond until he stood in front of her again.

"Maybe I didn't want to see you," she whispered. "I don't know."

"Do you know if you want to see me now?" He dipped his head down to her shoulder, and his tongue swept out, licking at her collarbone.

"Yes." She nodded, and he closed his eyes once more to trail his lips across the tops of her breasts. "I'm a little nervous that I don't look the same as I used to, though. I don't really have the body of an eighteen-year-old anymore."

"Neither do I." Back then, he was a lot thinner, and not

exactly in a healthy way. He had looked sick in comparison to the now lean but muscular build he had gotten from running.

"You look like you don't have trouble eating now," she noted. "You look good."

"So do you." He cupped one of her breasts, grasping as much as he could. "I like your bangs, and your tattoos, and all of this." He grabbed a handful of her ass. "I want to see you naked, but I have a fantasy I'd like to fulfill first." He dropped his grip on her and dipped his head to murmur in her ear. "Did you know people with ASD can be more prone to hypersexuality?"

"No," she gasped, her chest heaving and stretching toward him.

"It's common to have recurrent sexual fantasies about the same thing over and over and over again." His voice was low in his throat, his desire so strong that the aching of his body was near uncomfortable. "Do you want to know mine, Red?" Her head bobbed a yes before she spoke the word aloud, and he licked his lips. "You did so well by coming here tonight in red, because I still have that picture of you that I've gotten myself off to so many times since. I know I should have deleted it and it was wrong, but I can't take it back now."

"I should be mad that you kept it, but I'm too turned on right now, and I find that really hot." A giggle escaped Scarlett's lips before she lifted a finger in warning. "But I reserve the right to be pissed off about it when we're done."

"Right reserved," Colin recited.

"So that's your fantasy? Me in red?"

"And black." Her face sparked with curiosity, and he continued, "In my fantasy, you're wearing red, and you're tied up with my rope. Do you still like being held down, Scarlett?"

She released a breath. "God, yes."

"Good." Colin pulled away from her and went to his mirrored closet, sliding the door open and taking out his black duffel bag. He could hear the catch in her breath. It only turned him on more as he went to stand in front of her and dropped the bag with a thud at her feet. "Open it." Scarlett did as told and crouched down to pull the zipper, revealing the carefully wrapped black shibari ropes inside. "What are you thinking?" he questioned, watching her run her fingers over the ropes and twist an end between her fingertips. At some point during this interaction he had started to stim, rocking from ball to heel as excitement bloomed in his chest. This was really happening.

"Explain it to me?" she asked, rising to her feet.

"It's called shibari. Japanese bondage," he clarified. "I tie myself up, usually just my legs, as a self-soothing exercise before I read or lie on the ground, because the specific kind of pressure and the control I get from it feels good, but this would be more about displaying your body than anything else. I'll give you a rope cutter to hold the whole time, so if you're uncomfortable you can cut it off yourself. If all goes well, I want to tie your wrists so I can control you more."

Scarlett's cheeks were tinged pink, and her eyes were wide and alert, but he couldn't tell whether or not this idea was even remotely what she wanted. Even when she turned to kiss him, throwing her arms around his neck and pressing her body into his, he still wasn't sure, so he pulled away, breathing hard, and asked her point-blank. "Is that okay?"

"Yes," Scarlett said throatily. "That sounds like exactly what I'd be into." She kissed him again. "Please."

Eagerly pulling the rope cutter from the side pocket of the bag, Colin reached up to hand it to her, handle out. She took it, and he grabbed the first set of ropes from the bag.

FORTY-FOUR

Scarlett
23 Years Old

Colin's steady hands draped even sides of the rope over Scarlett's neck, and she felt like she might catch fire and burn his apartment to the ground. His fingers were so sure as he moved to her backside and did something she couldn't quite see, but when he was finished, she could feel part of the rope hanging between her shoulder blades as he moved back to the front.

"The first knot goes right here," Colin pressed his thumb just under the hollow of her collarbone, and it was torture to not have his hands all over her body.

"Okay," Scarlett squeaked out, gripping the rope cutter tighter. She wouldn't use it. She could already tell that this was what she liked. Whatever he was doing was exactly what she wanted. The wait as he tied the first knot was delicious, and she squirmed against him, her body searching for his hands.

"Stop moving," he chastised. "Stand still."

Hoping to relieve the ache and pressure between her legs, she squeezed her thighs together, grateful that she was wearing underwear, because it provided the smallest bit of friction she needed. "I'm trying."

"Try harder," Colin demanded, adjusting the rope with precision and leaning out to check behind her. "The second knot goes here." Instead of his thumb, his face pressed hard between her breasts, and he kissed her sternum. She was sure her breathing sounded erratic and noisy, but she couldn't bring herself to care as she clenched her thighs tighter. When he had tied that knot and inspected his work in the meticulous way he did everything, she wanted to scream out that he needed to keep going. That he needed to go faster before she lost her mind. Pulling the rope through the hole was the worst part, the way his veined forearms flexed as they dragged it through the loop he had created was painfully erotic. "And the third knot," he said, his voice barely restrained as he pressed his mouth between her breasts again. His wet tongue dragged down her body and the rope he pinned to her torso until he got to the center of her ribcage, where he stopped again.

"Colin," Scarlett groaned.

"Is that a good 'Colin' or a bad 'Colin'?" he asked.

A pang of guilt lodged in her chest for ever making him wonder if his name meant something bad. "Don't stop, Colin," she whispered. "I'll only say your name if I'm enjoying it, I promise."

"Thank you." He swallowed and started to tie again. She wanted to look down to see if he was just as aroused as she was, but when she started to tip her head, it shifted the rope. "Don't do that," Colin chastised.

"Sorry." Her voice came out high and squeaky, which would have been embarrassing if she was with anyone else, but Colin clearly couldn't care less if it sounded like she was going through puberty, because he was pulling the rope through the loop again, and she was back to wanting to lick his forearms.

"Next, your belly button." He held the rope down against her body and pressed a sweet kiss on her stomach before tying the knot with care.

"This is taking so *long*." Scarlett could hear how whiny she sounded, but this level of foreplay was going to put her in an early grave if he didn't get to the point sooner rather than later. Her thighs were burning from squeezing so much, and her core was molten lava, hot and achingly empty.

"Patience is a virtue," he said, pulling through the knot at her navel.

"I'm not a virtuous woman," she retorted with a small laugh. "I'm currently being tied up by my ex-boyfriend before I hook up with him."

"Good point." Colin chuckled. "Fuck your virtue."

"Would love it if you'd fuck my virtue way faster," Scarlett complained.

"This one's going to help you." He moved his hands down from the last knot, and she let out a small moan of relief when he pressed three fingers between her legs against her clit. "It's called a happy knot, because it goes right here." He pulled his fingers away. "Will that make you happy?"

There weren't any words left, Scarlett was so keyed up. She gave Colin a small, jerky nod of her head. The anticipation of this one was all-consuming, and watching him pull the rope through was so agonizing that she thought about throwing the entire thing out the window and demanding that he lay her down right this second. But she persisted, begging her body to calm down enough for him to finish. None of her need died down after he pressed the knot into her clit.

"God," she moaned, eyes closing. "I'm begging you to hurry up."

"Spread your legs, Red," Colin directed. She unclenched and did as told, whimpering at the loss of pressure. He bent and dragged the rope between her legs, moving around her backside to do something with the original knot he had tied at her shoulder blades. "We're almost done," he said. "Kind of."

Scarlett threw up her hands. "What do you mean, kind of?"

He separated the two strands of rope and pulled them around each side of her, under her armpits and to the front. "I mean I have to pull these through each loop on the front and wrap them around your back now." She huffed and puffed perpetually as Colin worked the loop, pulling each strand through under her collarbone and wrapping the rope tight over the top of her breasts. "Is this too tight?"

"No." It felt good, almost like his hands were fused to her body. If the rest of the rope felt the same, she was going to love this. He again did something at her back and pulled the strands to the front, yanking them through the second loop under her breasts and asking again if it was too tight. Every time until he reached the final loop at her belly button, she confirmed that nothing was too tight. He tucked the leftover bit of rope at her backside through the horizontal lines and met her around the front. The whole process couldn't have been longer than ten minutes at most, but by the end, she wanted to come so badly she was sure it wouldn't take any effort at all.

"Come look." Colin guided her to the mirror with a hand on the small of her back. Tiny diamond shapes formed down the center of her torso, and the lines of rope pressing into her body accentuated every curve of her breasts and hips. "What do you think?"

"I look hot," she admitted. "What do you think?" He grabbed her wrist and pulled her hand over to cup him between his legs. The hard jut of his erection traveled across his thigh, and she slid her hand across it all the way to the tip, liking the strangled sound it elicited from Colin and the wet spot on his boxer briefs where he had leaked precum.

"I want you so badly it's painful, Red." His voice was so hoarse she could do nothing but believe him. Moving around behind her, he pressed himself into her backside, gripping her with both hands, one braced across her collarbone to pull her in tighter and the other on her hip, his fingers indenting her skin like all the knots he had tied. Her head fell back against his chest, and as she looked in the mirror, she couldn't help but think they looked good together, like the rope adorning her body was tied around them both, linking them together. Her eyes fluttered closed in pleasure when he reached up to cup one of her breasts and brought his mouth down to her ear. "I want to taste you."

Without warning, she took the rope cutter and gripped the band to one side of her underwear, frantically cutting away the fabric.

"I could have pulled those off without ruining them," Colin said.

"I don't care. Ruin *me*," she pleaded. She was nothing but a desperate ache needing to be filled, and she didn't care if she had to destroy every single pair of underwear she owned if it meant his face was buried between her legs soon. Colin, who now seemed impatient compared to the methodical way he had tied her up, was already unclasping her bra. She reached behind her for the band at the top of his briefs and dragged them down over his ass as his erection popped free.

When Scarlett turned around, she was greeted with the sight of his strong, naked body. Colin was no longer the scrawny boy she once knew. Strong thighs, a sprinkling of chest hair, and a rigid hip bone cutting down to his cock felt both familiar and new, like déjà vu or an alternate universe's timeline. The part of his body that hadn't changed at all was as big as she remembered. She had had other men now, so she knew for certain this time that all her nervous spouting about whales in the past hadn't been in vain. Colin's cock, with its swelled tip and the thick vein running down its shaft, looked like it might hurt her when he finally pushed into her again, and God did she want it to hurt, just a little bit. Enough to make her sore. Enough to remember that he had wanted her so badly that they were both raw from it afterward.

"Give me your wrists," Colin directed. Eyes wide and excited, Scarlett held her forearms together and lifted them up as an offering to him, her bare breasts pressing together and lifting a bit behind the rope. It didn't take him long to tie this knot, and he was much less precise about it than the rope dress he had made her, wrapping the rope around her wrists quickly and only checking in once to make sure it wasn't too tight. His lips were on hers immediately after he finished, plundering her mouth. Her breasts felt full and heavy in his capable hands as they moved back to the bed. "Get on your knees and forearms," he ordered. Scarlett scrambled to heed his request, falling onto her elbows with her wrists pinned together and the rope pressing into her skin all over her body. Colin got in bed behind her and took no time at all to yank the rope between her legs to the side, his face buried in her heat and licking her.

She shouted his name, arching her back and pressing back into him. The knot on her clit rubbed her with each rocking swipe of his tongue, and the first orgasm felt like she was splitting herself in pieces between the sections of roped lines dividing her body. Arms stretched out in front of her, her shoulder blades pinched together and her face pressed forcefully into the pillow to muffle the choking cry of pleasure as she released the first wave. Each wave followed another stroke of his tongue until she could barely breathe.

"Red, how are you doing?" Colin rasped from behind her.

"Holy fuck." She heaved air into her lungs. The head of his cock knocked against her entrance, and she gasped.

"Scarlett, answer the question."

"Yes. Good. Perfect. Fuck if I know. Please, just don't stop," she begged.

"You said you wouldn't get annoyed when I asked too much," he reminded her.

"I'm not annoyed. I'm *dying*." Scarlett groaned dramatically. "I need you to push right now."

"Breathe, Red." The memory that slammed into her at the same time his cock did was almost too much. She had forgotten all the words he used to whisper in the heat of the moment, and hearing them now made the well of emotion in her chest hurt more than it should. The pleasure and the pain of it all made her eyes begin to water at the edges, leaking and wetting the pillow. "Tell me I'm better than everyone else," Colin demanded. "Tell me no one makes you come the way I do."

"No one," Scarlett croaked, her knees and thighs rocking with him and returning each of his thrusts, needing every push and pull of his cock and at the same time wishing she had never let him touch her again because it was *too* satisfying.

"I can't make this last. I've wanted this for too long. It feels so good, I—" he panted, his cocking snapping in and out of her in a rhythm she knew all too well. "I need to come. I'm sorry."

It didn't matter to her because the sorrow and the satisfaction she was feeling were already boiling over, the knot at her clit burning with friction and heightened sensitivity. As one last thrust had him twitching inside her, her spine crumpled and her body tensed, relieving her of every last drop of feeling and agony lodged in her heart. She came hard, blinded by her watering eyes, and when she was done, the comedown left her feeling empty and lifeless on his bed.

Colin did all the cleanup, untying her knots and tossing the rope into the washing machine. He wiped off his release from between her legs with a warm washcloth and discarded her torn underwear. She took a shower and found the answer to why he always smelled vaguely sweet, but not overly fragrant. The soap he used looked expensive and handmade, a honeycomb design on the top and oats embedded in the bar. Smelling his musk on her skin and scrubbing it away with the soft scent he used felt predictable—she could never seem to get rid of him fully.

When Scarlett finished showering and finally got her emotions somewhat under control, Colin lent her one of his shirts, and they curled under his soft, white sheets. There was a glass of water on the nightstand near her side of the bed that he must have poured for her when she was in the shower. The two pain reliever pills sitting beside it said he had anticipated the headache she had now from dehydration, and a well of emotion churned in her stomach again.

Colin asked her a few questions, and she responded to each one but fell silent afterward. She could tell he wanted her to elaborate and spiderweb her thoughts, but she couldn't pull herself out of the sadness that weighed her down. It wasn't that the sex was bad, it was that it was the opposite of bad. He was right, no one was as good as him. She would venture that nothing was as good as them *together*, and because of that, she felt cut open and flayed to the core. This was supposed to be just sex, and yet it felt like they had claimed each other again, a thought she was too terrified to speak aloud because she already knew how easy it was for him to leave.

Scarlett almost asked him. Almost begged for him to tell her why he had ended everything if not for all the reasons he had said back then, but when she had gathered the courage, Colin was passed out on the pillow beside her, gently snoring with a limp arm over her stomach.

She followed the first part of Colin's request and stayed until early morning, but she didn't wait for him to rise before leaving before breakfast.

FORTY-FIVE

Scarlett
23 Years Old

The ceiling of her uncle's house had a popcorn texture that they had slowly removed room by room as she was growing up, but Scarlett's childhood bedroom—now the guest room—was one of the last in the house that still had it. It reminded her a bit of Theo's paintings as she stared up at it from her old bed. She wished that they would remove it already, as if that would wipe the memories she had made in this room with Colin, but most everything in the room was the same. The furniture and the layout had remained untouched. The twinkle lights were no longer wrapping the curtain rod above the window Marty had replaced after Colin broke it, but even different curtains and bedding couldn't cover up the memories she wished she could repaint.

"Babe?" Kashvi's voice said from the doorway. Scarlett lifted her head to look at her best friend, face blank, even when she saw Harper and Saanvi were there, too. "Your mom called us."

"I slept with him," Scarlett said miserably. All three girls climbed up on her bed silently and maneuvered to lie back and look at her ceiling together. "I couldn't help myself."

"And how was it?" Kashvi asked, her usual excitement about sex void from her tone.

"Perfect," Scarlett whispered, her nose starting to burn. "Hottest night of my life."

"And he took care of you the whole time?" Harper asked.

Scarlett laughed bitterly. "He did. He wanted me to stay for breakfast, but I left before he woke up. I could just feel it, you know?"

"I *don't* know," Saanvi said. "Feel what?"

"Yeah, feel free to explain, because we have no idea what you're talking about," Kashvi agreed.

Scarlett sighed. "Like if I stayed for breakfast, I'd stay forever."

Harper spoke slowly, as if assessing the damage, "And you don't want to stay forever?"

"Forever sounds impulsive. It also sounds exactly like what I want. I can admit how naive and reckless I was back when I thought I was just going to drop everything and move to Maryland with him, but now it feels different."

"So, you're admitting that we were right, then?" a voice called out from the doorway, and everyone on the bed lifted up to see Nora with a slight smirk on her face and Eden beside her.

"Come on in." Scarlett chuckled. "There's no more bed space, so you have to sit on the floor. The topic of conversation might be too mature for Lindy's ears if she plans on joining us, though."

"I set her up with a movie in the living room. She will be fully engrossed in *Frozen* for the next hour and a half," Eden said, taking a seat on the floor and leaning against Scarlett's bed.

Scarlett's mother did the same and called up, "I take it you spent the night with Colin?"

"Yep," Scarlett exhaled. "How'd you know?"

"I told you back then and I'll tell you now, I was not born yesterday," Nora said. Her voice sounded like a smile, so Scarlett mimicked it, smirking at the ceiling. "Dear, you went to his apartment to teach a paint lesson, and you didn't come back home till five in the morning."

"I was never really good at hiding anything, was I?" Scarlett asked. A smattering of nos from the entire room made her wince. "Okay, well, Uncle Marty was clueless back then."

"Yeah, but he's usually clueless," Eden said, receiving a chorus of laughter.

"I feel like the dumb one now," Scarlett said to the ceiling.

"Why? Because you're in love again?" Harper demanded. "You are not dumb."

Scarlett sat up a bit to glare at her sister. "H, you're the one who has adamantly hated Colin since he's been back."

"I hate what he did, but I can't deny how he treats you now. I can't deny how he treated you before he left," Harper said. "I always kind of felt like I needed to protect you double the amount because you didn't have Tucker protecting you, too, and I felt like I'd failed miserably when Colin left and you were so depressed you barely got out of bed. I was blindsided because it really seemed like he loved you, and I was mad that I didn't see any warning signs before he broke you."

"'Broke' seems a bit dramatic," Scarlett said, knowing she was trying to rewrite history. *Destitute* would have been a more accurate and dramatic word to describe the slump she had slipped into.

"I walked in on you months after the breakup trying to give yourself bangs," Kashvi recalled. "You requested dressed and depressed eggs every day. It was bad."

"They turned out fine," Scarlett protested, ruffling the bangs on her forehead for show. "And I like deviled eggs."

"They turned out fine because I cut them," Saanvi said. "Friends don't let friends impulsively give themselves bangs without at least heavily supervising."

"All this to say," Harper took over again, "it took all of us to pull you back out into the land of the living, and I didn't want Colin to hurt you again. But Eden told me something about him the other day, and I might have been a bit harsh about my dislike for him."

"Leo chewed us both out, too. I guess he's been hanging out with Colin a lot," Saanvi added. "Not that I care what my brother-in-law has to say, but I do care what Piper has to say, and she seemed to think that Colin had a good enough reason."

"What do you know?" Scarlett asked, confused.

"You know he's autistic, yes?" Eden asked.

"Obviously," Scarlett replied. If he hadn't told her, she would have figured it out after all his interactions with Theo. "It's a non-issue. We just end up doing things a little differently and communicating more."

"I think he believes it is an issue. When he signed up for the mentorship program, I asked him out of curiosity when he was diagnosed, and he said the summer before he left for college," Eden said.

The air whooshed from Scarlett's lungs. "He didn't tell me that," she choked. "I assumed that he must have been diagnosed after he left."

"He should have told you," Kashvi said.

"That much is true," Harper agreed.

"I think he must have been very confused," Nora chimed in. "His parents died, and he was diagnosed, and at the same time, you were both so young and maybe a little too optimistic about your future together. You both knew virtually nothing about yourselves and the world back then and thought moving in together in the most tumultuous time of your lives was a fantastic idea."

"Like you and Dad?" Scarlett asked.

"Yes and no." Nora sighed. "I got pregnant, and yes, I was in love and moved in with him, but deep down, I saw his red flags and the writing on the wall and had to admit I ignored them until he left. The only time I listened was when I kept my maiden name after we got married and gave you girls and Tucker my last name instead of his. The fact that he didn't care should have been another warning sign."

"I wouldn't have any of the same things I have now if I went with him to Maryland," Scarlett said. "Not the art studio, not the program, not my place at the foundation. I don't know if it's just that I'm older now and think it was naive that I was just going to follow my boyfriend wherever he wanted to go, or if he broke up with me and I felt determined to do whatever the hell I wanted to do."

"Why not both?" Kashvi asked.

"It can feel both like he broke your heart and like he did you a favor, Letti. That's not wrong," Harper added.

"You're both more mature now. Maybe it's time to forgive and move forward. Or maybe it's time to get answers and decide you want to dump his ass," Saanvi said. "The world is your oyster."

"It always has been," Nora said.

"I still love him." Scarlett clutched her chest, feeling the weight of her words. "I don't think I ever stopped. He makes me feel like I'm important. And before one of you says something about me not needing a man to make me feel special, I know that. I don't need it, but I can want it, right?"

"Definitely," Harper said.

"I can do everything on my own, and I'm pretty sure I've proved that," Scarlett said. "I just don't want to."

"A little birdie told me that he's going to Tucker's 5K tomorrow," Harper cooed. "He's bringing his entire family."

"I think Leo would be really pissed that you called him a little birdie." Saanvi flopped onto her side, burgeoning belly on display. "I will not be there because this baby is pressing on my bladder, and I will end up peeing myself."

"Maybe you should get off my bed." Scarlett grimaced.

"I had to lend her underwear the other day." Kashvi cackled.

"What are sisters for if not to steal clothing?" Harper asked and turned an accusatory tone on Scarlett. "You had two of my cardigans for the entirety of fall."

"Where's the dress I lent you for the gala?" Scarlett shot back.

"Girls," Nora chastised from the floor.

Scarlett untactfully changed the subject. "All right, so, I'll talk to Colin, and if it goes poorly, I'm going to need another telenovela night."

"Done!" Kashvi said brightly.

The annual birthday run for her brother wasn't exactly the best spot to talk to Colin since he would be busy, well, running, but afterward, she would lay it all out on the line. If he loved her like he said he did, then he would do the same.

Forty-Six

Colin
23 Years Old

"Let's do this." Walker bounced on his feet beside Colin, who was casually stretching out his limbs and could care less about doing anything. The energy he planned on having today had left his body right along with the girl who had left his bed the morning before without even leaving a note.

"You're a dork." Talia socked Walker's shoulder, and he grinned at her before tugging on her ponytail. The happy couple was brimming with excitement over possible adoption prospects, and Colin wanted to be thrilled for them, but he couldn't find it in himself to drum up any excitement after his night with Scarlett had crashed and burned.

"Colin, Carter, Cooper," Walker called out. "You all look like someone pissed in your Cheerios. Buck up." Hearing his brothers' names in a row with his own made it seem all the more ridiculous to Colin. It was possible that he was just pissed off that morning, but at the moment, it was another dock on his parents for giving them all stupid matching names.

"I don't want to be here," Cooper bemoaned with a cold

glance at Colin. Colin sighed and kept stretching. Not even his brother's ire could worsen his mood. It was already sub-zero.

"It's too fucking early," Carter grumbled. He was still mourning his recent breakup and seemed to be in a depressive slump no matter what time of day it was. At least Colin would have someone to commiserate with.

"You need some fresh air," Pearl said sweetly. She balanced out the bad vibes of the family, splitting them evenly into groups of grumpy and peppy. Given that Piper, the most cheerful of their bunch, was at home with a broken arm, Colin decided that darkness would soon overtake them, and he would let it because he no longer gave a fuck.

"Leave me alone," Carter told Pearl.

Walker set a hand on Carter's shoulder. "I know you don't want to hear this, but Stella sucked, and you're better off without her."

"That's what I said," Colin finally chimed in, his voice no more enthusiastic.

"You all suck," Carter muttered. "Don't even come at me this morning, Colin. I know why you're in a mood, and it's also because of a girl who sucks."

Colin scrunched his nose and glared at his brother, making dead eye contact with him just to pull out all the stops. "Scarlett doesn't suck."

"Wow, that's a lot of suck," Talia noted.

"Care to share with the class?" Walker asked Colin. "Or am I still the only person who doesn't get to know anything?"

"You stopped being the fun, cool uncle when you became our guardian," Cooper declared blandly.

"Ouch." Talia cringed. "Do I get to know?"

"Nobody gets to know," Colin huffed, seriously second-guessing bringing his family to this event. If he hadn't signed everyone up already and it wasn't for charity, he would have bowed out yesterday morning like Scarlett had.

Cooper shrugged. "Colin hooked up with Scarlett, and Scarlett left before he woke up."

"How do you know that before I do?" Pearl complained.

"Eavesdropping, obviously," Cooper said. "Carter was talking on the phone loudly in his room yesterday, and I heard Colin talking to Leo earlier. I put two and two together."

"Fantastic," Colin deadpanned. Sarcasm felt like the perfect thing to bring into this conversation. Hell, he was ready to bring the house down with more negative commentary. The street at the start of the race was packed with people and getting way too loud for his liking, so he pressed on the plugs in his ears to dull the sound and readied himself to deliver another sarcastic comment about how much fun he was having when a voice interrupted.

"What's fantastic?" He turned to find Jessie and the two emo teenagers flanking one of her sides. Then, his gaze dropped to the one person who shouldn't be there at all.

"What the hell is Theo doing here?" Colin's eyes widened, then he jerked his head around to see the sea of bodies crammed into the small space.

Jessie answered quickly. "I asked him if he wanted to come because I knew you would be here. He likes you, and I thought—"

"It's going to be crowded, Jessie. You don't even have him wearing his headphones." Colin massaged his temples. He knew he was being harsh, but *what the fuck*. The crowd was starting to grate on *him*, so there was no way Theo could handle something this chaotic.

"He can't run with headphones on." Jessie looked at the ground. "We left them at home."

"This is a terrible idea. Theo really can't be here." Colin looked around again, his body tightening as someone beside him brushed his arm.

"I just thought it would be fun," Jessie choked out.

"Is this *the* Theo?" Walker came to stand beside him, eyes bulging from his head like a fish. "Isn't this too loud for him?"

"Yes. I need to get him out of here." Colin stooped down to Theo's height and saw how pale he looked. "Do you want to leave?" Theo bobbed his head, his shoulders curling in on himself. Colin rose back to his feet. It was too loud, and his brain was starting to get too foggy to think. He couldn't even see a discernible exit anywhere—no parting of the people in the crowd where he could escape to the side. "Shit. Um—"

The announcer with a loud megaphone at the head of the pack interrupted Colin's panic. "Thank you for coming to the Wallace Memorial Foundation's annual birthday 5K!" Nora Wallace was handed the megaphone, and he could now see Scarlett in a golf cart at the front of the line, his brain fighting for clear thought.

"Today would be my son's twenty-sixth birthday," Nora said into the megaphone. "His legacy continues to bring people together, and his memory lives on forever through all of you and the amazing research we're funding. We are so grateful to all the sponsors and donations that made this event happen. Special shout out to Wilton and Sons Metal Work. All that said, let's start the countdown, and we'll see you at the finish line!" The shouts of the crowd as everyone counted down from ten felt like they were counting down to Colin's imminent death. Theo was sitting on the ground covering his ears, and Jessie was trying to get him to leave, but he wouldn't budge.

"Do we need to pick him up?" Carter asked.

"Colin?" Walker touched his arm, and Colin flinched away from him.

"I don't know. I don't know!" he shouted. Theo didn't like being touched. That was what he had been told a hundred times. By Eden, by Scarlett, by Jessie, and yet Scarlett had had to pick him up to take him away from the fire in the studio, so maybe this situation was as dire as that one.

A shotgun went off to start the race, and Colin's hands flew up to press against his earplugs. Theo started wailing.

"Make a blockade," Cooper yelled to his family, and they all jumped into action, blocking Theo from the possibility of getting trampled by runners.

Once most of the runners had dispersed and Colin had his head on straighter, he ripped the earplugs from his ears and shoved them into Theo's. It didn't stop the wailing, though, and pretty soon he could feel tears sliding down his own face as he fought with his body against the loud noise Theo was making and the desire to help him. Warm hands pressed to his ears hard as Scarlett crouched down beside him.

"How can I help?" she asked, still holding her hands over his ears as he reached out to Theo. Her voice was muffled, but he could still hear it.

"I don't know," he answered honestly. "I think I'm going to carry him out."

"Okay." Scarlett nodded.

Jessie, still standing in the blockade with tears streaming down her face, was grasping at apologies he wasn't listening to, not that he didn't know that she was sorry or that this mistake was unforgivable. All his attention was on the boy in front of him.

Tentatively, Colin reached out to grasp Theo around his shoulders, pulling him into his chest. Theo didn't react by jerking away from his touch, and Colin gasped in surprise when Theo's small hand gripped him around his back so tightly for someone so small. And he knew exactly what Theo was feeling. Touch starved. A lack of pressure. A need for it. In a heartbreaking lurch of his chest, Colin wondered if Theo had ever been hugged on purpose before. If anyone cared enough to get past his revulsion to physical touch to see that it just needed to be a certain way. He wrapped his arms tighter around the little boy, and instead of carrying Theo out, he held on to him and sat on the ground more solidly. Theo's tears soaking his shirt and the way he had stopped screaming confirmed what Colin already knew. No one *had* hugged him. Or, at least, not in a long, long time. Theo wasn't stupid. He had to know that people avoided touching him when that was what he really needed. It had to feel, even to an eight-year-old, that no one wanted him. That no one cared. That he was too much to handle.

Theo's fingertips were digging into Colin's arms like Colin's pressure alone wasn't enough to satiate him. "Scarlett," Colin's voice broke. "Help me."

She had let go of his ears the second Theo had stopped screaming. "Plug your ears again?" she asked, tears streaming down her face, too. "Theo's?"

"No." Colin shook his head. "Hug him." Scarlett dropped to her knees and came around Theo's back, sitting fully on the ground in the street with them and wrapping Theo in a cocoon between the two of them. At some point, Cooper slipped Colin's headphones—which he must have run to get from the car—over his ears. The silence and peace he found between the three of them was a welcome distraction from his sour mood.

And finally, Theo stopped crying.

FORTY-SEVEN

Scarlett
23 Years Old

Scarlett's keychain with its random assortment of chunky knickknacks clacked together as she opened the door to her studio. She was exhausted, but she had one final thing to do. Colin bent behind her and picked up the flowers her dad had sent her for Tucker's birthday that had probably been sitting on her porch all day, wilting in the sunlight. She was grateful for the assist because she knew it would hurt if she bent down right now. Her knees were scraped up and scabbed over from her lack of care when she hit the asphalt that morning to hug Theo. She didn't regret it, even when Braiden had been the one to clean the dirt and pebbles from her cuts at the first aid booth. It was worth it. The rest of the day, she and Colin had companionably taken Theo to the lookout and fed him macaroni and cheese, the only food Theo never protested according to Jessie, who was in a guilty spell that would probably get Theo whatever he wanted for the next month.

Colin hadn't spoken much outside of Theo's care, and Scarlett could tell from the way he was barely present with her that she had hurt his feelings by leaving the other morning. But he had to know that whatever he was feeling now was tenfold for her when he had originally left. One morning wasn't years of abandonment. Even so, with his less than happy agreement to her request, he had followed her back to the studio she had finally gotten the okay to live in again.

"Looks exactly the same," Colin noted, staring at the wall where the fire had broken out.

"Yeah," Scarlett agreed. "Do you think Theo will be okay?"

"I think he'll be all right." He nodded, wandering over to the front of the room and setting the vase of flowers down on the cubby station. The easel didn't have a canvas on it, but the construction crew had moved it back to the center of the room after fixing the wiring and cleaning the burnt wall. She had missed this place, with all of its plants that were now half-dead from lack of watering. "Just give it to me straight. You don't want me, right?" Colin asked.

"What?" Scarlett blinked. "That's not at all why I asked you to come over."

"You left my bed after you said you'd stay."

"And you left town after saying you'd take me with you," Scarlett said.

"So, what? That was payback? That's not fair, Scarlett."

"No," she sighed. "It wasn't payback. It's not like I was going to avoid you forever. I would see you every Tuesday and Thursday anyway. I just needed to think, and I couldn't do it while I was still in your bed. I needed a clear head, and sometimes you make my brain shut off completely."

Colin sat down on her stool, his shoulders slumping. "You used to say you liked that because otherwise your brain was going a million miles a minute."

"I still like it," she murmured.

His head perked up a bit. "Did you make some sort of decision about me, then?"

Moving toward him, Scarlett took deep, steadying breaths,

preparing herself for something that she might not want to hear. "I need you to tell me what happened. I need to know why you broke up with me, because I'm still so confused. My aunt said that you were diagnosed that summer? But you never even told me you were being assessed for autism, so I'm clearly missing something."

"The same day." Colin's throat bobbed.

"What?"

"I was diagnosed on the same day I broke up with you." His hands started fidgeting in his lap, and he adjusted on the stool again as she came to stand beside him, not in front of him, in case that would make him think she needed eye contact when she didn't. She just needed the truth.

"Why would that be the reason?" Scarlett asked. "Did you think I would dump you because of that? Because that's insulting, Colin."

"I knew you wouldn't," he said quietly.

"Then why? What am I missing? I don't get it." She was on the verge of shouting at him to get to the point when he finally did.

"I knew how likely it was that we'd end up together. I knew how likely it was that you'd end up resenting me for the way I am. We had big communication barriers I didn't know how to cross, and I thought you deserved someone who wouldn't be so hard to understand." His voice was calm, but hers was anything but.

"That was it, then?" Scarlett demanded. "You dismissed me as a statistic? You were reckless with my heart, Colin."

"No." Colin stood up and faced her, his hand karate-chopping the air as he spoke. His calm voice was gone, replaced with frustration. "I was obsessively too careful with yours and completely destructive with mine."

"You were mean, Colin! You said awful things. You know that!" she yelled. "You have to know that. You never said anything like that to me before."

"You don't get it." He ran an aggravated hand through his hair and shouted back. "I needed you to give up on me!"

Forty-Eight

Colin
18 Years Old

The cool leather of the chair felt good against Colin's fingertips, but he lost sight of that a moment later when he met Dr. Thomlinson's eyes and counted.

One... two.

"That's uncomfortable for you, is it not?" Thomlinson questioned, clipboard perched in his lap as it had been for several months of sessions.

"What is?" Colin asked.

"Eye contact. You tend to not make it unless you have to or feel like you have to. When you greet me, you make eye contact. If it's been a while since you've looked at me, you make eye contact. If you're having an emotional session with me or an off day, you never make eye contact because you forget to. Sometimes you overcompensate and make too much. I've told you a few times that you don't have to follow social norms in this office if it's hard for you."

Colin swallowed and looked down at his fingers that once again felt like they were *too* there, and he could feel the fibers in his brain holding everything together and thrumming under the weight of pressure. "I count when I look at people. In middle school I took a record of when people looked at others and how long they looked and taught myself to do it."

"Masking," Thomlinson said, the exact word Colin feared he would, because after all of Colin's research, his behavior seemed to fit that word, and he didn't want it to mean anything. "I imagine you're very tired at the end of a day with a lot of socializing?"

"Yes, but isn't everyone? I'm an introvert. Sometimes I do the eye contact thing purely out of habit, not because I'm forcing myself. If it comes somewhat naturally to remember to do it, is it really masking? It's the same way with food textures and fabrics and smells. If I can handle it, doesn't that mean it doesn't really bother me that much?" Colin knew his voice was too hopeful and pleading, grasping at straws.

"Is it always uncomfortable for you?" Thomlinson raised his eyebrows. "Does it get easier to make eye contact or eat certain foods, or does it get easier to remember that you have to tolerate it?"

Colin wanted to throw up or toss out a new argument he didn't have as he replied curtly, "I tolerate it."

"It's taken me a long time to finish this assessment because you were so good at masking that I occasionally thought I might be wrong. Especially given your history when you were younger and another doctor with my same qualifications denying you a diagnosis. But you are so intelligent and so aware of your surroundings, I imagine even at five years old, desperate to fit in, you did some masking then, too."

"So you're going to tell me I have autism?" Colin ground out.

"It is my professional opinion that you have level one Autism Spectrum Disorder, yes. Meaning you require some support, but you don't have significant impairments to your cognitive or verbal skills."

Colin's head swam as the verbiage dipped in and out of his

consciousness. "No. My parents would have noticed," he finally said.

"Your parents were wonderful people, but they weren't infallible, Colin. They weren't medical professionals, and a lot of parents don't consider this likelihood because your autism becomes simply a personality trait, not a hurdle you constantly have to try to get over. Most people enjoy certain textures and don't like other ones, but for you it's more extreme, and often people don't catch that. You said your mom would volunteer on all your class field trips and pack you the right foods for a weekend so you wouldn't go hungry if you declined what the class was eating, yes?"

"She said I was a picky eater, but not like other kids because it wasn't like I needed to eat chicken nuggets every day simply because my parents didn't make me eat vegetables when I was little," Colin answered. "I like vegetables, they just have to be the right texture."

"Your dad dove headfirst into all of your hyperfixations on knowledge with you. Is it possible he didn't consider that your research was leaning toward obsessive because he loved you and wanted you to enjoy the things you were studying? I think your parents made a bunch of tiny little mistakes that added up under their nose. It wasn't intentional, and they trusted the medical system to do what it was supposed to."

"Or they just had to put up with me, so they did," Colin spat. His body was so stiff now, a numbness taking over. "I've read the statistics, and parents with autistic children have a higher rate of divorce. I was probably a strain on their marriage and a strain on my entire family."

"I don't believe that," Thomlinson said. "There are also plenty of studies that say there isn't a higher rate of divorce between parents with autistic kids and parents without. The divorce rate is always high regardless." Colin frowned and gripped the armrests of his chair. "I can see that you're angry, and I want you to know that that's normal. It's okay to feel that with such big news. It's normal to feel betrayed. It's normal to feel hurt. People with ASD can have emotional dysregulation as well, so it can even feel like nothing for a long time and then an explosion all at once like a delay timer."

Colin replayed the time he had broken down at the lookout and his prom night, when he had felt irrationally angry enough to punch Harden in the face. "I'm fine," he said, dread seeping into his chest. "What about Scarlett? What are the statistics on that? How often do people with autism last in relationships? How long is it going to take before she realizes that she hates me?"

"I have not seen any statistics on that that I'd deem relevant. You have a very highly charged emotional relationship with Scarlett. Typically when someone with ASD is grieving, they need to lean on others a little bit more, but since your entire family was grieving the same loss, it makes sense to me that you found someone to help you through it."

"So I used her?" Colin breathed, already knowing the answer.

"That's not the word choice I would use, but in a manner of speaking. You are allowed to have help, Colin," Thomlinson said. "It is good that she is a bright spot in a dark time for you."

"Is it good if I'm hindering her life?" Colin shouted. For what it was worth, Thomlinson didn't flinch, just sat calmly while Colin continued his rant. "If I'm making her cry with the things I say and not realizing when I've stepped over boundaries, how the fuck is that okay? How can that possibly be good? How can any of my relationships be good when I don't know how anyone is feeling ever? I don't understand when someone is laughing at me, and I don't know when I've said something offensive."

"You do what you always do. You ask," Thomlinson said simply. "I've known you for months now, and I can see you have your parents' kind heart, Colin. You are not a robot without empathy. You just don't know how to react with your empathy because you don't know when people need it. You want to do right by Scarlett. You make sure she enjoys sex. You ask her what's wrong when she doesn't. You worry when she cries."

"But if I'm the one making her cry, then what's the fucking point? I have a fantastic ability to fix what I already broke? What good does that do?" He scoffed morbidly. "That's just great."

"You bring more to the table than just your ability to fix and learn from your mistakes."

"Not enough. Scarlett is my only friend other than direct family members. What few options I have in friendship, I hurt without knowing it. I'm a fucking burden to people. Someone they have to put up with just because I exist." A tear slowly rolled down Colin's face.

"I think you need to call someone." Thomlinson leaned forward, his hand touching Colin's chair. "I think the most important thing right now would be to take a few days, to not make any big decisions, and to surround yourself with people who love you."

"And who would that be?" Colin laughed.

"You know people love you, Colin. They tell you to your face. They can't all be lying, now, can they?"

But his mind was already made up. Pity wasn't the same thing as love. Tolerance wasn't the same thing as love. Close proximity wasn't the same thing as love. And as far as Scarlett was concerned, not even good sex was the same thing as love.

Forty-Nine

Scarlett
23 Years Old

"Why would you want me to give up on you?" Scarlett asked, her voice so soft that she worried he didn't hear her question because it took him so long to answer.

Colin sat down on the stool again and leaned over his legs, covering his face with both hands. "I had convinced myself that my existence only brought people pain and suffering. That I was a nuisance and no one really liked me at all. That you took pity on me because my parents died. And maybe you thought you loved me, but no one could *really* love me because they were just fooling themselves." He took a steadying breath. "There was a reason I had no friends other than the people who were forced to live with me. There was a reason I destroyed any friendships I did have growing up with my lack of social skills. People thought I was rude when I wasn't trying to be. People thought I was weird and awkward and distant. I didn't like loud music or loud social gatherings, and everyone rightfully stopped inviting me to those things. I couldn't read a fucking room, Scarlett. I could look people in the eyes, but it was so uncomfortable that I couldn't think when I did it, and I counted the seconds till I could look away. I thought about how sad you must have been that I never looked into your eyes and actually wanted to. I thought about every time you cried because I inadvertently said something that hurt your feelings. I thought about how I couldn't dance with you at Prom because it was too loud. I thought about how I didn't see that you wanted to stop when we were intimate, and I just couldn't fucking do it anymore. It didn't matter how much I loved you, because I was just hurting you over and over and over again. I figured if I truly loved you, I'd let you go."

A choked sob left Scarlett's throat. "No." The tears rolling down her face as she shook her head fell faster. "I loved you. I still love you. You made me feel special and built me up more than any other person. You interested me. Everyone else seemed so boring by comparison because no one else researched all of my thoughts or cared as much as you. I felt *lucky*, Colin. In my naivety I thought you had taken pity on *me*. That you had chosen me out of anybody you could have because you were so smart and attractive and sweet and I—*God*—I was so in love with you I was willing to forget about any of my hopes and dreams to support you in yours. Because you told me to paint when I wanted to paint. You listened to my long, rambling stories when other people thought I was annoying, and you wanted me." Her breathing was so shaky that each breath was its own sob. "The same way you do now."

"I'm so sorry," Colin whispered, head hung low. "I hate that I made you think I didn't love you. I've always wanted you, Scarlett. You were the first person who *chose* to be with me, not because of circumstance or familial ties, but because you wanted to." He sniffed when she came to stand in front of him again, and he squinted his eyes shut, agony sinking into the lines of his now tearstained face. "There's more. But... I'm scared to admit the next part."

"Please tell me," she begged, pulling him into her chest. "Tell me like this. Where we're both safe."

"Okay."

FIFTY

Scarlett
18 Years Old

The boxes Scarlett had managed to pack were sporadically strewn about her room, and her entire closet scattered across her bed and the floor made it look like a bomb had gone off in there. Kashvi had helped her a bit earlier, but as soon as Colin arrived, he would know what to do with her mess. She was sure that he would make a list of categories or something and they would tackle the overwhelming chaos in an organized fashion that would make her question why she hadn't thought of it earlier.

"She's in here," Harper's voice called out from the upstairs hallway, and footsteps traveled to her room until her sister and Colin were standing in her doorway.

"My two favorite people," Scarlett chirped.

"Was your packing method just to throw everything on the floor?" Harper's eyes scanned the room with a judgemental gaze.

"Maybe," Scarlett laughed. Colin didn't seem to think any of this was funny, and just stood awkwardly to the side while she and Harper teased each other.

"Well, I'll leave you to it," Harper said, finally leaving Scarlett and Colin alone. Scarlett took the opportunity and bounded over to him, tossing her arms around his neck and kissing him. He stiffened against her, and she pulled back, confused.

"Ready to help me tackle this? I know it's a lot, but I—"

"Stop packing, Scarlett." Colin's voice was so cold, she immediately straightened her posture. He sometimes had that tone in bed, though, so she broke into a wide smile, realizing what this was.

"Why?" She dragged a seductive hand down his chest. "You have other things in mind?"

Colin jerked back from her touch and shook his head. "You aren't coming to Maryland with me. I'm going alone."

Her heart seemed to stutter in her chest, and she jerked her head back like she had been slapped, not even sure she had heard him right. "What?"

"This was never a good idea," Colin said, his voice still void of emotion.

"You're scaring me. What's wrong? You want to do long distance?" Her voice cracked. If that was what he truly wanted, then it was disappointing, but she could make it work. "Did my uncle say something? Because I've already told him and my mom and my aunt a thousand times that I can paint anywhere. They still want me to stay, but it's not their decision. I've submitted a few rental applications for those places we were looking at, and I think that one with the extra room is the perfect spot to—"

"Scarlett!" he interrupted loudly. "You're not coming because I don't want you to. We aren't going to work. We never were. I'm ending it."

"W-what?" None of this made any sense, and the whooshing sound pumping in her ears wasn't making it any easier.

Colin looked away and ran a hand through his hair. "I'm breaking up with you."

Suddenly her entire world was spinning. The tears rolling down her face and the fear that had started vibrating through her veins the second he had stepped into the room had finally collided, and she realized he was serious. "C-Colin," her stutter came back in full force. "Why? W-what did I do?"

"Nothing." His voice was so bitter that she didn't believe him for one second. "You did nothing, Scarlett. This was fun while it lasted. It was an experiment that worked for a little while but would never last in the long run."

She gripped his arm, desperately trying to make him see reason. "Colin, look at me! Please," she sobbed. Instead, he stepped toward the door, and she yelled after him, "You said you loved me."

He didn't look back, but froze in the doorway. "I used you, Scarlett. I used you to feel better after my parents died, and you did make me feel better. So thank you for that. You can move on with your life now."

"Move on with my—what are you even talking about? We—we were moving in together. You said you wanted to do this forever. You said you were *happy*. That you wanted me." Scarlett was hysterical now, her words coming out so frantic and pleading and angry, and every other emotion she could throw into the mix.

"Look at how I'm making you cry right now and think about all the times I've made you cry before, and I think you'll come to the same conclusion I did. I was temporary for you, and you don't need me. I have to go now."

"You know what?" Scarlett shouted. "Go!" She jogged over to her nightstand and jerked open the first drawer, plucking out their filled-out experiment charts and crumbling each one to throw it at his head. "Here, you can have your fucking experiment!" Another crumpled page flew across the room. "Leave me if you want to!" Colin bent to scoop up each balled paper, collecting them like they were his prized possessions. His little experiment that he had worked so hard on while she was just a variable he had thrown into the mix. "Get out!" she yelled, finally launching the last one at him. He didn't hesitate. Their entire relationship laid out on the crumpled paper in his hands, he left her standing among the chaos of her room, sobbing and falling to her knees, heart ripped from her chest and severed from all her vital organs.

"Letti?" Harper's voice came into the room, but Scarlett couldn't hear anything else she said over the sound of her own wracking sobs until she was lying on the floor with her head in her sister's lap, still crying, but the kind that lacked emotion. Staring into the distance and barely noticing that tears were still forming.

The dull numbness left over from when her brother died was back. Like an old friend, it slipped into place like a sweater she was trying on.

And it didn't come off for a long, long time.

FIFTY-ONE

Colin
23 Years Old

Most of the time, Colin's analytical brain worked in his favor, but when it didn't, it *really* didn't. When he was eighteen, his thoughts could go so easily from researching rock types and tectonic plates to calculating what the easiest, least messy, and least burdensome way to die was. The way that would cause everyone he loved the least amount of guilt and pain. He hadn't contemplated an obvious suicide. His mind was more crafty about it. It would be an accident like his parents. No one would be to blame. No one would know he had wanted it to happen. Everyone would be free of him. No more enduring his presence or humoring him.

Now, with his head resting on Scarlett's chest, he knew better. There was a reason Cooper was furious with him, and it wasn't because he didn't miss his oldest brother at all. There was a reason Walker and Talia called him every single Friday when he was away and painstakingly tried to make conversation with him, even forced him into FaceTime games of Monopoly. There was a reason Piper had an entire binder of ideas for his apartment at the ready with all his favorite textures and elements worked into each design. There was a reason Pearl had forgiven him so easily and Carter never questioned any of his peculiarities, just adapted to them with a smile on his face. There was a reason Theo kept painting his favorite things. There was a reason it took so long for Scarlett to know that he still loved her. He had broken her heart, and in order to break it, she had to have given it to him in the first place.

People could love him. They could, and *they did*. And Scarlett out of anyone deserved to know just how broken he was to be the kind of person who left her in her room crying that day. So he closed his eyes and whispered the words aloud.

"I wanted to die, Scarlett." Her arms wrapped around him tighter, and he could hear how hard she was breathing. "I had had thoughts like that before to a milder extent, but that day was different. People with ASD, myself included, often have dysregulated emotions. I remember how sad and pissed off I was that my parents didn't catch it sooner. And then I spiraled from there. My therapist said not to make any drastic choices and to call someone I loved. Instead, I dug myself so far into a hole of believing that I was hurting you and everyone else that the guilt ate at me till I ignored his advice entirely.

"The only way I felt I could get out of the hole was to end things with you and find a way to die by accident so I wouldn't hurt anyone else. I hyperfixated on it after I left your house. I left my car in your driveway, and I thought about Piper drinking a bunch and walking on the side of the road when Harden left her stranded at that party, and I thought that might be a good idea because then when someone inevitably hit me, it would be a clear accident, and Walker and everyone else wouldn't feel guilty about my suicide because they simply wouldn't know that I had begged for it to happen. But then I thought about whoever the driver might be and worried that they'd have lifelong trauma for carrying out my plan.

"So I moved on to other ideas till I was sick in the head,

miles away from your house and lying on a bench contemplating why I couldn't even come up with a good plan to off myself. My uncle's best friend Roscoe had every police officer on duty searching for me, and they eventually found me in Merrick, an entire town over, and they only found me because in some weird state of mind I had thought Carter might be able to help me think of ideas because we always came up with harebrained plans together. I somehow managed to call him and came back down to earth enough to realize that he obviously couldn't help me with my problem because then he'd know. The whole thing was chalked up to my reaction to being diagnosed, and no one knew what it really was. Walker, I think, looked at me differently from then on, and not because he knew I was autistic but because he knew something else was wrong.

"I went to college. I thought about my problem more. I changed my degree thinking that I could karmically make up for all the ways I'd hurt you, and I fell in love with cellular biology, both because of you and because it captivated me. I started seeing a therapist again after I listened to a seminar on autism in which I thought I would learn nothing, only to find out how high the suicide rates are for people on the spectrum. I graduated and painstakingly got a tattoo to remember when someone—*you*—laughed at something I said because you genuinely thought I was funny. I worked on myself and found better ways to self-soothe than diving headfirst into logic because I found that my logic was faulty. I started to see things differently with my family. That I wasn't a nuisance. That they did love me."

"And so did I," Scarlett murmured. She had been playing with his hair the whole time he spoke, he noticed, and his glasses were so crooked on his face that he couldn't see out of them. He rubbed his head into her like a cat.

"And so did you. I know that now. I promise." He laced his hand in hers as she pulled away from him.

"You better, because if you ever do anything like that again, I will hunt you down." She jabbed at his chest. "I really love you, Colin."

He adjusted his glasses back over his nose. "I take it you believe me now? That I love you, too?"

"Admittedly, the cyberstalking, the extra money you gave Theo, the paints you didn't give me, the tattoo, and your entire career change should have alerted me." Scarlett chuckled.

"And the flowers," Colin added.

"What flowers?" She screwed up her face, and he peered over at the vase sitting atop the cubby station to make sure they hadn't disappeared.

"The ones I buy you on your brother's birthday? The half-dead-looking ones over there?" He pointed. Scarlett's body stiffened under his embrace.

"You sent those to me?" For some reason, she was crying again after he thought they had worked through the brunt of their problems.

"Do you hate them?"

"I thought they were from my dad, Colin!" Scarlett snorted through her tears.

"Why would your dad send you flowers?" As far as he knew, her dad was still pulling his disappearing act and reappearing to send a quick text for holidays and birthdays.

"Good fucking question. But why would my ex send me flowers, and with my brother's catchphrase on it the first time, 'a great soul never dies'?" Her body grew rigid once again, and her humor-filled face lost all its color. "Was that an ominous statement about yourself?"

"What?" Colin shook his head. "No. I meant your brother. I left my name off the flowers so you didn't have to associate them with me if you didn't want to, but you told me Tucker's catchphrase at least twenty times when we were dating in one of your long stories, so it felt like an important phrase and one you'd know I knew."

"I don't even remember telling you that once."

"That's probably why you told me twenty times."

Scarlett giggled and bent to kiss his lips, chaste and sweet, hugging him close to her. "Thank you for the flowers, then."

"You're welcome." He pulled her head into his chest, wrapping her tightly in his arms. The touch finally made him feel grounded.

"Come lie down with me?" Scarlett asked as his fingers massaged her scalp in slow circles. He nodded, and they wandered up to Scarlett's apartment above the studio, only releasing their hold on each other because of the narrow staircase. Her place was exactly how he had imagined it—eclectic, with even more plants than the dying ones in the studio. She had macramé hanging off the walls and white lace curtains that looked like doilies hanging from the window in her tiny living room. A standing lamp with five differently colored light covers sat in the corner of the room, and a yellow sofa that could only seat two was currently occupied by a white cat with Play-Doh-pink ears. The sofa was front and center, facing a large framed painting of the lookout in a nighttime setting with a figure of a man standing on the flatter surface of the rock and looking out over the cliff's edge.

"That's you, I think," Scarlett said sheepishly. "I pretended it wasn't and that it was just a random silhouette of someone, but I was lying to myself. It's you. I liked the lookout best at sunset, but you liked it at night with the lights."

"I wish you were standing next to me in it." Colin peered at it and smiled easily.

"Maybe I'll add that." Scarlett grabbed his hand again and led him to her bedroom. She had hung shelves, paintings, and even more trinkets on the walls. Her bed stood out to him the most because the comforter was the exact same or a duplicate of the one he had been under so many times at her uncle's house.

An inexplicable wash of sadness drowned out the happy feeling in his chest. "Is this how you would have decorated our apartment in Maryland if you came with me?" It was so warm and happy that he felt the loss of her all over again.

"Maybe." She sat down on the edge of the bed. "But I've grown up a bit. I don't think I knew myself back then. Moving with you was never a good idea, Colin. I know we were in love, and I love you now, but I'm glad we had some time apart. I needed to learn who I wanted to be besides your sidekick."

Colin adamantly shook his head. "I never thought of you as a sidekick. You're a main character."

"I know that. But you always had more faith in me than I did."

Colin finally sat beside her, newly nervous as they both kicked off their shoes and crawled under the covers together, Scarlett curling into his chest. "Did you find faith in yourself, then? Or are you still looking?"

"I'll always be looking, but I know more now. I think what makes me special is that I'm a helper. I teach people to find joy through art. I help people find hope through my brother's foundation. I used to think it was bad that I was never the one changing the world directly, just helping people along the way to their own greatness, but there's nothing wrong with that. In every award or acceptance speech, the winners thank the people who helped them get there. I don't mind if my name isn't on the trophy as long as I helped someone else change the world," Scarlett said.

"That is changing the world," Colin replied simply. "Assuming you don't mean the ecosystem of it." She giggled and shook her head against his chest. "You changed my life after my parents died just by being you. You've changed Theo's, too. I worry about him because I don't want him to ever feel the way I did about myself, but I feel better when I think about how he has you. The current version of you that knows you're making a difference."

"He has you, too," she whispered.

"He does," he agreed. "And do *I* have you, too? You kissed me downstairs, but does that mean we're more than friends?"

"I'm pretty sure you're not supposed to want to fuck your friends." Her warm breath ghosted across his chest.

"So, you agree that we're soulmates, then?" Colin stiffened when Scarlett did, fear creeping into his chest once more.

"Soulmates?" she squeaked out.

He swallowed, but continued, "I don't want to just be your boyfriend." It was as simple as that. He was already her boyfriend once. This was different. This was forever, or he didn't want it at all.

"You think we're soulmates?" Her voice was less squeaky now and brighter as her body relaxed.

"There are eight billion people on Earth, and I only want you. I have no desire to search for anyone else. I don't want to be in a romantic relationship at all if it's not with you. You are my soulmate. You always have been. I just don't know if I'm yours." His heart tightened in his chest when she wiggled free of his arms, and he thought she might get up and leave him there until she instead reached beside her and pulled the first book he had ever given her from her nightstand, handing it to him.

"You're my soulmate, Colin. I wouldn't have kept this if you weren't. It still has all your sticky notes. I read those more than the actual book." Scarlett wiggled into his torso again, her hands burrowing under his shirt and pressing into his skin. He was momentarily distracted by the warmth of her body as he thumbed through the book, until he snapped to attention at the sight of a small splotch on the corner of a page and the way the book wanted to lie open on a certain page.

"You broke the spine! There are smudges everywhere. You—" His mouth propped open in horror. "You *doggy-eared* the pages?"

Scarlett was laughing. He couldn't see where the humor was in this at all. "But you still love me?" Her laughter died down.

"Of course I do. That has nothing to do with you being a book murderer."

"Book murderer seems harsh. Arguably, shouldn't this mean

that that book has received the most of my love because I've opened it so much that it's falling apart?"

"No," Colin said bluntly. "It just means you're a book murderer. You take care of plants okay, barring that fire emergencies don't force you to leave them behind. How do you manage that?"

"I just stick them everywhere so I know that I have to water them because they're always in my face."

"Then you need a bookshelf with so many books you don't end up reading the same one over and over again until you kill it," Colin decided, handing the book back to her. He watched as she set it on the nightstand with exaggerated gentleness. "We'll work on it. You can get a bookcase of your own at my place."

"I'd like that," Scarlett said, balling up in his arms once more. "Your place needs help. It's so boring."

"I've been putting it off because I want your help." He still had yet to make any decisions on Piper's designs, but he highly suspected that his sister had drawn up some of them with Scarlett in mind, given the bright colors. "I like what you did here, and Piper gave me a whole folder of options, but I want it to look like both of us. I want your half-dead plants everywhere and Pepto to have her own little cat house. You and Theo can use the spare bedroom I was going to put my books in as a home art studio."

"You want me to move in with you?" She shifted in his arms, but only to squeeze him harder. The pressure felt like everything he had needed for years.

"Is five years too long to wait to ask you to move in with me? Or is it now too early?"

"Your apartment is bigger, and it has a lot of potential, but I can't get rid of my apartment and the studio." Scarlett hummed in consideration. "But I do want to live with you."

"Then keep it. You can leave everything exactly how it is or use the apartment space for something else."

When Scarlett sat bolt upright with a start, Colin didn't get up with her, used to her livewire reactions to ideas that sprang to her head. "I could make it a showroom. A gallery! I've always wanted to hang some of the pieces in places that are open to the public other than Roaster's Republic, and if Kashvi helps me put together exhibitions, then it would make even more of a difference for sales of the pieces. I could use the kitchen for charcuterie because that's clearly the best hors d'oeuvre. Kashvi already gave me the hookup for wine for my paint-and-sip nights, so I have that covered if I want to get all classy about children's art. Someday we could just have a full-fledged Theo night, and he could have an exhibition all to himself. I do have some adult classes, so I guess it could have mixed-age exhibitions, too. Maybe you'll finally start painting, who knows." Colin didn't respond, content to let her talk at the speed of light until she turned to him, sobering. "You don't think it's a good idea?"

"I think it's a great idea," he replied calmly and closed his eyes, sinking into the pillow. "I just really missed hearing you ramble, and it's been a very noisy and emotional day. I'm tired and a little burnt out."

Scarlett flopped down beside him and whispered. "Do you need to retreat?"

"As long as you keep talking and I don't have to respond, I'll be happy," Colin sighed.

"I don't think I told you about how I started the program. That'll take me a solid hour with all my tangents. I'll start there?" He lazily bobbed his head, and she started to remove the socks from his feet while she spoke. "Okay, so, first off, I applied for a lesser art teaching job that I didn't end up getting, and I was kinda pissed about it because I was the perfect candidate." She started to unbutton his pants. "Then I realized I didn't even really want the job because it was just teaching art to rich people, and that's not as fulfilling. So, I said 'fuck it, I'll just do everything myself'—well, actually, I did have some help, but it was my idea, so I can give myself a little credit for that. I straight-up typed out 'grant writer' into a Google search and found this crotchety old man in a shitty apartment complex who worked for free as long as I brought him cupcakes. He was really grumpy, but I think he was just lonely. Sometimes I think about going to check on him. Maybe I'll make him some cupcakes tomorrow. Kashvi and I upped our game from boxed cupcakes and can make some pretty decent home-made ones. I'll have to make some for you, too. Anyway, back to the art program. So, we filled out all these grant applications, and..."

As Scarlett removed the rest of his clothes and spouted out her story in a roundabout way, Colin felt loose-limbed and spent. Once Scarlett folded all their clothing and joined him under the sheets and her naked skin was pressed up against his, he felt himself drifting off to sleep. Cocooned in warmth and listening to the other half of his heart ramble, he had never felt more comfortable. He finally belonged somewhere. Five years later, he was finally home again.

FIFTY-TWO

Two Months Later

Scarlett
23 Years Old

The studio felt so small now that all of Scarlett's close friends and family were crowding it. Even with the upstairs opened up to allow their guests to wander through the new exhibition she and Kashvi had worked tirelessly on, everyone was downstairs. She had underestimated how long people would linger while looking at children's artwork before they had seen all they could see and wanted to get to the other portion of the evening. The room seemed calm enough, but she sidled up to Colin and his easel anyway to verify.

"Is it too loud in here? If it's too loud in here, I can—"

"I'm fine, Red." Colin stooped to peck her on the lips, and she smiled before her eyes landed on the canvas he was painting. She quickly schooled her face into something less shocked and tilted her head to the side to try to get a better angle. The new perspective didn't help, and she still couldn't make heads or tails of it. "Do you like it?"

"Oh, it's very... abstract." Scarlett nodded.

"Dude, she hates it. What even is that?" Carter peered over their shoulders, chuckling.

"It's Scarlett," Colin said, seeming unoffended. "I think she'd tell me if she hated it."

Scarlett took another look at it and leaned into Colin's side to comfort him as her guilty conscience took over. She didn't hate it. That much was true. She couldn't hate it, because Colin had worked so hard on it, and she loved the effort he had made just to make her happy. But she definitely didn't like it. "You know what? I see it now. My hair is orange, and I'm wearing a red dress, right?"

"It was supposed to be a bra and underwear, but I used too much water, and it started dripping, so I made it a dress," Colin explained. A lot more than just the dress had dripped, but she kept her mouth shut.

"You were just casually painting her like a French girl in front of everyone?" Kashvi made her way over to them and peered at the picture. "Oh. I see. It wouldn't even matter if she was fully nude because we wouldn't be able to tell." Scarlett shoved her and gave a reprimanding look that said to play nice. Kashvi bowed out with a grin as she made her way across the studio to Varo, where the smile quickly turned flirty. The celibacy record her friend had been keeping for a while had recently been broken given all the explicit eggplant emojis Scarlett had received via text yesterday.

"I think you should stick to lab work," Carter told Colin with a sympathetic pat on his shoulder before he left to join Kashvi and Varo.

While Scarlett was experienced in pretending artwork was beautiful when it looked like it was made by a five-year-old, other people seemed to be unable to keep their cool when looking at Colin's array of bleeding blobs. He would have been better off with acrylic paints, but he had been adamant that he wanted to paint with watercolors like she did, even after an entire week of complaining and saying he didn't want to participate in the free paint she had planned for the evening because he wasn't any good. She had been pleasantly surprised when he changed his mind, but now she was really hoping that he didn't genuinely believe he was good at painting. If he did, it would render all his compliments about her pieces null and void given that his artistic taste was less than stellar.

One by one, everyone in the room seemed to decide that Colin's artwork was the next exhibition piece, and they put down their paintbrushes to make their rounds.

"Good lord, man. What is that?" Braiden peered down at Colin's painting with Jessie latched onto one of his arms, burying her face into his shoulder to keep from laughing.

"It's Scarlett, obviously," Colin said, unfazed as he gestured to something that was supposed to make the resemblance more obvious but did no such thing. The black splotch he had pointed to was leaking down what she assumed was her face. It looked a hell of a lot like tear-streaked mascara or clown makeup until she realized what it was.

"Oh, freckles! They look great, Colin. I like it," Pearl said, swooping in with a smile before returning to her own easel, where she was painting a bridal bouquet that was nowhere on the abstract side. Scarlett was thankful for Pearl's interlude between all the bad commentary because Braiden's smirk of amusement made her want to commit a crime or defend her boyfriend even more. It turned out she didn't have to because Braiden's expression quickly fell when Colin spoke again.

"Have you finished the book I gave you yet? For Jessie's sake, I think you should read it." Colin dabbed yet another terrifying freckle onto her blob face, and Scarlett had to press her hand into her mouth. This time, she wasn't in danger of laughing at Colin's art, but at the stricken look occupying Braiden's face.

"I read the book." Braiden sighed.

"What book?" Jessie asked.

"Nothing!" Braiden's cheeks tinged with pink as he quickly maneuvered himself and Jessie out of the fold.

Colin guilelessly called after them, "I'm told women like it when you tell them you're reading that!" He turned back to Scarlett. "Right?"

"I definitely like it when *you* read things like that." She bit her lip. Last week, she had been made aware of all the sex books Colin had read since they parted ways all those years ago, and like the creatures of habit they were, she pulled out lined paper and a ruler to build a new experiment chart. They had been frequently putting all his new knowledge to the test and recording it, not every time, but enough to remember everything they liked and wanted to return to.

"Think we should hang it up in our living room?" Colin asked, redirecting Scarlett's attention to his, for lack of a better word, masterpiece. Her heart dropped in her chest. Every painting in their living room had been meticulously chosen by herself and Piper. This not only did not match the uplifting vibe, but she was worried that people would think *she* had painted it. It was also the only suggestion Colin had made on the interior design of their home thus far, so it being ugly didn't feel like a good enough reason to not hang it up.

"Oh, um..." Scarlett floundered and widened her eyes in Piper's direction. Catching the hint, Piper and Leo swiftly came to her aid. "He wants to hang this in our living room. As our decorator, what do you think?"

Leo was the first to speak while Piper stood with her mouth ajar, no doubt thinking this painting was going to be the downfall of their entire design. "They're both too nice to tell you your painting sucks, but I'm not. It's really bad, Colin."

"Leo," Piper hissed, smacking him in the sternum before fixing her face into a bright smile. "I think it's wonderful, Colin."

"Faker." Leo chuckled, shaking his head.

"Asshole," Piper shot back.

Colin pulled his eyebrows together. "Is it normal to insult the person you love as much as you two do? Because I really don't want to start insulting Scarlett."

Scarlett shook her head and kissed his cheek. "Please don't. They're a special brand of weird."

Leo shrugged and gave Piper a salacious smirk. "Foreplay."

"I clearly entered this conversation at the wrong time," a voice said from behind them. Scarlett turned to find that Walker and Talia had joined their group, Walker scowling at Leo, who didn't seem to care at all that Piper's uncle was glaring at him and instead brought the back of Piper's hand up to his lips to kiss it.

"Oh, Colin, that's so... I can tell you put a lot of effort into it," Talia said thoughtfully. Walker started up a coughing fit that was clearly to dissuade his laughter.

"Maybe we could hang it in our bedroom?" Scarlett considered.

"Really?" Piper squeaked out.

The more Scarlett looked at it, the more she wanted the monstrosity to hang up somewhere in their home. Not because it was good, but because it was a display of how much Colin loved her. There were numerous black splotches all over her supposed arms and legs, which meant he had taken the time to put every freckle on like the way he kissed them when they were in bed, his hot mouth traversing her body. Her eyes in the painting were overly saturated, and the entire eye was green instead of just her irises, but it just went to show that despite hating eye contact, Colin paid attention. He had even made what she could now see were eyelashes, but he had painted them copper like her hair instead of black like she usually saw in inexperienced paintings.

"You must really love him." Walker choked on another laugh.

Scarlett bobbed her head and leaned against Colin's shoulder. "He's easy to love."

Colin kissed her fully on the mouth before looking over her shoulder to speak with someone. "Do I tell them now or later?"

Cooper sauntered over to the crowd around Colin's painting with his two best friends flanking his sides. "Later. *Fantastic painting*, Colin."

"Ew! What is that?" Camden pointed and gawked at the painting like it had personally offended him.

Straight-faced, Colin gestured off to Pearl, happily painting her flowers in the corner. "She said she liked it."

Camden shifted on his feet and cleared his throat. "I think it's the most beautiful painting I've ever seen. It took me a second to see the genius of it all."

After two months of being with Colin again, Scarlett had been informed on all the family drama, or lack thereof in this case. She had also been around the house enough to catch on quickly to the family dynamics. Pearl was as uninterested in Camden as ever. Cooper pretended that he didn't notice his best friend liked his sister at all and sidestepped any conversation about it. He also seemed a little too preoccupied by the only girl in their trio, who was currently sporting long goddess braids and a look of disgust.

"It looks like a radioactive orange and red turd is crying black tears," Jayla scoffed and elbowed Cooper. "Coop and Colin are just screwing with everyone." Scarlett narrowed her eyes as she looked between Colin and Cooper. Colin's face gave away nothing, but Cooper's...

Cooper threw up his hands in aggravation, and Scarlett's shoulders sagged in relief. The painting wouldn't have to adorn any of her walls if Colin was just screwing with her. "Jay, what the fuck?" Cooper glared.

"Language!" Walker and Talia shouted at the same time.

"You're easy to read." Jayla smirked.

"I'm not as easy to read as you think I am," Cooper muttered. Scarlett scooted closer to Colin, hiding slightly behind him because, as an honorary Hartrick, she knew Cooper and Jayla's history, and unlike everyone else who had secrets, she couldn't keep them from blatantly showing on her face. It was partially why she and Colin worked so well. Out of anyone he knew, she was the easiest for him to read. That, and they had made a pact to answer honestly anytime one of them wanted to know.

"What are you thinking about?" Colin asked her, grinning from ear to ear.

"I'm thinking that I still want this painting, but I want to hang it up in my closet so no one can see it." Scarlett bit her bottom lip. Colin smiled even wider, and it was all the confirmation she needed. "So you were just fucking with me, then? You don't legitimately think you're the next Van Gogh?"

"I don't legitimately think I'm the next *Scarlett Wallace*," he said sweetly.

The conversation around them had wandered away, bickering more about wasted pranks and inappropriate language for teenagers. The touch of Colin's hand on the small of her back along with her name said in reverence, as if her art were built for museums and high-end galleries, felt intensely intimate.

She blushed and entwined her fingers with his. "I still like the painting because you knew it would make me happy if you tried, and you tried really hard."

Colin shrugged. "If you say so. I think it looks like it was painted by a toddler. I bet your painting looks like a masterpiece."

"Not this again," Scarlett groaned. For the last two months, Colin had been on her ass about wanting to see the painting he had commissioned, but she had kept it hidden and threatened him with celibacy if he looked at it before it was ready. The painting had been done for weeks, but she couldn't bring herself to say it was done because there might still be imperfections she could fix before it was too late.

"What's your normal turnaround time for commissioned pieces? Because this customer service is lackluster at best," Colin stated, folding his arms over his chest. "I will need the reference photos back at some point."

She rolled her eyes with a huff. "You told me to take my time! And I normally don't get commissioned art pieces that make me cry this much."

He paled a bit. "It made you cry?"

"Yes. Not in a bad way, I just keep thinking of you requesting it and how beautiful the idea is, and then—" She gestured to her eyes, starting to water. "And then I get terrified all over again that I didn't do well enough."

"You could never ruin it. I know you'll do a good job. That's why I asked you to do it."

"That's a lot of pressure and expectation to live up to."

Colin pulled her into his chest and squeezed. "You know you're special. You know you're good at this. You know that I'll love whatever you came up with."

Scarlett blew out a breath and let her head rest against his chest. "I just want it to be perfect."

"Can I please see it?" Colin pleaded. As if they were waiting for the perfect inopportune time to make their grand entrance back into the party, her family members all filed out of her office and made a beeline for her.

"It's beautiful!" Harper declared as Scarlett removed herself from Colin's embrace and took her family's commentary with a light smile and a murmured thank-you.

"It's your best work to date." Nora nodded.

Eden hummed. "I agree."

Uncle Marty reached out to shake Colin's hand with a firm grip and smiled brightly. "You're going to love it."

Scarlett watched as Colin's expression soured during the handshake, and he jerked his head toward her. "You showed it to them before me?" The hurt look on his face made her wish she hadn't, but she knew at least Eden and her mom would tell her straight if she needed to redo it. Harper and Marty were solely there to boost her confidence. She wasn't above getting compliments she knew she would get regardless of if the painting was good. "Why can't I see it? I don't understand."

Scarlett winced and looked at the floor. "I needed to know what they thought before I showed it to you. You like everything I paint. I wanted constructive criticism, and now I know it's ready."

Colin brightened a bit. "Then can I see it now?"

She swallowed, nerves turning over her stomach. "Okay." She

lifted her hand, and Colin took it, practically dragging her along to her office, where she had her easel flipped away from the open doorway. He dropped her hand when he reached the easel and moved around the side of it so quickly she thought he might knock it to the floor. When he didn't and instead stood stock still in front of it, her anxiety ramped up tenfold. She slowly maneuvered to his side and confirmed nothing had happened to the piece since she had set it there before the soft opening of the gallery. Silently, Colin moved back toward the door, and she thought he might walk out completely until he did something much more in character: shut the door, silencing all their family and friends before returning to the easel and once again staring at it.

"Marry me," Colin said.

"W-what?" Scarlett blinked, her brain rebooting from shock.

"Marry me," he stated simply. "Or, I guess I should say, 'Will you marry me?'"

She floundered for a response. "I-isn't it a bit early for that?"

"Socially, it might be. Do you want to wait so our family and friends don't look down on us? I'm fine with that."

"I don't even—I didn't realize that this was an option. We just started dating again." Her voice was coming out all squeaky, but she couldn't wrap her head around anything he was saying when he hadn't told her what he thought of the painting. She looked at her artwork again, wondering what exactly had brought this about.

Colin cocked his head to the side. "I've been yours for five years. But yes, I suppose you are correct. Is that a no, then?"

Was it? Scarlett's heart desperately wanted it, but her brain said impulse decisions had gotten her in trouble before, especially with Colin. Her family would be more than shocked if she told them they were getting married so soon after getting back together. The first time she had wanted to make a rash decision and move across the country with him, they had protested it vehemently. She wasn't sure what their reaction would be to this, but she had a feeling they would think she was foolish, and she had enough of a self-preservation instinct to not want a fight with them again. She also had enough free agency to know what she wanted and take it without any input from her family.

Lifting a finger, Scarlett turned fully toward him. "Tell me what you think of the painting first."

"The painting makes me want to marry you." Again, it was so simple, and yet when Colin laid things out so plainly like that, it made her chest ache with affection. She loved his ability to get right to the point.

"But what about it makes you want to marry me?" she pried.

"Did you know they were lab partners after my dad bribed his chemistry teacher to be paired with my mom?" Colin asked. She nodded. "And you know they were each other's best friend and soulmate?" She nodded again. "I told you to paint them dancing, Scarlett, I didn't tell you *where* to paint them. You painted them dancing in the very place my dad proposed at the lookout. It's the same place that I would want to marry you. And the inscription on the bottom? It's perfect." She looked down to where she had inked her signature and written *a great soul never dies* in neat calligraphy above it, not so big that it overpowered any of the art, but enough to be legible if you were looking for it. "I have everything I want and all the facts I need to know that we'll last forever because my parents *did* last forever. I got to see the end of their forever, and they were still in love the day they died. If their souls are still alive, then I imagine that they're still in love. We already agreed we're soulmates. You were my lab partner. You're my best friend. I love you. You paint beautiful things, and I want you to paint the rest of our life together."

"Okay," Scarlett choked back her emotion. The beating of her chest was quickened and pounding in her ears like it wanted to rip free to be with her other half. She stepped toward him, and he bent down to press a languid kiss to her lips. "I'll marry you." They kissed again, and she added, "in a year. We can be engaged till then and keep it a secret until we're sure my family won't lose their shit."

"Perfect," he whispered and kissed her one last time. "You know how much I love rules. Does Kashvi get to know like last time?"

"This time, I think it'll just be our secret. No one else matters." She grinned.

"Great. Now that that's settled…" Colin trudged away from her, breaking up their happy bubble the way he did everything: abruptly. He jerked open the door and called out to the packed corner of the studio, "Pearl, come see the gift I got you."

Epilogue

One Year Later

Colin
24 Years Old

"Knowledge, pacing, skill, productivity, communication, and overall." Colin snapped his hips forward with a thrust as he listed off each category on their sex chart. "I want fives on everything."

"Make me come again, and I'll give you whatever you want," Scarlett gasped underneath him. She was completely naked besides the gold band and emerald wedding ring adorning her ring finger and sparkling in the morning light. Her hands had heated up enough to touch him. Cool metal against his skin, they had learned, was a mood killer.

He rocked into her again, hitting as far back as he could and lacing his fingers in hers to feel her even closer. "Tell me what you need."

"Compliment me."

"The dancing painting you did of my parents is so pretty that I pause to look at it every time I go hang out at the house," he panted.

"I meant about what we're doing right now, but that's nice." She arched her back, and he watched her breasts heave with her, jiggling with his persistent thrusts.

"You're so tight, Red." He switched tactics and meant it. Her walls were hugging him so well that he would come in no time. "And you did so good with your legs tied. I like it when you need my tongue but you can't move so you have to just take what I give you."

Scarlett moaned on another thrust as he pushed into her so hard that each jerk of his hips slid her back until the crown of her forehead was hitting the headboard. He knew when she was coming because she always told him, and it was no different this time.

"I'm there," Scarlett whined, arching her back more. And so was he, emptying himself inside of her as waves of pleasure wracked his body. He had barely finished releasing when Scarlett threw off the covers and clambered out of their bed. "We have no time left."

"You're the one that wanted me to try another knot trick." Colin followed after her into the bathroom.

"You really gotta learn to tie faster," she laughed out as she hopped in the shower. Colin wiped himself down with a wet wipe and deemed himself clean enough since it was just after he had gotten out of the shower when Scarlett loosed the towel from around his waist and started things off by dropping to her knees to suck him off.

"Rings, Red," he called out in a monotone voice, holding out his hand to the glass shower box. The door opened, and her hand popped out to drop her rings into his palm. She had lost one in the sink once already, and it had taken forever to get it back out of the pipes. He watched her happily for a moment as she used the oatmeal and honey soap they shared, scrubbing the suds into her wet, freckled skin. He was pretty sure he had kissed every freckle on her body at this point, but his view had him second-guessing himself and vowing to map her body with his lips more often. He stayed in the bathroom long enough to brush his teeth and left the bathroom before he was hard again.

Once Colin was fully dressed and ready, he waited in the living room with a water glass for Scarlett and Pepto in his lap, happily purring as he stroked her back. It hadn't taken Scarlett much longer before she was chugging the glass of water and sitting beside him as they both eagerly stared at the clock. Eden was four entire minutes late, and Colin couldn't fathom being more than two minutes late anywhere. Except to graduation, if you were otherwise occupied in the backseat of a car.

Soon enough, the doorbell rang, and Colin rose to his feet, ditching Pepto on the floor as he and Scarlett walked through their fully decorated apartment filled with plants that Scarlett over- or underwatered and colorful artwork covering each and every wall.

"Ready?" Scarlett asked, hand on the doorknob.

"Ready." He nodded.

When she swung open the door, Eden and Theo stepped into their home, Theo with a suitcase dragging behind him and a partial sign of *I hate being late*. Leo had been teaching Theo ASL any chance he could, but with his new film project starting soon, Colin and Scarlett had hired someone else for the job: a deaf girl from Texas who had recently moved to the area and happened to be Carter's roommate. Finley Moore was starting on Monday afternoon once Theo was out of school so she could teach them all how to communicate better with him.

"Want to see your room?" Colin asked, gesturing down the hallway. Theo nodded, and everyone followed Colin to the door on the right. What he once thought would be his office was now a second bedroom for their foster kid and the newest addition to the family—only in location, because Theo had practically been theirs for months. After they had taken all the foster care classes, gone through a routine home inspection, and gotten the necessary paperwork done, it was finally official.

Scarlett stood beside Colin, and he could tell by the way she sucked in a breath and he didn't hear it release that she was waiting for Theo's reaction. It wasn't going to be the same room that he had seen a bunch of times before. Piper had designed it specifically for him, with a sensory swing and, of course, an easel with a stack of canvas at the ready.

Theo immediately started to sprint happily around the room, pointing at things and grinning. Colin felt his wife finally release her anxious hold on his arm, and they both stepped into the room after him.

"It's official. You're foster parents. How do you feel?" Eden asked.

"I feel like that." Colin pointed to the almost-completed painting on Theo's easel, a portrait of his and Scarlett's wedding day at the lookout during a setting sun. It had been a small group, but perfect in every way.

"I feel like that, too," Scarlett said, folding herself under his arm as Theo ran up to the both of them, arms raised and expectant. They both stooped to his height and hugged him the way everyone deserved to be hugged: with a firm pressure and so much love behind it that when Theo pulled away, he told them they had practically suffocated him before he went to work at his easel.

The End

Resources

If you or someone you know is struggling or in crisis, help is available.
Call or text 988 or chat 988lifeline.org

Learn about suicide prevention, including helpline numbers, warning signs, risk factors, treatments and therapies, and resources for more information at:
https://afsp.org/suicide-prevention-resources/

For resources on autism, check out:
https://autisticadvocacy.org/

Consider donating to Lift 4 Autism, Romance Community in Action for Autism:
https://lift4autism.com/

ACKNOWLEDGMENTS

"In every award or acceptance speech, the winners thank the people who helped them get there." —Scarlett Wallace

At the end of every novel, I am terrified I will forget someone on my long list of people that helped me get here. So, here's to all the people that I remembered to thank, anyone I forgot, and the readers who will make this novel something special when it's out of my hands.

To my daughter, as always, you are the bright light in every day, and your joy helps fuel my imagination and gives me the spark I need to continue. Your artistic ability might be that of a five-year-old, but your artwork is still the reason I put so much emphasis on art and color in this novel. To the rest of my family, thank you for your continued support. I know a lot of creatives who don't have people in their corner telling them to go after their dreams, and I'm fortunate to have so many people cheering me on. I don't take that lightly.

To my sensitivity reader, Danielle, you are a phenomenal friend and person. Thank you for all your insights on ASD. I will always appreciate how open and helpful you were with each and every one of my questions. I truly could not have done it without you. To Melissa W., who provided much-needed scientific insight, thank you for being smarter than me and agreeing with Colin that nobody is allowed to hate science. As always, my brain self-edits nothing, and my editor, Maryarita, is to thank for making me look like I know how to use proper grammar. And to my other betas,

Melissa E., Kae, Cait, Lexi, and Crystal, thank you endlessly for all your commentary that helped me make this story all it could be.

The author journey is a hard one, but it makes it all the more fun when you get to go through it with friends in the same position. To authors Kelsey Schulz, Kayla Martin, Miranda Melanie, and Letizia Lorini, I'm so glad we can celebrate and commiserate about our books together.

Of which there are too many to list here, thank you to all the researchers that provided vital information, anyone who commented on the Reddit forums I frequented, and the authors of the books I read to better understand my characters. Special shoutout to Emily Nagoski's *Come as You Are*, which I read and based Colin's entire outlook on sex off of.

And finally, to every person who has loved my previous books, been loud on social media about them, been in my direct messages complaining about the sexual tension between my characters and the tears I provoked with my words, you make me want to continue. You make me feel okay about laying so much of my heart on a page. Thank you.

On to the next one.

DICK-TIONARY

Whether you wish to skip the smut entirely or return to it, that content can be found in these chapters...

By the Author

The Ones Series:
The Ones We Fight For - Walker & Talia
The Ones We Hate - Piper & Leo
The Ones We Remember - Colin & Scarlett

Coming Spring of 2025
Before We Were One - Prequel Novella - Cole & Paisley

About the Author

Katie Golightly is an Oregon girl who thrives on chaos. She lives happily with her husband, daughter, and overflowing bookshelf. In addition to getting serotonin from the outdoors and well-organized spreadsheets, she has always been drawn to the art of storytelling. Eventually, the endless emotional, funny, and spicy stories she fabricated in her head had to be written down somewhere.

www.ingramcontent.com/pod-product-compliance
Lightning Source LLC
Chambersburg PA
CBHW051253130726
47987CB00004B/1513